Battle for the Southland

JOHN DOUGLAS DAY

Copyright © 2015 John Douglas Day

All rights reserved.

ISBN-13: 978-1511899260

ISBN-10: 1511899263

No part of this novel may be used for any purpose other than personal use. Reproduction, modification, storage in a retrieval system or retransmission, in any form or by any means, electronic, mechanical or otherwise, for reasons other than personal use, is strictly prohibited without prior written permission of the publishers. A reasonable use exception is granted for excerpts needed for review.

This novel is dedicated to those who are weary and waiting for hope.

Table of Contents

ACKNOWLEDGMENTS		iii
MAP OF EHRYLAN		iv
MAP OF THE SOUTHLAND		v
MAP OF THE CENTRAL CRESCENT		vi
1.	THE RUSH TO TWOFORDS	1
2.	SAD TIDINGS	19
3.	BREACHED	40
4.	THE COMING OF THE KING	68
5.	WOLVES IN THE NIGHT	92
6.	TOWER PASS	127
7.	VALLEY ELOSAI	144
8.	NEW ACQUAINTANCES AND OLD	166
9.	ANCIENT ENEMY	191
10.	OF GRYHM, MOTHERS, AND BODYGUARDS	209
11.	STRYN	235
12.	THE WELLING	269
13.	THE CONQUEST OF EHRYNAI	286
14.	THE ROAD TO NEATH	300
15.	SEEING	316
ABOUT THE AUTHOR		342
BY JOHN DOUGLAS DAY		343

ACKNOWLEDGMENTS

E.L. Day and Deborah Bennet gave of their time freely and worked tirelessly on the proof of this novel. D. E. Kern, of Inkwell Enterprises, edited the final copy. I would also like to thank and acknowledge the many readers who read, enjoyed, and commented on the two previous books. No words could represent the gratitude I feel. Your enjoyment keeps me writing.

MAP OF EHRYLAN

MAP OF THE SOUTHLAND

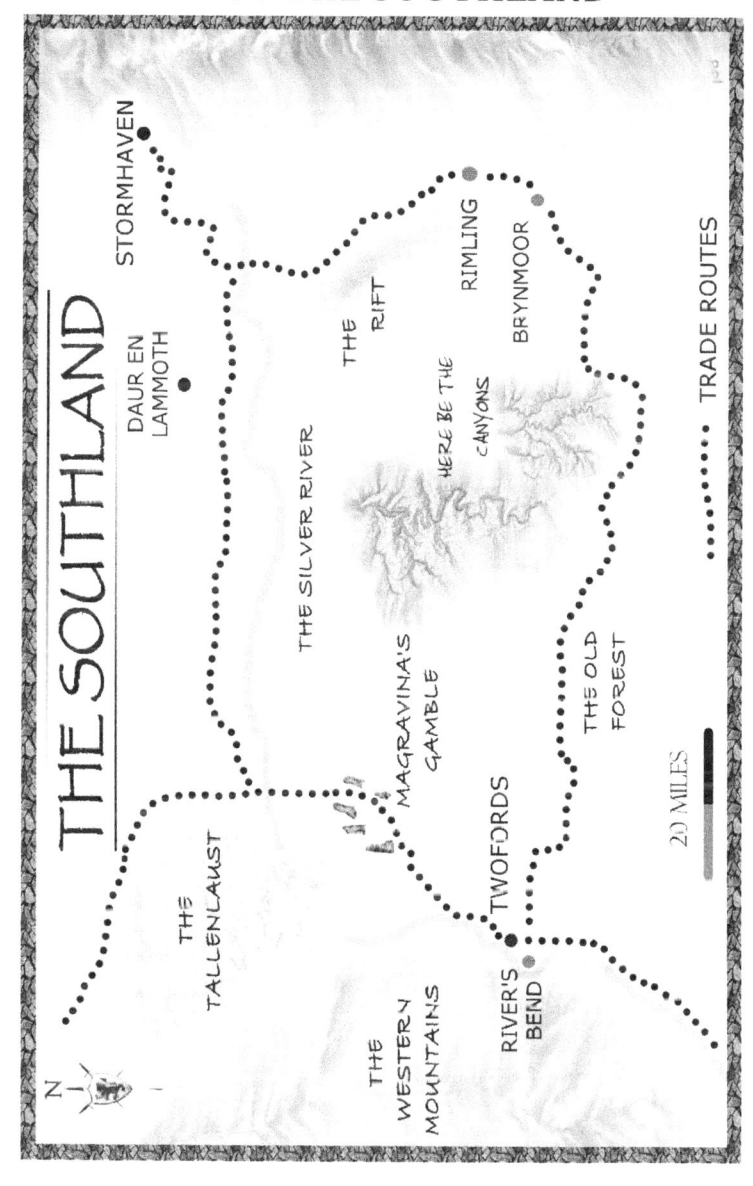

MAP OF THE CENTRAL CRESCENT

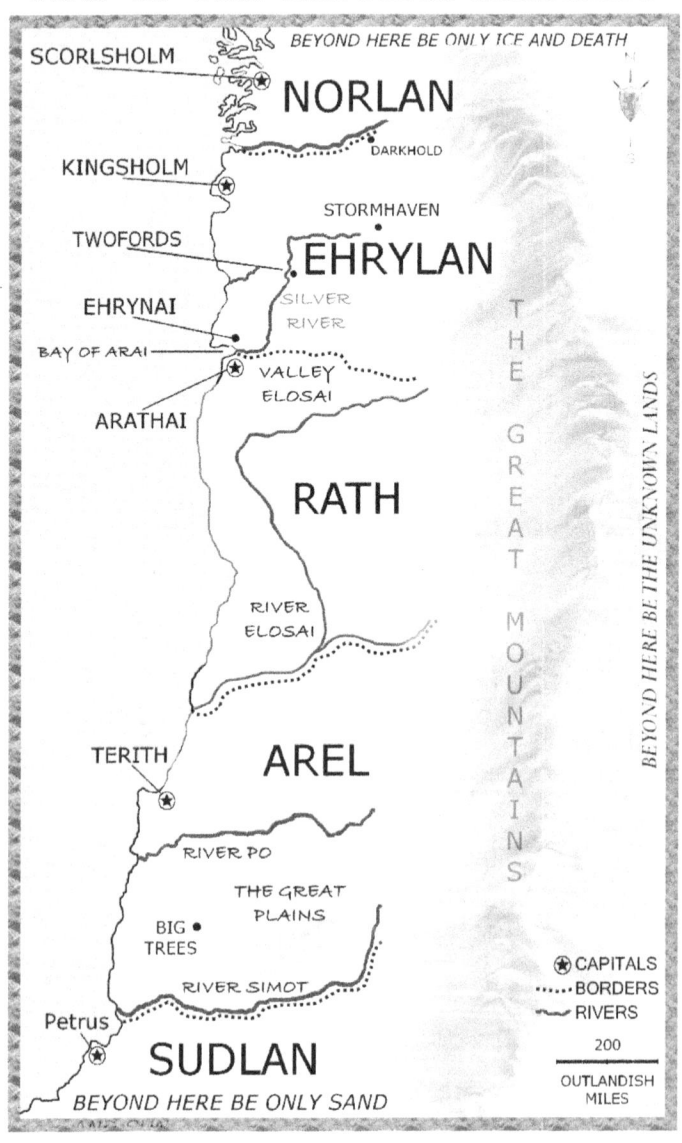

1. THE RUSH TO TWOFORDS

I.

The king's voice rang loud and true. The blade in his hand glittered as his exhortation echoed in my mind. Gazing at him, I imagined our armies pouring out of Stormhaven and thundering down the slopes of the Great Mountains, a wave of vengeance that flowed across the fractured reaches of the Southland and washed away the forces of darkness besieging Twofords. Dauroth's army was thrown back, a feeble, twitching thing that did not impede us. The city rose. It was battered and bruised, its walls pulled to pieces, but its people had withstood the test.

I saw the inexorable might of the armies of the sunrise swell to bursting as the Ehrylain flocked to the king's lion banners. Nothing could have stopped us save the hand of Ea as we marched on Kingsholm. There, before the gates of the ancient palace that had once been my home, the king himself slew Dauroth as ranks of freed men and women cheered.

Then came long years of peace and beauty that even Andur's reign could not equal. Gammin sired sons and daughters aplenty. The succession of Brand's house was assured. The Ehrylain thrived, living in an idyllic tranquility for which peace and prosperity are only pale descriptions.

Ah, me. That's what my mind's eye saw as the king's voice rang out in response to the unwelcome news the messenger from Twofords brought. But that is not what happened, not at all. Even at the time, sitting aback Avyansa amidst a throng of warriors on the road to Twofords, I did not mistake the vision in my head as far-seeing. It was only a fantasy brought on by the power of my friend's voice.

Others were moved as well. Ilmaren—the messenger from Twofords—felt it. His face lit up like a beacon of unexpected hope, and he straightened in the saddle. Though he had ridden with break-neck speed and little rest to warn us of Twofords' impending demise, the weariness seemed to wash away as cheers spread like fire down the lines of warriors filling the road. A ripple of excited voices spread outward. Soon the ranks were clashing swords on shields.

King Branden knew that, excitement or no, armies cannot move as quickly as renewed hope, even at the greatest need. They require preparation, planning, and above all, good leadership. This one had all of these, but there were things to accomplish before we could rush to the aid of Twofords.

Before questioning Ilmaren further, King Branden ordered a halt. He dismounted and made the travel-blasted messenger sit. Refreshment was presented to him. His horse was led away and another brought forward. When he had regained his breath and his composure, Ilmaren told us the full tale. The news was grim. Twofords was on the brink of disaster, would fall if help did not arrive soon. The king left the questioning to me, though I could see that he had to struggle to hold back. He knew I was more familiar with the situation in the Bend.

An army of ten hundreds is cumbersome, even when it is as trained and disciplined as this one. We split it. I would ride forward immediately with half the cavalry. The rest of the army would press on as fast as they could. I might come to the aide of Twofords three or four days before the main force.

Gammin stayed with Branden, as much as it pained us to be separated so soon. Nothing would induce Marin to leave his friend. Marin's parents would stay with their children. As for Merelina, I could not convince her to remain behind. She rode with me. I was proud to have her by my side.

By the time we were ready, afternoon was chasing hard on the heels of evening. A hundred riders were assembled, waiting to set out. That was nowhere near enough to assure us victory. It was a recklessly small number, but more could not be spared. Cavalry are the eyes of any army. Branden would be blind if I took them all. I could not leave my friend blind.

It was a pitifully small force with which to assail the army entrenched around Twofords. Yet twice that number of horsemen, which would have been the whole cavalry, would not have made much of a difference. Whether with one hundred or with two, there was little hope we could drive off Dauroth's forces. I would not know how we might help the beleaguered city until we got there and saw the situation.

As almost always, there was good news with the bad. The men and women who rode with me had been trained to the king's standards. Those standards were essentially the same as mine, since Branden and I had been trained together, side by side, from the time we were old enough to walk. I was able to lead them easier than might otherwise have been the case.

As I cast a final look back along the ranks of horsemen, I saw Marn and Arica riding toward me. We had made our farewell, so I had no idea what they might want. Quelling my impatience, I waited for them to approach.

Arica spoke first when the duo arrived.

"Do you have room for another rider, shinando? I have some skill with the bow, or so I am told."

I forced myself not to glance at Marn. Arica was old enough to make her own decisions. I would not go against the woodcutter's wishes as far as his daughter was concerned, but I owed it to her to weigh her request on its own merits.

"Arica, you are always free to ride with me if that is where you want to be." Having said that, I allowed myself to look at her father before continuing. "I thought you were riding with the others—with your father and mother. And with Gammin."

"I changed my mind."

"What does your father say to this?"

It was Marn who answered. "I would rather she stay by my side. Any road that bares you on an errand of import is lined with danger. But my daughter will make her own decisions. She has survived much without us to guide her. She has more than earned our confidence."

Arica flushed and lowered her eyes. She raised them again almost immediately. "I would not differ with my father, but I do not agree. Both of you were in my head and heart, as will ever be."

I saw a smile peak out of Marn's stern countenance. It did not escape completely before he captured it and stowed it away. In that unguarded instant, I saw something on his face that I could read for once. It was pride.

"Lady, the way will be rough. We will ride hard and fast. At the end of this road is only death, but, if you will, join us. This only I ask, that you ride by Merelina's side and fight next to her. Then I will have no fear for either of you."

I thought she might award me her smile for that, but she did not. Her face was colored with an unfamiliar sadness. It was a look that became all too familiar in the days ahead.

"Gladly," was all she said. She nodded to her father and nudged her horse into the formation. I saw the way she wore her bow. Though she was young and beautiful, she did not look like a simple maiden. She had the look of a haunted warrior, one who seeks something that must not be named.

II.

We did ride hard and fast. The way was rough. We hoped to come to Twofords on the third day after our departure. This would require the best efforts of the men and horses as well as a bit of luck from the weather. We received both.

Truth to tell, the weather proved a boon to us. Fall decayed to winter as we rode. Our exertions warmed us against the growing chill. There was enough moisture in the air to keep down the dust that dogs the heels of any army. Heat, dust, and thirst are the scourges of summer campaigning, even as cold, mud, and wet are the plagues of winter.

The first stage started late in the afternoon. We rode through the night. The road was open and distinct, if not well-kept. There was plenty of moon to light the way. I called a halt just after midnight. We entrenched our position, ate, and rested until the sun greeted us.

We set out at first light and rode until midnight, pausing for frequent short breaks and two long ones. When we stopped to make camp, we were all bone-weary. Despite this, we entrenched our position in the time-honored manner. I did not think we could mount much of a defense if we had to, but it was the right thing to do.

In all, we had ridden about eighty miles, the greater part of our journey. We could make the city by dusk the next day, but to do so would be foolishness indeed. It does little good to arrive at a rescue when you are so tired you cannot lift a lance or wield a sword. We would cover more than half the remaining distance the next day, stop early to recuperate as much as possible, then ride down upon the armies besieging Twofords with the dawn. It was a good plan. It might have worked, but I will never know. It did not live long enough for me to set it in motion.

We struck camp at dawn. The new sun revealed countryside that was comfortably familiar to me. We were far enough west now that the lay of the land and the features that covered it were consistent with the characteristics of the Bend. Gone were the steep-sided valleys and rifts. Now we rode over flat valleys that stretched between low, rolling hills.

In those parts, the road runs near to the edges of the Old Forest. That gave me a certain ease of mind. The Children of the Forest had not allowed Dauroth to establish a foothold in their woodlands. I planned to use that fact to our advantage that night. Still, we kept a good watch, and I tired several good men and women with aggressive scouting activities.

We stopped at midafternoon. The location we chose was well back from the road, nestled under the eaves of the forest. I did not think the Old Ones would mind; they knew me, and I had no fear of them, except the reasonable fear one has of what appears to be a friendly tiger. Only a few miles lay between us and the place where the road jogs due north for a time. There, the road meanders through a set of hills before arrowing straight west toward its intersection with the Old Road, just south of the city.

We did not pitch tents or indulge in other unnecessary comforts. I wanted to be up and out with as little trouble as possible in the twinight. Arica had slept in a tent with my wife and me since we left Branden and the main army. Tonight she would rest next to Lina under the stars and leaves.

As the sun set, I made a final inspection of our defenses and our preparations for the morrow. Once I was sure we were secure and prepared, I lay me down to sleep next to my wife. Arica wasn't with us. She decided to stand a watch, something she had insisted on doing since we left Stormhaven. I was not about to argue with her desire. She was a Tallean warrior, as well as an Old One. For all I knew, she might be the deadliest archer in the camp; she was certainly the quietest.

Our camp was nestled under the eaves of the Old Forest. Many sentries stood guard or walked patrols. Despite the lack of entrenchments, I was confident we were safe, and, tired as I was, sleep found me quickly.

I was dreaming of a tree. It reached up into the darkness, stars depending from its branches like sliver leaves. I heard a voice calling my name. At first, I thought it was part of the dream, the tree's voice, or maybe the stars'.

"Calen Farseer. I would speak with you."

Lina and I came awake at the same moment. She sat bolt upright. Her dagger was in her hand before I thought to reach for my sword. She extended it menacingly. Peering into the darkness, I made out the shadowy form crouching at our feet. It was the shape of a man hunkering down. Swathed in folds of gray, he was indistinct even at this short distance.

The figure extended a hand toward us. "Calen and the Lady of River's Bend need not fear me. I am Emen of family Traneal."

If the ranks of warriors had pressed in on us as closely as they did each other, even this hushed conversation would have attracted attention. But no one had noticed so far. All were weary from the ride. The patrols were concentrated on the perimeter; we were at the center of the camp.

But not all were oblivious. By the tree-dimmed light of the moon, I saw the form of Arica materialize out of the darkness behind the gray-clad figure. She stood a few paces behind the form, an arrow pulled to full readiness. It was aimed at the intruder. She had not made a sound.

The Old One at my feet retracted his hand. Raising his voice just a bit, he said, "Does the daughter of Lelan not recognize her father's brother?" I do not know how he knew she was there. I had been looking at her and yet did not hear her.

The bow complained as Arica eased the tension. Moving as silently as a star's thought, she knelt next to the man and touched her forehead to his.

"*Ahna e rhu*, uncle," she said. Share my breath. It is a greeting among the Children of the Forest.

The figure shifted, kissed Arica's forehead. "Truly you are Lelan's daughter. *Ahna e rhu*." There was pride in his voice.

That little scene gave me time to regain my composure. It also allowed me to think through what was happening. Obviously this man had not come to harm us. If he had, we would be dead already.

"You are welcome here, Emensa of family Traneal, though your coming is unexpected. Is your task urgent, or do we have a moment?"

"The answer to that is both and neither. My task will wait

until you have done what you now need to do."

"I thank you. May your sons hunt with the love of Ea in their hearts."

"May yours never stray from the Maker's path."

I could see by the moon that it was only a little past midnight. I found the captain of the guard and told him we had a visitor. This, as you might imagine, dismayed him. I gave him hasty assurance that I did not hold it against him. I suspected Emen was a Silanni, one of the Silent Assassins of the Old Forest. It is said that walls cannot hold the Silanni, nor can eyes see them when they do not wish to be seen. I gave the captain orders that we were not to be disturbed. Then I went back.

It was a strange gathering around our bed rolls. The four of us sat knee to knee as Emen told us what he had come to say. He had thrown off his hood. His face was bold, untarnished by falsehood and the scars it leaves in its wake. I did not see a family likeness to Marn, but Emen may not have been a sibling to the woodcutter. The Old Ones often refer to members of their clans, even distant ones, as brother, sister, son, or daughter. The fact that this man knew Marn's true name—Lelan—went a long way in easing any doubts I might have had about him.

"You ride this road to the city, Calensa." He added the "sa" to my name as an honorific. The Old Ones do that among themselves. It was courtesy to me.

I nodded. "I have been told Twofords is in peril."

"You must not take this road."

I knew better than to question an Old One when he was trying to impart information. "It will be as you say, Emensa."

Emen nodded. His teeth flashed in the moonlight. Maybe it was a smile. Among the Children of the Forest, trust without question speaks loudly.

"You send many scouts. We watch them come and go. Yet our eyes were not the only to have marked them. Yester eve, when you were still far from here, two of your scouts were observed by a patrol of the enemy. They followed your scouts far enough to see this army. Then they rode in haste back to their camp near the city."

Emen shook his head and sighed. "It is a pity. We had been hunting that patrol. We would have destroyed them in the night, for they had dropped their blankets not far from the edges of the forest."

"I thank you, Emensa. The news that we are detected is not unexpected. I cannot hope to hide a riding of a hundred warriors, even from the eyes of men."

Emen smiled again, this time at my partial quotation of an ancient wisdom, "The Children of the Forest do not see with the eyes of men."

The Old One shook his head. "You do not yet understand. I did not come to tell you that you had been discovered. I came to tell you that an ambush awaits you."

I wanted to ask him where, but I managed to hold my impatient tongue. He waited for the question. When I did not ask it, he smiled again before he spoke.

"Not far from this place, the road turns north and is hemmed in by hills. You know the place."

"I do, Emensa. How many?"

"Too many. A hundred horses, three hundred soldiers of the foot. The trap is laid. They are well-positioned. You will be destroyed."

I searched for something to say more than for a solution. This was bad news, yet there was a glimmer of hope. Three hundred soldiers and a hundred horsemen were a sizable part of the armies that menaced Twofords. That left us an opportunity to slip in and do some real damage to those who remained.

Emen watched me. I felt Lina's hand slide over my forearm, a caress followed with a squeeze. I turned my head and kissed her brow.

Then I asked, "What of Twofords?"

"The city will fall soon unless you come to her aid. She would have fallen today, I think, if you had not attracted the wolf's attention."

"That bad?"

Emen did not answer, even by nodding. He just stared at me, waiting for me to ask. I had played this game many times with the Children of the Forest. There were turns yet to be taken before he would speak more openly.

"I may not turn aside, Emensa, though it cost every man and woman in this command. Twofords is too important to me and to Ehrylan. We have friends there."

"You say true, Farseer."

We sat in silence as I calculated my next step. I heard Arica clear her throat. We all turned toward her. She looked uncomfortable under the scrutiny. Then she shook back her hair and spoke in a firm voice.

"When the road cannot take a woman where she needs to go, another must be found. Teryn needed such a rode once, and the Children built a bridge."

"Dara has taught you well, daughter." Emen reached up and placed his hand against Arica's cheek.

Merelina stirred beside me. Taking her cue from the younger woman, she said, "I have heard that the Children of the Forest know many roads that are hidden."

Emen chuckled. "Those who dwell in cities cannot see an obvious path." He paused, shook his head, sighed. "But you are right, Lady of River's Bend. There is a road."

"How can we find it? Our eyes are dulled." Leave it to my wife to cut right through the deer hide to get to the back strap.

"I will lead you."

I should have felt a gush of relief as he said these words, but it was more like a trickle. The game of words had siphoned off much of the emotion that had welled within me when Emen announced the news of the ambush. They are wise, the Old Ones. If their ways seem strange to us, it is usually because we are too young to understand.

III.

After Emen agreed to lead us on a safer road, he would say little else. It is frequently that way with the Children of the Forest. If they agree to help you, they take your trust in trade. It often feels like they take great joy in stretching boundaries of that trust, yet they have never failed me.

I summoned the watch commander and the other officers. It was still an hour or two before we were scheduled to arise and make ready for departure. Some of the men arrived with anxiety in their eyes, others with questions. A few faces showed curiosity accented with expectation. I marked those, for it was the look of veterans seasoned to the changing of plans.

A short explanation was all that was needed. Emen informed me that, for much of the way, we would be able to ride three abreast. There would be no galloping. The men were to stay on the course and not wander off. This last warning was probably unnecessary. This contingent had excellent discipline. But Emen stressed that detail to me. I had to make sure my men understood.

Within a very short time, we were mounted and ready to ride. My job was made easier by the two ladies. I returned from meeting with the captains to pack and ready the horses. Lina and Arica had done all that work. They were waiting for me to appear. Together we mounted our steeds.

And together we rode through the Old Forest in the dead of night under a nearly full moon. Unfortunately, these blessings did little to help us. We were under a thick canopy of branches that cut us off from the moonlight. The darkness was so complete that it was all we could do to see the man or woman in front of us or to either side.

Emen's course was by no means straight. It did, however, cut off several meanderings of the road that followed the borders of the forest. He led us back down the road to the east—the direction from which we had traveled—about a mile before turning south into the trees. I had not seen any opening in the forest the day before, nor had my scouts reported one. It was there, nevertheless.

Well inside the edges of the forest, Emen struck a relatively open lane that ran east and west. That is not to say the way was paved or plowed or even cleared. It was certainly not suitable for wagons or wheeled conveyances of any kind. I believe almost every step the horses took was on a thick carpet of leaves or an outcropping of rock. In the darkness, I could not tell if trees had been taken down to open the way. That mattered little to our purpose. It was enough that we were moving easily and without fear of attack.

On the other hand, we were not free from observation. I felt the eyes on my back. I am sure we were watched by other Children of the Forest. Some of my more perceptive men felt it as well. Lina and Arica turned to and fro, seeking the watchers as we rode.

We came to the Old Road before dawn. Emen gave us plenty of warning, so we were moving as quietly as one hundred anxious men and four hundred hooves can move. I was at the head of the column with Emen and met the other Old Ones who were waiting for us. I conversed with them as my captains ordered our formations.

The leader of these Old Ones was a man named Tamos. I had met him a time or two in the presence of Koppel, who, like Marn, was an Old One in self-exile. Tamos knew much of what transpired in the city and a great deal else. From him I learned that the field was mostly undefended. If we chose to, we could likely ride straight to the city without engaging the enemy. But that would have been an opportunity missed. We had come to help the city, not cower within its walls.

Lina and Arica played no part in that particular skirmish. They were never in any real danger, at least no more than any of the others behind the tottering walls of Twofords, which is where I sent them. I made my farewells to the two women whom I loved with all my heart and mind and left them in the care of Emen and Tamos. Both men knew of the secret tunnels beneath Twofords. The south entrance to those tunnels was currently accessible, which was not always the case. I had other duties to perform, so I was not there when the women and their guide actually got under way. They must have been within the city by the time I crossed swords with the first enemy.

We attacked Dauroth's army before the sun rose. Because of the ambush the enemy commander had set on the road we had not taken, he was not prepared for our assault as well as he might have been. There were no troops lining the palisades of his make-shift fort. There were few troops outside its protection.

About fifty soldiers and horsemen were deployed along the East Road, waiting for us in case we fled that way from the trap. But we came not from the East Road. We issued from the forest and rode with fury and hope north along the Old Road. The soldiers to the east scurried to mount their horses or grab their armament when they heard the roar of nearly four hundred hooves.

Thanks to a suggestion from Emen, many of our cavalry carried unlit torches or faggots of wood soaked in oil. When we came close the entrenched camp—which had sprung up between the city and the Old Forest in the scarce weeks since I had left the city—those riders kindled their fires and set them to blaze at the base of the gates, one south and one north. The primary idea was to keep the enemy's horses from coming out. With luck, the palisades themselves might catch.

By the time that was done, the sun was starting to light the sky. We could see the forces coming toward us from the east. Adjusting our plan somewhat, I wheeled toward them. If we could sweep them from the field, there would be that many fewer enemies to menace Twofords later.

It was a risky maneuver. If additional forces came around the city from the north, or if troops began to issue from the encampment, we might be cut off and have to retreat again. I was willing to take that risk. Our enemy had extended his hand to me. I would cut it off.

Now we were facing east as we rode, and the sun was

rising. Before long, it would be strong enough to interfere with our eyes. I adjusted course to the north slightly. That took me out of the path of a formation of four enemy spearmen who had taken a defensible position. Those following me would deal with them.

Straight away, I met two riders. The one nearest me was wearing a red cloak. It billowed out behind him as he charged. I guided Avyansa to the left with the pressure of my knee and hacked at the man as we passed. Our swords met, ringing in accompaniment to the other sounds that were filling the morning air. I turned quickly in the saddle to check the other rider. He was not in my way, so I returned my attention to the man in the red cloak.

The next time we crossed swords, I made sure my seat was firm. He rushed his attack, and his sword slipped in his hand. I won the encounter. He fell screaming from the back of his horse though I did not see it. I was moving on.

Someone else was engaging the other man that had ridden with my downed opponent. I moved closer and put the point of my sword between his shoulder blades. Like his fellow before him, he fell screaming from his horse. The man who had been fighting him looked at me wide-eyed, then nodded thanks. He was little more than a boy, not even Gammin's age. His name popped into my head—Andryg. I had spoken to him a time or two in the last week. It is important for the elder warriors to speak with the younger, especially on uncertain adventures.

That thought brought wings to the words in my mouth. I shouted above the din. "Well done, Andryg. Keep moving!"

He pointed with his bloody sword in answer. I could see the knot of men to which he was alerting me, and I could feel them. Several foot soldiers with spears and a cavalry officer were converging on us. Andryg took a place next to me, and, by then, my men were all around us. They were Branden's men, well-trained and up to their task, even if some of them were as young as milk in a dairyman's morning pail.

The spearmen were replaced by a parade of others as I

battled back and forth. Sometimes I rode to the aid of another. Other times, someone came to my aid. Avyansa, my friend and steed, bore me unfailingly though he was exhausted. As together we fought, I kept two things in mind. I must not stop moving. I must breathe.

By the time I had to look for foes to attack, we had carried the field. It was time to go. The fires had spread somewhat to the palisades, but the ground around the gates had been cleared. Fresh forces were issuing from the north entrance of the enemy encampment. They were not headed toward us; they were making straight for the city.

I stood in the stirrups and surveyed the way back to the forest. Enemy soldiers and cavalry were pouring from the southern gate of their encampment as well. Our retreat into the forest was already blocked by an accumulation of men and horses. We might yet make the forest, but it would cost many lives. Such a retreat would do almost nothing for Twofords.

I signaled my hornsman, who had somehow stayed near me without losing his life. He blew the notes that signaled the dash toward the city. That was our best hope now. I did not know if we could outrun the enemy riders who were already galloping that way. More troubling, I had no way of knowing if the people of Twofords would open the gates for us. That was Lina's battle.

My men must have seen the same thing I did. They were very quick to respond. Forming ranks as we rode, we headed toward the city gate with all the speed our weary mounts could muster. I could see men on the walls. No doubt they had sent word to their commanders. I could only hope that those commanders responded in a way that helped us. If they did not, my men and I would be caught between the weapons of our enemies and the walls of our allies.

Then I noted those walls. I was horrified. Twofords had changed much in the weeks I had been gone. The walls were battered almost beyond belief. Both towers astride the gate had been knocked down. Seeing her, I could only agree with Emen's estimation that Twofords could not stand much longer. The way it looked to me, the addition of my hundred men, or however many would be left of us after this morning's bloodletting, could do little to delay that fate.

I was not left to ponder these things further. We were approaching the city. The field was strewn with the wastes of war. Bodies were scattered about haphazardly. Half-burned shells of siege towers, battering rams, and throwers littered the ground like enormous turds in an overused cow pasture. Avyansa had to slow down to negotiate the maze. The oncoming enemy had the same difficulty. The race continued. The gate did not open.

We were not going to make it before our enemy. Fine then. We would fight. It was, after all, what we had come here to do. As we neared the place the two cavalry contingents would come together, I signaled again to my hornsman. He blew the command. A quick glance over my shoulder showed me that the riders behind were adjusting to it. Leaning forward, I shouted into my friend's ear. "Hold on, Avyansa. A little father now, a little farther to rescue and to rest!"

I sat up in the saddle, waved my sword over my head, and bellowed a war cry. We smashed into our enemy with the sound and feel of an earthquake. Horses screamed. Men fell, their mounts rolling on top of them in the confusion. Everywhere, steel cut flesh, and blood ran in rivers.

Then came the battle music.

What happened next lives in my memory mostly as a series of disjointed images. The two cavalries clashed about a hundred paces beyond the ditch we had dug around the walls. A chaos of sounds and smells swirled around us as bright metal turned red in the glow of a rising sun. I fought and fought, seeking ever a new opponent.

One memory stands out. I had just dispatched another rider. This came at the cost of a wound in my left arm. Some unseen opponent cut me as I killed his fellow. I turned toward the pain, seeking its author. The rider was no longer there, but I had a clear view back towards the Old Forest, back towards the encampment. What I saw threatened to suck the hope out of me. A wave of soldiers was marching toward us. Rank upon ordered rank, they were only a short distance away. We could not hope to stand against them.

I looked for my hornsman but could not find him. Desperate to sound a retreat, I tugged Avyansa around, searching. My friend responded sluggishly. He was utterly exhausted after days of hard riding. Standing in my stirrups, I surveyed the field. I saw few enemy horsemen. Free of any foe to fight, many of my countrymen were looking toward me. More were looking at the oncoming wave of death.

I was desperately trying to decide a course of action. Should we try to ride away? That would avail us little and Twofords nothing. North, we could not go because Dauroth's main force was there. West, we could not go because of the Silver River. The road south into the Old Forest was by now completely closed to us. And east… I looked that way, fearing that I would see the enemy's ambushing force marching back along that road. It was clear, at least for now, yet we dare not take that road.

Horns sang behind and above me, rich and sonorous, the horns of the Ehrylain. I heard the sound of the gate. The army of Twofords was coming out at last! The cheers of my men were so loud that they could be heard above the maelstrom that raged across the field.

Now my task was clear. We had to keep the area in front of the gate free so the newcomers could get out to help. Screaming at the top of my lungs, I pointed with my sword and kicked Avyansa. He responded despite his fatigue. He was a wonderful horse.

Leading the remainder of my cavalry, I charged towards the approaching foot soldiers. We crashed into them, a bolt of hooves and swords. They parted before us, and we were engulfed. That was fine. It meant there was no difficulty in finding foes to fight. Once again the battle music took me. Once again, I was left with only a jumbled assortment of disjointed scenes to remember.

When I came again to my senses, I was still aback Avyansa.

He was walking slowly toward the city, his head down. In front of me, only a few dozen paces away, the gate was open. The last of my cavalry was vanishing through it in orderly fashion. Each of them looked as depleted as I felt, but the brutal exhaustion was not reflected in their demeanor. They were hurrying and for good reason. Hundreds of enemy foot soldiers were rushing toward us out of the east. A flow of horsemen galloped before them. The thin line of Twofords' warriors who stood between us and the new wave of enemies would do little to impede them.

My hazed mind knew that it should recognize what those soldiers were. For a brief moment, it occurred to me that Branden had arrived to save the day. But if that was true, why were the men so unkempt and the ranks so ragged? Then I got it. This could not be Branden; he was still days away. These were the newly-returned ambushers who had come up the East Road from their foiled trap.

I kicked my horse for more speed. He shook his head, blew, and speeded up not at all. I chastised myself for my insensitivity and my foolishness. Did I want my friend to die beneath me? Summoning the last of my strength, I slid from his back and dropped the reins. I placed my right hand on his flank. Together, we passed under the gate arch and into the city.

2. SAD TIDINGS

I.

That is how I, Annen, a Justice of Ehrylan, came again to the small city in which I had made my home for many years. That homecoming cost many able warriors from my command, most of them in our effort to keep the gates clear while the forces of Twofords emerged. The city lost more than twice as many before all were safe inside the walls.

It was a hard price to pay, but it bought a fair exchange. Once they took the field, the warriors of Twofords had their way with the enemy, almost totally destroying the force that had been between the city and the forest at dawn. They were able to sack and burn the entrenched camp before the return of the soldiers that had been sent to waylay my cavalry.

As soon as I was through the gate, I was mobbed by well-wishers and people who thought they required my immediate attention. None of them knew that I required that same attention just to stay on my feet. I saw to Avyansa, leaving instructions with the groom for my good friend's care and comfort. Then, having been assured by my captains that our men and mounts were likewise under good care, I hustled to make sure my wife and Arica were safe. Along the way, I learned the worst news of the day.

I was making my way back from the stables to the castle proper. I found warriors who were familiar to me and sent one to let the council know I would attend them soon. I sent another to find Max or Breanna. I asked the third if he knew where I could find Torlan or Sheal. The look on the man's face stopped me in my tracks.

I set a hand on his shoulder. "What is it, Merrac?"

He looked down, then back up, shaking his head. "I am sorry, my lord. Sheal is dead."

My eyes closed, but that did not stop the tears. I opened them again immediately. As the leader of this army, it was important how I reacted. Tears were entirely proper, and I allowed them to run freely down my cheeks. But showing how devastated I was by this news was not proper. I hid it as best I could.

"How, Merrac?"

"He was shot in the back by an arrow, three arrows, actually. He died about a week ago. The enemy came upon us in the dead of night and without any warning. Sheal had the command that night. He took the men at hand and made a stand until others could arrive. His efforts kept the south gate from being breeched. The city would have fallen but for his bravery."

I forced a smile, squeezed the man's shoulder. "The city would have fallen long since but for the bravery and courage of all of you. He was a good man."

Merrac shrugged. "War harvests good and evil alike."

"Yes. King Brand used to say that war is blind and forever hungry. That is why we will end this one soon."

I thanked him, then went on my way, forgetting that I had asked about Torlan too. My feet carried me along without a destination while I struggled to force the grief into its room. Once it was there, I would visit it later, but not now. I had other things to do.

I did not find Lina in our rooms, which was the first place I looked. I could tell that no one had been there since we left. Chastising myself again for my stupidity, I realized I would have to force my weary legs to carry me back down to the south-side wall street. Of course she would be there. That is where the children were.

Before I left our apartment, I washed myself roughly and changed clothes. I felt a little better after that. Grabbing a shirt and tunic for my wife and a set for Arica, I hurried to the quarter of the city where Eanna and Lina served the people.

Merelina of River's Bend was there, surrounded by the children who were her riches. I came in quietly and watched until some clever little scamp found me out and raised the alert. During that time, I saw my wife smile and laugh. I saw her play and teach love in the playing. And I saw exhaustion in her face.

That observation was born out when she greeted me. I did not receive the usual hug or kiss. She did not even arise. When I crossed to where she was sitting, she only laid her hand on my arm as she looked up at me. The exhaustion in her eyes fell like a steady rain from the clouds of blue and gray. There was a great sadness too. A little of both those things melted away when she saw that I had brought her fresh clothing. For that I got my kiss.

I held her at arm's length and inspected her. She looked whole and no worse for wear. Then what I saw in her eyes seeped through my concern for her. I looked hurriedly around the room for the face I had not yet seen. I did not find it. My heart raced, yet I thought it might stop with the anxiety. It was a curious feeling. So great was the rapid tide of my rising fear that I had to clear my throat before I could speak.

"Merelina, where is Arica?"

Lina brought a hand up and placed it on my chest. It was a familiar gesture, and welcome. "Don't worry, Annen. She is here, somewhere. I think one of the girls took her to meet the new dog."

"New dog?"

Lina's beautiful eyes closed against tears. They tumbled down her cheeks anyway. Tears make an art of escape. "Maybe you don't know yet, Annen. I am sorry."

I lost my breath, had to catch it before I could question her. "No! Not Old Bil, too?"

The hint of a smile flickered across her lips. "No, not him. It's... it is... Annen, Sheal has been killed."

So many rivers of grief and relief converged within me that I had to drop my hands from her arms and let her go. I shambled to the nearest bench and sat down. My weariness found me there. So did Lina.

"I am sorry, Annen. I did not want to tell you like that."

I pressed my face against her. "No, lady, it is not that. I heard it already. But give me a moment. I am suddenly... tired."

Her hand came up and cupped my cheek. "You look tired, love."

She did not say anything more until I moved again. That is her way. My wife does not waste words where words will not help. She was completely content to sit with me and wait. That is what she did as I fought the exhaustion and sadness.

I was tired of fighting. That was unfortunate. The real trial had not yet started.

The children respected our privacy during this period. Such was their reverence for Merelina. The older ones, the ones who could see that something serious was underway, helped keep away the younger, who were oblivious to anything but their own desires. I did not allow myself to wallow in this muddy pit of fatigue mixed with grief. Questing with my lips, I found Lina's tiny ear and gave it a nip. She made a startled squeak and pushed away, but only a little.

I gave her a smile and gently pulled away the strands of her hair that had become attached to my four day's growth of beard. Remembering how this had all started with my question about the woodcutter's daughter, I said, "Help me. What does a new dog have to do with Sheal?"

"It is Sheal's dog. Now, since he is... is gone... it's come to live here. There is no one else to care for it. Just like the orphans."

I considered. That made a fair amount of sense. But there were three surprises hidden in the simple fact that Sheal's dog had come to stay. I had not known the man had a dog. I had not known he was unmarried and living alone. Most importantly, I realized that I was quite out of touch with important things in the lives of my friends. How little I shared myself with those around me! It took the death of a good friend to bring it to my attention. I would make sure to fix it.

I sat with the children as long as my tasks allowed. During that time, Max and Breanna found me. Remembering my recent promise, I asked them how they had been these last weeks. They wanted to call together their students right then and there to show me the progress they had made. Unfortunately, new resolution or not, I could not spare that much time. Promising I would visit him soon, I sent Max off with messages to various people and Breanna off to find Arica.

If I had let Max assemble his students, I would have learned much about Sheal's death and saved myself another trip. But I did not.

Little things in life make big differences.

II.

When Bre found Arica, she found Aldryn and Eanna, too. They were in a courtyard at the center of some nearby building used for housing the otherwise homeless. I hurried that way with the speed of someone three times my age, which was all I could manage. Arica was indeed brushing the dog when I got there. When it noted my coming, the beast stood up from the obedient sit it had been holding and growled menacingly.

It was a growl no one could ignore without peril. The beast bristled and showed it fangs as the fur on its back stood up. I saw in that instant that there must have been a silver wolf in its recent ancestry. It was not a child's pet. It was the companion of a warrior.

The aggressive posture did not last long enough for one of the people in the courtyard to speak it quiet. After a quick inspection of me, the large dog fell silent as death and crossed the space between us, its tail creeping higher with each step. I had to fight not to let my hand grope for the sword at my hip. I watched as the beast took a position directly in front of me. After sniffing my feet, it looked me right in the face, licked its muzzle, and lowered itself into a perfect sit. It's tongue lolled out, and it began to pant just like any happy dog might do.

"That's amazing," said Aldryn from across the square. He and I were old friends, long-time co-conspirators in the battle for Ehrylan's freedom. He and Eanna were married at the same ceremony as my wife and me.

I replied without taking my eyes off the calm storm of teeth and claws sitting not one pace from pieces of my body that were very important to me. "What is amazing?"

Aldryn said, "Watch."

His movement drew both my eyes and the eyes of the dog. Aldryn paused for a moment and nothing further happened. Then he took two steps towards me. Immediately, the dog was up and growling again. Aldryn stopped. The growling stopped. The man took another step. The two previous growls had been fierce warnings; this one was a sign of imminent attack.

Eanna's command echoed over the rolling ululation. "Faeryntha! No!" The growl stopped straight away. The beast sank once more into a sit. From my position, I could see that the fur on its back was still agitated.

Faeryn is a word in the Old Tongue that means friend. It has a flavor that is not only that of a friend; it tastes of a special friend, one who is cherished, one who is held with uncommon favor in the heart. I took this strange derivation of that word as a command that told the dog Aldryn was a friend. I was wrong.

Arica said, "Faeryntha, come!"

The dog looked at her. It turned back to me and gazed up at my face. Our eyes met. The dog moved close enough to touch me. It lifted its muzzle and gently licked my hand once.

Then it trotted over to Arica, presenting its back for more brushing.

"Amazing," said Aldryn and I at the same time.

My old friend crossed the courtyard. I could see he was keeping the corner of his eyes on that dog. Who could blame him?

After a strong hug and stronger slap on my back, the carpenter said, "Welcome back, Annen. It's about time. We were starting to think you were going to stay up there in that castle and drink this war away with the Defier!"

He was joking, of course. I had sent messages early on, letting the council know that the Defier was a good ally. My attention was still fixed on the wolf in dog's fur lurking so near my *faeryn*, Arica. I said, "Why does that dog mistrust you, Aldryn?"

It was Eanna who answered. She had come to stand with us. As she hugged me, she said, "It growls at everyone at first, especially men. You and Torlan are the only two it tolerates as far as I can see. I fed it for a full week before it stopped growling at me."

"Seems like a risky animal for an orphanage," I said, glancing at Arica. She was focused on her brushing. She bore a sad aspect, one that, until recently, had been a stranger to her.

"That's just it, though," replied Eanna. "You'd think every child was one of her pups. She rolls on the floor with them and lets them pull her ears and tail. She's even more tolerant of their indiscretions than Bil."

At his name, I looked around for Old Bilious, the one-eyed, tattered-eared hound that had been with Eanna for so many years. He was off to one side between Arica and where Eanna had been standing. When he saw me look at him, he struggled to his feet and came to me. I crouched down and received a good deal of fur and slobber in greeting.

When I stood up again, I said, "Old Bil tolerates her?"

"Oh, more than that," answered Eanna. "They are inseparable."

"That's good," I replied, thinking it was a fine thing for Old

Bil to have a new friend, especially one who could look out for him. He was quite old.

A youngster came into the courtyard. He was looking for Eanna to report this hour's minor emergency. Eanna and Aldryn took their leave. I was left alone with Arica and the two dogs.

"How are you, Arica?"

"I am fine, Annen. It is good to see you."

"And you, lady. I am glad that wolf has not eaten your hand."

She smiled in spite of her melancholy mood. "She does seem to be more wolf than dog. But she is well-trained."

"Yes, I can see that. Sheal was a wonderful man. He was a good warrior and a good leader. And he was kind."

I talked my way into a reminiscent silence. Faeryntha sensed my feelings. She voiced a tiny whimper and looked around the courtyard as if searching for the man who would never again be there for her. Arica immediately knelt and put her arms around the dog, burying her face in its fur. It was a compelling scene.

After a time, Arica lifted her face and looked at me. "I am sad for her. She lost something really important. Can you imagine how she feels? I can. Only, I don't have to imagine."

I mistook her meaning, thinking she was referring to her own spirit, which seemed uncommonly suppressed these days. Though I did not know it at the time, Arica had begun to develop the gifts Ea gave to the Children of the Forest. Those people have a way with all animals, as I have said time and time again.

"Arica, will you stay with Lina and me? You are welcome, as you well know."

"No, shinando. I would like to stay in the Grove. That is where my father and mother live. I will feel at home there."

Arica had never been to the grove. She, her brother, and Gammin left the city before her parents took residence there.

"As you wish. You know that you are always welcome."

I was trying to find a way to address the strange feeling I

was getting from her. That there was something amiss, I was certain, but I could not determine what it was. Not for the last time, I rued that the thing others termed my far seeing could not be focused when and where I wanted.

I reached down and tugged her up gently. Then I encircled her in my arms and hugged her for a long time. She was a woman now, coming soon to her twentieth year. She was almost the same size as Merelina. I wanted to talk with her more, but there was no time.

I was already over-long in my stay. It was always like that for me in the orphanage. To be there among the children seemed to be one of best things in life.

"I have to go, Arica. Max or Bre will show you to the Grove. If there is anything you need, you know where Lina and I are. Or, wait, no you don't! We are in the castle now. Max and Bre can take you there, too. We will expect you for supper soon, tomorrow or the next day at the latest."

I kissed her cheek. After saying my farewells to the two animals, I left in a hurry.

Though I was weary to my bones, I still had much to do before I could rest. There was even more to do after. I expected some response from the enemy. Its main local force was still comfortably occupying the sturdy fort they had built north of the city. What the response might be, I could not guess, but we had to be ready.

I met with the council next. There were a few empty seats. Sheal was dead. He had not yet been replaced. Dara and Marn were still with Branden. I brought with me the senior officer from among my contingent of the Defier's cavalry. That force was now a significant percentage of Twofords' forces. They deserved a seat and the representation that went with it. I could have represented them, but that did not seem politic to me. I informed the council that the man was a new member without bothering to observe their reactions. There was no time for niceties.

I told the council about the Defier and the plans I had made with him. I left out the news that he was actually the lawful ruler of this city and the entire kingdom. This was something the king and I had agreed to. He would choose the time and place for that little revelation.

The reports that I heard were bad, but not as bad as I had feared. The walls were in poor shape. Twofords' army was better. We had not lost as many as I would have guessed. The Defier had sent a hundred men and their horses to Twofords a month or so before when he had summoned me. Most of them had stayed in the city. Among them were trained and experienced officers. They had done wonders. The fact that they were obviously Southlanders, though of the odd eastern variety, helped.

The news that the Defier would soon arrive with almost a thousand men was most welcome. How soon that might be, I could not predict. It might be anywhere from two sunrises to five, depending on the weather and on what the enemy might do to hinder them. In the meantime, I suggested, we needed to see to the walls. The councilors did not protest. Perhaps, like me, they were too tired.

That is as far as we got. My fatigue caught up with me at that point. It was almost more than I could do to keep my eyes open. With apologies, I excused myself, promising to meet with them bright and early the next day. In the most strenuous terms I could muster, I abjured them to attend the walls. Then I went to seek a comfortable bed and a familiar scent.

The next morning, I had the energy to ask after Sheal's death. Koppel told me what he knew. He also told me that if I wanted it from someone who had been there at the time, I should seek out Max. That sent me straight back the orphanage with Breanna scrambling behind me to keep up. Fool that I am, I did not realize I could have asked her.

Along the way, I saw how truly depleted our city was. We had, after all, been under siege for two years. I passed through the market. There were many empty stalls and as many traders standing behind almost empty tables and shelves. Customers crowded the few locations that still hosted useful things. Prices were as high as the sky. That was to be expected. More troubling to me was what I saw in the faces of the people. Their eyes were as empty of hope as the bare tables. This I did my best to remedy. When greeted, I responded with as much good cheer as I could muster, fake though much of it was. When I saw someone who looked particularly downcast, I spoke words of hope to them, and, if they told me of their woe, I suggested places where they might get what they needed.

Max discovered I was on my way before I set foot on the wall street. He was waiting for me at the door to the orphanage. I had not yet learned of his system of sentries and the excellent communications system they had arranged. But good as it was, that system could not divulge to him the inner workings of the council, so he did not know my errand.

I took him straight away to someplace we could have privacy.

"Tell me," I said, "what happened the night Sheal was killed."

His head bowed for a time. He began speaking before he looked up. "Sheal was in command that night. I had duty at the south gate with the Young and the Old."

The Young and the Old was an affectionate label Max's two squads had been given by the regular warriors. It was an affection they had earned the same way they earned the right to stand watches. Those squads, mostly children and grandparents, fought with great honor at the Battle of the North Gate. That was now some two years gone, though it felt more like a yesterday from a hundred years ago.

"It was after midnight. I had just finished making the rounds." He lifted his head and looked me in the eye. "It sounds grand, doesn't it, making the rounds? I walked up the tower on one side of the gate, across the battlement, and down the other tower, checking on the watchers at each station."

He stopped. I took the opportunity to inspect him more closely. He had grown noticeably in the month or so I had been gone. He would never be taller than a boy, but I could see age adding to his body. More than that, he was carrying himself more like a man than a fifteen year old.

"It felt like a thousand eyes were watching me. I couldn't shake the feeling that something was wrong. I hadn't seen or heard anything, you understand, and the lookouts were alert. I felt strange enough that I found Bre and talked with her about it. She said we should go up together and look again. It seemed a good idea."

I turned to Breanna. She said nothing. Her lower lip pushed out just a bit. She nodded and fixed her adoring gaze on Max. The boy gestured to her.

"You tell this bit, Bre. I only went back up because of you."

Bre's eyes grew as large as saucers at being put on the spot. However, though she did not speak much in the presence of strangers or other adults, she was not frightened to talk to me. Children give gifts of love of which they are not even aware.

"Max decided we should go back up. I only suggested it. We climbed the tower stair and stood on the battlement looking out between those teeth-looking things. You know, the low and high places where the archers stand?"

"Yes, the crenellations. Go on." Strictly speaking, the crenellations were only the low spots.

"Creminations," she repeated, squinting with the effort. I did not correct her. "There wasn't much moon, so we could not see very well. But there was something. I don't know what." She looked at Max for help.

"I think it was a smell," he said. "Or maybe we could hear something out of place."

Bre nodded. "Anyway, Max sent me off to find Sheal, which I did pretty quickly. He took it seriously. He sent me to the east wall to warn them. I wasn't with Max when the attack came."

Max said, "She hadn't been gone very long when I did hear something. There was no mistaking it. I went back down in a rush and raised the alarm. After that, I guess I just sort of did what I thought might be the right thing to do. I sent the best archers from our group up the walls and organized the rest as best I could. You know how it is."

I did. I was astounded by this young man.

"By the time Sheal arrived, the attackers had crossed the ditch and were scaling the walls. They used the same ladders for both, which I thought was pretty smart. We were fighting them off best as we could, but there were more of them than us. They overwhelmed us. Then Sheal arrived with about ten men he had gathered on his way. That helped a lot, but it was not nearly enough."

No, it would not have been. According to Koppel, some two hundred men had mounted a surprise attack against the south gate that night, another two hundred against the east wall.

"Try as we might, we could not drive them off or kill all the ones who climbed over the wall. I thought we were really in for it. But not Sheal! He just raised a cry and fought harder. More of our men were arriving all the time—we had raised the alarm, you remember—so there was some hope. Still, the enemy soldiers got the gate open.

"Sheal organized anyone who was free enough to listen and went to defend the opening. I went with him. He managed to push the enemy back far enough so that others could start to close the gate. The bad guys had managed to wedge it open so it could not easily be closed. They just kept coming. At some point, I noticed that I was outside the gate. There were a lot of our warriors helping by then. Still, it got really nasty. Then we heard the call and knew the gate was closing.

"I beat it back in as soon as I could. Sheal came last of all. He was about ten paces from the gate when the arrows hit him. He fell right on his face, but he wasn't dead yet. He started to crawl forward, tried to get to his feet. Another arrow hit him, and he fell again."

Max's voice broke. His head bowed. If he shed tears, I never saw them.

Breanna said, "That's about when I got back from the east wall, which was also under attack. I saw Sheal go down the second time." She put out a hand to cover Max's where it rested on the table. "I saw Max go out to get him. Everyone was just staring at Sheal. We were kind of stunned. But Max didn't even hesitate. He charged right back out and tried to lift him, but there was no way. So he started to drag him. There were arrows everywhere. We had lots of archers on the wall by then. The soldiers could not come close, but they were shooting back. Max just ignored them as he dragged Sheal toward the gate."

Max had regained his control. "Two came out, after a while. They helped me. We got him back in, but he was dead already."

I looked at the boy. He stared right back. There was no need to make him tell anymore. I had heard the rest from Koppel. The assault on the east wall and the south gate had been driven off. But for this young man and young woman, the city might have fallen that night.

"You did very well, Max, and you, too, Breanna." Then, very formally, I added, "I am proud of you. More than that, I am proud to be your teacher. I thank you. You have brought honor to your names, to my name, and to this city."

Bre did her typical head bowing and lip pushing, embarrassed as always to be the focus of any attention no matter how much she craved it. Max's reaction was unusual. He did not look pleased. He looked sad, almost confused.

"Shinando, I thank you for the compliments, but I don't deserve them. I failed, twice over."

"Two things, huh?"

He smiled for an instant in spite of himself. "Yes, twice a failure."

"Tell me how. I will judge. Sometimes a man is harder on himself than is necessary."

"Well, I was guarding the gate, me and half the Young and the Old. The enemy got through. Many people died. Sheal died. A councilman lost his life because I failed!"

"I do not see it that way, Max. How can fifteen stand against hundreds? The duty of the gate warders is to keep the watch and raise the alert if the enemy attacks. You did both those things perfectly by your own account. As for Sheal, he died because he did his job, not because you failed him. You sent for Sheal on the strength of a feeling. You were right to do so. Sheal did the right thing by responding immediately and by sending men also to the east wall. The enemy was driven back. Good men died. That is war."

I came to a full stop, considered. Putting a hand on his shoulder, I made him look into my eyes. "I am the general of our army, and I tell you that I am pleased with you. You must put away the thoughts of failure and see your deeds in the light they themselves cast. Now tell me the second thing."

Max looked down then up again. I could see the second issue was harder for him.

"Shinando, I was scared! More than any of the other times I've fought, I was scared that night. I don't know why it was different, but it was. After all the training and all the battles, I was afraid!"

I had to suppress a laugh. "Max, listen to me. I am frightened every time I go to battle. Being frightened of the frightful is not a failure."

"You? Afraid? I don't believe that."

I looked at Bre for support. Her eyes opened wide. She shook her head. She did not believe me either. I did not know what to say.

"I saw you, shinando, at the Battle of the Bend. And, I was there when you leapt from the walls at the Battle of the North Gate. You did not look like a man afraid."

"Maybe not, *onando*, but I was." He brightened visibly at what I had called him, *onando*, one who follows in your footsteps. "Truth to tell, sir, I was mostly scared that I would break both my legs with that jump. And, I was scared that I would lose one of my favorite students, one of my best friends, if I didn't do something quickly. I thought you were very brave to go out onto that field by the North Gate. That took real courage, my boy."

"I thank you, shinando. I was not so brave that night at the

South Gate."

Images formed in my mind—Max struggling to pick up a large, dead warrior; Max dragging the lifeless body through the dirt and blood; arrows whizzing all around; other men, seasoned warriors, staring from the gate, afraid to go back out into the swirling death to help. Suddenly, I was the one holding back tears.

"Max, listen to me. This is important. Do you understand? I want you to hear me."

He nodded. Bre nodded. She screwed her face up in the effort to attend my words.

"There can be no bravery unless first there is fear. Good fear is the mind's response to danger. Bravery is doing what must be done in the face of that fear."

The puzzled looks on their faces showed me that I had not explained well enough. I struggled for an apt simile. "It is like this. One can't come of out of the rain unless it is raining."

Bre got it first, then Max. They looked at each other. I saw something pass between them that I had never noticed before. Breanna gave him a small nod. When he saw it, Max's face was washed by a flood of relief, sudden and complete.

III.

Later that day, I received word from Koppel. The scouts had returned. I went to see them right away. Their most important news, though we did not know it at the time, was that a party of some twenty riders had arrived at the enemy fort north of the city. There was little else of interest other than that the enemy on the south field had been reinforced with troops from the northern camp. They had already started to rebuild their enclosure. There was no word from Branden yet, nor could one be expected. I had sent a fast rider with the news of our victory, but at best, the man could only now be arriving at the prince's side.

As far we could tell, the enemy now numbered some fifteen

hundreds equally split north and south. That was fairly good news. Between the two of us, Branden and I had a matching force. Also, if the enemy did not increase the men in the south field, Branden would out-number them by a nice margin. Nice for us, that is. The men and women at arms within the city could hope to hold off an assault of seven hundred from the north. As long as our walls stood firm, we might even repel simultaneous attacks north and south, though that would be a test indeed. If our walls did not hold, we would be in for it.

The rest of the day, I toured the city and reviewed our troops. The men and women were the best of it; they put on brave faces and spoke proud words to me. The condition of the weapons and supplies were the worst. These had no words, save only those silent syllables spoken by notched blades, broken spears, and depleted storehouses. Everywhere, I saw the signs that accompany siege. The walls were a patchwork. I was reminded of garments that had been long used and frequently mended. Many structures within the city were in a similar condition. Some had been entirely destroyed by the enemy's catapults.

We did not see Arica that night. Lina had spoken with her twice during the day, so we knew she was getting along. My wife and I shared a meager meal of the food we had brought with us in our saddle bags. It was better than many in the city could hope for. The weather was warm enough that we did not need a fire. That was well, for there was now a shortage of firewood in the city.

Still exhausted by the week's labors, I slept through the knock on the door that awakened Lina. When I shook off the knots of sleep that bound me, she was standing over me by the side of our bed. I saw concern on her face. I chased it away with a kind word and a kiss of her hand.

Putting that hand to my cheek, she said, "A message has come from Torlan. You are to go to the council chamber right away."

I sighed and let my shoulders slump before remembering myself. "I thank you, love. You go back to bed. I'll be back as soon as I can."

She nodded, but she did not go back to bed. Standing silently, she watched me splash water on my face and run wet fingers through my sleep-snarled hair. She clawed gently at her own cascade of hair, something she did when she was anxious.

I put my hands on her shoulders. "I'll be back," I said, holding her eyes with mine and forcing a smile. I did not have to force it for long. Her eyes stole my breath and reminded me how lucky I was, even amid this hardship. Every day with her was full reward for a lifetime's labor.

She nodded and returned an equally-forced smile. I kissed her on her nose and began to leave. Reaching for the door, I heard her call out behind me.

"Wait!" She hurried to the table and picked an apple out of the bowl. It was old and wrinkled, ugly. "You'd better take this. You might not get a chance to eat for a while."

I accepted it, thinking how new and lovely she was by comparison. I took her in my arms and held her. We communicated a great deal without any words.

The council chamber was fully lit. Guards were positioned on either side of the door. Koppel was there, and Torlan. I was pleased to see Garlean, the officer from the Defier's cavalry I had added to our little group. Two scouts were seated on one side of the table. The councilors were on the other. My chair waited. I dragged it next to one of the scouts and collapsed into it. The man nearest me spoke immediately.

"Lord Calen, there was a disturbance in the enemy camp north of the city."

Hope flared within me. "An attack?" Perhaps Branden had sent another contingent after all. If so, it would have to be a mounted party. There was no way foot soldiers could have covered the distance in so short a time.

Even as the scout answered, I was calculating in my head. How long would it be until the main army of foot soldiers could get here? I had performed this mental calculation about three times each hour for the last two days. The answer never changed. We would see three more dawns before the king arrived, probably four.

I wondered if it might be Branden's Black Guard. They were a set of elite warriors, six men and six women. They were something new the prince had cooked up in the last three decades. As far as I knew, King Brand had not used such a corps. My eager heart connected some imaginary dots. Perhaps the disturbance was associated with the arrival of the small party the scouts had reported yesterday. Had they been the Black Guard in disguise? Maybe they had infiltrated and were fighting out from within! If so, we needed to do something to help them right away.

I came through the haystack of thought back to a table of men looking at me expectantly. "I am sorry. What did you say?"

"I do not think it was an attack. If it was, the attack came from within the camp, my lord."

Hope began to spread from my heart to my head. "What did you see?"

"Sparks and fires, lord. It seemed to me that fire leapt into the sky from within the palisades, almost like lightning going the wrong way. But it was fire, not lightning. It was quickly over, except for the screaming."

"Screaming?"

"Two or three men, lord. They were screams of pain and of terror, I think."

The other scout spoke for the first time. "I heard them too, Annen. I thought men were being burned alive. I am not sure why. Perhaps such an ill thought fit the fright that was on me."

That last sentence made me focus all my attention on the second scout. If I had not already known him, his words would have given him stature. Few men willingly admit fear to their leaders. His name was Rehlys. He had been in the Resistance for years—one of my five officers—which accounted for why he called me Annen rather than Lord Calen. Now, he was captain of all our intelligence gatherers. He was a stalwart warrior and a very good scout.

"What frightened you, Rehlys?"

"I am not sure." He shook his head slowly as if in deep thought. "There was nothing in particular, just a feeling in the night. Perhaps it was a bad smell or an ill wind? I cannot say, but it is true, nonetheless. An unreasonable fright was on me."

I was going to offer him words of encouragement, but the other scout jumped in.

"I felt the same way. It was as Captain Rehlys says. There was no menace that I could see, but I felt oppressed, almost like there was a ravenous wolf behind every tree."

All at once, I saw. My mind leapt over the chasm of unknowing and into a pool of certainty. There was a Gryhm. Damn. The Gryhm were Dauroth's most-dreadful servants. Like him, they were inhuman; they were demons inhabiting human bodies. Neither of these scouts was old enough to have been in the great wars, so I did not voice my realization to them. There was no reason to add to their fear by naming it.

"I understand. What else did you see or hear?"

Rehlys, like any good leader, let his subordinate speak first. "There was nothing, Lord Calen. Though there was not much to go on, I felt the news needed to be brought back to the city. I hurried, too. I was relieved when I met Captain Rehlys at the mouth of the tunnel and learned he carried the same report."

The man realized what he had said and threw a hasty look around the chamber. A wash of relief flooded his face for an instant, then his eyes returned to Garlean with a start. The tunnels were by no means common knowledge. I had not known of them before this war broke out two years ago. There was no harm in Garlean knowing, so I waved the scout's self-reproach away with what I hoped was a reassuring smile.

There was nothing more from either scout. We dismissed them with our thanks for a job well done. I might have told them to be extra careful from now on. What good would that have done? They were scouts. Their whole job was an exercise in being especially careful. Their lives depended on it.

After they left, I told Koppel and the others what I

thought. Nay, that is almost a lie. I told them what I was sure of, though there was no proof. A Gryhm had come to Twofords. They accepted it without question. I was both gratified and discomfited by their ready confidence in me.

We doubled the guard and put the first responders on alert. The council agreed that we should prepare for an all-out battle as soon as might be. If a Gryhm was here, it was not to parley. That is not their purpose or their way.

I went back to my wife in hopes of finding two more hours of sleep before the new dawn ushered in its share of misfortunes. She was not abed when I arrived. She was sitting next to an unlit hearth, staring into its cold depths. I took her into our bed, but sleep did not find us there. We lay in each other's arms until the fingers of morning pushed around the shutters. I thought I felt her body trembling occasionally. Maybe it was my own. When we were together like that, with her head on my chest and a leg draped over mine, it was difficult for me to determine where she ended and where I began.

3. BREACHED

I.

I was standing on the north wall. The sky was darkening behind a layer of brooding clouds. The day had passed. Directly below me was the gate. Behind me and to either side were ranks of Twofords' finest warriors, archers, and cavalry. The empty killing field stretched below me, from our ditch—which was not grand enough to be called a moat yet—to as far as our bows and catapults could hurl their missiles. Beyond lay the assembled army of our enemy. The air between us was tight, expectant.

The troop movements had started before the sun rose. The enemy general sent his forces out in numbers so great we could not go out to do battle. He must have emptied his camps, both north and south. Likewise, we emptied our barracks, houses, and armories. We filled our hopes with prayers.

It was a scene we had witnessed many times before, but it was different this time. For the first time, the enemy army stretched in strength all around the city walls. Boats without number, filled with soldiers and the various devices of assault, crowded the shallow waters between the two fords. They were so many and so thickly set that I thought one might walk from bank to bank without getting wet feet.

The enemy was about to launch the greatest assault we had yet seen. Their sheer numbers were enough to put fear into the hearts of our men and our leaders, too. I was not immune. I tasted that fear. It was familiar to me. Had I not stood outnumbered at Branden's side time and again in the great wars? But Branden was not here. We would have to make do on our own.

My belief was that the Gryhm had punished the general and officers who had failed to keep our cavalry from entering the city. If I was right, he had burned them. That told me who we were up against. Perhaps what we were up against is a better description. Chilshan, an Arch Gryhm, was the Fire Gryhm in King Brand's day. I knew him. He was clever beyond reckoning. His delight in evil knew no limits.

The Gryhm had to know of Branden's army, had to know that help would soon arrive at Twofords. He could ill afford to sit and wait for it. If I were in his shoes, I would attack the city now with all I had in hope of overcoming it before Branden got here. If I was right, we were in for the fight of our lives.

As the last light bled from the sky, trumpets blared within our enemy's ranks. A selection of soldiers stepped forward, one about every hundred paces. Each of them held a tall, wooden pole that looked like a giant, unlit torch. The ranks directly across from the gate stirred. A single rider emerged from among them. He was dressed in yellows and reds. His horse was black as night and fitted with a mask that resembled the snarling face of a wolf.

The rider sat unmoving as the horse walked forward. He was well into the killing field when he stopped, as if he had no fear of arrow or stone. For a long moment, the Gryhm sat silent. Of a sudden, his voice thundered across the space between us, inhumanly clear and loud.

"Where is Calen Farseer?"

The voice carried a gust of terror, as if the very words were weapons that could destroy us. Around me, I felt men's hearts begin to cower. Fear is a tool that all Gryhm use. Some say it is part of their magic. Whether that is true or not, I knew I must not delay.

"I am here." I laid my hand on the pommel of my sword but did not draw it.

The rider raised one hand in an abrupt motion. The long poles held by the selected soldiers burst into flame at the top. Two pillars of fire erupted from the ground on either side of the Gryhm. The ground trembled so that the rocks of the wall shifted. Then, just as abruptly, the tumult ceased, and the pillars of fire vanished. Only the giant torches stayed lit, sputtering and coughing in the night breezes.

Once more, the voice boomed out. "We have met before, Calen Farseer. Do you remember?"

"I remember you, Chilshan. I defeated you before. I will do so again. The Defier sent your brother back into nothingness. Your fate will be the same."

The Arch Gryhm, the Fire Gryhm, laughed. It was a cruel laugh. There was no mistaking the malicious mirth it contained. "Where Charshan has failed, Chilshan shall succeed. What hope do mortals have against the seed of eternity?"

"The future does not exist until mortals turn it into history, Gryhm. Get you gone, foul stench of evil. If you stay, your armies will be defeated."

"Words," he returned, scoffing. "I offer the people of this city their lives." The last word echoed, though there was no reason for an echo. "Lives... lives... ives... ives... sss...sss."

When the sound died, he continued with his show. "All they need do is lay down their arms, submit to my master, and deliver you to me. That is not much to ask for so many lives."

"You ask everything, Gryhm. We will not submit."

Chilshan's voice turned silky. "Is it your choice to make, Calen? Perhaps your people will make a wiser decision."

Rehlys was near me. He had his bow at the ready. It was a long bow. He leaned close. "Shall I put an arrow in him, Annen?

He did not know the ways of the Gryhm.

"Nay, my friend. Your arrow would not survive its flight, and then you would be open to his reprisal." I thought about that for a moment, decided to be more specific. How else would he learn? "To his magic, you might say. That's something to avoid if you can. This is all a show. It will end soon. He already took his best shot with the earthquake. Our walls stood the test. So will we."

I turned my back on the Gryhm, which is never a clever move. Drawing my sword, I held it aloft and cried out to those assembled within the city. "What say you, countrymen? I would rather die fighting for a free life than live to die in chains. Will you surrender or fight to live as the Ehrylain of old?"

A huge cheer floated on the breath of my countrymen, a mixture of "Annen," and "Calen," and "Ea," and "Ehrylan," and "King Brand!"

This went on for some time. When finally silence lent its ear again, the Gryhm spoke. "So be it, then. Die!"

He stood in his stirrups and gestured toward me. The rumble of catapults leapt across the open space. The sound arrived just in time for me and the others on the wall to throw ourselves behind merlons, the raised teeth between crenellated spaces. Most of the rocks fell short. A few landed within the city, leaving death and destruction in their wake. One struck the wall.

I shouted an order. Our throwers responded. The battle began.

II.

We tossed giant stones back and forth for a time. Then, at the signal of a trumpet, Chilshan's army began to move forward. They did not come in a measured march. They had learned that much. They charged through the killing field screaming as they came. Many fell with Southland arrows through their bodies. Far more, many times more, came through to lay ladders and ramps across our ditch. We tumbled rocks onto them, shot scores of arrow into them. They fell only to be replaced by the next man and then the next.

Sooner rather than later, ladders and ramps bridged the ditch. Enemy troops streamed across. They threw grappling hooks. We cut the ropes. They pushed ladders up against the parapets. We shoved them backwards. All the while, our archers and warriors showered them with arrows and rocks. Still they came, heedless of the deadly rain. They were driven by fear of the Gryhm, a worse fear than death. I could see him sitting on his horse, illuminated with an unnatural light of his own making. He was laughing.

All round the city, the walls were washed by waves of soldiers. We fought them off. They battled back. For every ladder we pushed away, another popped up somewhere else. We fought on, killing and being killed, until a trumpet called the enemy back to a safe distance. Some of the men and women on the walls cheered, thinking the battle was won.

Then came rocks. They had moved their catapults to new locations and were safe from ours for a time. The rocks fell fast and furious. It was fully dark now, so their task was harder. Most of the first two volleys fell short. Two stones from the third volley struck the wall midway to the top. I was rocked and had to put out a hand to keep from falling. Sections of the wall broke loose, leaving a gap half way up. We responded with our smaller, more accurate throwers, forcing the enemy catapults to move again. I saw one of our boulders drop out of the night sky and smash into an enemy catapult. It was a direct hit. The machine disintegrated, its shards creating deadly havoc among the people nearby. The crew of that catapult had been using torches to light their work. As I smiled at their foolishness, another wave of soldiers dashed across the killing field and hurled themselves like living stones against our defenses.

The cycle repeated. I fought against the soldiers who made it to the top of the wall until my arms were weary. My voice was horse from the screams and orders I bellowed. So far, I was not wounded, though a lance had pierced the leather of my jerkin.

I was working on one of the ladders. Though I had given it my best effort, I could by no means dislodge it under the current press of battle. The ladder's hooks had done their job and fallen into place over the top of wall. The weight of the climbing men pressed against the hooks, so they were difficult to remove.

A soldier's head popped up above the wall. I looked up from my struggles with the hooks to see his torso looming over me. He raised a battle axe with one hand while he held to the ladder with the other. Our eyes met for an instant. It is one of those strange little memories that stayed with me. Grabbing my sword in both hands, I struck at his head with all my might. Sure and I knocked him off the ladder, but his helmet made me pay for the effort. My right wrist complained so that almost I dropped my sword. I had to fight left handed for a while, something King Brand's weapons masters had insisted we do two days each month in the practice hall. I thank you, weapons masters.

By the time the enemy retreated the fourth time, the dead lay everywhere. Inert forms and writhing bodies crowded the base of our wall. Bodies floated in the spiked waters of our ditch. They were done with this war; those who still clung to life were not.

I had the rhythm of it now, knew instinctively how long we had before the next wave. I shouted some unnecessary orders to the captains near at hand—make sure the men drink some water, rotate the archers, see to the wounded—and scrambled down the stairs. I needed to get to the east wall to see what I might see there. I could have sent a runner to gather a report, but I wanted to see the situation with my own eyes.

I made the trip there and back before the next wave of soldiers descended on us. The east wall was faring better than we were in the north. They did not have catapults hurling stones at them. They did not have a Gryhm driving the soldiers against whom they fought insane with fear. There were casualties among the Ehrylain there, too, of course, but the officer in charge assured me that we were holding fast on that front. When I left them, I was feeling better than I had expected. That feeling evaporated like dew in the hot sun as soon as I got back to my station in the north.

The enemy catapults had scored more hits against our wall. A section had crumbled from the parapets to half-height. The gap was a good twenty paces across. When they came again with their ladders and hooks, we could only defend that section with arrows. We would kill most that made it to the top of the fractured section, but some were sure to get over and throw themselves down upon the warriors below. The North Wall had failed. The city was about to be entered.

Standing in my place atop the parapet, I directed forces here and there in the ways I thought best. I was grinding my teeth in the effort to concoct some defense for the breached wall. None had made it over alive yet, but there was already a pile of dead soldiers below the fracture line inside the wall. It was only a matter of time.

Suddenly, Breanna was by my side.

"Shinando! They are breaking through the south gate. There's a battering ram. Torlan says you must send help."

My mind shrieked. I looked out over the field, glanced quickly at our warriors lining the battlements. We had suffered many losses. Below me, ranks of foot soldiers and cavalry stood waiting. They had had little to do so far. Now, with the gap in the wall, they were sure to be needed here soon. But they were needed elsewhere right now.

I shouted orders. The cavalry officers responded, and the sound of galloping horses filled the air. Company captains billowed commands. Foot soldiers turned in orderly unison and marched off toward the south. Once they were gone, less than half of the forces I had stationed at the north gate remained. The night was still young.

I glanced over the field, calculating. I gave Breanna a message and sent her off to the orphanage. That is where Lina was. Moving toward the tower and the stairs within it, I issued orders to officers. The defense of the North Gate was now in Rehlys' hands. I went to help in the south.

As I neared the bottom of the winding stair, I met Arica. I was surprised to see her. Lina had told me Arica was going to stay with her in the orphanage to help defend that quarter of the city from any soldiers who might come over the wall there. But here she was. She had her beautiful black bow and three overfull quivers of arrows. Her face was cold, almost empty. I had seen that look many times, but never on this maiden. I knew what it meant. The knowledge chilled me to the bone even in the heat of battle.

"What is wrong, lady?" It was a stupid question, but she took my meaning. I had wanted to ask her this for days, but had not had the time. No, that is not right. I had the time. I just used it in other places.

"Don't you know, Farseer?"

She had never addressed me that way before. My disquiet grew. "I do not, child. Tell me."

Her face fell, pulling her gaze downward. She stared at the steps while precious time dissolved into the growing calamity. I waited for her. At last, she looked up. When she met my eyes, I saw tears.

"It's Gammin."

Sudden panic rushed over me. A chill walked up my spine. She went on before I could speak.

"I don't mean that he's hurt. How would I know? I have been here with you. As far as I know, he is still with his father, the king."

I saw a tear fall from her chin. It caught a shaft of torch light and glinted for an instant.

"That's just it, though," she continued, looking up at me beseechingly. I was stunned by her beauty, by how much she looked like a young Merelina. "He is a prince. He will be king. Anyone can see he was born for it."

"Yes? What of it?"

"I am just a woodcutter's daughter. That is what I will

always be."

The sounds of men screaming in agony and fury pulled at my attention. They were hurling rocks at us again. I had to go, had to get back into this battle. Things were not looking good. But I had a job to do here, as well. Maybe I could not save this city, but I might be able to save Arica, my friend, the woodcutter's daughter.

She pushed the back of a hand across her nose, smiled, laughed a tiny laugh. Then she looked me square in the eye. "I love him, Annen."

Ever slow on the uptake where women are concerned, I said, "He loves you, too, Arica. You must know that. Where is the problem?"

"Yes, he loves me. I think so, too. But... he is... he has to... If we get through this mess alive, he'll have to marry some princess or something. It will be the best for Ehrylan."

Ah! Now I saw it. I reached out, set a hand on her shoulder, tried to smile away her anguish. As I started to say something, the rock from a catapult slammed into the wall about two dozen paces from where we stood. The whole tower jerked. Pieces of stonework fell from above. Showers of dust rained down on us. I wanted to tell her that I'd rather see her on the throne than any foreign princess I had known. I wanted her to know I thought she would be an amazing queen, that I would gladly see her wed to my boy, my prince, my king. But there was no time for such talk now.

"Arica, I have to go."

"I know, Annen."

"I want to tell you something."

Another rock, this one smaller, hit the wall near the top. Again the tower jumped, though this time it was not so bad. The sound covered what I had said. I had to repeat it after we caught our breath.

"Listen to me. The feelings you are having are real. You have to deal with them. But, dear heart, the thoughts and fears causing those feelings, they are just imaginings."

I could hear people screaming my name.

"We don't know what Ea will put before us tomorrow. We've got enough to worry about today. Leave the future to worry itself."

I looked deeply into her eyes. They were swimming with tears, but there was no fear in them, not for today. It was tomorrow's pain I saw.

"Arica, will you do that for me?"

She stared at me for what seemed like a very long time, though it probably wasn't. Then she nodded. "I will try. For you, I will try... sir."

"I thank you, lady. Hear me. Has Gammin ever betrayed you? Has he ever given you reason to doubt his love for you?"

She shook her head.

"No? I thought not. Nor has he failed to be true to me. Let us honor that."

She nodded and forced a winsome smile.

I grabbed her and gave her a bear hug, holding her more tightly than ever I had before. Then I held her at arm's length.

"I am glad to see you. We could use your bow. Will you help defend the breach in the wall?"

She nodded, wiping away tears. I wanted to say more, to encourage her, to help her navigate the dire straits she was enduring. I started to do so. Another rock struck, this one within the walls. I dropped my hands from her shoulders.

"Find good targets, lady."

I pushed past her and bounded down three steps. When I turned back a last time, she was still watching me.

I pointed at her. "And don't forget to move!"

Later, near the end of the battle, I saw her standing on the rampart, a solitary figure clad in a white dress with a gray shawl about her shoulders. Her arrows were spent. She was just watching the field of death that stretched before the North Gate, heedless of the occasional missiles that whizzed by her. Below her and to one side, fires ate greedily at the mobile assault towers the enemy had pushed against the walls. The glow of the flames shone red on her dress and in her face. She looked like a glowing spirit of the night.

I saw this with my own eyes. Others saw her, too. They had watched her stand fearless in the face of the oncoming storm, shooting arrows at the beast that threatened us while men twice her age cowered in fear. That is how Arica became known also as Urymbehel, which is Flower of the Flames in the Common Tongue, or Fire Blossom.

That night, she won the hearts of the people.

III.

The reinforcements I sent to the South Gate made a difference, but it was only the difference between immediate destruction and temporary delay. By the time I arrived, the battering ram was breaking through. I saw the gates begin to buckle, saw enemy bows shooting blindly through the fractured opening. Soldiers began to wedge themselves through. The ram hit again. One side of the gate broke asunder. A section of the wall cracked where the iron hinges had been hammered into it. Pieces fell, indiscriminately crushing friend and foe beneath a shatter of wood and rock. I heard screams—men's screams, boy's screams, the screams of women.

Soldiers poured through the gap, stumbling over the rubble and bodies. They were met with a phalanx of Ehrylain. The two groups surged into each other. The front of the battle held for a while as the fighting spread sideways beyond the gate court and into the wide street that ran along the wall. I looked out through the opening in the wall from well back, trying to see what might be seen. I think that I was willing the Defier to appear. We needed him now. Twofords was falling.

A cross bow bolt ripped by my ear so closely that I felt and heard its passing. I decided I had been standing in one place too long and threw myself into the chaos.

There were a few moments where I was unable to get through the general press. I pushed forward, sword in hand, knowing my moment was coming. I laid my left hand on the shoulder of the man in front of me. He was a warrior I recognized. I was leaning forward to shout something into his ear when he collapsed in a gush of blood.

Cursing, I labored to get around the dying man so I might have revenge on his killer. I need not have bothered. In his death throws, the warrior stabbed out and up, catching his killer in the groin and driving the sword into his abdomen. Slashing at the falling soldier's neck, I leapt over him and found another opponent.

Someone stabbed at me from the side. Irrational anger took over, and I turned to face that attacker. He was hauling back his sword for another go when I chopped his arm off. I had to leave him to bleed out, though it is not my custom to leave an adversary alive once we have crossed blades. Another man, two men, in fact, were already upon me. I did not have to face either of them. Other warriors got to them before I could. I moved to a new position and offered the same assistance to others.

The front surged, the enemy pressing us back into the city a dozen paces or so. We recovered ourselves, made a stand, slowly fought back toward the gate. It continued for some time, this back and forth. We killed each other; the Ehrylain of Twofords and the River's Bend strove against the Ehrylain who peopled Dauroth's armies. I agonized with each man I slew. Every time Ehrylain killed Ehrylain, the Gryhm won a small victory. It did not matter one whit if Twofords stood firm or fell. Dauroth's purpose, the malice that is the Faceless, was satisfied as we killed one another. Thankfully, the battle music descended upon me at some point, and my thinking was done. After that, it is only a dance of death.

We were almost able to push them out of the city at one point. Someone poured precious oil from above onto the ram and tossed a flaming brand into the mix. For a while, the thing burned so fiercely that additional soldiers could not get through the gate. Eventually, they dragged the burning ram away, and we were in for it again.

I was running out of hope. The North Wall was breached.

The South Gate was smashed. My friend had not come in time. There seemed to be an inexhaustible supply of soldiers to pit against my exhausted strength. It was the same with my men. We were coming to the end of hope, where desperation breeds brilliance and folly. I heard someone calling my name through the tumult of battle which is death's maniacal laughter. It was Breanna.

"Shinando! They are coming over the wall! There's fighting near orphanage! You need to help Max!"

Breanna! I had sent her to Merelina with a message. How long ago had that been? I had no clue. It was deep night now. The smells of blood, smoke, sweat, and fear were everywhere.

I yelled, gestured to the nearest of our warriors, and darted toward Breanna. She was jumping up and down, wringing her hands in agitation. Her tunic was covered in blood. A small sword rode at her waist.

As we approached—myself and the handful of men who now followed me—the little lady turned and fled down the wall street. My anxiety for Merelina and the orphans, which overwhelmed my dismay at having the enemy come over the walls, pushed my weary legs. I had some notion of sprinting all the way there, something I could not have done in the best of times. We had not gone far before that notion vanished. We slowed to a brisk walk.

I wanted to question Breanna about the situation. Information is golden in any battle. Unfortunately, she had outdistanced us and was already out of sight around some slight bend. She had not noticed we were no longer behind her. She was that eager to get back and help. After making sure the men with me, five foot soldiers, had caught their breath, I hurried them along until we came in sight of the trouble.

There was a swirl of fighting in the street beneath the wall. I could see perhaps two dozen enemy soldiers. Opposing them were what was left of the Young and the Old, who had been deployed in this section of the city. Where better? We tend to fight hardest for our own homes and for the ones we hold dear. Ropes dangled over the wall, betraying how the soldiers had come down. There was sporadic fighting along the battlement, but it looked to me as if our men had repelled the boarders, as it were. There were no more soldiers on the ropes, no one coming down the walls inside the city, at least not in this place. That was the good news. It was my lot to see if I could help with the bad news.

I led the five men into the mix. We fell on the soldiers with such fury that the whole front rippled. Our little group moved through it. Before we knew what was happening, we were surrounded by the enemy. That certainly lent eagerness to our fatigued arms and legs. Still, it was lucky for us that the youngsters and oldsters defending that part of the city took courage from our coming. It was fortunate that the soldiers against whom we fought seemed to believe more than six tired swordsmen had arrived to oppose them.

They gave ground. We pressed them back to the spot where the main building of the orphanage bordered the street. Lina was in the doorway—the window would have been a safer choice—taking aim with her long bow. I watched her loose a single arrow, then turned back to my business.

We fought on. It seemed quite sudden when I realized we had begun to prevail in that small battle. There were fewer soldiers than Ehrylain standing in the street. The ropes had been cut. There was no activity along the battlement.

I glanced at Merelina. She was still in the doorway. Trouble was headed her way. A group of soldiers was rushing down the path, perhaps thinking to barricade themselves in the building. They were already past the little gate, so they were inside the yard. There was no way I could get there in time.

Merelina brandished her horned bow. I could see she was out of arrows. It was obvious why. Bodies lined the low, stone wall that escorted the path to the door. She was no longer alone. Next to her was Temay. He was holding the short staff we had given him as a token. A sharp object was not the right tool for that young man, who was more than touched with mental difficulties. Beside Temay was Faeryntha, the wolfdog. On Lina's other side was Old Bil. Both animals were as bristly as festival wreaths, with fur standing on end and teeth bared in ferocious growls. Bil's growls were interrupted by deep-throated barking. Fearyntha's were not. She only growled, her eyes wild and baleful. She was an animal from a child's nightmare of a trip in the forest gone horribly awry. Between them and the oncoming soldiers stood Breanna. Her sword was raised in a defensive posture. Her gentle face was set with determination. Ea! This was worse than bad.

I bolted toward them. I was just at the short wall that separated the yard from the street when Temay attacked. He had taken only a little training from me, just a lesson here and there when he had accompanied Lina to my house in the Stone Gate on some training days. Max and the others had taught him as well, though none of the effort was in evidence that day. Temay rushed past Breanna and fell upon the advancing soldiers in a flurry of arms, legs, and nonsensical utterances.

The front-most soldier brushed him aside with his sword. Temay stumbled, rolled, lay still. I screamed at the top of my lungs to get their attention. Two soldiers turned toward me. The others kept straight on to their goal, whatever that was.

I took too long to deal with those two men. They were better than most of Dauroth's troops, and I was very weary. I can say truthfully that I almost lost my life three times in the short altercation.

After they fell, I staggered toward Lina, passing Breanna on the way. She was engaging one of the soldiers. He was almost twice her height. There was no way she could have stood toe to toe with him and survived. She was darting in and out, avoiding his strokes—not blocking them—while delivering her thrusts when she was able. The effectiveness of her strategy was evident. A second soldier lay unmoving nearby. That man must have underestimated her. The other was not doing so.

I ended that fight as I passed by, sliding my sword into the man's back. Breanna saw the opening his surprise created. She darted in and sliced open his abdomen. I did not see what she did next. I was already gone.

I arrived at the place where Lina stood. She was

brandishing her bow, keeping the sharp tip of horn on one end between her and five soldiers. She had closed the door behind her, the door into the orphanage and the children it contained. There was no way for her to retreat. I got there about the same time they did. Breanna and Temay must have slowed them. Old Bil was by then a vibrating mass of angry fur, fangs, and drool. Just as I arrived, he launched himself across the space between Lina and the nearest soldier. The man fell backward, screaming and shoving against the dog with his hands. Faeryntha did not attack, and I wondered why. Then it hit me.

I looked at her and bellowed, "Fearyntha! *Delaura*!"

She launched herself at the nearest soldier. Her teeth found his throat. Her back paws raked his abdomen. He went down with a gurgling scream. *Delaura* is a command in the Old Tongue, an imperative. Kill! She did. That was a well-trained dog.

One of the three remaining soldiers turned to help his companion. Old Bil was on top of the man he had attacked. The helping soldier delivered a violent kick to Bil's abdomen. The old dog yelped, whimpered, but did not release his teeth from the downed man's throat. The helper stabbed at the animal with his sword. That is when my blade took his sword arm off just above the elbow, cutting sideways deep into his torso. So great was my fury that I delivered a second blow that was unnecessary. It took the man at the top of his shoulder next to the neck, slicing down into the body where the first cut had stopped. As I pulled my sword back, that whole quarter of his torso fell way.

My eyes went to Old Bil, who was an old friend and very dear to us. Unless I missed my guess, he would grow no older. I only had time to see the blood on his fur before my battle senses alerted me to the death that stood behind me. Whirling on the balls of my feet, I brought my sword around in a blocking guard. One of the two remaining soldiers was there. His sword smashed into mine, sending a shock into my already tender wrist. I started to lose hold of my blade, but I did not let it go. Concentrating, I brought it up again, hid behind it. The man cringed and lurched toward me half a step. He turned his head to look over his shoulder, away from me. I hacked at him. When he fell, I saw Lina behind him holding her bow as if it were a staff. The hook of horn on the end was red.

Looking into her eyes, I saw fear. She was glaring over my shoulder. I whirled around, again bringing my sword up to block an unseen blow. This time I did lose hold. The blade fell to the ground at my feet, but it had saved my life. My wrist and arm flared in agony as I stared into the face of the enraged soldier. His sword was leveled at my throat.

I was about to throw myself at his knees when I saw his eyes go blank. There was a question on his face. He looked down, his sword dropping from his hand. We both saw the outline of the tip of a blade pressing against the inside of his leather jerkin. Someone had stabbed him from behind. As his hand came up to touch the offending object, Temay stepped around him and began to assail him with a flurry of blows and a storm of words.

"Oh, no you don't!" He punctuated the sentence by slamming the staff against the man's head. "You can't attack us." Smash. The soldier went to his knees. "No you can't!" Crack, crack, crack—one with each word. The dead body fell on its face. Temay moved to straddle it and raised his staff.

I reached out and put a hand on Temay's arm. He stopped immediately. His eyes fixed on mine with an unspoken question. A sound interrupted what he might have been about to say. We both looked down at Breanna. She was tugging at her sword, trying to get it out of the dead man.

I glanced up at Lina, opened my mouth, and sighed an unspoken apology. I stooped, picked up my sword with my left hand, and went back to help fight the soldiers in the street. I attempted to vault the wall, which should have been as easy as a high step. My lagging foot came down too soon and caught the top of the stone, sending me rolling in an undignified tumble. I scrambled to my feet, thinking I was lucky to have kept from impaling myself.

Then I was upon them, fighting with desperation, too tired

to use the skills and finesse I had spent a lifetime acquiring. The fighting there was mostly done, and it was a lucky thing for me. Soon, there were no more swords swinging at me, no more soldiers to cut down. I looked around. Max was standing next to me. Had I known that? I was not sure, could not remember the last... hours? Minutes?

"Max, how are you?" I had to push the words out between gasps for air. I could not hear my voice amid the groans, weeping, and vomiting. Somehow he understood.

"Fine. I am fine, shinando."

He was a mass of cuts and scrapes. Blood oozed down his face from a horizontal cut on his forehead. His jerkin was ripped. It hung open at the front half way to his waist.

"You look like you have been in a battle," I said. It was a strange thing to say, but I knew I needed to say something.

He laughed, which took me by surprise.

"What's so funny, Max?"

"You should see the other guy."

That brought a laugh to my lips, but I did not let it out. Instead, I looked round the street. It was literally covered with bodies. Most of them were soldiers. Some were Ehrylain, the Young and The Old, Max's squads.

I returned my gaze to Max, said, "I see him, sir." I reached out a hand and gripped the young man by the shoulder. I opened my mouth to tell him how proud I was of him and his people, his students, his warriors. I tried to tell him that they had saved the orphanage and who knows how much else, but nothing came. Words failed me.

Max stared back at me for a moment, then bowed his head. "I thank you, shinando."

Once again, I opened my mouth to say words that did not come. Sensing the order that was coming, Max raised his head and squared his shoulders. "There's two things we need to do. I'll get the squads reorganized and send for some healers. Where do you want us, Lord Colen?"

"I think you should keep doing what you were doing. You have done a good job. And stop calling me that!"

"Yes, Lord Calen. As you wish, Lord Calen." Max's eyes twinkled through the collected layers of grime and blood.

"Get yourself seen to, while you are at it, boy. I don't want you dying from a scratch."

I started to tell him that I could not afford to break in a new runner, that good messengers were hard to come by. Looking at him, seeing what he had accomplished here with his band of followers, I realized the truth. He was no messenger, not any more. This man was a leader.

He saw something in my eyes that made him uncomfortable. He gave me a half-bow, which was completely unnecessary. "Well," he said, "I'll get going, then."

He turned, but I could not let him go like that.

"Max."

He spun round. "Yes, shinando?"

"Well done, sir. I thank you. We all thank you."

He beamed and brought his sword up between us in a formal salute. Then he moved off.

I surveyed the street again. The survivors were already moving among the bodies, helping where they could. Three of the five men I had brought with me were still on their feet. One of the other two had a bad wound. After a moment, I saw the fifth. I need not worry over him; he was beyond pain, beyond any help I could give.

I crossed to the nearest of the three.

"Well done, Mathyr. Get the other two together. We'll be heading back to the gate."

"Yes, Lord Calen." The man looked weary, but not half as bad as I felt.

I walked back to Merelina. Breanna and Temay were at her feet, crying over the dog. I did not look down at them. I could not afford that right now.

"Lady, are you well?"

"I am, sir."

"And Temay? He took a hit."

"He's alright. It is not him I am worried about."

I thought she meant Old Bil, or maybe Breanna, who was

sobbing. I wanted to kneel down and console her, but time was pressing, and the city was falling. I had to get back to my men.

"Lina, I have to go. I'll send more men this way in case soldiers come over the wall again or if they…" I stopped, considering the words I was about to say, thinking of the implication. "Or in case they come down the street from the gate." If that happened, it was very likely all was lost.

Her face grew stern. "You will do no such thing, husband."

"No? You are that confident in the Young and the Old? Well, I suppose Max earned that trust."

"That is not what I mean, you big bag of wind." Her voice was exasperated, almost fierce, as if she knew already that I would not listen to what she was going to tell me. "You are not going anywhere until you've rested. I saw you fall over that wall. If you try to fight again, you are going to get yourself killed and for no reason."

A litany of replies lined up in my mouth. It doesn't matter how tired I am. We are all exhausted. A commander cannot rest while the men toil. I managed to hold them in. She was right; I was only a danger to myself at the moment.

I sighed, remembering that I was carrying almost sixty years on my shoulders. I did not feel that old, but I felt twice that tired. Nodding to her, I said, "Yes, dear."

She pushed a hand against my chest, the familiar gesture. Both of us were surprised when the slight force of it set me off balance. I had to step back to steady myself. If that wasn't enough to convince me, the pain in my sword arm when I lifted it to call Mathyr over did the job.

I told Mathyr to take the others back to the gate and to send word to me of the situation there. I watched the three warriors until they rounded a bend that took them out of my sight. They were brave men and had fought well. I wondered what they had been before this war started. Farmers? Tradesmen? It did not matter. I was honored to serve with them, proud to fight by their sides.

Turning my gaze and thoughts from those three heroes, I sought Lina's eyes. What I saw in them nearly broke my heart.

There was deep concern and something much worse. It was fear, not for herself or her children, but for me.

I lifted my left hand to cup her cheek and thought of how much I loved her. She said, "I love you, too."

A forlorn whine broke in on my thoughts. My eyes went toward the sound, which was down at my feet. I saw a jumble of two children and two animals. Breanna was sitting with her arms around Old Bil. She was stoking his fur, though she avoided the places that were slick with new blood. Faeryntha was licking at the wound on Bil's haunch. It was she who was whining, not Bil. At first, the sight shocked me. Then I realized the truth. She was not interested in the blood. She was offering her love and help in the only way she knew how.

There was not much blood. It would not be the sword wound that killed the dog. The soldier's kick must have broken ribs and ruptured vital organs. What a terrible way for such a gentle beast to die. My heart started to break.

Kneeling, I pushed my hand against Old Bil's head, moving the fur so that I could see his eye—he only had one. It had the look of eyes that could already see the doors of forever open and waiting. His tail moved in the parody of a wag, all he could muster, a single shift.

"Old Bil. Good boy, Bil. You did fine, old man. We thank you." Those words did little to empty the ocean of sorrow. "You were a great dog, Bil, a great friend. I am so glad to have known you."

His tail moved once more, for the last time. His tongue flicked out and touched my hand. Then, he lifted his great head toward Breanna's face. I saw his tongue again as he gave her cheek a little kiss. After that, almost lazily, he laid his face on his paws. He seemed to drop into an easy sleep. The labored breathing slowed, stopped.

Faeryntha raised her muzzle and sang him into eternity.

I had to leave before Merelina was satisfied I was recovered. We agreed to wait until the report returned from the south gate. When the runner came, he told us that we were holding the entrance against the soldiers, neither driving them away nor yielding before them. According to the man, there was no fighting within the walls when he left.

This was excellent news. I had expected the worst; he had brought me the best I could have hoped for. Lina brought him some fresh water and a morsel.

With a less dark heart, I bade my wife and shorter friends farewell. Quickly as I could, I headed back to my original position on the north wall. Though the rest had done me a world of good, I could not make as much speed as I would have liked. As I neared the court inside the North Gate, I could see the flickering glow of fire reflected off the roofs and walls of adjacent buildings. I glanced at the sky and did not see the moon. She must have set already. Sunrise was gathering. We had fought all night. Perhaps we would yet live to see another sun as free men and women.

I rounded a corner (I have always thought that a funny phrase—rounding a corner) and moved into the gate court. Expecting calamity, I had drawn my sword and was carrying it. But there was no fighting within the walls. There were ranks of ordered warriors, some of whom were seeing to the wounds and wellbeing of their fellows. There were scores of bodies, most of whom were dead.

I looked up at the battlements. I could see it in the subdued light that precedes dawn. Our archers were there. The warriors who stood next to them did not have swords drawn. There were no ladders to fend off, no hooked ropes to cut. Occasional arrows hissed over the wall or shattered against the upright merlons. Whenever that happened, three or four of our archers responded.

My eyes followed the ramparts westward, toward the gap in the wall. There, standing at the edge of the crumbled section, stood Arica. No one was within two dozen paces of her. She was staring out over the field, motionless, her hands at her sides. She did not stir when arrows hissed past her or ricocheted from the stone wall. She might have been a marble statue on whose surface danced red paint that had come alive. She might have been a young woman devoid of hope, waiting for death to release her from sorrow.

Through the gap in the wall, I could see the remnants of siege towers. Some were engulfed in flame. Others had bled out in the flames, were just embers. At the base of the wall, a heap of bodies told me how hard the Ehrylain had worked to keep out the enemy. As I stood dumbfounded, I heard my name from above. It was Rehlys. He pushed by the men who crowded near him and rushed to the tower. I moved to meet him at the bottom of the stair.

The smile on his face told me that he was delighted to see me. "So," he said, clapping me on the shoulder in a way that was not quite appropriate for a captain to strike his commander. It was very appropriate for one warrior to greet another. "Now the fighting's eased a bit, you decided to come back to us?"

Involuntarily, my head bowed. "I would have been here sooner, but..."

He interrupted me. "I need no excuses from you, Annen. One look tells me there is plenty of fighting elsewhere. There was here, too, until little while ago."

"What happened?"

"They just up and left! I am not sure why. It was fairly abrupt. One minute, we were fending off an attack. Another, the Gryhm was gone, and the troops were leaving. They seem to have moved to the south."

I cursed, asked forgiveness, and told him of the breached gate. When I had answered his questions, which took me longer than the city could afford, I asked one of my own.

"What of the west wall and the east?" The leader of the North Wall was the collection point for messages. In my absence, they would have continued to come here.

"The east is in no danger. The west was hard pressed, but they held. There's no gate there, as you know. Now both have reported the same thing we saw here. Their foes have moved south.

"I've got to get back there, Rehlys. What do you need here? I'll send it if I can. But..." I glanced over my shoulder foolishly. I could almost feel them coming.

"But what?"

"Be ready to defend an attack from your rear. I do not know how long we will hold the south wall."

"We will be ready."

Trumpets blared somewhere out on the north field. I heard the same from the east and west. Remembering the broken gates, I tasted the agony of impending defeat. But not yet. I was not done yet. There were lives to save and soldiers to kill.

"Look to Ea for your salvation, Rehlys."

He saluted me formally, holding his sword in front of him. "And you, Annen."

As I turned to go back across the city to the disaster at the South Gate, horns rang out in the distance. Their sonorous voices lilted out of the south, contrasting with the brazen trumpets. I wondered that Dauroth's army would use such musical signals. Then, suddenly, I realized that I knew the meaning of the signal. The horns were signaling a charge, the initiation of a preplanned stratagem. They were no device of Dauroth. Those were Ehrylain horns.

Branden had arrived.

IV.

Even now, as I write these words in fulfillment of a dead king's last request, I can still feel that wild emotion. The memory visits me often. When I hear horns calling or when I see a sunrise, fierce joy spills like clear, bubbling water from deep within my heart. For he came at sunrise, did King Branden, with the sound of horns and an army riding on that hopeful music, chasing away the despair that had almost consumed me.

I wheeled back around and bolted up the stairs with more speed than I thought I could muster. Yanking out my sword, I turned my back on the field of the fallen and faced my countrymen.

"Hear me, Ehrylain! Take heart! Our deliverance is at hand. Allies from the east have arrived! We begin this new day fighting for freedom!"

A roar rose up to meet me. I shook my sword and had to stop myself from jumping up and down with excitement. The coming of Branden explained why the Gryhm had shifted his troops. Enemy scouts had no doubt reported the approach of the army, one that he could not hope to defeat with his forces divided. So he had drawn them together and arrayed them for battle in the fields between the city and the Old Forest.

Now, no matter what the situation at the South Gate, I had an important job to do, one of which Branden could not know. How could he? The opportunities of each day—like the troubles—do not reveal themselves until mere mortals stumble across them. I had not seen this opportunity until it appeared fully wrought within my mind but a moment before. This was the far seeing for which I have earned a name. It is a sudden flash of insight, a swift image of what might be. I shook my fist at the Gryhm, literally, not figuratively, and looked for my captains.

Rehlys was moving along the rampart. He came to me before I had sheathed my sword. He spoke first.

"You knew of this, Annen?"

"Only as much as I told you, Rehlys. I did not expect them for another day yet. That army moves with more speed than I have ever seen in one that size." I considered my own words as Rehlys processed them. "We must move with equal speed. I have a mind to gamble."

He did not answer, so I continued.

"Assemble the cavalry we have here, all of them, and two thirds of the foot soldiers. Half the archers, as well."

"Yes, sir. We move east around the city to fall upon our enemy's rear?" A wide smile lit his face.

"Nay, not that, not yet."

The smile turned into a shadow of uncertainty.

"I will lead the horsemen and the others. We will take the enemy stronghold. When he is pushed back and seeks his refuge…"

He interrupted me. "He will have no place to go! We will hold his fort against him. Brilliant!" Then he thought a little more. "You are sure our allies will carry the day?"

"No. There is no certainty in battle. If I take the fort, I will send back some of the warriors, for we do not have to hold the fort against them, not for long. An army will be chasing them. That is, if they are driven back at all. I believe they will be. I have ridden with that army."

"And if you do not take the fort?"

"Why, then, we will come back and help the army just the same."

I thought he would delight in the simplicity of this scheme. Instead, his face grew stern.

"You've got one thing wrong, Annen."

"What?"

"You are not the right man to lead the assault on the fortress."

This statement caused my mental gears to seize. For a moment, I could not think. "Why not?"

"You are not familiar with the lay of the land around the fort. You've not even seen it recently. All sorts of roads and paths have sprung up." He let that sink in for two breaths. Then he said, quite firmly, "I have."

I exhaled a chuckle that sprang from realization. "You have, indeed," I said, clapping him on the back. Who better to lead that assault than the head scout, particularly when the head scout was Rehlys? He and his men had been spying out the ways and means of that place for many months. There was no better choice.

As he readied his forces, I sent messengers to the other three commands within the city. I gave the messengers strict instructions to hurry back with the information I wanted. Information and time are weapons in war. One of those grew shorter with every heartbeat, and there was nothing I could do to change that. The other, the knowledge of what was afoot on the different fronts of this battle, was a tool I could refine and use. Now I could only watch and wait as others did their jobs. It was unsettling. I had time to first ponder and then to worry. When we walk in fields of thought, we trip over imaginary monsters. It is much better to be in battle, to be in the thick of things where there is no time for thought.

Though it felt otherwise, Rehlys and the other captains quickly arrayed the forces. We sent out the cavalry first. They cleared the field of the few soldiers that had remained to watch the gate. We sent mounted scouting parties east and west to make sure there were no forces waiting there to ambush us. While they were about this, the rest of the men began to issue from the gate. In ordered ranks, they set off at a brisk pace for the enemy stronghold. As the last foot soldiers set foot outside the gate, I saw the scouts riding hard toward the rest of the horsemen, who were well on their way. That meant there was no apparent threat from either flank. Good.

Satisfied that we had done all that could be done, I headed back into the tower and met Arica on the stair. I stopped and watched her come down, picking her way through the crumbled steps. Her tears were spent or burned away. She carried herself erect, and her face was set. She stepped around me, which was not easy in that narrow space. It came to me that she was going to pass by without speaking. That thought troubled my heart. I could not let it come to fruition.

"Arica?"

She stopped and turned back.

"Will you speak with me?"

"I am sorry, Annen. I... I did not see you. Or, I did, but..."

"Never mind, lady. Are you well?" Foolish Annen! A blind monkey could see she was not well.

She nodded without breaking eye contact.

"Arica, where are you going? We could use your bow. The fighting is not done here, for better or for worse. One way or another, we will see soldiers on this field again today."

"I will stay if you want me to, Annen. I was going to the

South Gate, to see the army."

"The army?"

One corner of her mouth turned up in a half-hearted smile that didn't make it unscathed past the suffering. "I thought I might..." She sighed and shrugged. "I want to see him. From the walls, I mean."

"Go, then. Your bow will be welcomed there, I am sure. But there is one thing."

"What's that?"

"Don't forget to pick up some arrows."

4. THE COMING OF THE KING

I.

Rehlys arrived at the fort without encountering opposition. The most difficult part of that ride was avoiding the masses of bodies littering the field near the city walls. The dead enemies proved more of an impediment than the living who guarded the approaches to the fort. Most of the live ones broke and ran as soon as they saw our horsemen sweeping down on them. The rest ran or surrendered when our foot soldiers appeared.

Chilshan had left only a token force to defend the fort. I think the Gryhm never considered that those men would see action. The defenders put up a feeble resistance. They shot a few arrows from the palisades. Our troops had picked up discarded ladders and grappling hooks at the base of Twofords' walls. The fort was so quickly overwhelmed that we later speculated most of the defenders were eager to join us.

I could scarce believe it when I saw a contingent of Ehrylain riders appear from beyond the north edges of the field. Bolstered by the good news they brought and the equally good news my messengers returned with, I sent most of the forces that remained to me around the east wall. It was a gamble, but we mitigated the risk by using our scouts effectively.

Having sent for Avyansa, I galloped with reckless speed through the streets of the city to the South Gate. What I found there was encouraging. There was little fighting near the walls. The craftsmen among us were already erecting a new barrier to bar the opening.

Most of the action was farther down the Old Road toward the forest. I had sent word for our forces to be prepared. As soon as we saw the men I had sent from the north come around the east wall, we issued from the gate. Fed up with the anxiety of watching and waiting, I led that charge. If I was already tired, my friend Avyansa was fresh and spoiling for a fight. Together, an eager tide of Ehrylain at our backs, we charged into the battle, trapping Chilshan's army between three attacking forces. On the fourth front was the Old Forest, where the Children of the Forest waited. Into that place, our enemies dared not go.

This battle was like many another I have fought. What stands out in my memory is not the fact that we routed our opponent. We had done that before. The difference this time was in the performance of the warriors from Twofords. Even as we charged into battle, I noted their discipline, their resolve, the way they performed cohesively. Once we encountered our foe, I saw that the Ehrylain of Twofords fought with ferocious spirit and good technique. Foolish as it sounds, I realized only then the extent of how far they had come, these farmers and merchants. They were truly an army now. My tired heart soared. Ea's name came unbidden to my lips. I roared a war cry. This was taken up by others as we fell upon the backs of the men who had besieged us.

There was still killing to be done, and there was still the chore of staying alive. To these things I applied myself. There was much chopping and poking, stabbing, slicing, blocking, and moving. I led those who followed me to wherever our swords and spears were needed.

At some point, I caught sight of my king's banner and began to fight my way toward it. That is when I saw Gammin and Marin. They were, as was to be expected, in the thick of it, fighting alongside the king's personal guard. What I saw so captivated me that I might have been killed but for the fact that I was surrounded by my own men and women at that point. Gammin and Marin, my students, my *onandi*, my dear friends, fought like two swords joined by one mind. The soldiers and cavalry they faced fell before them like wheat before the scythe. Gammin had warriors at his back, and he was leading them. The tide of battle swept us apart. I had to return my attention to where it belonged lest I lose it forever.

We fought on and on, gradually bringing Chilshan's army to its knees and then casting it on its face. I kept my eye out for the Gryhm but never saw him. He was a clever Gryhm and would likely be miles away by now. I did not know the ways of the Gryhm. Maybe he wanted to die and so take a new body. Maybe when a Gryhm fails, there is no returning to Dauroth.

The sun rose in the sky. Men died. The air was filled with the smell of blood, sweat, and some things worse. Eventually, the pace slowed, which was a good thing for me. I was riding steep trails on the far side of exhausted. There came a time that, having dispatched the man I was fighting, no other was near enough to replace him. I surveyed the field. It was much the same for the other Ehrylain. The fighting was mostly done. Turning to my left, I saw Branden. He was sitting erect on his horse and staring straight at me. I started to nudge Avyansa that way, but as usual, my hooved friend felt what I wanted and started that way without a hint from me.

I wanted to hail Branden as the victorious king he was, but this was neither the time nor the place for that. He had warned me not to call him king yet. I rode up in silence and waited for him to speak.

He reached down and caressed his horse's neck. "You fight well for an old man, Calen. You fight well for a young man, too. How is that possible?"

"Practice, practice, practice," I returned, matching his

forced jocularity with my own. It was important for those around us. "I am glad you made it. Your army travels fast. I did not look for you until tomorrow. That would have been too late."

"Too late for Twofords or for your foes? I've been watching your farmers fight. I can see that I have a thing or two to learn about farming."

He said this in an almost contented tone. There were so many emotions on his face that I could not read the story. He looked pleased, though he grew serious. "What's to be done, Calen? I've a mind to storm their entrenched position. We are all weary from the march, but I don't want to wait."

"No need." The end of the sentence hung oddly on my tongue. It seemed curtailed without the sire at the end. Then I remembered what he had told me and added "my lord." He raised his eyebrows at me.

"We took the fortress as soon as you came to the field. We hold it now."

"Excellent, Farseer." His face echoed of the pleasure in his voice.

"Your thought is well-placed, my lord. I recommend we send a strong contingent that way immediately. We should send another to guard the North Gate. I'll find some men to lead both so that there are no unfortunate misunderstandings."

"See to it." He nodded and smiled. I could tell some private humor was banging around in his head. He did not hold it captive. "It is your army, after all, General Calen. Shouldn't you be about the business of leading it rather than sitting here chatting with an old friend?"

I had not thought about that responsibility for days! How many? I started to ponder that, then remembered where I was. "Aye, aye, lord."

I began to nudge Avyansa around. He beat me to it. Sometimes it seemed that horse could read my thoughts and see through my eyes.

I moved across the field issuing orders to the various captains I came across and offering suggestions to the warriors who looked like they needed them. Just because the battle had ended did not mean the work was over. Our labors had just begun in earnest. If we had been busy before, now we were hard-put even to consider all that had to be done. There were wounded to tend, captives to secure, squads and companies to reform. The people in the city had to be told of the situation and reassured that their rescuer had no bad intentions.

The eastern army, which was experienced with what needed to be done after a battle, was already functioning like a well-greased wheel. Specially designated people, most of whom had not fought, were moving among the casualties, selecting the wounded that might be saved, dispatching those who could not. Three or four tents already been set up, each with a different focus. The wounded were carried to which ever was the best for them—arm and leg wounds, abdominal wounds, head wounds, and the like.

Aside from tending the wounded and the dead, the largest single need was to accommodate almost a thousand newly-arrived warriors. We could have let them make camp upon the north or south fields, but those were filled with the dead and dying. Warriors, even those who follow Ea, are a superstitious lot. Few of them would want to sleep where death was feasting. In all my years, I have never spent a contented night on a killing field.

There was no way a small city like Twofords could absorb so many. For one thing, we did not have the food. From what I had recently seen, Branden's army was eating better than the townsfolk. Further, a thousand hungry warriors could easily destroy the local food supplies, particularly this close to the snowfalls. An alternative had to be found. I had one in mind.

To tell you the truth, the housing and feeding of the king's army—my army, I suppose—was the primary reason I had wanted to secure the enemy's fort. After a good cleaning, the place would provide the perfect haven for the easterners. There would be room for them. The fort was bound to be stocked full of victuals and other winter supplies. The fields nearby would be just right for their livestock. Branden's army, like any army, travelled with much of their food supply still on the hoof. It is ancient wisdom that no army should set out on a campaign without their pigs, goats, sheep, oats, and corn. An army that did so would most likely come back on their shields rather than behind them.

I moved through the field, navigating the knots and waves of soldiers, doing what I had seen my father and King Brand's other generals do dozens of times. Even while I was about it, I was struck by how simple it all was. I did not have to consider what needed to be done. It was all right there before us. The issue was not in determining what, but in determining when. Time was the limited asset.

The more direction I gave, the more I became the center of a seething hive of captains and messengers who came and went with alarming frequency. It seemed to me that for every message I sent, three came in reply, and for every command I issued, six clarifications were needed. There is a lesson in that.

Working together, we began to make a dent in the list of things that all had to be done at the same time. With a little breathing room, I began to consider how best to get the king into his city. With that thought came the realization that I had not spoken with any of my old friends. Where were Gammin and Marin, Dara and Marn? That thought, as is the way with such thoughts on the heels of battle, quickly swelled into apprehension.

The concern was soon cast aside when I saw them, all four, in a small cluster with the king. They must have been talking about me. As my eyes lit upon them, Gammin turned and looked straight at me. Avyansa began to make for them. Gammin nudged his huge war horse my way. Thus, after a few days and a few battles, we met again, my boy and I, and shared a few moments alone on a field choked with bodies and blood.

For a moment, we sat on our horses simply staring at each other. I was waiting for him to speak, and I could see he did not know what to say. I helped him out.

"It is good to see you, Prince Gammin."

He rolled his eyes. "Do you really have to do that?"

"Yes."

"Then what am I to call you?"

Father was the name I wanted most from him, but that could not be. "Annen will do nicely, your highness. It has always been enough, and I have not changed. It is you who have sprouted a new identity."

I tried to hold a straight face and failed. The sheer, magnificent joy at just having him within reach again bubbled out of me. He grinned. All of a sudden, we were grasping at each other across the space between the horses.

"Are you injured, Annen?"

"No. I can see that you are not, either. That is good."

"And Lina? Is she all right?"

"Last I saw, she was." Then I remembered the two sadnesses. How many more were there now, I wondered, deaths about which we had yet to learn? My face must have fallen. Anxiety blossomed in my boy's eyes. He leaned closer.

"Arica? Is she injured?"

"No, she was not injured when last I saw her. She was heading to the south wall with her bow."

I saw relief wash over him. "Who, then?"

As quickly as I could, which is not the preferred way to deliver the news of the death of friends, I told him of Sheal and Old Bil. The loss of Sheal hit him hard, but I could see he had lost friends before. He shrugged it off. About Old Bil, he was more philosophical.

He said, "Bil was old. He must have been fifteen or sixteen at least. He was full grown when I met him. I think he might be lucky to be spared the lingering death that sometimes comes. I am glad he made a stand for Merelina. He was a good dog."

We chatted only a moment longer. There were, as I have already reported, many things to be done. As we made our way over to the king, messengers rode up on lathered horses. Their news was good news. The North Gate of the city was secure, free of attack. Likewise, the east and west walls were now unmolested. As for the fortress, the additional troops we had sent found the place under attack by a remnant of Chilshan's army. Those soldiers were killed, captured, or put to flight by the additional warriors.

I reported to my king that we had won the day, with the exception that there was no word of the Gryhm. That was typical. Gryhm are as elusive as they are powerful. As in the other battles where we had come away the clear victors, many survivors were eager to join us. These we dealt with as before, using truth tellers where they were needed. But that came later.

With the battle won and the fort taken, it was time to give thought to how the king should enter the city. Slinking through the gates in disguise was not an idea Branden would even discuss. It was not safe to use the tunnels with so many running about. After a short debate, it was decided that he would come openly into the city unaccompanied by fanfare. If anyone asked, we would name him the Defier. He thought it best to introduce his true identity first to the council and then to the city dwellers. The plans of men are like arrows in a strong wind; they often go awry.

We could not allow ourselves the luxury of rest without inspecting the enemy's fortified positions. The one in the south field had been much damaged by fire and fury we had brought a few days ago. It was little more than a row of encircling stakes ringed by a ditch. Inside, we found clusters of mean lean-tos and other shacks. The structures were so choked with dirty blankets, furs, skins, and refuse that no one, no matter how tired, would have wanted to sleep there if there were any alternative. Fortunately, there was.

The northern enclosure was a finished fort. It was soundly made and very appropriate for the uses to which we intended to put it. Within the circular enclosure were avenues of barracks, each sleeping twenty or so. There were kitchens, warehouses, smithies, and armories—each stacked with goods that would be useful. There was a tremendous store of food and weapons. One thing that can be said of Dauroth is that he did not starve his soldiers. Indeed, they were well-fed. The heavy taxes that bled dry our local economies and left us in want and ruin fed Dauroth's war machine.

When at last we had assured the welfare of our troops and the disposition of the field, we mounted our horses and started down the North Road toward the city. I was riding next to Branden, Avyansa walking proudly beside a horse fully three hands higher than he. On Branden's right was Gammin. Marin was next to Gammin. As we came to the wall, I was pointing out the gaping hole to our right, describing how the woodcutter's daughter had taken her place there. We hardly noticed as we rode through the gate. There were horsemen in front of us and horsemen behind. We were just one more school of fish in a busy stream. We had not even made it out of the gate court when I heard a cry to my right, which was where Branden was riding.

"Prince Branden! It's the prince! He lives! The prince! Ea be praised!"

A curious thing happened. Stillness and silence descended on the busy crowd as if someone had pulled a plug to drain away the clamor. A gray haired warrior pushed through the mass of people. He came right up to the head of the prince's horse and gazed up at my friend, the rightful king of Ehrylan. A look of doubtful dismay on his face dissolved into amazement. His hand reached up longingly, then retracted. Bowing his head, he sank to his knees.

"Sire," was all he said.

Another voice rang out. "It is the prince!" And another. "Prince Branden!" There was a general swirling from all directions as gray haired men and women pushed forward. One by one, as they came close enough to see, they dropped to their knees.

Then the crowd exploded. A ring of riders formed around us, shielding the king from the thronging masses. Branden looked at me. His shoulders rose and fell as a wry grin formed on his lips. He leaned over and pulled me close.

For my ears alone, he shouted, "I've been waiting a long time for this, my friend."

He slipped off his horse and reached out to the first man

who had recognized him, pulling him to his feet. A hush chased away the rumbling articulations of the crowd.

"You know me, sir?"

"I was with you in the wars, sire, in the Old Forest and other battles, too. I would have been at Kingsford, but we had other orders. I was a only foot soldier in your father's army." Tears streamed down the man's old, weather-beaten cheeks. He dragged a sleeve across his nose. "We all knew you, sire, Prince Branden the Bold. But now you are king! King Branden!" A look of fright bolted across the man's face as he realized how bold he was being. He bent his head and lowered his eyes.

Branden would have none of that. "Only a foot soldier, is it? Foot soldiers are the backbone of any army, sir. I am proud to meet a warrior who fought with us."

Branden took a knee, which brought a gasp out of the observers. He reached out and lifted the man's hands in his own, then rose to his feet again.

"I welcome you, friend. Now you shall be in my army."

"Gladly, sire." The man looked at me with a sudden guilt. "Your pardon and no offense, Farseer."

Branden did not give me time for a reply. He was into his job now, a king among his people. I could almost see the hope and love pouring from him into his countrymen and women.

"What is your name, foot soldier?"

"I am called Feal, sire."

"Long may you be remembered, Feal, for your memory and your courage." He lifted Feal's hand above their heads and turned to the crowd. "Long may you all be remembered, *folani*, for your courage and valor. The people of Twofords and River's Bend were the first to throw off their shackles. The Southland has again shown its true strength. Today marks a new hope. Together we shall reclaim our birthrights. Together we will drive the Outlanders from our land. Together we will rebuild the lives we lost. Are you with me?"

Cheers broke out from those who recognized him, then from the rest of the crowd as they exchanged disbelief for hope. I saw Feal gesturing with his left hand, pushing his palm toward the ground repeatedly. The crowd got it, first by twos and threes, then by tens and twenties. Before long, they were all kneeling. Not completely too late, I remembered myself, dismounted, and did the same.

So it was that, in the backwater city of Twofords, Prince Branden, who had been the Defier, became, after many journeys and many years, the king of his father's country.

II.

A leader who wins a large battle and frees a besieged city seldom has trouble making himself rather popular in that city. This is particularly true when that leader's charisma swirls about his body like an iridescent cloak. Nor did it hurt that he had my backing, and I led Twofords' army. There were many among our warriors who had either fought in the Great Wars or were sons or daughters of someone who did. If Calen Farseer was remembered as a hero, Prince Branden the Bold was held as a legend. I think we benefited from a good deal of backlash as well. The people had lived long under rigid conditions where even discussion of the old days was a crime. When those controls were removed, the people of the Bend embraced Branden with a frenzy of wholesome debauchery, if there can be such a thing.

We were so busy that first day that I did not have time to consider how the council might react. They had known only that the Defier was coming. Now that he had appeared, that same warlord claimed to be the long-lost prince. But there were no problems there either. Koppel immediately recognized Branden by sight.

Branden had wisdom as well as charisma. He did not insist upon the first seat at council, nor did he reach out his hand to take control of the city. In the first few days, he did little in council beyond listening. When he opened his mouth, he spoke softly, and his advice was useful and effective. He recognized that the leadership team we had cobbled together was doing a splendid job. He tended to sit back and observe rather than to guide.

One last item and I will move on from this tedious business of relating how power was transferred into the rightful and capable hands. There were few changes in how the council went about its business. The only major change was that, instead of me having the final word and controlling vote, now Branden had them. It was his nod that gave the stamp of approval rather than mine. I could not have been happier!

That was a very satisfying time of my life. To be the second in command was far better than being the leader. I was free to recommend risky policy and radical endeavors knowing that someone else could weigh the worth and make the final decision. Even better, there was someone to whom I could admit it when I did not know the best choice.

The first night after the battle was not a comfortable one. No general should sleep in comfort while his troops make do in an enemy's captured stronghold the night after a battle. It was particularly important for me. I was still new to the troops. They knew I was willing to die with them; they had to be shown I was willing to live with them. To that end, I told Lina what I was going to do. I had intended for her to stay in the castle. By now, you will know her well enough to predict what she had to say about my suggestion. So the general and his wife spent the night wrapped in furs in the enemy's captured stronghold.

The third day after the battle found us back in our own rooms within the castle. There was no sign of the enemy. We had made good progress in reapportioning the fort. For Lina's sake, I agreed to sleep in the castle. Gammin had taken rooms next to the king. It was fitting, though it did not please either of us overmuch. Arica and Marin joined their parents in the Grove.

Lina and I had just finished breaking our night's fast. She was massaging my sprung wrist with liniment. I was listening to her hum, feeling the love pour from her fingers into mine. It was a wonderful moment. There was a knock at the door, one we both recognized.

"Come in, Gammin," called Lina. "You don't have to knock." He had been to see us twice the day before, and we had spent time with him as we were about our duties.

The door opened. Gammin stepped in as he said, "I know."

After kissing Lina's cheek, he settled himself on the hearth and said nothing further. It was as if he had come just to be with us. That was enough.

He looked every bit a prince now, though it was not overdone. His mantle was off-white, hanging loose over a close-fitting shirt and leggings of gray. A dusty red cloak draped his shoulders. His father's ring was on his finger; his mother's hung from a chain around his neck. Only the thick gold chain was visible, but I knew the ring was there near his heart. The only other adornment was a broach fastening the cloak at his shoulder—a red lion against a black background, ruby over onyx. Since he was of the House of Brand, the eye of the lion was an emerald.

This was not much finery for a prince, but it was enough to make Gammin uncomfortable. He had to put his foot down to keep it that simple. His father wanted him to wear a slender circlet of finely woven gold strands. When the boy refused, Branden asserted that such a sign was entirely appropriate for a prince. The people, so he said, deserved to know who their prince was. Gammin argued back that he would be taken for an obnoxious turd by those who had known him before. Those who did not know him would get an entirely wrong impression of who he really was. Branden made some rebuttal I no longer recall; it is Gammin's clever victory that stands out in my memory. He won the day in his typical fashion by declaring that he'd feel much better about wearing a prince's circlet when his father was wearing the king's crown, something Branden was not yet prepared to do.

When Gammin related this episode, Lina and I were delighted. Though it was not typical of what one might expect between a king and one of his subjects, it was exactly the sort of thing any normal father and son might go through. Of course, neither Branden nor Gammin were normal.

It was not long before the young man asked about Arica. He told us that an uncomfortable strangeness had been growing between them lately. He did not know what to do about it. He had not seen her yet, though he had tried several times. It was in his mind that seeing her today was what he wanted to do with the little free time he had. Whatever the issue was, he wanted to get over it so he could share her company again.

Truth to tell, it eased my mind to know that he was longing for Arica's company. She was surely aching for his, even if her want was tinged with despair. She had given up on her heart's desire before giving it a chance. Gammin could ease a heavy heart. That was an aspect of his charisma that exceeded Branden's. The king inspired others with his presence. Gammin inspired too, as I have noted many times, yet he also comforted. He was like a tidy brook on a hot day. You could sit next to him and simply enjoy being there, or you could partake and be refreshed by the water.

I had told Lina about the disturbing conversations I had with Arica in the tower during the battle. It is not good to keep secrets from your mate, especially when she can read you as easily as my wife reads me. Once Gammin had spoken his desire to her, Lina wasted no time.

She said, "Arica will be with the children today. Annen and I are going down there this morning. Why don't you come along?"

Gammin accepted the invitation. I had not known we planned on that excursion. I kept my mouth shut for once and let the tide bear me along. Moments later, we were out the door and on our way.

I entered the orphanage first, followed by Lina and Gammin. Arica was at the back of the room talking with Eanna. We headed that way. One of the little children delayed Gammin. He was not with us when my wife and I reached Arica. I looked back and saw him. He'd made it to the center of the room. He was smiling down at a young boy that might have been eight.

A shriek erupted to my right. Every eye in the place turned that way. We all saw Temay.

He screamed again, but this time there was a word in it. "Gammin!"

Temay raised his hands and waved them wildly above his head. The unfortunate tray he was carrying clattered to the ground, completely forgotten. Temay charged Gammin, who, in addition to Marin, was his closest friend. His lead foot trod upon the tray. The tray slid backwards. Temay fell hard, face-forward. However, he did not hurt himself, which surprised us all. He tucked his chin down and executed a perfect roll. Well, it was prefect for Temay, anyway. In a flash, he was back on his feet and charging toward Gammin like an amorous bull.

The delay was enough to allow Gammin to push the child with whom he had been talking to safety. I saw my boy turn and take a strong defensive stance. He could have simply stepped away at the last instant or deflected Temay with one of the many defenses he had learned, but that might have caused Temay to hurt himself. Therefore, Gammin rooted himself to the ground and waited for the limbed tempest.

When Temay struck him, Gammin did not move at all. His arms engulfed Temay, who was gesticulating wildly. Temay eventually calmed down enough to participate in a hug. Then they were talking. At least, Gammin was talking. Temay continued to shout an insensible mixture of questions, answers, and exclamations. He was very excited, having not seen either Gammin or Marin for a long time.

Gammin looked toward us when he had a chance. His eyes sought Arica. She was turned elsewhere at the time and did not see. At just that moment, Marin and his mother entered the room. Temay saw them. Once again, he threw up his hands and shrieked. Like the tray before, Gammin was forgotten and discarded without a thought as Temay threw himself toward the door.

As soon as he was free, Gammin set off for where we

stood. There were many young people who wanted to greet him. They were understandably curious about his fine attire and the amazing rumors that had reached them. He was soon at the center of a crowd.

I glanced at Arica, intending to smile at her and shrug my shoulders. She was looking down at her feet. A dark curtain of hair hid her face. She did not look up as she turned to leave the room. Sure I could fix the crumbling situation, I started to follow her but felt a firm grip on my arm. I looked back at Lina.

Her eyes spoke very clearly. "No."

My heart was pounding. Every beat screamed, "Yes!" Plainly, Arica thought Gammin had snubbed her or, at a minimum, just wasn't interested enough in her to come greet her. Nothing was further from the truth. I had to tell her.

I stayed myself and felt Lina's hand relax. She kissed my shoulder tenderly as I watched Arica leave the room, a graceful shadow dissolving into the darkness of another doorway.

When Gammin freed himself, he hurried to my side. I could see the confused disappointment in his face when he saw Arica was not there. I moved my head in the direction she had gone. Gammin nodded a greeting to Eanna and murmured an apology. He took a single step in that direction, but it was too late. Marin and his mother arrived. With a barely perceptible slump in his shoulders, Gammin put on patience and greeted Dara.

By the time we followed Arica from the room, she was long gone. Later, Gammin took me aside and told me that he did not understand why Arica had not waited for him. I think that, so great was his trust in her friendship, he was not yet hurt by the action. He was simply perplexed. The hurt grew over the next two days as Arica continued to avoid him. I might have eased his concern by sharing with him what she had told me. Lina cautioned me about trying to steer their lives in the direction I wanted for them. She told me to leave it in the hands of Ea. I remembered, of course, that it was Lina and Dara who had plopped Arica right in the middle of Gammin's adventure in the first place. I kept the thought to myself. I was learning about being a good husband.

I have deliberately left Max and Breanna out of these events because they deserve a place all their own. No teacher could be more proud of his pupils than I was of them. The smallest of my students, they displayed courage and skill out of proportion to their stature.

In the days that followed the battle, the valorous deeds of Max and his squads gained much notoriety in the city. The warriors I had brought into that fight described it to their comrades and to their wives and families. I told the king. Branden showed them great favor and even asked me to assign Max a real place in the army, which I did. But it was not the thanks of the king or the adoration of the people that brought a quiet smile to Max. He reveled in the fact that he was, at last, accounted among the warriors, a battle-tested veteran among battle-tested veterans. At last, I say, though Max, in spite of his slight stature, rose very quickly, outpacing many an older man. He was too young for anything to have taken very long in his life.

So, while the woodcutter's daughter became the darling of the townsfolk for her quiet grace and deadly valor, Max became the toast of the town for his pugnacious bravery. To his credit, the young man bore the new-found fame well. He did not swagger or boast, as do so many who find sudden notoriety. Rather, he grew more silent, less ready to find some slight offense to his honor. Truth to tell, he was the very personification of the Warrior's Code as it is accounted in the Tales of Andur: Warriors must be strong when they feel weak, courageous when frightened, and gracious and humble in victory.

Breanna garnered her share of glory, too, but she did not relish it. She took to hiding much of the time when she was not helping me. She stayed mostly in Eanna's quarter. She began to spend time with Arica. She even went so far as to sleep in the grove on occasions when Max was away from the orphanage—which was common now that he was assigned to a regular unit of the army. Perhaps the two young ladies shared a silent kinship, the bond of people who love deeply with little hope of love returned.

III.

In one way or another, all of my friends were consumed in the rebuilding and reordering. We each had our jobs. One of the first things I needed to do was introduce Branden's quartermaster, a man named Prunel, to Simon.

Prunel, though he tried to be kind and gentle, almost scoffed when I presented him to Simon. Simon was twenty, only a few moons older than Arica. He was a quiet man, unassuming even for his height. He did not have the cocky assuredness that accompanies quartermasters like a shining aura. He was, in point of fact, contrary to the norm in every way. His face was emotionless, as if smiles and frowns were afraid to contest upon that placid field.

As his way of taking control—as far as he was concerned, everything in the city belonged to him—Prunel began to tell me of the goods and services he needed for the men and women in the fort. He wanted so many bails of this or that. Simon calmly stated that two thirds the number would be more than enough. The quartermaster gave him a surprised look. Then, still nonplussed, he said he wanted new blankets for the thousand warriors out there.

Simon corrected him. "It's eight hundred seventy five warriors and cavalry. You also need blankets for the seventy-three support personnel. And you will need replacements for some of the horse's blankets."

"Yes, quiet so," was Prunel's startled reply. "How do you know that?"

"I counted." For an instant, Simon's eyes flicked to mine before returning to the man he was addressing. Did I see a glimmer of a smile hiding there?

"Ah, you have been out to the fort, then?"

"No."

"Then when did you count them?"

"I saw them ride there after the battle."

Simon refused to speak about his gift with numbers to anyone but Lina, Eanna, and me. He knew it set him apart. Having been bullied as a boy by more-assertive lads, he accounted the gift as something that made him less rather than more. This is one way the Faceless separates us. His malice twists the little differences Ea gave to each of us so that they are accounted curses rather than blessing.

I knew this might go on for some time, so I put a stop to it. We did not have time to waste.

"Prunel, when Simon tells you what you need, you can be sure he is right. If he does not know something for certain, nothing you or I can do will make him guess. Trust me in this. And trust him. I certainly do."

Prunel snapped to attention, a new respect for Simon coming into his eyes. "Yes, Lord Calen. Thank you, Lord Calen. It shall be as you say."

I had to keep from laughing at such a reply.

"Fine, then. I am glad that is resolved. I'll be off. Simon will get you squared away. But remember, Twofords has been under siege for years. It may be that you can help them more than they can help you. Have a care what you ask for. I make no doubt these good people would give you the food from their plates without grumbling."

Prunel stamped a foot in answer as I began to leave. It was good military etiquette. As for Simon, he had already forgotten I had been there. He was reaching for his book. I heard a little bell ring behind me as I walked down the hallway. A moment later, a young clerk scampered past me on the way to see what Simon wanted. He carried a book in one hand and a quill in the other. I noted with some amusement that there was a look of excited anxiety on his face. I wondered if he knew that Simon was a well-trained warrior, even more deadly because he was able to act without emotion in time of crisis.

When I made it back to our rooms after the day's work, Lina was not there. She had set places for three. That meant we were to have a guest tonight for dinner. I did not know who, but it did not matter. There was still time before the customary hour at which we ate, so I decided to do something I had not done in a long, long time.

I changed into loose clothing and stretched my muscles for a few minutes. Then, I started moving through the forms of empty-handed combat. Similar to the sword and staff forms I had taught my students, these were a collection of moves strung together—some offensive, some defensive—against imaginary opponents. When done slowly, such forms, especially those from the empty-hands style, can be a moving meditation. They can bring serenity and healing to a tired mind, body, and spirit.

That afternoon, I was moving through them very gently and slowly. My wrist was not even close to being healed. I had, perhaps foolishly, not consulted a *nemen*—a Healer; they had more than enough work. As I moved through the forms, I tried to empty my mind and leave it open for Rhua, Ea's healing breath. I must have been successful, for when I finished and opened my eyes again, I found that Lina was sitting cross-legged on the hearth watching me.

I went to her and kissed her.

"That was lovely," she said.

"There are more where that came from."

She pretended a nip at my chin with her fine, white teeth. At least, I think she was pretending. "Not the kiss, love. I was talking about your forms. I recognize them, but I've never seen you do them like that before—so slowly. You looked like you were floating on a breeze."

I did not know what else to say, so I just thanked her and took a seat next to her. I knew her; there was more coming. I waited for it.

Presently, she said, almost in a whisper, "Annen, I really mean it when I say that was beautiful. I would love to be able to do that if… if I could do it the gentle way. Will you teach me?"

Lina knew this was an enormous request. She knew that I had no desire to be her *shinando*—her teacher—no desire to set myself above her, even for that noble cause. We were equals, a man and a woman united in one life. I feared to violate that. But what could I say?

I nodded and said, "I will, but there is one condition."

"Yes?"

"You must promise to be very patient with me."

She laughed and set her hand against my chest. Then she put her other arm around me and snuggled close. "I will try."

We sat for a few minutes. There was a little talk and a lot of silence as we discussed the important points of our day. When she did not mention it, I knew Lina was waiting for me to ask, so I did.

"Will you tell me who is coming to supper, or is it a surprise?"

"It's Arica. It was a surprise to me, which is why I did not discuss it with you before I invited her. I could not get her off my mind while I was cooking. She's so glum lately."

Lina pulled her head away from my chest and looked me in the eye. Frowning, she said, "I don't like that one bit! I set three places and went to tell her she was coming to eat with us tonight. She tried to say no." My wife shook her head again and struck her small fist against my chest. "Annen, when did Arica ever say no to spending time with us?"

I shrugged, not wanting to interrupt her, eager to learn what she would teach me.

"It seems odd to me," she continued. "You'd think she would be happy for Gammin. You'd think she knew him well enough to know he would not… set her aside."

I sighed and started to tell her that it was difficult to predict how any woman might react at any given time. At the last instant, I caught the foolish honesty before it broke cover and scampered into the danger zone. Instead, I said, "I feel the same. I am glad you invited her. Do you have advice for her?"

"I don't think she needs advice. She just needs to listen to the right voice in her heart."

Arica arrived while I was freshening up. When I came out, she was helping Lina. I welcomed her, then put the finishing touches on our meager table. The shortages in the city had eased slightly in the last few days, but we still had far to go. Branden had sent word to Brynmoor and the other enclaves in the east of the Southland, but no supplies could be expected from that quarter for a week or more.

If supper was fine, it was not because of the quality of the conversation. Arica had changed completely from the vibrant young woman we had known. She asked almost no questions and volunteered little when answering. More than once during the strangely silent meal, my eyes looked for guidance in Lina's. What I saw there was troubled concern that could have been a mirror of my own. I also saw a quiet patience, so I dammed my concerns though they steadily built as the meal progressed. Finally, we were done eating. Almost never have I enjoyed a meal less. We moved away from the table, each trying to hide the relief that retreat gave us.

We were very blessed, Lina and I, in comparison to how most folk in Twofords lived. Our apartments were large and well-furnished. The sitting room boasted a low couch that could provide comfort for three. At either end of this was a chair. Amidst this collection of sit-upons was a sturdy table of some local hardwood. My wife put Arica on the couch. We took the chairs.

Lina maneuvered the conversation toward the place where we could address Arica's malaise. The woodcutter's daughter seemed to recognize where we were headed and shied away at every opportunity. I am not sure how it would have turned out if we had not been interrupted by a knock on the door.

"Come," I called.

The door opened. Gammin stepped in. His eyes searched the room for us. They locked on mine for a moment. Then he noticed Arica. A rain of looks splashed across his face—pleased surprise, uncertainty, self-doubt, apprehension, then resolve. He opened his mouth to say something, but Arica spoke first.

"Are you following me?"

Her tone was pensive. It contained an aggravation I had not heard there except in the early days when she argued with her little brother. The words ricocheted into a sudden silence that seemed to echo off the walls. My heart cringed, knowing the question would wound my boy. And perhaps they did do him a grievance, but I underestimated him.

Gammin let the words resound in the silence for the perfect amount of time to indicate that he had heard them and knew them for what they were, what they meant. He took three quick steps so that he stood in front of the seated young lady. Then, with silky grace, he sank to a knee and reached out for her hand. She started to retract it, but even in his gentleness, he was too quick. There was no softness, no hesitation, in his voice when he answered her.

"Yes, lady. I am following you."

Here was no boy suing for pardon from a play-yard infatuation. Here was a man, a knight, a blooded warrior true-born to leadership. He had the heart of a lion. No, that's not enough. He had a dragon's heart.

The forthright answer took Arica by surprise. To cover it, and to give herself time to think, she said, "Why?"

"I want to be in your company, Arica. I thought you would know that."

She tried to pull her hand away. He held it until she gave over, then set it free. When she pulled it away from him, I saw real hurt in his eyes.

Gammin bowed his head for a moment. When he raised it, he said, "Arica, if you wish, I will leave. I just want to know how I displeased you. Please tell me."

Arica did the most sensible thing possible. She burst into tears. That was very unusual for her; she was an exceedingly strong you woman, physically, mentally, and emotionally. As I sat staring like a simpleton, Lina rose and touched my hand. She pulled me up and led me out of our apartment.

The last thing I saw was Gammin rising up and settling himself around Arica. He placed his arms about her, gathering her into his embrace. Arica went willingly, as if that was the place she most wanted to be, but she drew her hands up in little fists, tight across her chest, the way a frightened child protects herself from a nightmare.

My wife and I took the opportunity to visit the children in the orphanage. After a nice time, we judged it safe to return home. Arica and Gammin were gone. The dishes had been cleared. There was a short note on the table. Both of them had written in it and signed it. The note did not contain anything about what they had done or talked about. It was only a thanks and an apology.

I never asked Gammin what had occurred. It was not necessary. After that day, there seemed to be a peace between them. Things returned to the way they had been for years, Gammin, Arica, and Marin were seen most often together. If there was any difference, it was that Gammin and Arica seemed to speak less—at least publically—to each other, though their eyes were tender and they stood closer than was strictly necessary. I believe it is safe to say that each knew how the other felt.

5. WOLVES IN THE NIGHT

I.

The king and his son set out for Mendolas with five hundred warriors. That was a much smaller force than we should have sent. There was nothing to be done about it. We could not leave Twofords undefended. Likewise, Snow Moon was not the best month for making the journey, but Branden would not tarry. He was eager to build upon his recent victories in Daur en Lammoth and Twofords. He could sense the momentum building and did not want to let it abate.

I was ordered to stay in Twofords. My tasks were to rebuild and improve the defenses, to integrate the two armies that were left with me, and to ready them for the next phase of the plan. It stung my heart to see Gammin riding away, but he had his own life. He had a father to get to know, and he had the responsibilities of a prince to learn. Arica did not go. She elected to stay in Twofords.

Marin went. He and Gammin reminded me so much of the young Branden and Calen that it almost hurt me. I wanted to spare them the pain and heartbreak that life had in store for them. Even if I could do that, it would only rob them of their greatest pleasures. Pain and pleasure are two sides of the same golden coin. The things that give us our greatest joy are also the causes of our most grievous sorrows. Of these, love is the principal. Life is very strange.

As before, Marin kept a log in his book. That was something that gave him pleasure. We did not know whether the book would provide the same interactive experience for me as it had done with their previous adventures. When, after hundreds of leagues and many battles, the book came again into my hands, we discovered that it did. Lina and I were able to relive the young men's pain and pleasure, the gains and losses that matured them. Branden's scribe kept the official record. I read both accounts. That is how I can now relate to you what happened.

The last report Torlan had received told that Mendolas and Ehrynai were held by forces loyal to King Brand. That might have changed. We had no way of knowing. There had been no word for some time. Both cities were besieged. We sent scouts to gather information. They had not returned by the time Branden set off. I do not believe anyone ever accused him of being a patient person.

The passes above Mendolas might already be covered in snow. The peaks and shoulders of the Western Mountains as far as we could see from Twofords were white, though we could not see as far south as the pass below the peak known as the White Tower. If the road over Tower Pass was snowed over, travelers and traders would not undertake the southward trek along that route. That possibility did not deter the king's army. Though an army cannot go as quickly as a small party, it can sometimes go where the less equipped cannot. Branden's army was very well equipped.

They set off one wet, chilly morning about three weeks after Branden arrived in Twofords. Marn sent word to the various families of Old Ones along the forest road that would take the king to Teryn's Crossing. The army was careful to respect the Old Forest. They refrained from hunting as much as possible. Three times during that portion of the journey, Children of the Forest appeared out of nowhere to greet the king. As he marched to war, Branden was sowing the seeds of rebirth.

The Old Ones told Branden that Mendolas was still under siege by about fifteen hundred soldiers. It was uncertain whether the enemy would have remained there given another choice. Dauroth's army was essentially trapped between Mendolas and the sea. The way north was closed by the Old Forest and its Children. The way west was blocked by the mountains. The Silver River led to Ehrynai, and the soldiers had no large ships, for those had been captured with the city and were held by loyalists. South into Rath, the soldiers could not go. The king of Rath, King Kappelli, had stationed his own troops along the border and the trade roads that lead into his country. There was word of fierce fighting in those borderlands.

The soldiers surrounding Mendolas were fighting all the harder to regain possession of the city before the winter cold became an issue—if ever it did. Mendolas was far enough south and low enough on the mountain reaches that the city does not suffer as cruelly from the snows as does Twofords during hard years.

Branden's army came unopposed to Teryn's Crossing. While they were crossing, the scouts we had sent earlier came down from the icy fingers of the mountains to confirm that Mendolas was surrounded. To say it was besieged would be an overstatement. It is difficult to besiege a walled, fortified city that sits hard by the banks of a large river, especially when you do not control access from up or down river. However, the enemy's control of the land-based approaches to Mendolas was effective.

This situation was not unexpected, but the news that Dauroth's commander had sent a portion of his army to Tower Pass to meet Branden's force was very unwelcome. There were already six hundred enemy soldiers holding the pass and more on the way.

The king held a council of war with his captains. Gammin and Marin were afforded seats at that metaphoric table. The major topics of debate were obvious. If Branden continued his current course, he and his men would be fighting against an opponent who both outnumbered them and held the higher ground. Further, the enemy would, by the time the king's army climbed to the pass, have had time to secure their position. Gammin, who had less experience with Branden's ways than any of the captains, raised the concerns the others must have been feeling. Fortunately, the young man did not bring up the Precepts of War in his arguments. Despite Gammin's well-reasoned arguments, the king was not dissuaded from his intended course.

After allowing the army to rest for the night, Branden set off for Tower Pass, the northern gateway to Mendolas. Knowing that a formidable force waited above him, he arrayed his small army for battle. He sent out scouts and platoons of riders to range ahead of the unmounted warriors. Before the main body of the army had crossed the few miles that lie between the bridge and where the road begins to climb the ridge, a scout returned with an awful report.

Approaching the king on his horse, the scout bowed his head and spoke so quietly that only those very near could hear. Gammin was at the king's side. Marin, as ever, was with Gammin.

The scout said, "We found bodies, sire, men hung from trees along the side of the road. They look like Children of the Forest. I do not think they died from the hanging."

Branden nodded gravely. "A message."

"So we thought, sire."

The king dismissed the scout, who rode in haste back the way he had just come. It was not long before the column of warriors came to the first of the dead men. He had been gutted the way a hunter cleans his kill. There was almost no blood beneath the body.

By the time the army reached the rising switchbacks, they encountered six such bodies. Branden was enraged, though that was only apparent to those close enough to see his eyes and the set of his jaw. He caused each victim to be cut down and wrapped in a blanket. The king would not abandon the unfortunate Old Ones to the wild. Instead, the bodies were treated as any wounded warrior would have been treated and carried along by the men and wagons charged with such things.

The warnings did nothing to deter the king, but the message was clear. Dauroth's army was here to fight, and the Old Ones would be of little help.

II.

The delays with the dead and the labors of getting a large force up a mountain road in winter kept the day's progress relatively small. They encountered snow about half way to the pass. The snow had not yet accumulated on the road, where it was open to the sun. It was the mud that made the going difficult. That day, they made it only about two thirds of the way to the pass. There, a fold in the ridge provided a relatively level expanse where the army could camp for the night. Knowing there was no more suitable place below the top of the ridge, the king stopped the ascent earlier in the day than might have been normal.

The first attack came as Branden's forces were entrenching their position. The king was not caught by surprise. He had been expecting such a ploy, and his scouts gave plenty of warning. The battle raged until darkness consumed the sky. When, after a ferociously energetic confrontation, the enemy withdrew up the road, Branden's exhausted warriors did not give chase. They immediately set about finishing their fortifications. Those duties, as well as the work of retrieving and treating the many wounded, meant that few warriors got the rest they needed by the time the sun rose.

The enemy attacked again at first light. This frustrated the king. He had intended to be the aggressor; now, he was forced respond rather than initiate the action. All through the day, the tide of battle surged up and down the mountainside, both on and off the road. The king's forces managed to gain a good deal of ground, but at much cost in life and effort. When the sun began to set and the enemy withdrew, the king's forces had to set up new entrenchments on the newly captured ground. The location was less suitable than the encampment below.

The next day, the king's men did not take any new ground. They were forced to give up the second encampment and fall back to the first one. Tactically, the first encampment was a much better situation, but the retreat felt like a bitter defeat to each of the warriors who had fought so hard. It did not help that the weather worsened in the afternoon. The evening was wet, cold, and dreary.

The spirits of the men were beginning to droop. The king was not immune. That night, he ate alone in his tent, not even allowing his son the accustomed place at his side. No one knew what was in Branden's mind, but Gammin had thoughts of his own. Accordingly, taking Marin with him, he approached the king's tent. Branden was seated in his camp chair. He seemed to be staring into space. His gaze did not stir when his son and Marin entered.

When Gammin said nothing, the king glanced at his son and said in a pensive tone, "What?" Then Branden closed his eyes and shook his head as if to clear it. He rose to his feet wearily. "Forgive me." He gestured to the empty chairs that sat close by. "Sit. Have you eaten?"

"Yes, father."

The king, who could read men as if they were open books, said, "You have something to say?"

Gammin nodded and took a seat. Marin took a place next to him, the one that was farthest from the brooding king. When the silence had endured almost long enough to hurt, Gammin said, "Father, we were talking, Marin and I. We have an idea."

The king's head jerked around. He looked at his son fiercely. "Yes? Let's hear it, then. I could use some ideas."

"It seems to us, sir, that we are caught in an impasse. We

cannot fight our way up; they cannot dislodge us from the mountain. All the while, winter grows heavy up here, and good men die on each side."

"So you can see what is plain to see? That is good."

Branden glared at Gammin, holding his eye until Marin, who was growing exceedingly uncomfortable, shifted in his chair. The slight noise seemed multiplied by the tension. The king blinked and rubbed his face with his hands.

"I am sorry, my son. Again, forgive me. I had not expected to be stifled here. Dauroth has seldom prevailed against me since I returned to Ehrylan."

"I understand, sir."

Gammin cleared his throat and threw a look at Marin. The expression of anxiety on his friend's face almost made him laugh. That eased his own discomfort. "May I tell you what we were thinking?"

"Certainly," answered the king. He was taking himself in hand and had regained some of this composure.

"We were talking—Marin and I, that is. Marin said that he felt like a child at the mercy of a watch dog."

Branden snapped a quick reply, perhaps more emphatically than he'd intended. "This army will not retreat!"

"No, sire, of course not. If you'll let me finish, you may find another alternative at the end of my words." Gammin's tone was more appropriate for a son talking to his father than for a subject counseling his king. Marin cringed in preparation for the king's scathing response.

Branden laughed, fully and loudly, from the depths of his chest. "You are my son, indeed, Gammin. I'll wager you did not learn to confront a king that way from Calen."

"No, sire, of course not," said Gammin again, an echo of his last statement. He shook his head and looked grave, though inside, he was feeling rather excited. With each passing moment, he was more sure the plan Marin and he had devised was a good one.

"As I was saying, Marin brought up the watch dog. While we were talking about it, I thought of Old Bil. He was a dog at the orphanage in River's Bend. One time—this was years ago—we were playing out the story of Andur and the cave bear. Old Bil was the bear. It was going pretty well until Bil refused to give way when Max, who always played Andur, confronted him. Bil knew Max. He knew that Max was not going to hurt him, so why would he turn and run when Max menaced him?

"Anyway, little Breanna got up from where she was sitting and crept behind Bil while he was trying to figure out what Max wanted. By that time, the rest of us were jumping up and down trying to make Bil budge. Breanna reached down and pulled his tail. The dog whirled around in surprise with a snap and a growl. When he saw it was Breanna, he cowered down as if he expected us to be mad at him. Poor old thing." Gammin, who was openly smiling now, looked at Marin and laughed. "The point is that a dog will turn its head away from the threat in front of him when someone steps on its tail. A dog or a wolf. Marin and I think an attack on the enemy's rear while the rest of the army surges for the ridge might be just the thing."

The king was not unmoved by the honest pleasantry of the story. Still, he frowned and shook his head. "You believe I did not think of this, Gammin?"

"No, father. I believe you considered this and many other things we have not. We just wanted to discuss it with you. May I ask why you do not favor such a plan?"

Branden might not have condescended to offer an explanation to someone else. In this case, he was dealing with his son. As a father, if not as a king or commander, he owed clarification to the young man. How else was the boy going to learn?

The king spoke slowly, straining his frustration through a sieve of patience. "Attacking the flank of another army always involves splitting your own forces. We are already outnumbered, as you pointed out at Teryn's Crossing, and fighting up hill. Those are the most obvious reasons for not implementing your plan. Consider this, as well. Whoever I send to attack the rear is most likely going to die. Our opponent is not a friendly old companion. When the wolf—maybe a viper would be a better illustration—turns back to bite the pest pulling on its tail, it will neither miss nor cower in regret. It will destroy the pest utterly. Aside from the many warriors we would throw away needlessly, which of my leaders shall I send to their certain death?"

The king's voice had grown darker with each sentence of his explanation. As he lapsed into a mournful silence, he plucked a grape from the nearly-full plate of food that sat nearby. Seeming to have forgotten that the boys were still present, Branden inspected the grape for a time before setting it on the arm of his chair. He smote the grape with a closed fist. A spray of juice and disintegrated grape jumped to each side. Branden lifted his fist slowly. His eyes inspected the wet spot on the arm of the chair. Without moving his head, he looked at Gammin.

The two young warriors had watched in silence. Marin was ready to slink out of the tent and lick his wounds in less-tense circumstances; Gammin was not.

"Sire," he began, then started again. "Father, there is truth all through what you say. Yet, your words are only what may be, not what must be. Can you agree to that for a moment?"

Branden sighed. "I will listen, my son. But first I will tell you this. Now I understand what my father felt when Calen and I used to pester him with our young hopes and ideas."

Suddenly, Marin spoke. The words were the first he had spoken since entering the tent. "Is it that hopeless, sir?"

"Hopeless? Who said anything about that?" The king abruptly rose to his feet, which caused the other two to do the same. Branden impatiently motioned for them to reseat themselves. They did.

"I have not lost hope of restoring our kingdom. Nor do I believe our present situation is hopeless. Never think it, young seer. I have only lost hope that we can take our opponent swiftly and ride down upon Mendolas like a cleansing wave. That possibility seems lost to me now. What remains is a grinding battle where the lives of Ehrylain are lost at every step. That is not what I want for my people. I am not king only of those who fight under the lion banner. I am king also to those who fight unwillingly under the banner of the wolf. I mourn their deaths as much as I mourn the deaths of our own warriors."

"We understand, father. So we have been taught. We feel the same." Gammin stood and crossed to where his father was standing. "I say again, what you have said is only what might be, not what is. I will described a plan that might work to distract the head of the wolf—or, the snake, if you will—long enough to allow the main forces to gain the ridge."

"I am listening," said the king pensively. His tone was not fatherly. It was the tone of a king who has grown over-tired of listening to his councilors about matters that have already been decided.

"Marin's idea is that we take a hundred men south across the spur ridges that fall from the heights." Branden began to speak, but Gammin silenced him. "Of your courtesy, sire, allow me to at least begin before you finish me."

Branden recoiled. His eyes widened. Then he remembered who this young man's father was, remembered that these two young men had faced more than one Gryhm in their short lives and come away with their lives intact. Their council was worth listening to on that count alone.

He nodded once.

"I thank you, father. Now, Marin and I are aware of how difficult the valleys running west to east are. We've seen them from above, twice actually, and even seen them from the Old Forest from an angle few get to see."

"An angle? You refer to when the woodcutter brought Calen back from the south of the forest? You were with them, I recall."

"Yes, sire. My point is that Marin and I have seen the lay of the land below the ridge road. We've ridden over Tower Pass in both directions. We even spent several nights up there. We are familiar with the ground, sir."

Branden motioned for Gammin to take his seat. After

refilling his wine glass and calling for two more from the guards, the king asked for more information.

Marin, who was the better story teller, explained. Annen, Merelina, and the rest of the children had paused for a few days at the top of the ridge during their return journey to Twofords after a trip to Mendolas and the port of Arai. The snow had melted by then, and the weather was as fine as one could have wanted for an outdoor excursion. They had tarried at herders' huts on the south edge of the pass.

Everyone had been in a fine mood, and no one wanted to get back to Twofords before they had to, most especially Merelina and Annen. Those two had seemed to be on some journey of their own, a mysterious dance that had no steps and no accompaniment. Gammin, Marin, and the others had been left to roam where and when they would, as long as they stayed together. Exploring the hidden valleys that reached down toward the Silver River was just the thing to keep everyone occupied and happy. Marin had written down some of the adventures they had during that happy time, making them into little stories suitable for the children in the orphanages to read.

The king was not interested in knowing what a fine time they had. He wanted to learn more of the valleys that fell from the eastern approaches below the pass. The two young men told as much as they could recall, even going so far as to describe the potential route they might take. By the end of their descriptions, it was obvious the king was hooked on the idea of a strike from that region.

They talked through the various finer points. When should the raid leave the main body of the army? What was the goal? Where would they strike? When should they hit the enemy? This last was one of the most important aspects to nail down. The raid and the onslaught of the rest of Branden's army had to be synchronized to be successful. Otherwise, it would be a disaster.

The next task was to choose the correct warriors for the raiding party. There would be one hundred. More could not be spared. Any fewer could not hope to succeed.

More to test his son than anything else, the king asked, "What skills will the men need?"

Gammin replied immediately. "They must be the best climbers and the best at moving through the forest in mountainous terrain. They must be able to move silently and fight like dragons. They must be able to do all these things on light rations and no sleep."

Branden said, "Is that all?" Irony dripped from his word.

"There's one more thing, sir."

"What's that?"

"They must all be brave as lions."

Though Branden was fully invested in the idea at that point, he was less convinced that Gammin or Marin should lead the surprise attack. The king's hesitation was not based on any doubt in Gammin's abilities. The king knew that Gammin was an excellent rider and an outstanding swordsman, even when compared to grizzled veterans. The king had also seen that Gammin was a natural leader, one whom men seemed to follow almost instinctively. But the father was not yet convinced that his son should lead such a desperate raid. Branden's reluctance may have been equal parts the concern of a father and the fretting of a monarch with a single child.

Gammin was Branden's son by blood if not by upbringing. He had inherited both his father's and his mother's stubbornness. This he kept well-hidden, though when he knew instinctively that he was right, the obdurate streak appeared with a vengeance. He argued for the chance to lead the raid.

The king said there were other tried and true leaders within the army to lead such a raid. Gammin asked if any of them had been in those valleys within the last few years. The king claimed that a prince had no business leading such a dangerous venture. Gammin recited a list of the various exploits he had heard Annen relate. Flustered and somewhat outwitted, Branden stated that there were others more suited to such an adventure. That is where he lost the battle. Gammin calmly reminded his father that, as a captain in the Tallenlaust, he—Gammin—had often successfully led more than a hundred men on desperate missions against Dauroth's soldiers in heavily wooded areas.

Marin, whose head had been turning to and fro as each opponent shot their verbal arrows, saw the recognition finally seep into Branden's eyes. The king, who must have at last realized the truth in the young men's council, shook his head and sighed as if exhausted.

"Fine, then. Have it your way. But you must promise me one thing."

Gammin did not answer. He waited in silence.

Setting his hands on Gammin's shoulder, Branden shook him firmly. "If I give you this, you must agree here and now that you will not argue with every pronouncement I make. I've waited a long time to be king. I am not ready to pass the scepter on to you just yet. Now get out of here, both of you. You've got your work cut out for you."

Dismissing the boys from his attention, Branden bellowed for his attendant. He sent the man away in a rush to summon the company captains.

III.

The enemy did not attack the next morning. Perhaps they were as busy licking their wounds as Branden's army. More likely, the nasty conditions prevented the attack. It was an altogether gloomy daybreak that followed an altogether gloomy night. Rain had fallen in great torrents from time to time, but most of the time, it had just piddled down in that annoying way rain falls in the mountains. Fortunately, though the air was by no means warm, it was warm enough that no snow fell.

All through the night, Gammin, Marin, and the captains had worked to choose the right men and women. About half were from Stormhaven. The rest were drawn from the warriors of Twofords, both the locals who had been living in and around the city when the war broke out and the men who had previously served Dauroth and received amnesty from Annen and the council.

There had been no significant trouble from the liberated troops. Most of them were true Ehrylain who had been pressed into service by the hand of evil; they had taken to calling themselves the Redeemed and were too happy to cause trouble. A few were true foreigners from elsewhere in the Crescent. Of that group, more than one was rough around the edges.

Midmorning on the day after Gammin had approached his father, a sizable portion of the army's train began to make their way slowly down the mountain. Wagon's laden with food and supplies, blacksmiths, carpenters, stonemasons, and all manner of support personnel headed back toward Teryn's Crossing. The caravan, with its guard of slightly more than a hundred unmounted warriors, resembled the first stages of an orderly retreat. The inclement conditions added another verisimilitude of truth to the ploy. It could be hoped that the enemy would believe that, battered, wet, and cold, the army had decided to pull up tent stakes and make for the river.

Early on, the caravan stopped. If enemy scouts were watching closely, they might have wondered why such a resting was taken so soon after departure. The place was well-known to those who traveled that road and well-chosen for Gammin's purposes. A stream fell from above, its waters collecting in a chilly pool that routinely provided refreshment for people and animals.

While the others were about their watering, Gammin and his force melted into the forest, hopefully unnoticed in the shadow of the quite commotion. If they had been birds, the flanking party would have flown directly south. However, the undulating folds of the mountain spur ridges did not allow a straight course. The men, who were split into smaller groups of about ten warriors each, made their way on a southerly course by switching back east and west as the land allowed.

Much of the time, the forest was so thick or the land so craggy that no landmarks could be discerned to reassure the leaders that they were on the right track. Occasionally, glimpses of the shimmering waters of the river below or the white peaks above helped chart the way. The places where the land opened enough to look upon things distant were also the places where the men had to be the most cautions. If the warriors could see up or down, the eyes of an enemy who was above or below might also be able to spot them.

The weather began to turn again, as it does so often in the high places. All through the afternoon, the clouds rolled back. Before long, the sun was peaking through. Later, those clouds were blown away, leaving a blue sky. By midafternoon, it was as pleasant as before it had been uncomfortable.

An hour or three before sunset, Gammin, who was in the leading group, called for a halt and waited for Marin. The woodcutter's son soon appeared. The two had prearranged this before they started. After a brief discussion, they came to agreement as to where they were in relation to where they wanted to end up. As the warriors rested, the prince and the seer made the rounds, being careful to visit every unit.

They were almost done with that activity when they came across a spot of bother. Most of the men and women were sitting, taking rest and refreshment while it was there for the taking. A knot of people had formed around one man. That man was talking rather loudly. His voice instantly set both Gammin and Marin on edge. It was obvious from his rough appearance and rougher accent that the man was from somewhere in northern Ehrylan, one of the rougher parts. He was one of those who had accepted clemency after some previous battle.

Marin stepped forward, breaking the ring of men.

"Is there a problem here?" The woodcutter's son eyed each of the surrounding men before turning on the man who stood with him at the center.

The man looked hard at Marin, then at Gammin, who were the youngest in this contingent by several years. The man turned his head in a peculiar way, his chin jutting marginally. "No. T'was nothing." The words did not seem to mirror his thoughts.

Gammin stepped forward. The ring of men drifted apart as he approached, giving him a wide berth. In a quietly firm voice, he said. "It was something."

The man sighed, looking to his friends for support. That did not help. Everyone else was focused on Gammin, the prince.

The man sighed again, shrugged his shoulders. There was something dismissive in the movements. "I was a'sayin' that I did not think we was needin' to go farther south."

Gammin held him with his eyes. "Why do you think that?" His words were not accusatory, nor aggressive, but there was no weakness in them.

Gammin was frustrated with this loss of time. The whole endeavor—the survival of his father and the rest of the army—depended on speed and stealth. Debating strategy while the last light of day bled away contributed to neither of these things. But Gammin knew he had to hear the man out. This was not the first time he had been forced to earn the respect of seasoned warriors years older than himself. He also knew that the man might have something valuable to add. The trick was getting it out of him without destroying the discipline that had been building.

When the man did not respond, Gammin repeated his question more forcefully. "I am really interested in your thoughts. Why don't we need to go any farther south?"

The man, who had been sporting the beginnings of a smirk, drew himself up to his full height. "Why would the enemy guard the route back down to Mendolas? They just come up road. They know it be safe in their own hands. And, further south we go, farther north we return. We be exhausted by mornin' if we keep a'goin'." After an awkward pause, which might have been entirely intentional, he added a belated, "Yoor Highness."

Gammin nodded. "What is your name?"

"My father called me Leanord... yoor Highness." Each time he added the title, Leanord managed to stress it in such a way as to make it sound like some sort of wasting disease.

"Leanord, have you ever been down the ridge road to Mendolas?" Gammin did not pause to give the man a chance to answer. "I have, and I can tell you that there are at least two good places to shelter dozens of men on the crest before it starts down the south slope toward the river. We won't be able to distract the soldiers facing the king if we are being attacked from behind ourselves. As far as being exhausted by morning, you are right. If every man and woman here isn't exhausted by the time we complete our mission, we have not tried hard enough."

Gammin stepped into the man's space. His eyes narrowed and his lips pressed into a tight line. His voice very quiet, he asked, "Do you understand me?"

Once again, Gammin did not pause to let the man reply. He continued, his voice now as sharp as the sword at his side, "The truth is, I don't need you to understand me. I don't even need you to agree with my decisions. What I require is that you follow my instructions without debate and that you do so to the very best of your ability. If you can't do that for me, Leanord, can you do it to support the rest of the men and women with us, or for the king, or even for Ehrylan?"

Leanord stammered a hasty, "Yes, yoor Highness!" This time the title sounded like it belonged to a prince.

"Are you certain?"

"Yes, yoor Highness!"

Gammin insinuated himself even closer to the man. He gripped Leanord's upper arm with hard fingers and pulled him away from the others. In a voice only Leanord could hear, he said, "Good, because if you can't, I will kill you where you stand."

Suddenly Gammin's blade was in his hand. It glittered in the forest sun, a shaft of fire. He did not menace the startled Leanord with it. Instead, he spun around to address the others in the squad.

"We are not playing at some fool's errand. We are not just hoping to distract our enemy. We are going to wound him. We are going to crush him between our swords and the swords of the king. We can do that, but only if we do it together."

The group of men who had been clustered around Leanord had been joined by other men and women. Some began to cheer. Marin raised his hands to quiet them. As Gammin turned and walked away, the woodcutter's son motioned for the group to break up. Catching Leanord's eye, Marin gave him a look that was as much an appraisal as a warning, then headed back.

When the force set out again, it took a course upward, across the spur ridges and the tree-choked valleys that lay between them. In time, Gammin crested a ridge and saw what he had been searching for. To his right, at the top of the next ridge, a bare shoulder of rock rose above the surrounding trees. Down the north face of that rock cascaded a diminutive waterfall that vanished into the shadows.

Gammin set out for the bubbling pool that waited at the foot of the falls. There, in times past, he and his friends had spent a pleasant afternoon. Marin had already written down that adventure before the war started in earnest. It was one of his first attempts at true story telling. Neither the woodcutter's son nor his friend needed to review the story to recognize the place. The rock, the falls, and the little pool were etched firmly in joyful memories of days gone by.

The sun was beginning to slide behind the peaks when they arrived. One hundred warriors gratefully took off their packs. The pool was an excellent place to shelter while they rested. The raiding party was hidden from above and below. Any reasonable noise they made would be disguised by the tumbling waterfall, and there was plenty of fresh, clean water, always a good thing after a hike.

The most-important reason Gammin had made for the pool was that he knew the valley in which it lay led up to the pass half way between the north and south shoulders. An overgrown, seldom-used path wandered in and out of existence as it led to the top of the ridge about a mile distant. With any luck, the whole company would be able to follow it, making their way more easily and quietly.

As the warriors rested, Gammin gathered his squad leaders, one from each unit of ten. Together, they selected scouts, two to head up to the ridge and two to go down toward the river. Marin took the duty of scouting the southern half of the pass. He knew the path and wanted to see what could be seen. One of the Defier's trusted scouts, a woman of some fifty summers, drew the duty of scouting the northern end of the pass. It was a difficult and dangerous task; that was where most of the soldiers were likely to be.

IV.

Once Gammin cut him loose, Marin briefed the men in his team. After appointing one of them to be the acting team leader while he was gone, Marin checked his weapons and his water bag. Then, a whispered prayer to Ea on his lips and in his heart, he set out.

Soon, Marin was travelling in darkness. He didn't notice when the crepuscular gloaming turned to the true darkness that can only be found where men have not built cities. The moon was strong and yielded some illumination, but Marin did not need its light. He was a creature of the forest and knew its ways from instinct and long practice.

Marin was moving quickly and quietly when he noticed a glimmer of moonlight that broke through the trees to splash the forest floor up ahead. Instinct slowed his steps. He proceeded more cautiously. As he approached the spot, Marin saw a smallish clearing through which the track he was following travelled. Conscious that every delay made his task more difficult, he slowed to a stop. If he were late in returning with the scouting report, he would fail Gammin, fail the king, even fail himself. He could not let that happen, but cutting corners with caution could lead to even greater failure. He stopped and listened. He sniffed the air and tried to feel what lay ahead in the night.

There was something, a hint of disquiet in the air. Marin

closed his eyes, opened his mouth a fraction. He heard nothing out of place. He smelled no hint of man or beast, yet he sensed something. It could have been an echo of the raiding party, or even a reflection of the enemy occupying the pass. Maybe it was a hint of some unknown danger that was still far away. He did not know.

Cautiously, Marin insinuated himself through the trees that described the edge of the clearing. He was just one more shadow in the night. He made no more sound than a shadow would make. The open space was smaller than he had anticipated. In a few steps, he could have been across it and out the other side. Something stopped his feet.

He felt a hint of anxiety. A mist of fear drifted through his heart. As he recognized the feeling for what it was, the breath caught in his throat.

Quickly, his eyes searched for a good tree. He needed low branches to get started and a nice set of dense branches higher up in which to hide. A soon as he found what he was looking for, he moved. Instead of heading straight across the clearing, he followed along the edge of the trees. No sense in showing himself in the moonlight to whatever was coming… or already watching.

With a thoughtless ease that bordered on grace, Marin, the Old One, the Seer, pulled himself off the ground. Up and up he went, two levels higher, and sat himself where a sturdy branch emerged from the trunk. Craning his neck this way and that, he made sure he had a good view of the clearing. Satisfied that he was concealed, the woodcutter's son lapsed into stillness.

Marin felt the blanket of mental unease settle around him. It was nothing like the aching terror and revulsion that had accompanied the two Gryhm he had encountered. This was a wholesome disquiet, not the cloak of dread that surrounded undead demons. Marin was not frightened in the least. That could not be said of his encounters with Gryhm. With both Grachul and Charshan, he had been terrified from his hair to his boots. The sensation he was feeling now was different. It was natural, not the product of some dark magic. This was more like a nagging anxiety that washed over him as the oncoming tide covers a beach, bit by bit, a pace at a time with each successive wave.

Despite the urgency of his mission, Marin knew he had to hold his position until he better understood what his intuition was telling him. There was something out there above him on the ridge. It was coming his way.

A dim shape appeared out the darkness. It halted at the edge of the clearing. Marin felt it more than he saw it and smelled it. It made no sound. In the darkness between the trees, it was difficult for his eyes to tell him that the shape was a wolf. He knew it just the same. The wolf stepped from the dark edge of the woods into the silvery bath of light that pooled in the open space.

The animal was injured. It moved with a pronounced limp. Its head and tail were down. The wolf stopped abruptly and raised its muzzle to the breeze; its head turned to the place Marin had emerged from the forest looking for the source of the scent. Marin understood that the wolf recognized the smell of a friend. He felt the pressure of anxiety lessen in his mind. A breath of grateful surprise wafted over him, then vanished.

Slowly, the woodcutter's son raised one hand.

"Friend, I am here." His voice was barely a whisper.

The wolf's head jerked toward him. Marin saw the hind end bunch in preparation for flight, saw the wince as pain shot through the animal. He felt the echo of its agony in his mind. The wolf's eyes found him. He saw recognition in them, felt it in his heart. The animal relaxed, though it retreated closer to the far side of the clearing. Marin let himself down from the tree. Though he jumped from twice his own height, only the wolf could have heard him land.

With quick steps, he crossed to the wounded animal. It stood bravely at his coming. Only the bared, moonlit fangs betrayed its instinctual fear. It held its ground, a suppressed growl fighting for freedom deep in its chest. Marin went to a knee near the head of the animal and extended a hand.

"Sister, if you permit it, I will help you."

Carefully at first, then with more confidence with each moment the wolf did not bite off his hand, Marin stroked its head, scratched behind its ear, explored further. After running his hands over the beast's body, he amended his words.

"You will be alright, I think, little mother." The young she-wolf was very pregnant.

Someone had tied the wolf's leg with a cord. The animal had chewed at the knots until it was free. In doing so, it had grievously wounded its own limbs. That was an older wound, on its way to healing. When Marin ran his hands over the animal's torso, they came away sticky. He did not need the smell to identify the thick gore matting the fur as blood. There were several gashes along the back and flanks. A noose, still cruelly tight, encircled its neck. The leash terminated in a ragged end where the wolf had chewed it away. That end was wet, sodden with saliva. She must have just escaped.

"Whip marks and a noose around the neck. Who would do such a thing?"

Marin was in the process of loosening the noose when the answer to that question announced itself. A spate of words and the hushed noise of careful feet tumbled down through the silence. From the sound of it, the owners of those feet were headed straight for where Marin was kneeling.

"Of course, they are coming right for me. I am almost in the middle of the path," he thought with chagrin. From the taste of hatred in his mind, Marin felt sure that those same men were the authors of this wolf's agony.

There might have just been time enough for Marin to climb a tree or lose himself in the darkness, but he did neither. He spent the time reflecting on how this chance encounter had placed the fate of the surprise attack and the fate of the Branden's army in jeopardy. The woodcutter's son had just time enough to laugh at the fact that, by extension, the fate of all Ehrylan might, at that very moment, lie between the mangled feet of this poor, pregnant wolf.

"So be it," Marin thought, and drew his sword.

Looking down at the wolf, he whispered, "Stay here. I need them to see you. Don't worry, sister. They will pay for what they have done."

He knew the wolf could not understand the words. He believed she might understand the intent of his communication. It was new to him, this ability to feel the thoughts of some animals. Not all the Children had it, though his parents certainly did, and Arica, too. This particular blessing came to the Old Ones only after they reached adolescence and sometimes not at all. It was a gift that took a very long time to develop, a lifetime to master. The ability had started to grow within Marn during the last year or so. Until this moment, the budding ability had been more often a frustration than a boon.

Marin was uncertain he could make the wolf understand him, but he could understand what his ears told him. As he moved into concealment at a location good for an ambush, he heard the unmistakable racket of three big men. He could also hear their conversation. They were not Ehrylain.

"Blast. I think she's got away for sure this time."

"Nar. You give up too easy by half, Glum. Besides, you've told me a hundred times as how you wants a wolf pup. Here's your chance. An' anyway, I ain't come this far down this cursed mountain to turn back. Least wise, not yet."

"Ha, you fat, old fart," retorted the first man, who must have been named Glum. "We haven't walked more than a quarter mile."

"That's what you say. I say a quarter mile walked down is a mile we have to walk back up. So says me."

A third voice interrupted. "If you two don't stop jabberin', we ain't standin' a chance to catch that wolf. It was only dumb luck that we catched her the first time she got away. I'm guessin' that whippin' you give her did more harm than good."

"Luck, is it?" Glum snorted derisively. "I'll take dumb luck in place of whatever it is you got. I'll warrant your mother cursed her luck after she saw your face the first time."

There followed a gaggle of laughter. The three men were

still patting each other on the back when they stepped into the clearing. One of them saw the wolf immediately. With a delighted cry, he leapt toward her. That one had to be Glum. In one hand, the man had what was left of the broken leash. He passed directly in front of Marin's hiding place. The animal lay completely still as if she were already dead. Maybe she was.

The second man, the fat one, rushed across the space. An instant later, the third stepped between where Marin crouched and where the wolf lay. The woodcutter's son struck with silent precision. The man was already dying by the time he started to fall. Unfortunately, the fat man turned back with his mouth open. Perhaps he was going to make a jibe about the fattest not being the slowest. What he saw stopped his words and pulled a gasp out of him. He clutched at the shoulder of the first man, who was kneeling by the wolf, as his other hand went for the sword at his side.

Gliding forward, Marin jabbed at the fat man's face, the target that was farthest from the protection of the sword he was raising. Like many fat men, he was quicker than he looked. His sword made it up in time to deflect Marin's. The man also blocked Marin's second attack, a mid-level swipe at the protruding belly.

The man moved to the offense. He stepped forward nimbly and slashed at Marin, who jumped back out of range—just barely. With a mixture of trepidation and excitement, the woodcutter's son realized that this corpulent soldier was a fine swordsman.

Not waiting for the man to strike again, Marin leapt forward. He attacked with a storm of ferocity. The fat man moved sideways in an arc, deftly blocking Marin's attacks and responding with his own. Striking and parrying, the two blades sang out in the night.

Marin did not have time for this! His peripheral vision caught a movement from where the wolf lay. The fighting had shifted the two combatants several paces to one side. Marin suspected that Glum was about to come to the aid of his friend. That made Marin's plight even more urgent.

The woodcutter's son faked a stumble, then launched himself toward his opponent. At the last instant, just as he came in range again, Marin spun unexpectedly. His blade took off the fat man's sword arm with the first stroke then sliced into his neck with the second.

As the man collapsed with a strangled cry, Marin caught the flick of movement out of the corner of his eye. Twisting away, he felt a searing pain in his side. Instinctively, Marin brushed across the space with his sword. The blade bit into the wooden shaft of the spear that had wounded him. Marin stepped sideways, away from the spear and the agony. He could not allow the last remaining soldier to sound the alarm. Knowing that it is seldom wise for a swordsman to close with a spearman, Marin turned his retreat into an advance and a new attack.

He suppressed a wince at the pain in his side. How bad was the wound, his mind wondered? Maybe it was bad enough to kill him, he concluded. It certainly felt that way. That did not matter now, not while he was still standing and able to fight.

Refocusing his attention, Marin knew what he had to do. Whether he lived or died was not the most important thing. He had to kill this last soldier before the man alerted anyone else.

That killing did not prove easy. The man was good with his spear, as good as the fat man had been with his sword. The spearman used the length of the weapon to keep Marin at a safe distance. For a moment, they circled. Twice Marin sought to slip inside the protective net woven by the point of the spear. Twice he was repelled. Why the man did not yell for help was a mystery to the woodcutter's son, but it was a fortunate mystery.

As Marin was summoning his strength for another assault, his opponent gasped, staggered forward, and fell. Marin saw a gray-silver flash as the wolf let go the leg she had bitten and jumped on the man's back. The wolf's fangs groped at the soldier's neck. When the man turned over to dislodge her, she sank her teeth into his throat and jerked her head from side to side savagely. The man's screams emerged as liquid gurgles, stifled by the ferocity of the she-wolf's onslaught.

The man rolled again, frantically trying to free himself of his terrible foe. As soon as Marin saw the exposed neck, he moved in with the tip of his sword. With a sharp spasm, the soldier jerked and receded into stillness. That did not stop the wolf. She continued to tear at the inert body with her fangs and claws. It did not look to Marin as if she was feeding. It looked like revenge. That impression was confirmed by what he felt in his mind. Whoever this man was, it was certain that he was the one who had tortured her.

Marin left the wolf to her pleasure. After glancing at the other two bodies to make sure they were dead, he knelt and pulled aside his shirt. Probing the wound with his fingers, he found a cut along the muscle on his side. The spear had not pierced his abdomen, as far as he could tell. He considered for a moment, looking around at the three bodies. Discarding the idea of using some of their clothing for the task, he cut a strip from the bottom of his shirt, then cleaned and staunched the wound.

The wolf appeared at his side. At first, she nosed at his wound, trying to lick it. Marin gently pushed her away. "I thank you, sister," he murmured, "but your tongue carries the blood of my enemies. I don't want that in me."

With a slight whimper, the animal sank to the ground next to him, where she lay licking her paws until he finished.

After he had done all he could with what he had, Marin stood up. Sweeping the clearing with his eyes, he looked at the three dead men. Glum, the man the wolf had attacked, could be of no use to him; the body was a mass of tattered rags and flesh soaked with blood and gore. For the first time, Marin noticed that the man wore the black uniform of an officer. Each of the others did, as well. That accounted for why the spearman and Glum had been so proficient with their weapons. Marin should have noticed the uniforms straight off. That might have saved him some trouble. Or, maybe not. There was no sense in fretting about it now. Shaking his head at his own thick-headedness, Marin resolved to be more careful in the future… if there was one.

He crossed to each of the other bodies and inspected them. The fat man had a wide sash. Marin took the sash. After assuring it was relatively clean, he tied it around his abdomen under his shirt to hold the make-shift bandage in place. More than that, he could not do.

After searching the bodies for plans or other documents, Marin pulled them into the sheltering trees. Then he returned to the wolf. Confident in the animal now, he knelt and caressed her head and ears with his hands. Seeing the noose, he finished loosening it and slid it over her head, freeing her at last. For that, Marin received a series of strong licks on his hand. He smiled in spite of the urgent situation.

"You are welcome. Little mother, I must go. I think you will be fine, but you must leave these parts. Soon, many men come." He concentrated on an image of the king's warriors marching up the path.

"If you will take my council, go down to the water." He imagined the river. "Cross it where you can. You will find other friends there." He imagined the Children of the Forest.

The wolf stared at him unblinking. Marin did not have a clue whether she had understood him or not. The seething anxiety was gone from his mind and heart. In its place, there was a feeling he could not quite identify. It was something like realizing that friends were closer than he thought. The woodcutter's son stared into the eyes of the she-wolf for a long moment while he tried to determine if she was communicating or he was just imagining things.

With a sigh, Marin shrugged. It was time to go, past time. He had not wasted more than half an hour here, but that was more than he could afford. And now, he was wounded. With a last glance at the wolf, he decided the time had not been wasted.

Rising without another word, he started up the path. When he looked back to make sure he'd hidden the bodies well enough, the wolf was gone.

V.

Marin was vaguely familiar with the narrow track, which was quickly becoming a fairly distinct trail. He knew from personal experience that it led to the top of the ridge. With each turning, the night-shrouded landscape came back to his mind more clearly. Soon he was remembering what was around the next corner before he got there. In a few minutes, though he had been moving slowly to maintain silence, Marin found himself near the foot of a shelf that stood between him and the level of the pass. He was less than two hundred paces from the road.

The shelf was a flattish promontory jutting from the mountainside some five or six vertical paces from the ridge top. It was an excellent place to post a guard. That is exactly what the soldiers had done. From his concealed position in the trees, Marin could hear two men talking and one man snoring. All around the edge of the shelf, rocks had been carefully piled into a wall that gave shelter against the wind. The enclosed area was big enough for three or four big men to sleep side by side. Marin, Gammin, and their friends had found the spot when they tarried in this area. Annen had told them it was likely a place where hunters waited for elk and deer. He'd called it a blind. Little Breanna had wanted to know why such a thing should be called a blind if it was a good place from which to see. Good old Max had called it a fortress. They had based several adventures from it. Marin smiled at the memory, then frowned. Now, their imaginary fort was held be the enemy.

Marin had suspected this place would be occupied by lookouts. Accordingly, he had left the trail some distance back down the mountain and made his way through the forest. The darkness and the trees gave him excellent protection from the guard's eyes. The silvery moon shone down on the shelf with enough light that Marin could see the rock wall clearly and, from time to time, the movements of heads and shoulders behind it. The night breeze was blowing over the shelf and into

Marin's face. He had smelled the men well before he arrived.

The woodcutter's son had achieved the first of his goals. The easy part was done. He had determined that this approach to the pass was watched. But was it guarded? Was there a detachment of soldiers waiting close above? What were the positions of the other accumulations of soldiers? Marin had to get up to the pass and walk unseen among his enemies to complete those goals. After that, his final goal was to get back to Gammin without being detected. Without achieving that, the other goals were meaningless.

As he sat considering how best to do these things, Marin heard the unmistakable sound of footsteps. His hand started to move toward his sword. He stopped it. Any movement might betray him. An instant later, he realized he was not in trouble. The feet that were taking those steps were coming down from the pass to the shelf. They were halting and irregular, as if the walker was taking care. There was no real path or trail from the top of the ridge down to the shelf. One had to trundle down an eroding face of mud and stone to get there.

Abruptly, the snoring stopped. With a snort, the sleeping man came awake, presumably after one of his comrades elbowed him sharply in the ribs.

A voice rang out from the shelf. "Who goes there?"

"It's just me," came the reply from above.

"Me who? Give the password!"

"Wolf puppies! Good on you for asking."

"Thank ya, cap'um. You'd up'n have me whipped if I ain't askin'." After a slight pause, the guard added, "No offense, sor."

"None taken. You are entirely correct."

By that time, the captain had reached the shelf. The three guards stood up to meet him. From where he was hidden, Marin could just see them. None were looking in his direction, so he was safe from detection, at least for a time.

The captain asked, "Anything afoot?"

"No, sor. It's been quiet as a grave yard, so it has. We ain't seen nothin' since Cap'um Glum come down."

"Captain Glum?"

"Yes, sor. He come down with his wolf. Cap'um Sammel and Cap'um Binner was with him too, so they was. Said they was gonna take a look round. Cap'um Glum say he had him a strange feeling."

"How long ago was that?"

"Oh, an hour, maybe two. It be hard to tell sittin' here in the dark."

"Fine. I am glad he is out and about. If he passes this way again, tell him I'd like to see him."

"Aye, aye, sor. Cap'um Glum to see Cap'um Middon soon as may be."

There was a moment of silence before Middon spoke again.

"You are doing a good job, you men, though I can see that at least one of you has been sleeping." He kicked something with his foot. Marin could not see what because of the rock wall. "Here is something to keep you warm. It's not much, not enough for even one of you to get drunk—and that's on purpose—but it will help. If I were you, I would wait until it gets coldest, just before the dawn." Middon slid a small bag from his shoulder and handed it to the guard with whom he had been speaking.

"It's Rathian Firewine, the best I've ever tasted, I must say. That's one the nice things about fighting in these parts. Good wine, nice vegetables. Hunting's good, too. I've been thinking I just might settle around here after the fighting's over. Maybe take a local girl for a wife."

Abruptly, the captain realized he was rambling to his men. In a brusque tone, he said, "Your relief will come at dawn. They'll give you the new password."

Hearing that, Marin perked up. If these guards needed passwords to get back into camp, he knew there were other guards somewhere up on the pass. Knowing the guards were changed at dawn should be useful, though he wasn't sure why yet. He needed to think about that. But not now! Refocusing on the tasks at hand, he stowed the notion about trying to have an idea in the back of his mind for later.

Marin waited a good fifteen minutes after the captain left and the look outs settled back down. He rued each minute as it passed away never to be regained. The night was pressing on toward midnight and there was still far to go, much to be done.

Marin checked his wound as best he could in the dark. His bandage was holding. He did not find any fresh blood seeping over his hip. That was good. Once he got back to Gammin, he might be able to find some arrenil, a healing plant that grew where there was plenty of water. That would help.

When he had waited long enough, Marin melted back down the mountainside to a safer distance, then headed south. He wanted to mount the pass near its southern edge. He terrained across the narrow valley that would forever be Little Mother Valley to him, made his way up and over the crest of the next spur ridge, then turned west again and climbed toward the pass. If he was right—and he knew he was—he should now be at the southern extreme of the pass. Above him, maybe fifty paces away, were two huts that stood back from the place where the road started to switchback down to Mendolas.

It was time for the real fun to start.

This high on the mountain, snow lay heavy on the ground. Crusted over with the night's cold, it crunched at every step. Marin avoided it where he could. He knew the trees thinned out as they approached the pass, where the mountainside leveled out into a broad shoulder, allowing sun its teeth. There would be much less snow up there, he was sure. All he had to do was get there.

The moonlight was strong enough to cast shadows. That was good on the one hand because he could see what was where and who was watching. On the other hand, those same whos could see him. He stayed within the shelter of trees as long has he could.

It was with a sigh of relief that he finally saw the huts. He lurked within the edges of the wood, watched, and listened. No one seemed to be about. He could hear nothing from within the structures. From somewhere to his right, he could hear vaguely the sounds soldiers make during the night, but they came from a good distance.

A large pile of firewood stood between him and the huts. That was something he had not anticipated. He could certainly use it to his advantage. Marin made a dash across the open space. He crouched low, moving almost on all fours. Once he was at the wood pile, he hunkered down, pulling his cloak across his face and hands to hide their paleness. When he had been just a boy, his father had taught him that hiding face and hands was one of the most important things when trying to avoid detection.

Hunkering blind behind a pile of wood on a cold night was not the way to achieve his mission. When he was sure no one had seen him and raised an alarm, Marin peaked out from under his cloak. There was still no one about. Swiftly, keeping his face bent and his hands covered, he scampered the rest of the way to the huts.

He paused momentarily to listen. There were no sounds. The hut against which he cowered might have been empty but for the trail of wood smoke rising from a hole in the roof. His eye flicked up toward the top of the other hut, just a few steps away. That one was smoking, too, though not as much.

He thought "It is a poorly tended fire if it still smokes this late at night. The horses are in this hut." There were very likely soldiers, probably officers, in the other hut.

Careful as a fox outside a henhouse, Marin crept around the wall until he was near the door. His nose and ears now told him that his guess had been right. There were horses on the other side of the wall he was hugging. He could not feel their thoughts. Perhaps they were sleeping.

Having verified that the huts were occupied, he had to scout the rest of this side of the pass along the road to see where the troops were stationed and count their numbers if possible. That should not be too difficult if he could avoid patrolling guards. He had not seen any so far, but they had to be out there, somewhere.

Marin heard coughing from within the other hut. The cough was followed by the groan of a man getting up from his less-than-comfortable bed roll. The doors to each structure stood across from each other, separated only by a few paces. If someone opened the door to the other hut, he would see Marin.

For an instant, Marin was paralyzed with fear. Then, his instincts took over. He clutched at the near door, lifted the rough latch, and stepped inside. Pulling the door closed, he heard the other door open and knew despair. He might be able to deal with whoever came in to inspect the stabled horses, but Marin doubted he could do it without attracting at least some attention. That would be a catastrophe. Alerted to the presence of a spy in their midst, the enemy would be even more vigilant. Gammin would be doomed.

Marin hastily put away his panic. Breathing deeply, he thought, "I am a friend, my brothers. Do not be afraid. Hide me if you can."

Would the horses understand? He did not know. But, as the instants flew by, they did not whinny or raise a ruckus. That was a start.

Drawing his hunting knife, Marin crouched low and waited for the door of the stable to open. When it did not, he began to wonder what was happening. Then he heard a queer sound. It took a moment for him to figure it out. The man who had emerged from the other hut was urinating against one of the side walls of the stable.

Casting aside his disdain for such a fool, Marin breathed deeply again and sent reassuring thoughts to the horses followed by images of himself moving among them. There were four. The fit was very snug. Someone had put up a low half-wall to separate most of the single room from the small fire pit. Marin climbed over the wall, pausing only long enough to run his palms over the backs of the two closest horses. He shoved himself up against the rear corner. Hunkering down beneath his cloak, he hid his face and hands again.

The door to the stable opened with a sudden shudder. Two of the horses shied at the sound. Marin was nearly crushed against the side wall in the jostling that followed.

"You buggers alright in here? Eh?" The speaker spit, then said, "That bleedin' fire's smokin' again, ain't it? Damn. Nothin's ever easy, is it?"

There came a sound of scraping and prodding. A log was added to the fire none too gently. A swirl of sparks leapt up to meet the darkness. Marin gripped his knife and readied himself. He would have to take the man in the throat with his first attack. The horse below which he squatted shifted nervously. Marin cursed at himself and returned to thinking reassuring thoughts.

"There, that'll do it. Now, how are you, Spots? You warm enough?"

The light from the flame as it began to catch on the new log glittered off a ring on a hand that was rubbing the nose of the horse beside which Marin hid.

"You hungry?" The voice was only a whisper then. "I'll get a little something for you."

Marin heard the man rip hay from the bundle.

"Too bad for the rest of you, I guess."

The horse's head moved as it took the morsel from the man's hand. For an instant, Marin could see the man's shoulder. Then, remembering himself, the woodcutter's son hid his face away again. He gripped his knife even tighter.

One of the horses further down the line whickered.

The man jerked his hand back. "Here! What's this, then?"

Marin knew he was discovered. He tensed his legs, readied his arms, focused his mind—all in an instant—and he tasted the bile of failure. Though he might overcome this one man, he would doubtless be revealed to the others by the sounds of combat. He had failed himself and failed Gammin. With that thought in mind, the woodcutter's son readied himself for his final battle.

Before he could even move to push himself upright, Marin heard the man's voice again. "There'll be none of that, you horse. You'll get your feed from your own master or not at all. That's what I say!"

Marin forced himself to unclench his teeth. His heart

started beating again, the pulse thundering in his ears. He fought against the desire to gasp, the need to suck in great draughts of air. Any amount of time might have passed while he collected himself.

The next thing he heard was the closing of the stable door. Marin waited for several minutes after he heard the door to the other hut open and shut, signifying that the man had gone back to his bed. The delay was just as well. Marin could not have gone anywhere during that time. He was shaking, breathing in short, ragged breaths.

Now that he was free to move, he wiped cold sweat from his face with his cloak. He slid out from beneath the horses, stood slowly, and climbed over the wall. Once he was standing by the fire, he had to bend over again.

With some alarm, he realized he was going to vomit.

6. TOWER PASS

I.

Marn's son was exhausted by the time he finished his scouting mission. A full day's march up and down steep-sided ridges followed by a full night's scouting will do that to even the most vigorous man or woman. Exhausted or not, he was not done contributing yet.

After adding his report to that of the other three scouts, Marin spent some time with a nemen, the only healer in the company. He managed to secure about an hour's rest before Gammin commenced the final march to the pass. By the time the company reached the place Marin had encountered the wolf, the woodcutter's son had considered the notion he'd had about exploiting the password. It was a stroke of genius.

Marin showed his friend the three bodies and explained the idea. Gammin needed no convincing. He called a quick search for the stoutest warrior in the company and one other who was the size of the third dead captain. Marin's idea was that these two would pose as Captain Glum's friends and would be dressed in their clothes.

Glum's clothes could not be salvaged, but the other two yielded enough usable clothing to accouter the two stand-ins convincingly enough—or, so it was hoped. Marin did not resemble Glum overmuch, but he would have to do. He was the only one who had heard the man speak, the only one who could hope to imitate him when the three imposters confronted the guards on the shelf. When the time came, Marin would follow behind the other two and present the password when challenged.

Marin and his two accomplices took the guard post rather easily. The facts that the guards were anticipating Glum's return and that they had enjoyed the Firewine must have assisted in their demise to some degree. It was as easy as three throats cut; there was almost no commotion or extra noise.

Marin used a very similar ploy to obtain the new password and eliminate the fresh guards that came with the sun. After arranging the dead bodies in natural positions along the rock wall on the shelf, the only thing to do was to wait. A few minutes after sky began to brighten with the first extremities of morning, three men came slip-sliding down the steep embankment above the shelf. As soon as he heard them, Marin, who was crouching out of sight, demanded the password. He made an attempt to emulate the voice of the guard he had heard earlier that morning. The imitation was only marginally successful, but it worked like a prayer. It was a stroke of fortune that the guards provided the new password in the same sentence as the old one. Luck follows intent like the shadow of good planning.

With a good plan, thorough preparation, excellent execution, and a large dollop of luck, the three guards who had come to relieve the others were eliminated without too much noise. There were a couple of startled grunts and a single muted cry as nine arrows simultaneously struck three soldiers. After that, several tense minutes were spent waiting to see if other soldiers had heard and were responding. But they hadn't, and they didn't.

Things began to happen rapidly after that. With the benefit

of the information provided by Marin and the other scout, Gammin and his captains knew where the enemies had made their camps and where their guard posts were. The scouts provided an estimate of the enemy's troop strength. Most of the soldiers were forward-deployed farther down the north side of the ridge in closer proximity to Branden's army. Those who occupied the wide saddle of the pass were the reserve troops and those who had served the night watches and were beginning to take their rest.

Gammin knew his father was supposed to have attacked the front along the road about an hour before dawn. It was to be an all-out effort; the king was attacking with everything he had. If that had happened, the enemy's attention should by now be fully focused to the north and further down the mountain about a quarter mile or so. This was a crucial part of the plan. If too many soldiers were left on the pass, or if soldiers were free to be summoned back up in defense, Gammin's slight force of one hundred was doomed.

At the appointed time, Gammin sent several men to free the enemy's corralled horses. This was another unplanned improvisation. Marin and the other scout had both reported that the animals were not guarded. The most difficult part of freeing them was crossing the open ground without raising the alarm. The men sent on the task achieved it, though not without detection. The two soldiers who saw them joined the others as the first casualties of the engagement.

Horses running wild and free caused quite a commotion among the enemy. Soon, dozens of cavalry men were running about in attempts to recapture the beasts. Most of those men, who had until moments before been sleeping or eating, did not carry weapons with them in pursuit of their steeds.

That is when Gammin struck. Like an ancient dragon, his timing was perfect.

The Prince of Ehrylan hit the two nearest encampments with overwhelming force. This far back, near the middle of the pass, the enemy had not erected palisades or dug any protective ditches. The few soldiers standing guard had been distracted by the horses. The rest, though they were not slow in responding, were left to fumble for their weapons while shaking slumber from their eyes.

Gammin's warriors swept across the pass, a wave of muscle and steel that left only the dead and dying in their wake. They mowed down the soldiers who managed to grab weapons and face them. The raiding party drove the enemy before them in a tide of screams.

Many of the retreating soldiers bolted for safety. Others fell back northward along the road toward where other companies had been sleeping. The men in those camps, alerted first by the commotion accompanying the horses and then by the more tumultuous rumor of Gammin's attack, leapt to form their ranks. If they had known the force confronting them was only one hundred men, the enemy commanders might have used a different strategy. They did not have that knowledge, and their enemy, who seemed to have materialized out of nowhere, did not let them ponder. Accordingly, the captains of Dauroth's army sent their men into the fray as fast as the ranks formed.

From the scouting report, Gammin knew there were four camps on the pass, each with about fifty men. Before hostilities began that morning, he had been outnumbered at least two to one. By the time he met organized resistance, the odds must have been almost equal. The Ehrylain were flushed with success, driven by the single purpose of cutting through all resistance and coming at last to the rear of the army opposing King Branden. The soldiers on the pass were off-balance. They were dismayed, disunited. They were dying.

As the early morning aged, the soldiers began to see they were overmatched. With this realization came hopelessness and fear. At first, in ones and twos, the most timid began to flee for their lives, skulking back through the forest to take the pass road down toward Mendolas. The few became many. Soon, the soldiers who still fought saw they were severely outnumbered. Recognizing what he saw, the only remaining captain called for a retreat. He led his men northward, down the pass road, toward the safety of the larger force holding

Branden's army at bay.

A great cheer went up from the Ehrylain. They surged forward and would have charged down the road in pursuit if Marin and Gammin had not stopped them. As it was, the horns had to be blown before the most-eager heeded the call and returned.

As they stood surrounded by their warriors, Marin looked at Gammin, waiting for him to speak. Gammin gestured with his chin. Marin understood.

Stepping forward and raising his hands, the woodcutter's son projected his voice above the joy and elation.

"Warriors of Ehrylan! You have succeeded in your first task. You have broken the back of Dauroth's reserves." He paused to let that sink in. A murmur of silence dribbled across the gathering as the implication of his words became evident.

"The soldiers you drove away will join with the rest of the army. That army must have heard rumor of us by now. If not, the men you defeated will carry it to them. They will move to defend their rear."

The last of the chattering voices fell silent. This was not the kind of talk they had expected, not what they wanted to hear.

"Now Dauroth's army will have to fight on two fronts. You have been wholly successful."

A round of cheers broke out. That was more like it.

"Hear me. We will reform ranks. We will march down the road with discipline and resolve. We will meet our enemy face to face in battle and cast him from the mountainside. Do you hear me?"

Cheers turned to a disambiguated roar. Marin turned to Gammin's hornsman.

"Form ranks!"

Gammin's company fought their way down the road toward the king. From the strategic standpoint of distracting the dog by attacking its tail, it was a good move. From the tactical perspective, it certainly put Gammin and his warriors in a difficult situation. Now there was the possibility of being stuck between the two hands of the enemy's army, one below and one above. Sure and the hand above was bloodied and wounded, but if the any of the soldiers had the will to reform their own ranks and attack, it would spell trouble for Gammin's company.

That is what happened. If Gammin could have spared the troops, he would have left a contingent on the pass to guard it. But there were no warriors to spare. Fortunately, the enemy contingent that followed behind never amounted to more than a token. Mercenaries from foreign lands and men pressed into service seldom sacrifice their lives in such an endeavor. The remaining enemy captain put together three units of about ten men each. That was enough to make Gammin's warriors pay attention.

By the time the three units of soldiers came down from above to menace his rear, Gammin's company was already facing a strong detachment from below. Even with Gammin and Marin to lead them, the raiding party was hard pressed to defend both fronts. But there were many among them who had fought long in the service of the Defier, many who had trained hard and fought in Twofords' battles. The seasoned veterans stood out from the less experienced like bonfires among candles as brave men and women whose names are not reported in any tale fought valiantly and died.

Gammin's rear guard, which was led by Marin, prevailed. As soon as the last soldier to their rear had fallen, Marin threw his men into a bold flanking maneuver that, if it had not been successful, would have meant obliteration for all the warriors involved.

With the dragon at their backs, the lion before them, and Marin's warriors attacking their flank, Dauroth's forces stumbled and broke. The breaking took the rest of the morning. It was noon by the time the fighting began to slacken. An hour or so later, the Ehrylain were mopping up the few remaining pockets of resistance.

At some point, Gammin saw his father and went to meet him. The king was, at first, too flushed with victory to notice the lack of a smile on his son's face. When he did, he asked,

"What is amiss, my son? We have crushed our enemy!"

Gammin gazed unblinking back at the king. "Yes, father, we have. It cost many lives. Fathers, brothers, sisters, and wives with whom we ate only yesterday will never come again to their homes. I feel the sorrow of their families in my bones."

The king frowned briefly. Then, the elated smile returned, irrepressible. "You say true, Prince of Ehrylan. That is a cost of war. War is the cost of regaining freedom for our people."

Gammin blinked and lowered his gaze. In a voice barely loud enough for his father to hear, he said, "I find I do not like war." He wandered back to do what must be done among the men and women of his command.

By midafternoon, the grinning king sat aback his horse unopposed at the top of the pass under the White Tower. Next to him was his son, Gammin. Beside Prince Gammin sat Marin, the Old One, the Seer, who just might have been asleep in the saddle.

II.

The battle for Tower Pass went well for Branden's army, though well is a bad description for any conflict where so many Ehrylain lost their lives. But, no, that's not right. The warriors who rode under Branden's lion banner did not lose anything. They sold the only thing they truly possessed to pay the price of freedom for those they loved.

As always, when things went the way of the Ehrylain in battles with Dauroth's armies, many and many of the soldiers took their first opportunity to declare for the loyalists. At the end, when the mercenaries and Outlandish captains were abandoning the field, whole units within Dauroth's army had thrown down their arms and declared for the king— though they did not know it was for a living king. There was little difficulty in telling which of these soldiers were in earnest and which were just being opportunistic. The joy in their faces and the hope in their voices were sure signs for all to read.

The king had ridden from Twofords with five hundred warriors. Almost two hundred were lost in the conquest of the pass, a high number, but not as high as could have been expected in those difficult circumstances. By the time the king reached Mendolas, his force numbered almost five hundred again. The newcomers, who might be called either turncoats or escapees depending on whose side one fought, were welcomed with open arms and open eyes. They were given new weapons and clothing, fed, and watched very carefully by their new captains.

A more timid leader might have stopped on the pass to let his men rest and regroup for a day or two. That was not Branden's way. He had the enemy by the tail and would not let go. After only a pause for a few hours to collect and array his forces, Branden set out for the kill.

A hunting eagle will fly twelve leagues between Tower Pass and the gates of Mendolas. Warriors must walk a road that stretches closer to twenty. The king had not travelled half the six leagues that would take him down to the river before he had to call his army to a halt. This was not because an enemy force opposed him. A solitary figure stood in the road. It was a woman. Her long hair was loose and blowing in the mountain breeze. With her feet spread shoulder-width apart and her hands clasped behind her back, she might have been an officer in some well-disciplined military. She appeared to be as fearless as if she were queen of the wood.

As soon as he saw her, Branden understood why none of his scouts had reported her. He knew that, if she wished it, they could not have seen her.

"Hail, Old One," called the king, raising a hand and halting his horse. When she nodded, he dismounted, gesturing for Gammin to do the same. Unasked, Marin followed.

"Hail, Branden, son of Brand," said the woman as Branden approached. She nodded to Gammin with as much respect as she had shown the king, maybe more. Then she addressed Marin.

"*Ahna e rhu*, brother."

"*Ahna e rhu*, sister."

When Marin failed to add anything more, she addressed the king again. "I am Hamea, daughter of Bellea. May your children walk ever in the light of Ea."

"I thank you, Hameatha, daughter of Bellea. May my son meet your children there and dance with them."

Hamea relaxed. She did not smile, but there was a perceptible change. Gammin, who found that he had been holding his breath, breathed again. There was no risk, no penalty, for failing to exchange greetings with the Old Ones in this traditional matter, but it did grease the wagon wheels. And, niceties have a way of being nice.

Hamea said, "We received your messenger. Know that he is well. We sent him on his way to the city where Lelan waits in the grove. He said that was your will."

"I thank you, Old One."

She nodded. "We come for our brothers. We will take from you."

Marin had a moment of disquiet, thinking he and Gammin were to be sent away. Then he remembered.

The king, who had sent a messenger to inform the Children of the Forest of the six brutal hangings, sent an aide galloping along the formation with word that the bodies were to be brought forward. There was no need. As soon as the aide reached the wagons where the honored dead were kept, a dozen Old Ones appeared out of the forest at the very spot. With great reverence, they took their dead and carried them back to the head of the column.

Hamea was exchanging bits of news with the king when the men with the bodies arrived. Cutting the conversation short, she whistled. No man or woman in the king's train could have told that whistle from the song of a real bird. Some who heard the call wondered if, perhaps, Hamea was a real bird dressed as a woman.

There was a slight commotion in the woods down below the road. The king's guards began to stir, thinking that some attack might be imminent. Branden held up his hand, stopping them. Many of the warriors who saw this thought him the bravest man alive. Branden was brave, it is true, but he was also wise. He knew that if the Old Ones wanted him dead, he would be dead. He also knew that if Hamea was standing here in the middle of the mountain road chatting with him, it was extremely unlikely that there was danger from Dauroth's troops.

Groups of Old Ones began to appear out of the forest along the steep-sided road. There were men and women, boys and girls, though not in equal numbers. In all, twenty-four came. Wordlessly, they arranged themselves into six groups of four. Each group had what appeared to be a *cheshano*, which, in the Common Speech, is sensibly called a drag-sled.

The bodies had been treated by Branden's morticians with plants and oils, then wrapped in cloth. Their faces were not evident. As the identity of each body was discovered, the body was wrapped in clean, well-brushed furs and deposited on the proper *cheshano*.

As they watched, Marin and Gammin realized that the four Old Ones around each *cheshano* must have been close friends or direct family to the dead men. Gammin found solace in this. The weight on his heart lessened just a bit as a glimmer of love peeked through the thick mantle of war.

When the Old Ones finished their arrangements and were ready to set out, Hamea addressed the king again.

"We go to show our fallen brothers how we have honored them. Wait here for one hour. You need fear nothing on this road. There is no danger for you between the pass and the gates by the river. I have said it."

Branden the Not Usually So Patient nodded and laid a hand on Hamea's shoulder. "We will wait, Hameatha. Go, honor your dead. May their sacrifices not be in vain. May Ea give us victory over the evil one."

The mysterious lady, who, though slight, looked very strong and able, wished the king good will and the Maker's love before turning to Marin.

"*Faenea*, I have two messages for you."

Astounded, Marin could not find his voice. *Faenea* was a label that had been applied to very few individuals in the long history of the Children of the Forest. In rough terms, it means "Voice of Ea" or, more properly, "Ea speaks." In the Common Tongue, we would say Seer. It was very formal. Marin was so taken aback that he had to ask Hamea to repeat what she had been saying once he could talk.

"I would speak with you alone, Marinsa."

Marin's tongue stumbled out of the gate, but he managed to rein it in as he looked around. Only Gammin and his father were near.

"Sister, these two men are my friends. Gammin is my brother. The other is his father, the king, as you know. I have no secrets from them. If it is permitted, they may hear anything you have to tell me."

Hamea nodded once. "It is well said. You are wise for one so young, Marinsa. Perhaps that is to be expected from a *faenea* who talks with sister wolf. The Children have not seen such a one in nearly a thousand years. It is my honor to speak with you and to bring you words that will give you joy."

She waited for him to reply, but Marin was still struggling to master his voice. He had not even grown used to being thought of as a seer by his closest friends. To hear one of the Children—one of his own people name him so was almost overwhelming. And, how did she know about Little Mother?

As if she could hear his thoughts, Hamea said, "My first message is this. There will be new children in the forest because of you. The little mother is grateful. She found us. Because of her, justice was done among the servants of evil. For that, we are grateful, as well. The Maker blessed your tongue. We rejoice with you."

Marin managed to stammer, "Justice?"

"You will see, *faenea*." She paused a moment. Perhaps she was laughing at her own unintended jest.

"My second message comes from the Tallenlaust."

Marin inhaled sharply. His discomfort dissolved, pushed aside by anticipation.

"Tell me, Hameatha!" He stepped forward, unknowingly pushing his chest out and his chin up. Gammin thought he looked just like Max.

Now, for the first time, the lady smiled. With a tender expression, she held out a small object. It fit easily in her hand. Marin took it with a slow timidity, his mouth and eyes open in an eager wonder that was the antithesis of his movements. He studied the object intently. It was a piece of wood, roughly-carved to resemble a miniature lacanaria blossom. His friends, the army, and the war had suddenly vanished.

When Marin finally forced his eyes back to her, Hamea continued. "She who sent this bids us tell you that she is well and that she remembers your face."

Marin opened his mouth to respond, but Hamea cut him off. "There is no time for questions, Marinsa, and I have no answers to give. But this I know. Ea is gathering his people. He has raised a *faenea* to walk with kings and talk with wolves. Rhua is blowing across the land. You are a sail for Ea's wind, my young brother. Your path will not be easy, but you must keep to it. May the Maker guide your feet, Marinsa, Seer of Ehrylan, son of Lelan and Dara!"

Hamea nodded to the king and his son, stepped away, and began to lead her brethren down the road. The king, who had not heard about the wolf, started to address Marin. Gammin, laying a hand on his father's arm, interrupted.

"It is a long story, father. Shall we save it for later?"

Branden caught Gammin's unspoken meaning and nodded. Maybe, after all those years, the boys were teaching him patience.

The king was less put out by the delay than he might have been. Hamea had informed him that Mendolas was essentially free of the siege. Apparently, the enemy commander had sent the bulk of his troops to stop Branden on the pass. It was a sensible enough move. For some reason—Hamea mentioned a large conflict on the border between Rath and Ehrylan—the two or three hundred troops left around Mendolas had been called away a day or two before.

The soldiers who had fled the pass in hopes of gaining the safety of the siege army would be forced to move away from Mendolas. There would be no haven for them there. If he had had a larger force, Branden might have split it and sent cavalry charging down the ridge in chase of the remnant. With only a bit more than three hundred troops he fully trusted, he could not afford to send any away.

When an hour had passed, Branden's army started for Mendolas. Once again, they did not get very far before they had to stop. At the top of the next switchback, where the road started to drop steeply east, two scouts waited, sitting somewhat uncomfortably aback their steeds. When the king came near, one of them nosed his horse a few steps back up the road.

"Sire. There is something to see on the road around this bend. We do not think there is any danger, but…"

The king nodded. "I thank you, Rendol. Go back to your duties."

"As you wish, sire."

The scout pulled his horse around and trotted it down the corner of the switchback and out of sight. The other scout followed.

With Gammin and Marin by his side, the king rode around the bend. On that particular switchback, a section of the Silver River was visible straight ahead, glimmering far below. It should have been a beautiful sight, but the distant view was spoiled by the near.

On each side of the switchback, the road was lined with dead bodies hanging from low branches in the trees. The bodies had been hung in pairs, one of each pair on either side of the road. In most cases, they still wore the clothes in which they had died. From that, it was easy to see that these were Dauroth's soldiers, men who had fled from the battle above.

Here, stretching out before them the whole length of the switchback, the king and his warriors saw how the Children of the Forest honored their dead. Unlike the six Old One's who had been first gutted and then hung out as a warning, these bodies had not been eviscerated. Indeed, they had not been mutilated in any way. A few of them bore outward indications of how they had died, broken arrows protruding from the heart or throat. There were no other targets and no indication that any arrow had missed its target by as much as a finger's breadth. In four cases, throats had been cut; on those bodies, there were no other visible wounds.

Most of these soldiers had died from the hanging. Hanging can be made more merciful by the snapping of a neck. That is not what the Old One's had done. The soldiers had been strung up to just a hand span above the ground—probably fairly slowly—and left to fight against the inevitability of death by strangulation. Scuffs marked the layers of pine needles beneath the bodies. More terrible still, the soldiers' hands had been left free to grasp at life even as it fled from them. On some of the bodies, lifeless fingers were still clutching at the rope above their head or the loop around their neck. And the faces, shall I tell you of those? I saw them only in the miracle that is the magic of Marin's book, yet I can see them still in my mind, eyes bulging, teeth bared in a rictus that captured hatred, terror, and agony in a single expression.

Gammin and Marin were wondering how best to comport themselves for the benefit of the warriors behind them. So grim was the scene, with bodies as silent as death swinging gently in the mountain breeze, that the two friends wanted to hang their heads and stare at the ground. They had to do better. Instead of giving in to their desire, they looked at each body as they passed it, gazing into the eyes if they were open, else looking at the arrows or clothing.

Aside from any other benefit that may have accrued from that, Gammin noticed one thing in particular. None of these soldiers wore the black uniform of an officer. He did not know if that was significant. He wondered if it meant none of the officers had fled the battlefield or whether they just hadn't been captured by the Old Ones.

Gammin said a silent prayer for the dead, asking Ea to comfort the loved ones who were left behind. They would never know the fate of their husbands or fathers or sons. What Marin thought, none can say. As for Branden, he focused his eyes front. Perhaps he was being a good leader and looking for an ambush or some sign that danger lay ahead. Maybe he was suppressing tears with the strength of his will. After all, most of the dead soldiers were likely Ehrylain, men who would have had a rightful claim on the King of Ehrylan in better times. Even that was not right. The Ehrylain had a rightful claim on their king in the worst times as well as the best. Old King Brand had believed that. He told me that himself. He died believing that.

As they rounded the end of the switchback and started back to the west, each of the three leaders—a king, a prince, and a seer—was desperately hoping that the carnage in the trees would come to a stop. The final demonstration was yet to come. As awful as the hangings of the soldiers had been, the execution of their leaders was worse by far.

About half way along the westering switchback, the Old One's had felled trees to clear a small area adjacent to the road on either side. In each of the open areas, two black-clad officers were staked out with their torsos and faces to the sky. Each man's arms and legs were buried beneath the earth. A stout wooden stake protruded from the ground at the terminus of each limb. Whether the hand or foot was tethered to the stake under the ground or whether the stake had been hammered right through the appendage was unknown. No one wanted to stop long enough to find out.

Each of the four men had died from the same cause, though most could not have understood it. Branden, who had hunted the wilds of Ehrylan in happier times, had seen similar signs. The king stopped his horse and stared at one of the bodies. The eyes were gone. The cheek and teeth from one side of his face were missing, leaving a roundish hole that gaped like a nightmare. Branden did not have to investigate more closely to know that the tongues would be missing. The brutalized side of each face seemed to be grinning. It was wholly grotesque, almost obscene.

Marin, who was also no stranger to the forest, said, "Bears."

The king nodded. "Yes. Well-fed bears."

Gammin asked, "How do you know that, sire?"

"A hungry bear would have torn into the abdomens. This bear was not hungry. He went only for the tender morsels—the tongue and the eyes. He must have eaten well before."

"There is no need to wonder on what," added the woodcutter's son, thinking of the feast any battle leaves for woodland creatures. It would have been quite a bounty for bears that would so soon go into hibernation for the winter.

Marin's tone made Gammin look at him. Gammin did not see either revulsion or adulation in his friend's face. In fact, for almost the first time, he could not read Marin's face at all.

The king's voice stopped Gammin's uncomfortable wonderings. "There is more to be read from this riddle. Do you see it?"

Gammin did not return his eyes to the gruesome scene. He moved them directly to his father's. "The men were alive when the bear ate them."

"How do you know?"

Gammin sighed, but not because he was bothered by the question. He knew what his father was trying to do. The king was just a new father trying to teach his new son.

"You can see that the men struggled with their arms and legs. The dirt is churned up around them. And, there is some blood on the shoulders of their tunics."

"Excellent," said the king. "The Old Ones staked them out here, left them to be eaten alive. I wonder if they knew the bears would only eat the good bits." He heeled his horse gently to move it on.

As the king moved away, Marin said, in a voice only Gammin heard, "They knew."

In all, there were thirty pairs of soldiers hanging in the trees. That made sixty bodies, ten soldiers for every one of the Old Ones that had been killed and hung up. The two pairs of leaders staked out on the ground were left as visual—and visceral—punctuation. It was a terrible demonstration of revenge. Gammin wondered for whom the message was meant. Was it to other soldiers who might follow? Was it to Branden and his forces? Or, was it really just a demonstration by the Old Ones to show their dead brothers they had been avenged?

Whichever it was, that was the retribution of the Children of the Forest. Good or evil, make of it what you will, but be warned.

7. VALLEY ELOSAI

I.

Hamea had been right. Branden's army encountered no danger on the road down to Mendolas. That is not to say the trip was completely uneventful. Three twisted ankles were the worst of it. There was also a tussle between two of the newly joined soldiers. They almost came to blows over which of them had hated the enforced service in Dauroth's army the most. The difficulty was soon set right by a strong admonition from their team leader. If they did not behave like warriors in the king's army, they would not be warriors in the king's army.

When Branden came to Mendolas, he found the gates well-defended by a force of loyal Ehrylain, city-dwellers most of them. There was a testy bit while each side determined that the other was truly friendly. In the end, they got it right, and peace prevailed.

Despite the fact that his army had driven away Dauroth's forces, Branden's entry into that city was less triumphant than his entrance into Twofords. There were a good many suspicious looks from the local Resistance, many of whom had become officers in the city's now-official military. Likewise, more than one member of the city council frowned at the coming of the king. However, like Twofords, there were old warriors and townsfolk who remembered the king as a young, heroic prince. The king had little trouble in establishing his identity. After that, the rest was easy enough.

As in Twofords, the king made no demands. While his weary army rested, he met with the city's leaders and military commanders. Messengers were dispatched to points north, west, and east. Strategies were debated. The more promising of those were reworked, massaged until they little resembled the original design. At last, a single cohesive plan took shape.

Gammin and Marin were permitted a seat at council, though they seldom had the opportunity to speak. Both were wise enough to recognize that compared to the other men and women present, they had travelled very little, seen much less of the world and how it works.

The king was the main architect of the plan. He had been thinking of this war and these moments for most of his life. In his head were a map, a set of ideas, and a single hope.

To start, he arranged an exchange of forces. Many who flocked to Branden's side in Twofords had already burned through their desire for such service. The king knew that much of his growing army had recently been farmers and merchants. They were men and women who had been caught up in the excitement of the moment. They had jumped into the pool of savagery to find they were floundering. There was no shame in this. Warriors and farmers are not always made of the same stuff.

The king acted with grace to preserve the dignity of these people. They were encouraged to lend their support to Mendolas or Twofords. Branden thanked them with gifts of gold or silver. It is a matter of record—the king's quartermaster tracked every copper that left the treasury, even before there was a treasury—that a good portion of that set refused the payment.

Most of the citizens of Mendolas were elated that a king

had come again. Hundreds of the city's warriors flocked to Branden's banners. Some were anxious to join the campaign to free the rest of Ehrylan, others eager to let the fight for freedom take them to far-off places of which they had only heard.

The records show that Branden did not spend much time in Mendolas. He found it in good order, though disheveled from the repeated battles. The city had been back in the hands of loyalists for some months. Much work had been accomplished, even under the burden of continued siege. With his rear guarded, the king could concentrate on the war in front of him.

Branden's initial plan was to take ship for Ehrynai, the main city of the region of Ehrylan known as the Westland. The Westland is a wide swath of ridges, valleys, fields, and forests that flow down from the Western Mountains to the sea. From Ehrynai, the southernmost reach of Ehrylan's coast, Branden intended to fight his way up the coastal plain while I punched up from Twofords on the other side of the mountains.

News poured in from a flood of scouts. The king, master tactician that he was, seemed to change his mind twice as the result of each piece of intelligence. When word came that demanded immediate action, it was almost a relief. The attention-grabbing news was that all of the forces at Stone Bridge's garrison had picked up stakes and fled. It seemed, on the surface, to be good news, but the fair wind that brought freedom to Mendolas blew a gale over Rath.

There had been activity for some time on the border between Rath and Ehrylan south of the Old Forest. The conflict had escalated. The Rathian Border Guard had been pushed back by Dauroth's troops, and there was a major battle raging in Valley Elosai. The additional forces from Stone Bridge would tip the scales. If they were successful against the Rathian Guard, there was nothing to stop the Outlandish army from marching south and east to Arathai.

Rath had become more active in its support of Ehrylan with Branden's unveiling a few weeks before. All pretenses had been thrown off. Rath was now at open war with Dauroth. The evil usurper faced significant conflict on multiple fronts; redirecting efforts and assets toward the most valuable targets was prudent. The capital of Rath was certainly more valuable strategically than Mendolas.

The repositioning of troops from Stone Bridge was a strategic move by Dauroth's commanders, not a retreat in the face of King Branden's might. Dauroth had no fear of either Branden or the Ehrylain. He was simply turning his attention from southern Ehrylan to Rath.

Branden knew that wars are not won by allowing the opponent to dictate the battle ground. His intention had been to sail in strength for Ehrynai. But the strength of Rath is not in its armies. She has long depended upon her friendly neighbors to lend their support on land as she gives hers on the sea. The king of Rath had been a loyal friend to Ehrylan. Branden would not suffer any foe to march freely across his border and into Valley Elosai.

There had been word of other allies responding to the situation. A host of riders from Arel had arrived on the scene. The horse warriors of that land had managed to quell the invasion, but the new reinforcements from the garrison at Stone Bridge would put them over the edge. Now, the Arelese were fighting as much for their own lives as for the Rathians. Fighting and losing.

Branden changed his plans. He set out south by land rather than west by water.

II.

The sharp escarpment upon which Marin sat was the official border between Ehrylan and its southern neighbor. The valley below was a cauldron of tumult. It was the biggest military engagement Marin had ever seen. Thousands were fighting in the verdant basin that described the northern portion of Valley Elosai. They were arrayed like pieces in a gigantic strategy game.

Marin could make out the divisions in the opposing armies, though he was still too far away to discern individual combatants. To an almost startling degree, the scene below him resembled many of the drawings he had studied. From this vantage, it seemed he could reach out and move a unit of Arelese cavalry here or there to meet the oncoming rush of Dauroth's soldiers. That was just a fantasy. This was not an illustration in a text on military strategy. This was real, far too real. The thunder and stench of death rose up on the gossamer wings of dawn, a disconcerting contradiction.

Marin was all too familiar with Dauroth's forces. He picked them out easily. They were the most numerous, by far. Next were the Arelese. Marin knew they fought almost exclusively from horseback. Their horses and attire were markedly different from any the woodcutter's son had seen. He searched for the name the Arelese called themselves but couldn't pull it from his memory. Last and fewest of all were the remnants of the Rathian Border Guard. There had never been many of them. Marin could only infer their identity because they were not riding against Dauroth's soldiery. They were fighting on foot, scattered throughout the field in unorganized knots usually no larger than a handful of people.

Marin heard Gammin's voice. It was lowered in a needless whisper. They were still miles from the action. "Things don't look good for those horsemen, do they, Mar?"

Marin did not look away from the carnage as he answered. His eyes were chained to the living violence.

"Nope," was all he said. Maybe he just thought it.

Gammin continued. "Those must be the Arelese. They look pretty perky, considering how badly they are outnumbered."

He was referring to the horsemen. How many were there, two thousand, maybe three? It was difficult to count. They were separated into several cavalries that were in constant motion along a straggling front. The Arelese were obviously skilled fighters, but they were in danger of being overwhelmed by virtue of sheer numbers.

Dauroth's forces lay across the valley floor, an enormous serpent of men and malice stretching east to west between the Arelese and where Marin and Gammin sat at the head of King Branden's army. The horsemen could not hope to prevail against the masses of Dauroth's troops. Even with the addition of King Branden's army, they would be outnumbered.

Marin and Gammin were thinking the same thought. The probable outcome of attacking Dauroth's army was the total ruin of King Branden's army. The Precepts of War state that a general who hopes to win must not engage in a conflict without the benefit of overwhelming numbers. The Precepts said very little about loyalty or about doing what is right despite the cost; they were a road map, not a religion. Sometimes one had to do what had to be done, no matter the cost.

Silently estimating that, all told, the Arelese and Ehrylain could field perhaps two-thirds the numbers of their enemies, Gammin muttered "We've seen worse."

Marin exhaled a muted chuckle. "Too right. Just once, I'd like to fight a battle where we hold the greater numbers."

"Just once? I'd like to have the superior numbers every time."

"That's because you are lazy."

Marin pointed to a section in the front where a bulge was forming. A bubble of Outlandish soldiers was pushing into the Arelese line. If the maneuver continued unabated, the Arelese forces would be split.

At the moment, the Arelese center was holding. However, they were also in danger of being flanked north and south. They were too outnumbered to do anything about that. Even the added mobility and speed of their horses could not counter the disparity. They were doomed if someone did not soon come to their aid.

That someone was King Branden of Ehrylan. His voice broke in on Marin's thoughts. Both young men turned to face him in their saddles.

The king gestured with a twist of his head in the general direction of the bulging line. In a voice meant only for his son and his seer, he said, "Before my time, it had been long and long since a king of Ehrylan rode to the aid of Arel or Rath. I did so once before, in Arel, when I was a toddler just a little older than you two. Now it is my lot to do so again in Rath. I will take my army and all the hope of Ehrylan to fulfil oaths made long ago by the fathers of my fathers. So be it."

Gammin started to speak. Marin voiced the thought first. "Not all hope, King Branden. You're only the instrument of Ea. We all are, I guess. Ehrylan's true hope is in him. And, do not forget. Many of your countrymen fight elsewhere. They will fight on, no matter what happens here today. Your task is to take the next step. What follows is in the hands of the Maker."

This was so like a voice speaking from out of legend—something Teryn might have said to Andur—that both Branden and his son looked at Marin with startled eyes. The king's brow clouded momentarily, but the storm passed. After the lightening faded from his eyes, he grunted and fixed Marin with his gaze.

"You say true, seer." His words were agreeable, his visage less so. He nodded once and pulled his horse around to a location where he would be more visible.

As the king moved, Marin glanced at Gammin. What he saw in his friend's face made him laugh out loud despite the grim situation. Gammin's eyes were opened wide. His mouth had dropped into what looked like a caricature of a startled gape. The woodcutter's son might have said something then, but things were starting to happen.

The king now sat on his steed a few steps above them. He squared his shoulders. Silence pushed out from him, an invisible wave that swept over Gammin and the other captains near at hand on its way down the troop lines.

After sweeping his royal gaze over them, the king's stentorian voice called out, "It is time to pay back debts."

His arm swept out in a gesture that encompassed the rambling basin below. The ocean of death it contained flowed and ebbed in tides of violence. The sounds rose and fell like waves, first swelling, then running back out only to be replaced by another swell.

"Warriors of Ehrylan!" Branden's voice rose to a roar as he drew his sword and held it above his head. "May the tale of your valor outlive you all!"

He began to issue orders. His army and his hopes began the descent.

By the time Gammin, Marin, and the king arrived at the edges of the battlefield, the sun had moved half a hand higher in the sky. It was coming to midmorning. The presence of the battle dominated everything—sight, sound, smell, taste, feel.

Marin's horse was skittish. Its rider was restless. Compared to this one, the other battles in which he had been involved had been only small tussles.

The all-encompassing view of the battle had been lost as they descended the Ridge, which is what Southlanders call the high places along that part of the border. The last clear view had not been promising. The Arelese had been fighting valiantly to keep from being surrounded by the larger hosts of their enemies. The front had disintegrated to a sea of unorganized chaos.

The riders had done well to resist so long. They would not have lasted this long but for the arrival of King Branden's host. The enemy commander had been forced to redeploy assets to defend his rear. The troop movements had been easy to see from the vantage provided by the higher switchbacks on the face of the Ridge. Now that advantage was gone.

Marin surveyed the lay of the land as his horse moved down the last switchback and on to the valley floor. Companies of Ehrylain were flowing southward to meet the enemy soldiers who had been sent to stop them. There was no need for the various captains to await the arrival of the rest. Each contingent had its mission already, each leader his or her orders.

The Fifth Company, Gammin's company, had been held back, assigned to assist the king. That did not mean they were kept from the action. Being safe was the last consideration on the king's mind. Branden the Bold was not a commander who took his place on a hill overlooking the killing fields to direct men and mayhem here or there as the battle dictated. Not Branden. His aides and his captains had been able to dissuade the king's desire to ride in the vanguard of the attack. They could not keep him from following close behind.

Marin took his position. A horn sang. Horns from the other companies answered, left, right, and center. It was a curious music, another incongruity. There was a brief moment when the woodcutter's son thought he heard the flapping cheer of the lion pennants that danced at the ends of lifted spears. He caught the smell of smoke and blood as his horse surged forward.

Gammin, his eyes fixed on the battlefield, checked his weapons one last time. His hand travelled to his right hip. There was a new tool there, a curious hand axe Branden had given him. Gammin had not had time to practice much with it. He had plenty of experience using an axe—one could not spend much time in the company of Marn the woodcutter without finding an axe in one's hand—but he had never trained with a hand axe. His fingers caressed the weapon briefly before the hand moved to his left hip, where it found an old friend.

The young Prince of Ehrylan pulled his sword free. He lifted it above his head, voiced the battle cry of a seasoned warrior, and spurred his horse on. The men and women of the Fifth Company spread out beside and behind him, the wings of a young dragon.

Then came battle.

III.

The king did not sweep his enemies from the field. Nor did his army stab into the enemy's hindquarters to make it squeal and scamper away. The initial charge broke upon a force that had taken the time to dig in and prepare for just this kind of fight. Units of Branden's cavalry slammed into hastily laid earthworks. These low fortifications were festooned with nests of pikes, javelins, and spears. In some places, the onslaught of the Ehrylain was so fierce that the shafts of these fixed weapons snapped, the splintered ends killing as indiscriminately and as readily as the iron points.

Ranks and ranks of Ehrylain foot soldiers followed. The plan—which is to say, the hope—had been that foot soldiers would flow through the enemy lines in gaps made by the preceding cavalry charge. Instead, the charge was rebuked, thrown back upon itself in a chaos of men, horses, blood, and broken weapons. The king's line surged against the enemy's defenses, sagged, broke, and gave way back toward the Ridge. Horses screamed; warriors died.

The Ehrylain attempted to reform their lines. A flood of Dauroth's soldiers pursued them. To slow the enemy's advance, an entire company of Ehrylain stood their ground to cover the retreat. That was the Third Company, Eamehr's command. Eamehr was the king's most-trusted captain. He had been with Branden during his entire exile across the sundered seas. His company was consumed.

The sacrifice was not in vain. It was no rabble army the king brought to the field that day. Sure and there were hundreds of new recruits, many of them green as new grass. But among the farmers, merchants, and villagers in the king's army were also trained warriors whose whole lives had been spent in preparation for this chance to strike a blow for their kingdom and for themselves. The experienced warriors, many of whom were not officers or designated leaders, kept their heads. They gathered stragglers, carried away the wounded, offered order where order could not exist. That is how it is. True leaders lead whether a title accompanies them or not. Sometimes, these small, improvised units banded together with others and fought their way to some island of temporary safety where there were more friends than enemies. Others fought on, taking targets of opportunity wherever they found them, until they were overwhelmed by the sea of enemies and slaughtered. Of these brave individuals no tales tell. Therefore, we remember them here, the warriors who died without a friend in sight, save Ea alone, who was beside each of them that day and always.

Marin, the woodcutter's son, surveyed a battlefield gone decidedly wrong. The quick snatches of the field he was able to catch spoke only of impending disaster. Marin was spared the task of brooding. He was too busy staying alive.

Marin had little opportunity for coherent thought. Stubby, desperate vestiges of thinking flickered across the surface of a mind devoted to survival. An enemy rider was attacking him with a long, curved scimitar. Even before Marin put a stop to that one's breathing, another closed in behind him, only to be dispatched by a flick of Gammin's glittering blade. There was a group of enemy pike men moving closer to the king. Marin rode them down and was immediately beset on all sides.

A spear passed close to Marin's shoulder. He started to haul on the reigns, but the horse was already turning toward the threat. There was no way to tell where the spear had originated. Marin chose an opponent at random. The man, a foot soldier in a filthy robe that looked as if it might have come from some rich merchant's closet, was pulling his sword back to strike at one of the king's men. Marin hacked off the man's arm as it started forward. Before the soldier could scream with the pain of it, Marin's backhanded swipe silenced his voice.

Movement caught his attention, something of an absurdity given that there was movement everywhere. That something screamed danger to Marin. He threw himself forward, stretching low across his horse's neck. A sword slashed through the space that had recently contained his neck. His own sword lashed out reflexively. He felt it slide into flesh, felt a gush of hot insides burst out, saw a flow of deep red spatter his leg and the side of his mount. There was no time to see more. He was moving on.

At some point, Marin's horse received a death blow. He jumped off the animal as it was stumbling, its death screams reverberating in his mind so clearly that he had been jumping before he knew why. As soon as his feet hit the ground, he was fighting again, his horse forgotten until later, when there would be time to drink from the grail of sadness that was on the brew.

So it went for eons. Time did not exist. There was only the blood and the stink, the screams of the living and the groans of the dying. The nightmarish lamentation had long-since ceased to register on his mind. His ears were filled with the pounding of his heart and his ragged breathing.

Gammin's voice cut through the maelstrom.

"Marin! To me, to me!"

IV.

Gammin forced his hips around. His shoulders followed, then the keen edge of the sword. The blade connected with a satisfying thump. There was an accompanying sound, something like the sound a butcher's cleaver makes. At the butcher, the venison never falls to the ground to writhe in agony. One never heard screams at the butcher, at least not on a good day.

Gammin perceived the fallen soldier's screams. They blended with others to make a terrible music, death's theme. He heard them, but they failed to draw the smallest bit of his attention. Gammin was already fighting a new enemy by the time the soldier's screams faded from terrified shrieks to moans of anguish. When the soldier was too weak to draw another breath, the final sound his dying body made was a soft, choking gurgle that spewed blood across his lips. No one was there to mark his dying, no one to speak his name a last time. Gammin, the man who had caused his death, had already forgotten that they had ever crossed swords.

The fighting continued as the sun rose to its highest and began to make its way down. It was a fine winter's day, the kind we sometimes have in the Southland, a faded echo of spring. But who noticed? Not Branden, King of Ehrylan. Not

Marin, the woodcutter's son, the Seer of Ehrylan. Not even Gammin, who had loved to skip rocks along the surface of the Silver River on similar days in the time of his youth.

The weather was not on Gammin's mind. Exhaustion was. He had fought all morning and into the afternoon. His company had received new orders several times. As the day progressed, he found himself farther and farther from the king. Each new mission was a response to some development that had to be dealt with—flank that line; attack here; defend there. Now, he was not even sure where his father was or even if the king was still alive.

Feeling rather than seeing a moment's relief in the action in his immediate area, Gammin allowed himself a respite. He took three deep breaths, intentionally holding them longer than his heaving chest would have liked. He shifted two paces to the left. One never knew when an enemy archer had one in his sights.

His eyes automatically quartered the field from left to right. The afternoon sun shone on a battle that was coming to its end. Things were looking better for the loyalist allies. In this part of the field, Dauroth's troops were falling back, though there was still action near at hand.

Gammin and his company had performed each of the tasks assigned to them, most of them successfully. The last, an all-out push against a large contingent of soldiers, had taken them far from the king's position. That fight had been furious, the tide turning back and forth so fast that it did not pay to try and keep up with it. Eventually, Gammin's company had destroyed the soldiers, driving them backward in a disintegrating collapse. Now, the Fifth was regrouping, reforming ranks. Things were looking better for the good guys, but the fighting and the dying were not yet over.

Gammin's eyes searched out and found a handful of his unit and squad leaders. He caught one's eye, signaled for the reformation he wanted. He turned his attention elsewhere. Unconsciously bending lower, he took three more random steps. That is when he remembered his horse. What had happened to it? He could vaguely remember climbing to his feet while trying to avoid being crushed by the struggling animal and simultaneously fighting off the soldiers who had brought him down. Had it died? He could not recall. His hands automatically checking his weapons, he reached for more memory.

A pallet of raucous sounds drew Gammin's mind back to the present, which is the best place for it if you want to stay alive on a battlefield. Off to his right, three Arelese warriors were beset by a flurry of soldiers. More Outlanders loomed in the near distance. Only one of the Arelese was still on a horse. The other two seemed to be protecting him, or trying to. The three Arelese were facing in Gammin's direction. They could not see the additional soldiers converging on them from behind.

Looking around, Gammin found Marin almost immediately. That seemed to be a special ability they shared. If the thought had occurred to him at a better time, he might have explored it, but now was not that time. He shouted Marin's name. When his friend looked at him, Gammin pointed at the beleaguered trio, then at himself. He pointed to the group of on-coming soldiers, then at Marin.

Marin nodded. Fifth Company was gathering behind him, drifting in as the fighting eased and their various assignments concluded. Even with the quickest of glances, Marin saw that few units boasted their full complement. Anger tinged with sadness infiltrated his mind. But he could spare no time for the emotions. He gestured to the nearest warriors. Bellowing for them to follow, he sprinted to meet the oncoming soldiers.

The young prince did not see. As soon as Marin nodded, Gammin started his own race for the lives of three people he did not know. As he ran, he took in as much of the scene as he could. The three surviving Arelese must have been the last of a larger company. The remains of their countrymen were strewn amidst gruesome heaps of Dauroth's soldiers. The figure on the horse was the oldest of the three, his beardless face lined with age. There was nothing other than the horse to distinguish him from the others. His clothes—well-tanned, handsome animal skins, mostly—were no finer, his mien no more noble. Like the other two and most of the Arelese warriors, his hair fell in a thick braid at his back. It was stained white with the passage of years.

Of the other two, Gammin could tell little save that one seemed much smaller than the other, shorter, more slender. Perhaps he was younger, the son of one of the others? It mattered little. The sword of an enemy did not discriminate between the young and old. Just before he arrived, Gammin had time to decide that if the smaller man was younger, he was no less valiant than the others. What he lacked in weight, the man made up for in speed and agility. But those two traits were not going to be enough, not unless he, Gammin, could....

The Prince of Ehrylan slammed into the conflict with the violence of an ocean squall. His sword ripped into one of the soldiers attacking the mounted man. When that soldier collapsed, Gammin turned his back on the mounted man. He had a mind to help the others. The man on the horse seemed to be someone they were protecting. If that was true, who was going to protect them?

Gammin shifted his feet, slid sideways to avoid an attack from a soldier. He skipped forward twice. In another setting, one might have thought he was a dancer, not a swordsman. That grace is something they share, dancers and fighters. One celebrates life, the other death. It is the way of things. Ea makes soup from ingredients mere mortals cannot fathom.

Whatever the Almighty was cooking at the time, Gammin's hop, skip, and jump—during which he avoided tripping on at least four inert bodies or large pieces of same—delivered him to the side of his intended rescue. One of the soldiers menacing the slight man wisely shifted his focus to the newcomer. This wisdom prolonged his life exactly five breaths, three while he was still on his feet, and two last gasps as he lay forgotten and dying in a collecting pool of his own blood.

Gammin redirected his attention to another of the soldiers attacking the younger man—or, maybe he was just a boy. He saw an opportunity, raised his sword. Before the prince could strike, the man collapsed. The Arelese boy had knocked him on the head with some short weapon.

Breathing very hard, Gammin spared an instant to recover. He was relieved to see that none of the attackers were still standing. The youth tugged on the handle of the weapon he was using, some sort of hand axe. It did not come free. The boy put a foot on the dead soldier's neck and yanked. When death did not release its grip on the weapon, the boy squared his shoulders and tried again. He leaned well back, gripping the haft with both hands. In the moment just before the axe head came free, Gammin saw that it was not a small man, nor even a boy. It was a girl, a young lady. Startled by this realization, Gammin came to a full stop. As he did so, the head of the axe jerked free.

A gout of ichor jumped off the axe head. It described a low arc through the air before landing on Gammin's boot. Involuntarily, his eyes were drawn down. He stared at the blot like a bemused chicken until he regained his senses. Purposefully setting aside his confusion, Gammin shook his head rapidly. Droplets of blood, sweat, and dirt flew from his nose and chin. They were the consistency of thin, pinkish-brown cream.

The girl was gazing at him. She had the face of a maiden, soft and unmarked, save for a single thin line of off-white next to one eye. The narrow scar stood out on skin hued curiously bronze. The scar might have been cosmetic, some form of decoration painted on the face of a… child?

Did the Arelese send out their sons and daughters to fight for distant allies and foreign kings at such a young age? Gammin was forgetting in the heat of battle that he was little older than he thought this woman to be. In truth, she was older by a year or two.

The Prince of Ehrylan opened his mouth to speak. A baleful look in the young woman's eye stopped him. Her words chased away whatever he had intended to say.

"Shall I kill him, father?"

She spoke in heavily-accented Common Tongue. Her voice was almost conversational. Her eyes did not waver from Gammin's as she stepped forward, halving the distance between them. In one hand, she wielded the hand axe; in the other was a long knife. Sunlight danced off the metal from gaps in a quilt of blood.

She raised the axe menacingly and moved the knife toward Gammin's throat. Her mouth was smiling as if it was sharing a private joke with her mind. Her eyes were not. Gammin was unsure whether she was jesting.

Others were arriving now. A rank of horseman made an effective barrier behind the old man and his two… children? Many of them had horse tails flying from their lances. They were obviously Arelese. They were just as obviously watching the group that contained Gammin with eager fascination. The men and women of the Fifth were catching up to their captain. Marin was arraying them. The prince felt very safe from Dauroth's army, less so from this girl.

He took two steps back, using the movement to inspect his surroundings. Only the young woman was in his primary zone of defense. She was between him and the single horseman— her father—who was sitting aback his steed as if he had not a care in the world. Gammin shifted his eyes to the third of the trio he had come to rescue. That warrior stood watching with the dozens of horsemen who now lined the developing spectacle.

Another cluster of Arelese horsemen thundered up in a fury. They placed themselves between Gammin's forces and the group that contained the older man on the horse and the young woman. The nearest members of the Fifth Company started to respond. Marin held up one hand and voiced a sharp order. The Fifth held their lines. Marin held his position. He was itching to get next to his friend where he could help, fidgeted uncomfortably with his sword as he glowered at the nearest horseman. Three Arelese warriors held lances pointed at Marin's breast; three held short bows bent to their limit with arrows. Marin knew that there must be twice as many arrows aimed at the Prince of Ehrylan.

Gammin did not see any of that. He was watching the young woman. She moved closer, reducing the buffer zone again. It was the tactic of someone who knew they were fighting with shorter blades than their opponent. Opponent? Looking into her eyes, Gammin felt more like prey than opponent.

Though it was difficult, he did not raise his sword to defend himself. Instead he dropped it, stepped back, and held his hands up. It would have been more prudent to step back before dropping the sword, but that mistake—it was a pretty big one, truth to tell—did not cost him. Sometimes we are lucky.

The action of dropping his weapon likely saved his life. The Arelese are protective of their king and his offspring. None of the mounted warriors, now arrayed several deep in a wide arc, would have suffered anyone to harm Theramina, the Princess of Arel, daughter of King Theros.

V.

Gammin did not know this man was the King of Arel. He looked back and forth from the father to the daughter. "If you kill me, you kill one who came to help. You were under attack. I thought…"

The horseman shook his head, frowned. "Those men were not attacking, young warrior of Ehrylan. They were fighting for their lives against being captured. One of them killed my standard bearer." He uttered the last sentence as if it was a complete explanation.

The accent was thick, but Gammin had no trouble understanding the Common Tongue as it is spoken by the Arelese. He did, however, miss the implication connected with the words "my standard bearer."

"I saw…," he began.

The man on the horse cut him off.

"The standard must be lifted again before we sit in victory with the memories of our fallen. It is our custom to choose the new bearer on the field of valor. Our warriors contend for the right to defeat the one who killed the previous bearer." His eyes flicked to one of the bodies at Gammin's feet. "But you have done that for us."

The prince missed the glance. He was still trying to piece the puzzle together. Not under attack? Capture? These people had been fighting for their lives! He was sure of that. Or was he? He replayed the scene in his mind.

How easily the older man sat his horse, how calm and collected the three of them looked. Realization came to him. He understood most of it, though not all, not yet. He, and Marin at his direction, had interfered in a custom, something associated with the warriors of Arel and the bearers of their standards.

Staring up at the man on the horse, empty-handed and muddle-headed, Gammin finally understood. He had made a mistake. The rider and his two companions had been in no real danger. Immediately, his head cleared and found the firm ground it was seeking.

"I see," he stammered. "Surely... surely, an active battle is a strange place for a ritual." His words tumbled to a halt, then broke loose again in a small, rushing avalanche. "Even for a people as fierce and noble as the riders of Arel."

The man on the horse looked right and left in what might or might not have been an intentional parody. Laughter splashed across the other horsemen. He spoke the moment his gaze fell once again upon Gammin.

"This is no longer a battlefield. Now, it is the resting place of the victorious fallen, the beginning of new labors for the living."

Gammin managed to tear his eyes away from the rider. He swept them in a wide half-circle. There were no living enemies anywhere to be seen. Though he did not have a view of the whole battle field, it was enough to close the gap in his understanding.

He had no need to look toward the other half of the circle, the one directly behind him. Gammin had unconsciously noted the sounds that indicated his company, a full one hundred—or, they had been one hundred at dawn—had been assembling. He recognized a voice, the jingle of a harness that was just a little different from all the others. These were familiar sounds. They should have made him more comfortable, but they did not. This was a very dangerous situation, not only for him personally, but for all the warriors around him, both Arelese and Ehrylain.

There is a mischief that haunts battles, a laughing imp who delights in turning friends into enemies. The hundreds of warriors now facing each other had all fought for the same cause, some side by side, others on distant parts of the field. Despite this, with the smell of death hanging in the air and the terrible energy of battle coursing through their veins, the slightest spark could set off a bonfire of death that would blaze out of control in the blink of an eye. Whatever he did, Gammin, the Prince of Ehrylan, had to ensure such a tragedy did not happen.

The last words of the King of Arel hung in the strangely quiet air. The two contingents faced each other over bloody ground. For some reason, Gammin's mind chose that moment to flit back to a morning not so very long ago—though it seemed like forever—when he had faced a group of bullies in the Bendwood. Marin had been with him that day, and Annen, too. That day, he had felt like a dust mote floating within a lighted crystal, waiting to see what would be.

Gammin held up his left hand. He tossed a glance over his shoulder without turning.

"Hold. Lower your weapons, warriors of Ehrylan. There are only friends here." He used his command voice. Normally, he would have spoken to the captains or just told Marin what he wanted. Now, he needed everyone, Ehrylain and Arelese alike, to understand. He tried to will away the tension.

The air behind him sighed with the begrudging complaints of unconsummated bowstrings. Gammin sighed himself and sucked in a fresh breath. The fate of two nations was now a little more secure, and he was free to concentrate on the formidable maiden before him. She was close enough to strike him. For all her studied nonchalance, her chest was heaving. The muscles of her forearm stood out with the pressure of her grip on the axe.

"Shall I kill him, father?" Again, her voice was light, containing a hint of mocking humor, though she was still showing her battle eyes.

Theros, the King of Arel, laughed. He shook his head vigorously, as if he feared she might do just that before he could stop her.

"Nay, daughter. The King of Ehrylan would doubtless mislike it. This young warrior is my brother-in-law's son. He is your cousin, my sister's son. Do you not see yourself in his face?"

It had often been said among the Arelese that Theramina resembled more her aunt than her mother. There was no way for Gammin to know this. The thought that he might meet blood-kin this terrible day was far from his mind. He had not even conceived the notion. Accordingly, he was knocked off kilter by the statement. This man was his uncle? The young woman was his cousin? Gammin had known, in some vague and unexplored part of his mind, that his mother had a brother. He had not let himself realize what that meant to him personally, not until now.

Gammin blinked several times very quickly and shook his head again to clear it.

"How do you know Branden is my father?" He searched for the name, found it. "Theros....er, King Theros? I do not look all that much like him."

Again, the king laughed. It was the kind of laugh one usually reserves for the simple. "That may be true. It has been a power of years since I saw Branden, so that would not matter anyway. You wear my sister's countenance, sir, or so my fond recollections insist."

Mostly to allow his mind to catch up to his racing heart,

Gammin started to throw out another question.

"I've heard that, particularly from my father. Isn't it also true that…"

Theros cut him off. He was a king, unused to being questioned by strange boys on battlefields.

"Now is not the time for a recitation of lineage."

The king continued to speak, but the call of nearby horns blurred his words so that Gammin did not understand them. Without conscious effort, the prince recognized the horns. They were not signals. They bore no message other than "Get out of the way."

King Branden had arrived.

8. NEW ACQUAINTANCES AND OLD

I.

The first meeting of the two kings was brief. There were greetings, a comment or two on gray hair and waist sizes, all things that had little or nothing to do with the current situation. The two monarchs separated again, departing with their troops to do the things that must be done after a battle. Gammin, relieved to be excused from further encounters with his murderous cousin, took his place at the head of the Fifth.

Throughout all the rest of that day and the next, the warriors of each nation went about their appointed tasks. Whole companies from Branden's army were assigned to guard the approaches to the valley. Others roamed the macabre field, executing mercifully enemies who could not be saved. Those who could be saved were taken into custody. They would be dealt with later, when the bleeding, bandaging, and dying stopped. The wounded enemies were tended with as much care as the wounded allies. It has always been thus with the armies of Ehrylan.

The Arelese took a different path to the feasts of victory.

They executed wounded enemies wherever they found them. That, at least, was understandable. More troubling—and almost incomprehensible to the Ehrylain—was the fact that seriously wounded Arelese were killed, as well. These were sent into death with great reverence and ceremony. The wounded Arelese went willingly, even gladly. The Arelese do not suffer themselves to be a burden on friends and relatives. To live on after a battle, reduced by injury to the point of needing a long-term caregiver, was the grossest of insults. By the standards of Ehrylan, it was a curious belief, perhaps related to the worship of barbarous gods.

Of wounded there was no lack. There were thousands. Healers from Branden's army established field hospitals in central locations that provided access to good water. Corps of engineers and other support personnel descended from positions high on the Ridge now that the battle was won. Some set to digging the trenches in which the dead would be buried. Others began to erect structures. Tents and corrals sprang up. Hammering and sawing intertwined with a melody of moans.

Here again, the differences between the Arelese and the Ehrylain were made evident. Instead of burying their dead, the horse warriors built innumerable pyres and gave them to the flames. This, too, seemed strange to the Ehrylain, but it was a sensible practice that saved effort. It caused a fair amount of discussion among troops eager to be rid of trench detail.

The Arelese also burned their fallen enemies. Rumor had it that they burned a substantial quantity of enemies who had not quite yet fallen. Who can blame them? No pyres were built for that purpose. The dead from Dauroth's army were piled into heaps, dosed liberally with oil and pitch, and set ablaze. The windborne stench of burning flesh was smelled miles to the south. The Chinenyeh of Valley Elosai made a song about it. But one cannot trust the song of a Chinenyeh. They are the Dancing People, the Laughing People, the Travelling People; they sing to ease the way.

Gradually, chaos retreated against the assault of so many hammers, saws, spades, and nails. About midday on the day after the battle, the wholesome smell of wood smoke began to mask the aromas of death and destruction in Branden's camp. By that evening, the winter wind—which is a capricious friend that far south rather than a freezing monster—blew through a carefully laid-out grid of lanes upwind of the battle field.

Gammin did not see King Theros or his daughter again until the evening of the day after the battle. That is when the victory feast was held for kings, captains, and warriors. A cavernous pavilion was erected between the two camps. The structure was of Arelese design; it both delighted and confused the Ehrylain, few of whom had seen its like.

All the surviving Rathian warriors were accorded places of great honor in the pavilion. The three senior commanders of the Rathian Boarder Guard had fallen in battle, along with most of their men. The remaining contingent was represented by a young captain. He looked distinctly uncomfortable with his place at Theros' table.

It was difficult for Gammin, who sat at Branden's right hand, to converse with the Arelese royalty. There was little opportunity. The kings had much to talk about and many warriors to honor. Immediately after the food was served—it went to the warriors first—both kings rose and began to circulate through the celebration. Gammin might have taken that opportunity to speak with Theros' children, but he was too busy watching his uncle. Then, waking from his daze, the young prince was up and out of his chair, making his own pilgrimage among the survivors. Marin went with him without out even considering if it was proper.

The kings, Gammin, and Marin did not make it back to their tables in time to make amends with their food. The kings wandered among the feasting throng, spreading a tincture of praise wherever they went. The prince and the seer followed at a discrete distance. Like their elders, the two young men accepted morsels from each cluster of men—and women, among the Ehrylain—they visited. So it was that hundreds of Arelese, Rathian, and Ehrylain warriors could claim from that time on that they had dined with kings, princes, and seers after the Battle of Valley Elosai.

Following in the slow wake of that procession came Nandea, a *faelyth* of the Crescent. She had come up from the south with Theros. She blew through the pavilion like singing breeze, tarrying wherever the fancy struck her. She played her flute here, her five-stringed finalla there. As evening passed into night, she settled into a central location outside the pavilion, among the main assemblage of warriors. She told legends of the Crescent, north to south, as well as specific favorites from each of the three represented kingdoms. She even improvised a telling of the battle that had just concluded, much to the delight of her audience, many of whom figured prominently in the tale.

This was the first time most of the warriors heard the full account of the battle. The Arelese heard of Branden's mad dash from Mendolas. Even the meanest serving boy—to be a humble server that night was accorded an honor—was already aware the Ehrylain had delivered the victory. It was a surprise to many that the Arelese had likewise saved the Ehrylain.

It had been a classic example of what Gammin had described to his father not so many days before. When you pull a dog's tail, it is likely to turn and snap at you. That is exactly what had happened. As Branden approached the battlefield, the enemy commander was forced to redeploy significant portions of his force. That relieved the pressure on the Arelese. The horsemen regrouped and gained the offensive. Soon enough—just barely soon enough according to Nandea's song—they pushed back the enemy lines, turning the whole field into a confused melee.

Meanwhile, Branden's army was taking it hard, having been swamped by waves of retreating enemies. Once the Arelese perked up, those same enemies were caught between the horse and the lion. The arrival of scores of horsemen at just the right moment turned the tide, and, though it took the rest of the afternoon, the allies had driven Dauroth's conscripts from the field.

II.

Gammin and Marin were hungry by the time they left the feast to the warriors, who would likely celebrate until daybreak. All was not lost for their stomachs, though. The kings reassembled in a private setting. As midnight loomed, Gammin was seated uncomfortably on a pile of furs, picking at the lonely survivors of strange-looking Arelese food on his plate. He was conversing with the young woman who had offered to kill him. Twice.

The two kings sat apart. They were chatting with each other and with a few senior commanders. All the additional men, some Arelese and some Ehrylain, had been with Branden in Arel decades ago. There was a lot of catching up to do. Eamehr was not there. He was still under the care of Elma, the king's own nemen. He had played an important part in the defense of Branden's fall back. Grievously wounded, he was still unconscious and unable to tell his story.

Gammin and Marin were sitting with Theramina and her brother, Theden, who had been the third of the trio Gammin had thought to rescue. Theden was a few years older than the other three. He turned out to be an interesting fellow. He could be solemn, almost regal, one moment, jocular the next. The changes seemed random and instantaneous. Behind his bubbling, often sarcastic mirth, Gammin sensed a lake of strength. Theden, son of Theros, was already a great leader; he would be a great king.

The four of them lounged in a tight little group. They had been left to fend for themselves, the older warriors too engaged in their own gray-haired memories to mind them. In the beginning, Theden monopolized the conversation. He spoke mostly with Marin and Gammin. Among other things, he provided a wonderful rendition of Gammin's attempt to save the Arelese royal family. In particular, Theden's portrayal of his cousin's confusion, complete with facial gesticulations, was hilarious. His thick, luxurious accent improved the telling.

As interesting as Theden was, Gammin would rather have

listened to the two kings and their captains. Their reminiscent footsteps were landing on many stones that were of interest to Gammin. He heard the names Gilmarun and Therana several times. They pulled at his attention with velvet talons. However, as odd as it sounds given his fractured childhood, Gammin had been raised well. More than that, Gammin was well. He was attentive to his companions, smiling in all the right places. He joined the other three youngsters—Theden was younger by two decades than the next oldest person in the tent—in laughter when the occasion demanded it.

It was that laughter that turned the focus of the conversation to Theramina. After one particularly funny remark by her brother, the young lady expressed a colorful gush of laughter. Gammin's eyes were pulled to her face. They were caught there as he noted the oddly pleasing slope of her eyes, the aquiline tilt of her fine nose, the bronze tint of her skin. He stared at her without knowing he was doing so. She did look startlingly like the portrait in his father's…

"Is my face displeasing to you, cousin?"

"What?" Gammin stammered as he regained his composure. "No, of course not. Your face…"

He stopped, collected himself. He set down the hunk of bread he had been nibbling. It was Arelese bread, heavy and flavorful, neither in a good way. Glad for an excuse to be rid of it, he produced a smile.

"Princess, your face is not displeasing. On the contrary, you are lovely. You know that."

"Then staring is polite in your land?"

"No, lady, not at all. I was just thinking how pretty your laugh is. It is very… what? Marin, help me!"

The desperation in Gammin's face almost made Marin laugh, but he was too disquieted to laugh. What had Gammin called her? Lady? That's what he called Arica. Marin unconsciously adopted the mental equivalent of a battle stance as he searched his memory. Did Gammin call other women that? He entirely forgot to answer Gammin's question.

Gammin, seeing he'd get no help from that corner, started

again.

"You have a beautiful laugh, lady. It is full of joy and... well, it's just full. Maybe that describes it best."

Theramina's face was impassive as he described it as lovely. She smiled at the description of her laugh.

"Then, thank you, cousin." She stopped, frowned, pondered. "Wait. You say, what is it, brother?" She looked at Theden, uttered a spate of words in what must have been the native tongue of the Arelese.

Theden replied in the Common Tongue. "I thank you." He turned to Marin. "That is it, right? I thank you, not just thank you?"

Marin did not get a chance to answer. Theramina burst in. "Yes, that's it! I thank you."

There followed a long discussion of the varying customs of the two peoples. They covered clothing and food for the most part, and fighting, of course. Of special note was the discussion of standard bearers and their selection rituals. After that, and for no reason in particular, Gammin produced his mother's ring. The only jewelry he wore voluntarily, it depended from his neck on a simple loop of braided silver and leather strands. Much oooing and awwwwing followed as the siblings inspected their aunt's token. The Arelese, by and large, do not decorate themselves with their wealth. They account family and horses of more worth than jewels or gold. Bravery they value almost above all else, and strength of body.

A smattering of applause and cheers drifted in from outside the tent. Reminded of Nandea, Marin described how, when he first heard her new tale, he had been struck with the resemblance of what happened at Valley Elosai to what happened above Mendolas.

"At Mendolas," Marin told them, "it was an intentional maneuver. We struck from behind to make the enemy turn, like a dog whose tail has been stepped on. Here, at Elosai, there was no ruse, no significant advanced planning. The strike from the rear that turned the dog's head was blind luck. But the outcome was the same. That's the point I want to discuss.

How much does blind luck figure in any battle?"

Gammin's immediate thought was that luck was not blind, but he did not get to voice it.

"It was not luck!" Theramina asserted pugnaciously, her face split by a severe grin. "The *Themera* won the day. We are mighty warriors."

Themera is what the Arelese call themselves. It means "Horse Riders" in their tongue. They account it a great honor to be defined by their four-hooved friends.

Marin said, "What is it I've heard? Luck is the residue of planning? Luck is the happy bedfellow of preparation? Something like that."

Theden shook his head. He sighed theatrically. "It's good to be lucky? Is that all you infants can learn from this lesson?"

"How can there be a lesson from only two different instances?" Theramina's retort was sharp as a knife.

Gammin recognized the look on Theramina's face. He had seen it on Arica's many times. It was the look a sister flings at her brother when he falls into a behavior that long ago became irksome.

Theramina continued. Her eyes flicked to Marin's. "We know it is good to strike at an opponent's …" She paused, digging for the word. She found it with a little spasm of satisfaction. "It is good to strike at an opponent's flank. That is hardly a revelation, brother."

Marin nodded.

Gammin did not. He was staring at Theden, thinking that it is not always good to strike at the flank. If your opponent was prepared for it, expecting it, wanting it, there would be trouble. Presently, Theden spoke again. This time the tone he used was that of a disappointed tutor, something with which each of them was only too familiar.

"You have all missed it, my young children." He smiled, showing twin rows of startlingly white teeth. Only one of them was missing. "In your search for the meaning of meaning, you stumble past the juicy Mellon of Wisdom."

Now Theden's companions were less interested in the

lesson than the performance. Theden was enjoying it as much as they were.

"The lesson, my brave companions, is that it is not good to be the dog."

Having delivered his sage pronouncement, the Prince of Arel held out his hands palm-up, as if he were holding out a saddlebag full of wisdom. He put on a smile that was as ingratiating as it was irksome.

Marin started a quip but swallowed it back. He'd caught the tiny shift Gammin sometimes made when his mind snagged a feisty thought. For a moment, the laughter of two kings in the background was the only sound. Theden waved the back of a hand at them dismissively and nursed his smug look. He turned his head to cough. Marin did not think it was a cough he was hiding.

Theramina made a rude sound with her lips. "It does not pay to be the dog? That is too obvious, brother, even for you. I know you too well. There's more."

"You're right and right, Theramina," said Gammin. "That is obvious. Don't be the dog. And, there is more."

At that moment, King Theros asserted control over the festivities.

"You four are making new acquaintances old, I see. This is good. The road to friendship runs between new acquaintances and old. Victory's hope will be built on the ties made here."

The king's voice had the effect of splashing the four youths with warm water. They turned their heads toward Theros in a chorus of movement. Marin looked around the tent for the first time in what seemed like a long time. They were alone with the two kings. The others must have left quietly.

Branden waved them over. There was a general shuffling as four bodies moved from one pile of furs to another. As he was about to sink once more to the floor, Marin remembered the pillow he had been using. He started to go back for it. As he turned, Gammin pushed it against his belly in what was almost a swat. Marin nodded and dropped into something that wandered halfway between sitting and reclining. Not for the last time, he wondered how the Arelese could ever get comfortable without chairs. It was just one of the many differences he was learning to appreciate—or not.

As soon as they were relatively comfortable, King Theros pinned Gammin with his gaze. "I said before that a battlefield is not the place for recitation of bloodlines. Upon consideration, I find my statement untrue. I have declared the names of my fathers to opponents in the field many times. How else would they know whom to thank in the After? But, no matter, that. You asked me how I knew you. Do you remember?"

"Yes, your majesty."

Theros looked at Branden. "Shall we dispense with that, my friend? You know we are less formal in my land. I have always wondered why the kings of foreign lands need to be so often reminded of their rule."

King Branden nodded disinterestedly. That was a field the two of them had plowed long ago.

Theros turned back to Gammin with an unspoken command in his eye.

Gammin was relieved. He had not been around any kings until recently and had little idea of how one addressed the monarch of a far-off kingdom. After an afterthought, he added, "Very well, sire."

Theros frowned. The theatrical displeasure was wasted. A single exhaled chuckle escaped his intentionally pursed lips.

"This one reminds me of my son," he said, glancing at Branden. "Are they all alike, these sons of ours? Is this how we appeared to our fathers? By all the gods that ever were, I hope that is not true!"

Branden started to answer, perhaps to suggest he did not know because he had only just met both young men in question. Theros raised a preemptory hand. He dropped it when Branden held his silence.

Turning to Gammin once again, he said, "In the field, you asked how I knew you. Now, in this more pleasant place, I ask you, what do you know of the hand axe you carry?"

Gammin's hand went instinctively to his hip. The axe was not there. He had left his weapons outside with everyone else's. There were no weapons in the tent, save only the knives which any man or woman takes to a meal.

"My father gave it to me, Theros. He said that you gave it to him."

Gammin just managed to keep the honorific silent. The result did not feel right. Truth to tell, Gammin was in quandary as to what to call his uncle. At least with King Branden, he could fall back on "father." That also felt wrong, but it seemed to make everyone happy. And, it was the right thing to do. That made it easier.

"That is true, nephew. When I was your age, it was mine, and dearly bought, too, though not with coin. I would have known you by the hand axe alone. But I did not need that. You have the look of your father on you, though it is mixed with the look of mine. The blood of Brand flows in your veins. That is good for Ehrylan and for her allies."

Gammin's emotions flared at the thought, suddenly strong, unquestioningly true. The same blood in my veins? The blood of King Brand? The House of Brand traced its origins back to Andur. Pride swelled in his chest, turned to chagrin, dissolved into an unquiet watchfulness. It would be foolish to take pride in his birth. He had no control over it. It was just a blessing. Or a curse.

Theros, unmindful of Gammin's epic emotional journey, pressed on.

"You have also the look of your mother."

"Not just his mother, Theros," Branden agreed. "Now that I see you both together, he has your look, too."

Gammin spoke out, his voice brimming with new-found confidence. This was not because he was Brand's grandson. It was because King Theros had deftly shown him the way out of his difficulty. It had been a masterstroke of on-the-spot diplomacy. Now he knew what he could safely call the Arelese king. Gammin's respect for his uncle doubled in that moment.

"Uncle, you also mentioned that Princess Theramina and I

share the same face."

"Yes, it is true. Little Terror looks more like your mother than her own."

"Little Terror," repeated Branden. "That is an interesting label."

Theros laughed, as did Theden. Theramina looked defiant, but amicably so.

"Little Terror, yes. That is the translation. It has somewhat of a different flavor in Arelese. It is a beautiful phrase, and strong. *Samerelda*, we say, which is Small Wind in the Common. The *Merelda* is a killing wind that comes some years out of Sulan and Yar. The sands of that wind can blot out the sun, eat paint off stable walls. Perhaps Little Storm would be more accurate, but Little Terror is often how I feel."

Theros eyed his daughter, willing her to keep her retorts unspoken. His gaze, though commanding, was warm with an elixir of love and pride. Hers was equally full, brimming with respect.

"Theramina and Theden came to me through my second wife. The first, with whom Branden rode on many pleasant days, died a year or two after he came to kill the fiend. She died in childbirth, as did the baby. It was a boy. He would have been king after me. My second wife gave me another boy before she died. That was Theden. Now he will be chief in the land after me."

The aging Arelese king shifted his gaze to his son, who had long ago outgrown the description of boy, except in the most obvious sense.

"He will be a better king than I, better than his grandsire, too, I think. Our people are fortunate."

Theros words tumbled out as if he had forgotten he was speaking, a rare thing for a king. The tone upon whose back they rode changed as he spoke, sadness turning to pride, muddy water clearing as it ran from a river into the wide, trackless sea.

Unease washed over Marin, a tide of anxiety. It was sudden. The light of the candles and lamps seemed tenebrous rather than cheerful, their flames fighting against overwhelming shadows. Inhaling sharply, his hand moved for his sword. It was not at his hip. He searched the tent with his eyes. Though large, it was not big enough to hide even a single assailant. He listened. There were no unwelcome sounds. He listened again, but there was nothing.

Marin had no fear about being attacked unaware or from an unprepared rear. There were at least three sets of personal guards lurking somewhere very near the tent—Theros', Branden's, and Gammin's. Theramina and Theden were likely represented as well. The occupants of the tent were, for that moment, as safe as they could be anywhere.

Still, something had touched him. He felt short of breath, as if his heart had been caressed with a flutter of raven's wings stained by ash and blood. His mind spun about the same axis again—look, listen, wait. Again, he could detect no threat. Then, he realized that the sense of dread was gone. It had vanished as quickly as it appeared.

Marin looked at Gammin, expecting to find his friend's eyes on him. But they weren't. Gammin was doing just what Marin had been doing, quartering the tent with his eyes and ears, looking, listening, moving on to the next quarter.

What Marin did not know was that Gammin had been watching him earlier, had seen him go on alert. Gammin felt nothing untoward himself and was a bit mystified. When he looked back at his friend, their eyes met.

In the foreground, Theros was still talking about losing his first wife.

"I was very sad when they died, my wife and my first child. I had no desire to wed again. I wanted only to mourn, and to take that emptiness with me into the After. But the needs of a kingdom do not await the desires of its king or queen. Custom would have me wed again and get an heir as soon as possible. Yet I was young and stubborn. I did not remarry for years. My love is not slave to custom."

Theros dropped his eyes. He inspected his plate, which waited not far from his elbow. After a moment, he plucked a morsel from it. With a distasteful smirk, he tossed it backhanded at his daughter. She caught it, looked at it, feigned frustration. Then she popped the thing into her own mouth. Gammin saw a brief glimpse of the food and recognized it. It was some kind of meat. Of that, he was pretty sure. But of which animal and what part, he had no clue. He had purposely not taken anything off that particular platter when it had been presented to him earlier. He was relieved that Theramina had not offered it to him now.

She looked at him as if she felt the pressure of his eyes. Seeing the look on his face, she laughed. "It is a game we play, my father and I. I serve him not only what he likes, but also what is good for him. Usually he eats both. Sometimes, not."

A sudden thought smote Gammin. It ran from his brain—or maybe his taste buds—right out of his mouth.

"Hey! Do you have *raushyt* in Arel?" He was referring to a healing medicament famous for its foul taste as much as its amazing restorative properties. The fact that everyone else in the tent shuddered at the word made Theramina's response unnecessary.

"Eeewwww. Yes!"

She dissolved into silent laughter that sent her shuddering softly against Gammin's side. Sitting up again just as quickly, she buried her face in her arms and shook her head vigorously. "Let's not talk about that! What father just threw at me tastes wonderful."

As if in contradiction, the young lady reached straightway for her cup. She gulped, swallowed, and sipped in rapid succession. Then she set the cup down and smiled prettily.

There followed a comfortable time when no one spoke. Eventually, Branden shifted his weight to his other side and repositioned a pillow. He grimaced, poked the pillow twice, then grunted as he packed it against whatever was ailing him. When he was finished with that, he said, "Tell my son of your children's mother, Theros. I would have him know her tale. The women of Arel are strong and true." He held Theramina with his stare.

"As you wish, brother," replied Theros. "Where was I?"

Gammin answered first. "You were telling us youngsters how important it is for a ruler to put the needs of his people before his own desire. The last thing you said was that you refused to remarry in defiance of ancient custom."

Theros sat unmoving just long enough to make a point of it. Then, he turned to Branden.

"This one is truly your son. I see you in him, Branden. That is understandable. What I do not understand is why I see you also in my son." He glanced at Theden, then back at Branden. "It makes one wonder."

Branden did not reply. He was a wise king, after all. The younger set did not reply either. They must have been wise kings, too.

"No matter."

Theros inhaled, collecting the moment. With the exception of Gammin and Marin, everyone in the tent knew the story they were about to hear. It was a tale of sadness piled upon sadness, not the sort of story that fit well into the jocular mood that had developed in the tent.

The quiet settled in. A slow counterpoint of camp sounds told out the time in the background. A warrior complained that no beans had actually been used to brew the *kef* she was drinking. An officer barked some slight reprimand, his voice hushed because he knew how close he was to the king's tent. Much closer, almost just outside, a finalla was playing a happy country trifle. It was now very late, but still they danced, the survivors. The others rested already in beds of earth and stone.

III.

"My wife was called Eramena. That would be Lovely Flower in the Common. I have always wondered if that was a jest her parents played. Though she was beautiful, one could not look at her without seeing she was a warrior all the more. She must have had the look by her Naming.

"I might have waited longer to wed despite the weight of custom. My father was not yet so old. He was still able to ride to war. I had no desire for any woman but the one I had lost. However, once I came to know Eramena, the rest didn't matter. We were wed later that same year. Eramena gave us a son and a daughter."

Gammin held up a hand. "Hold up, there!" Hearing the imperative in his own voice, seeing his offending appendage extended, he shed a regret. He softened his voice, quieted his mind. "You skipped a bit, uncle."

Theros did not look angry at being cut off so curtly. He looked puzzled. The King of Arel turned first to Branden and then to Theden. Finding no help, he returned his gaze to Gammin and stared blankly.

"Uncle, I am asking you to tell us more about Eramena."

Theros hand fell from where it had been supporting his face. It struck the floor with a slapping sound that brought a guard's head and shoulders through the tent flap. The gesture would have been a good, old-fashioned knee-slapping if the king had been sitting in a chair rather than reclining on furs.

"Now I understand, nephew. Forgive, please." He did not stop and suffer Gammin to accept the apology. "In Yar, where there is only wind and sand, they have a saying. In the Common, it is, 'Oh, gentle lion, my friend, my companion.'"

Gammin was not sure what to make of that. He kept his mouth shut and his ears open.

"Eramena was daughter to the headman who kept his lodge at Big Trees, a village half way between River Po and River Simot. Simot is in the far south of Arel. It is the border with Sulan. The village of Big Trees was a… what do you say? Ah, yes. It was a strong place. No, that is not right. Stronghold. That is it. It was a stronghold where we kept vigilance over the Great Plains and the river to the south. Though we were at peace with Sulan, one must maintain the tradition of readiness. And, there were the raiders who come out of the north.

"I had ridden to Big Trees many times with my father when I was a boy. When I was very young, the head man was called…" He searched for the name. "Well… it matters not. At some point, the head man died. The new head man was Eramena's father. I do remember his name, though I can't recall how old I was at the time."

He cocked an eye at Gammin.

"You will have to forgive me if I am too vague for your liking here, nephew. My old memory does not remember my younger days as clearly as I would like. The result of all these comings and goings was that I had known her many years before I got to know her, if that makes sense. That might never have happened but for luck, if there is such a thing.

"One day, we arrived unexpectedly, having ridden to Big Trees after repelling a party of Norlan raiders along the shores of River Simot. We had a mind to protect the village in case, as sometimes happens, the raiders sent a force across land, or up one of the river's tributaries. When we arrived at the village, Eramena's father was not there. He was off east and south with his riders, farther inland along the Simot. He was doing the same thing we were—protecting the territory of his lodge.

"Eramena told me that she was leading the village while her father was away. It was not long before I knew she was telling the truth. It was not long before she let me know she would consider me suitable to share her horse. The rest happened quickly, with no time between the beginning and the end, though there is proof otherwise. My father was too old to oppose the match. But he had no need. It was a good match for the kingdom and a good match for me. The head man of Big Trees was a strong chieftain, known throughout the land for his courage. More importantly, I think, he was loyal to my father and his line. Theru, my father, had no objection."

Theru's son addressed Branden, who had known the old king, though only for a short while. "Sometimes, I wonder if it was not an accident that brought us to Big Trees that day. Maybe Theru was craftier than I knew."

Branden said, "I am guessing all people are craftier than we think. We are just too busy unwrapping our own cleverness to notice."

Theros grinned, then continued.

"Eramena could hope for no better match. My father had only one son, me. His daughter was gone, off to a foreign war with her lover. Therefore, I would be king of Arel. Eramena would be my queen. We wed. We had babies. Life went on.

"Sea-rovers from Norlan attacked three inland villages along the Po. That is south of Terith, where I keep my lodge, as did my father. In the time of my grandsire, such a thing was almost unheard of. Since the great Evil came again to the Crescent, we see them perhaps three years in five."

Norlan raiders were well-known throughout the Crescent. Unlike the huge merchant ships and the sleek, many-masted fighting vessels of Rath, the raiders' ships were shallow of draft. They could carry many men—only men, for Norlaners do not allow women to board ship for any reason—on the wide ocean as well as navigate inland on many rivers. Norlan *farafyk*, which is Sea Wolf in their harsh and unlovely tongue, could move quite happily under either sail or oar in water that was too shallow for any vessels other than turcs or small boats. That is a shallow draft for such a powerful weapon. Therefore, they are much feared by those who dwell close to the sea and the shores of even smaller rivers.

"In the last years of my father, we refitted the towers that guard the mouths of certain waterways and other strategic points. These had been empty for many years. They were ready and served us well. Or, so we thought.

"They came in their farafyks. The Coast Guard saw them. We had a good start, once we were sure where they were going. By the time we got to the first village, the raiders had split into three groups, which was not uncommon. We had planned for that, my father and I. I led a third of our forces against the first landing, my father the second, and a senior captain the third."

Branden started to ask a question. Theros cut him off with a gesture.

"Save it, brother. I told him the same. King Theru was too old to be riding to war, no matter how much he liked it. My father was stubborn, and he was king. Yet it was no toothless, old man who led that troop. Theru was still hale enough to wield his axe and command his horse. His arrows flew true. He was no less a warrior that day than any of the younger men. If his arm was less strong, his mind was stronger."

Branden assented. "How old was he, Theros?"

"My father was riding hard upon ninety summers on the day we set out to destroy the raiders along the Po. He rode east while I stayed and fought at the first village. I did not think of him again for a long time. When I did, we were putting the last details to rights. We defeated that set of raiders—three farafyk full of those freakishly large, hairy Norlaners. It was not a big incursion, only about one hundred men. I was about to set out for the second village with my riders. The last report said fighting was still fierce there. We did not want to miss it."

Theros picked up his cup. He looked to see how much it contained, then swallowed deeply from it.

"As we prepared to depart, a rider came out of the north. He bore the blanket of the Coast Guard, so we knew there must be trouble on the horizon. He told us that another set of raiders had been spotted. This one landed very near where Branden came ashore. Terith, my father's village, was forewarned, but there were not sufficient numbers to drive so many raiders off our shores. Nine ships they counted, nine ships with one sail and near fifty men each.

"We had drained our village of the bulk of its riders, judging that Terith was too far from the river to be at risk. That much was likely true, but we had forgotten about the ocean. Never in living memory had a farafyk landed upon the beaches of Terith.

"We set out at once with great speed, though we were weary already. After we had covered about half the distance, another rider came up the road toward us. Her blanket was that of the Village Guard. I knew her well. She was grievously wounded. The news she brought was not good. The raiders had beaten back the shore patrols. A dozen riders cannot hope to hold ground against five hundred axes. Yet, even a few

Themera can play havoc with a landing. They delayed the raiders long enough for the Village Guard to respond. Even so, there were too many raiders, though we had the horses and could move faster. The messenger had been sent as the barbarians neared the village, having fought their way from the waves to the lodges of my people. We hurried all the more, yet we were still too late.

"We drove them from the village, destroying them utterly so that there were none left to stop us burning the ships. We might have kept the vessels, maybe sold them to some other nation. Perhaps they could have been the first Arelese navy. But, we did not do these things. The Themera who were left piled the Norlaner corpses on their boats and set them adrift with flame, as is their custom. We did not want to offend the strange gods they worshiped, for the raiders were warriors of great worth and prowess, though they were our enemies, too. The gods of Norlan are far away, but what is distance to a god?"

Theros paused. He lowered his eyes, stared at his hands. They were nut-brown, laced with a network of pale scars, the adornment of war. The fingers were strong, ringless.

Marin thought, "Here it comes."

The king sighed. He began the part of the story he had so long delayed to tell.

"We were too late to prevent most of the sadness, but I think we mitigated the worst of it. I must hope that much. I returned home to find my wife dead and my son injured. Theramina was untouched. That, at least, turned black night into a lessor shade of evil. But there was other sad news. My father, the king, had been killed. He was pierced by a javelin while cutting down the raider's standard. I was not distraught over him. He was a very old man. I think we both knew that battle would be his last. If you would ask me, I believe he set out for the ending he found. Can you blame him? Who can ask for a better?"

Marin thought there might be any number of better endings for an old king, but he held his peace. He understood. He had discovered that good, better, and best have different meanings in different places.

"I was king. My people were safe for a time. That was good. I needed time to discover how I would be the man I needed to be without my greatest asset by my side."

Gammin and Marin spoke at the same time.

"What of Theden, lord?"

"Theden was injured?"

The resulting jumble was nearly indecipherable. Somehow, Theros got the gist of it. A smile tugged at the corner of his mouth unsuccessfully. It turned, climbed his face, and escaped from his eyes.

"What of Theden, indeed? There is a tale worth telling. When they found him, he was standing over his mother's body, a hand axe in one hand, a knife in the other. He was not yet eight. The weapons were too heavy for him. They were mine. I had left them with his mother for her protection."

The women of Arel are of equal stature as warriors with their men. The men took war on the road. The women, who were famed in song and story, formed the basis for home defense. They were brought up alongside their brothers in weapons training and other necessary arts. Therefore, the matter-of-fact announcement took no one in the tent by surprise.

"Injuries, you ask, as if losing one's mother was not the worst of all blows to a young boy. My son's ankle was broken, though he was standing on it when they found him. His arm was bleeding badly from a cut. His cheek was cut, too, and one tooth knocked out. Someone about three times his size must have backhanded him. I hope he gave him steel in return." He looked at Branden. "Your steel, brother. The knife was the one you gave me all those years ago."

"Then something good came of that knife," replied the King of Ehrylan. "I got the better of that exchange. You gave me a princely weapon. I gave you a tool I picked up along the way." Then, softly, but suddenly, "You gave me two treasures, Theros, one very much more precious than the other. I thank you for both."

Silence bloomed like an uncertain odor, soft at first, growing in strength until it could no longer be ignored. Theros raised a cup to his lips, drained the last swallow.

Theramina started to arise. According to their custom, she attended her father at social occasions. This being a celebration of kinship, she had allowed herself more freedom than might have otherwise been usual. Her father's cup was empty, as should not have been. The purposeful grace with which the princess moved showed everyone that she intended to remedy the slight right now.

Fast as she was, her brother was faster. Theden stood a fraction more quickly, waved her back down. He grabbed a flagon of Rathian wine. As he poured, the smell of the ruby-tinted liquid chased away the ambiguous silence. Refilling his own cup last of all, Theden turned back to the kings. He put a hand to the knife at his hip.

"I have it here… uncle." He paused to emphasize the last word, observing Gammin out of the corner of his eye, where a smile might have been lurking.

What came out of Branden in response was a toneless vocalization of surprise, a miniature gale. Theramina twitched.

"What, the trinket I gave your father? That's preposterous." He turned to Theros. "Are the armories of Arel so poor that her prince must wear a sailor's dirk?"

Theden produced the blade. He handed it to his father, who held it as if remembering forgotten secrets with an old friend. After a moment, Theros set it on the cushion between them and said to Branden, "Hardly a dirk, unless I misunderstand that word."

Branden did not respond. His eyes remained on the knife, which was not a dirk by any definition. The blade was not particularly long, nor particularly slender. It was, in fact, a well-worn, much-used hunting knife, though small for its type. That made it handy for life aboard ship. Branden had picked it up somewhere on his long journey home; he did not remember where. That is not to say it was in any way a poor specimen.

The fact that a warrior of Branden's caliber had selected this knife to carry at his hip day in and day out spoke for itself.

"Interesting," Branden said at last. He tossed the knife back to Theden, who caught it by the haft with less apparent concern than he likely felt. "We both gave to our sons the gifts of our youth."

Theros watched his son re-sheath. He said, "Perhaps we give the things we love most to the ones we love best. Or, maybe they are the things that bring us the most joy."

Gammin thought of Annen, who had given him the knife that waited at his own hip. In that instant, he had a brief moment of insight, maybe his version of far-seeing. His eyes flicked to Branden. He was not surprised to see his father looking at him.

Theramina had tired of sitting so quietly. She was tired of talking about knives and axes as if they were treasured foals. Inspecting the end of her braid pointedly, she stated, "I suppose that's just fine if you are a son. It sits not so well if you are a daughter." She crossed her arms over her breasts and grimaced with the perfect amount of imaginary ire.

Theros was unmoved. "It is as I have told you these many years, Samerelda. Son or daughter, it matters not. The one I love best gets my treasures."

Instead of looking aggrieved, the young princess clapped her hands. She cried out with what sounded like glee. She rose to her feet so rapidly that her pillow tumbled against Gammin's cup. He caught it almost quickly enough to avoid spilling any of the wine it held.

Once she had established her feet, Theramina wasted no time. She addressed her father, her face radiant. "You've beaten me again, father."

She dipped into something of a contortion. Marin thought it was her equivalent of Arica's courtesies.

Theros gave no indication he had seen or heard Theramina. "Where was I?"

Theramina replied instantly. "You seem to be forgetting yourself even more than usual tonight, father."

Theros ignored her. "The villages were safe, my son was injured, my daughter was safe, and my wife was among the victorious dead. We built her pyre in the high places and gave her to the flames. You asked me to tell her story, Branden. It has ended now."

Branden nodded slowly. It was the first bookend to a long stillness. The sounds of camp life drifted in to fill the space. Someone was looking for their boot. Another suggested that he might have had that boot for dinner. The finalla had stopped. The player had moved on. There came the unmistakable sound of the watch changing.

Quietly, Gammin said "Uncle, may I ask a question?"

"Certainly." Theros' voice was deep. It rolled like the prairies of his homeland.

"Did you wonder if it was an attempted invasion?"

"I thought about that a lot. The Norlaners hit the three biggest villages along the Po, then struck my father's lodge—which is what you would call our capital, I think—once we had ridden away. If that was their plan, it was a good one. At worst, the raiders could hope for some booty. At best, if they won the day, they'd have control of the Po as well as the area's major village, the capital."

"That could be a kingdom in its own right," said Branden, "if they could hold it."

Gammin said, "That would make a great beach-head."

Marin said, "For Dauroth."

Theros agreed. "Aye, yes, and for any band of merry warriors who could hold it from the Themera. We thought of those things. That was many years ago. I have revisited those thoughts more times than I can count. Even though I have now the grace of hindsight, I am still not sure. It may have been that Dauroth was reaching out for Arel. It may be that the king of Norlan had turned his eye our way of his own accord. That much I doubt, but it is possible. It is also possible that Dauroth had some kind of influence over the ruler of Norlan. What I believe now is that it was just raiders doing what they do."

The king fell silent again. Far across camp, where revelers still enjoyed the victory feast they had earned, a cheer erupted.

Theros inhaled a slow breath, then finished. "That is the tale of Eramena. I mourned her passing for the customary time. I mourn it still. She was queen. She was mother of Theden and Theramina. She was my councilor, my confidant. I have had two wives. I will have no other. I had only one sister. You stole her away, Branden."

Theros turned toward his daughter. "This young princess of Arel has had no queen to guide her, no mother or aunt to teach her the ways of a woman. I fear she was raised to be a prince more than a princess. If she is over bold, how can I assign her guilt? I know nothing of princesses. It is no wonder this one is the Little Terror?"

Theramina smiled. Her eyes were very green. They tilted slightly upward at the corners. Even Marin thought her beautiful. And, she looked tired.

Just as Marin had that thought, Gammin yawned.

King Theros said, "It is late. My tale is done. It has been a long day. Let us each to bed so that we may greet the new sun with joy."

There were four nods of agreement. Only Theden failed to acknowledge the statement. He was already dozing.

9. ANCIENT ENEMY

I.

The sun had not pulled itself above the horizon that same morning when a messenger rattled the flap of Gammin's tent. The two young men who shared the accommodation seldom needed to be called to their duties. They were usually up and out by the dawning, circulating among their warriors, seeing to the things that needed to be seen to. But this day, both Marin and Gammin were still fast asleep.

After acknowledging the message—Prince Gammin to report to the king's tent immediately—they did not arise with their customary alacrity. Marin groaned. He covered his face with his hands. Gammin turned over and hid his head under a pillow. From that haven of safety, he said, "I feel terrible."

Gammin's voice conveyed a good portion of the discomfort Marin was feeling. The woodcutter's son replied, "I would have to improve to feel terrible. Was it the wine, do you think, or the food?"

Gammin did not answer. There was really no need, since there was no doubt. Both had consumed more wine than was usual for them. They had drunk much of it later than normal. The stuff was just so good!

Despite their discomfort, the young prince and his right-hand man were up and out in good time. Marin made his way to where the Fifth Company was billeted. He checked with the cooks and the officers. He moved among the men and women, offering a word, sharing a morsel of camp grub with those who offered. Soon enough, his discomfort was forgotten.

Gammin went to his father. He was not the first or last captain to arrive. As he took his place, Gammin saw the king watching him with a stern face. He wondered what he had done wrong. Maybe he was supposed to arrive first, being the prince and all. Who knew? Branden seemed to become more surly with each victory.

The young prince forced himself to eat, though he was, for once, not hungry. The assembled captains and advisors shared the bread, cheese, and fruits, marveling at how such fine produce could grow so late in the year in Rath. As they ate, they talked of what was to come.

This battle was over. The border between Rath and Ehrylan was, at least for a time, safe from Dauroth. That was not true for the two cities on the Bay of Arai, where Arathai and Ehrynai faced each other across a deep, blue harbor. Arathai was where old King Kappelli kept his court. Ehrynai was the largest city in southern Ehrylan. Both were consumed in war.

Branden was champing at the bit to get on with it, but his plans had changed. It was not practical to march all the way back to Mendolas to take ship. The army would make the journey by road, not by water.

The northern bank of the Silver River—the Ehrylain bank—runs hard by the mountains for many leagues south and west of Mendolas. The mountains rise out of the water in austere cliffs of white and gray. There were no westering roads suitable for an army on that side of the river.

On the south bank were roads aplenty. Successful trade requires fast, easy transport. Trade was Rath's lifeblood. The kingdom was crisscrossed with as fine a network of roads as could be found anywhere in the Crescent. They were kept in excellent repair by the local governors. Branden's army would make excellent time on those roads.

Apart from the mode of transport, the lion's share of the king's plan stayed the same. After arriving at Arathai and fighting off whatever opposing forces were there, Branden's army would rest and recuperate for a time, then focus on Ehrynai. That city was allegedly in the hands of loyalists, but no one knew how willing they would be to bend a knee to Branden. After Ehrynai, Branden would head northward and free the rest of the Westland.

The part of Ehrylan that lies between the sea and the Western Mountains is not considered part of the Southland. We call it the Westland. The Ehrylain there have strange accents and odd customs, as might be expected from an area so accessible to the sea roads.

Once the agenda was set, the rest became easier. The decision was made to set out on the morning of the second day hence. Preparations began. Efforts were redoubled.

Marin and Gammin were too occupied to visit with their new friends and relatives. Twice, they saw Theros and Theden at a distance during the day. They did not see Theramina.

Night fell. The opportunity for socializing returned. They met again for a private supper. This time, the Arelese came to call at Branden's tent. Marin was happy about that. He would understand the food.

Though Theros left his cooks behind, he brought a variety of wines, each in its own leather bag. These were better in every case than the best wine Branden had with him. It was much easier for Arel to trade with Rath than for the Defier, which is who he had been publically until recently.

Gammin, who had not until recently known that wine had varieties other than red or white, thought it all a bit strange. He watched with amusement as the others sniffed and sipped their drinks. This one, they said, had the taste of lemons, that of plums. To him, they all just tasted like grapes and smelled like wine.

Though the reveling was more subdued than the previous evening, the revelers in the king's tent enjoyed themselves just as much. They were joined early on by Nandea, the faelyth. Much to Gammin's disappointment, she did not bring her flute. When he asked, Nandea told him that her flute was not made for such a small space. Here, in the tent, her finalla would serve better.

"You must use the right instrument for the audience and the space," she said.

"Is a Chinenyeh flute better for a tent?"

Gammin was very interested in hearing the instrument his mother had played. He had no idea what such a flute might look or sound like. He had never seen a Chinenyeh before, much less a Chinenyeh's flute.

"Yes," replied Nandea patiently, "A Chinenyeh flute would work just fine. The Dancing People call Rath their home, more often than not. That would make a Chinenyeh flute a good choice for this occasion. Do you have one? I do not."

Gammin hid his disappointment. He shook his head. "No matter." He waved his hand dismissively. His voice and intonation were the perfect imitation of his uncle and what seemed to be his uncle's favorite phrase.

That set the room to laughing, which is how Nandea wanted it. Happy kings are more generous than unhappy kings. The same was true of farmers, merchants, soldiers, and butchers. There was something to that, she thought, tuning her finalla, an almost impossible task amidst the animated banter.

When she finished her preparations, she sat and waited, smiling amiably while the others came to a natural pause. There were not many of those, for there were several conversations going on at once, so she did not waste it.

"Shall I tell your guests a story, King of Ehrylan?"

"By all means," replied Branden, draining his cup. Before anyone could move to refill it, he raised a forestalling hand. Reaching out, he snatched a bag at random and splashed fragrant redness into Theros' cup before filling his own.

"Very well," the faelyth said. "I shall start by improvising a work on the bravery of Princess Theramina. I understand she fought in the battle?"

"She did," cried Theden. "She almost killed the Prince of Ehrylan!"

"Now, that is a story I have not heard. Tell it to me."

Theden did. As he talked, Nandea watched the others, taking note of where they laughed and where they frowned.

As Theden finished, Nandea nodded. "I think that will be enough, your Highness. Give me a moment." She bent close over the neck of her finalla, strummed, listened. With a satisfied grunt, she made one small tweak to the tuning. Marin thought she was stalling, perhaps to work on her rhymes, meter, and the other things faelyth's think about but common folk don't.

When she was satisfied, Nandea looked up and nodded. "Is it cold in here?"

She did not await an answer. Instead, she launched into a lively tune that frolicked like a country barn dance. The stately words she used were entirely at odds with the irreverent accompaniment. That was just the first of many songs and stories Nandea gave them that night. Before it became very late, she begged permission to leave, claiming some commitment. Before she left, Branden gave her a fine ruby and three uncut stones that might have been emeralds. She accepted these gladly, without a trace of self-consciousness.

Last of all, Marin bade her a good night.

"May your sleep bring you peace, Nandeatha." He used the proper form of her name when he addressed her. He was the only one in the tent who remembered she was an Old One.

After she was gone, the conversation naturally pertained mostly to Nandea for a good while. Branden asked if the faelyth had been visiting Arel when Theros got the call from his son, who was already on the northern border of Rath, fighting not very far from where they sat now.

Theramina jumped in before Theros could answer. "We happened upon Nandea in southern Rath. She was walking along the road as if she had not a care. If we may believe my father's scouts, when first they saw her, she was skipping, dancing, and playing her flute. What was the word they used, father? Oh, yes, never mind. She was skipping and dancing, playing her flute as she frolicked."

The young lady rose to her feet in a very graceful motion. Watching her, the word "supple" came into Marin's mind. That changed as she began to pantomime how Nandea might have looked. Theramina held her hands out as if she were playing a flute. She even pursed her lips in an imitation embouchure, her face a perfect caricature of an enraptured—if somewhat peculiar—artist.

That was just the start. She began hopping from one foot to the other, moving across the tent as if she were dancing down a path. For her final embellishment, Theramina turned in slow, narrow circles as she danced. Somehow, the princess managed to imbue her performance with the tiniest hint of village idiot. All told, it was a masterful performance. Everyone who saw it was impressed by her balance and charm.

Even Marin laughed, though he was negatively predisposed to the young lady. He knew his disposition was entirely unwarranted, for she had, as yet, done nothing wrong. But that did not seem to matter to him. There was just something about her he did not like.

Theramina lowered herself onto the furs, a graceful heron returning to its nest. After sipping her wine and dabbing her lips, she continued her story.

"That changed when she learned what we were about. She said battles mean stories that need to be told. She said it so dispassionately that it gave me the chills. Almost, she seemed then like the carrion-eaters of the field, watching and waiting for her next meal."

"Nay, daughter," interrupted Theros. "She is not a carrion-eater. She is a warrior in her own right. A warrior of words, I suppose."

"Yes," added Branden, "I have come to believe that nemen, faelyth, and warriors are all the same."

There followed a lively discussion on the nature of words,

swords, medicaments, and their various usages. When that had run its course, other subjects followed. They enjoyed each other until the need for sleep forced an end to the enjoyment. Theros left the remaining wine for the Ehrylain. He selected one in particular, perhaps identifying it by the design on the bag. He put that one into Gammin's hands without an explanation.

King Theros strode from the tent, his children and guards flowing after him into the torch-lit darkness like a cape.

II.

Gammin and Marin stepped out of their tent and into the chilled still of the night. Perhaps in penance for the previous day, they were out even earlier than usual. One went right, the other left. Marin was off to make the rounds. Gammin moved down a lane that ran straight as an arrow between the rows of tents and lean-tos. He was headed to see if his father was up.

If the king was awake at this tender hour, it was likely because he had not yet gone to bed. You could never tell with that one. He slept in starts and fits. Sometimes, the king did not sleep for days on end, or so it seemed.

As he moved by tents filled with darkness and snores, Gammin checked the moon. He sniffed the air, trying for what might have been the thousandth time to catch the flavor of dawn on the breeze. Marin had tried to show him, then Marn, when the son made no progress in the teaching. For the thousandth time, he was disappointed. It was a meaningless exercise, if practice can ever by meaningless. Dawn was still hours away, perhaps two, maybe three.

The camp was laid out in an ordered grid. Intersecting lanes of bare earth and mud separated the whole thing into what the engineers and architects called blocks or sometimes cells. Gammin strode past smithies and collections of stalls that housed the accoutrements of the various trades necessary in war. It was a jumble of iron, wood, rocks, mud, sweat, and effort. But it was an ordered jumble, built on designs used in antiquity by Andur.

Gammin had no difficulty in understanding camp layout. In his younger days, he had read the most credible texts over and over, spending whole days with Marin and the others studying maps, moving little pieces of string, candle wax, and even figs to represent companies, battalions, barracks, tents, corrals, cavalries, and the like. For reasons unknown to him at the time, the figs always represented Dauroth's troops.

The two young men could have stayed closer to the king, in the king's block, in fact. But Gammin and Marin had decided to sleep closer to those for whom they had responsibility. Most of the other company commanders held to the same policy, though it was not mandatory. Gammin was very careful not to let his status as the prince interfere with his military responsibilities. The truth of it was that he felt his duties as prince interfered with his duties as captain. He did not care for that.

It was a fine winter's night, the type they have in Rath, where the cold clears the sky so the stars can shed a dust of frost upon the earth. When Gammin felt the chill, he did not mark it; he just pulled his cloak closer, thought no more of it until later. What he was thinking at the time was that, though this was his battle cloak, it was the finest cloak he had ever owned. It was not the prettiest or the most fashionable of the cloaks his father had given him to wear, but it was the finest, in his opinion.

He was mulling over this fact—which seemed queer to him—as he walked by a group of men and women sitting around a fire. They were preparing to eat either an early breakfast or a late supper. Perhaps they were a squad who had the next watch or one that had just completed the last watch. Gammin had learned that an army never sleeps.

Warm smells danced through the night air. A rabbit, stuffed and trussed, was spinning on a spit over the flames. A man turned the spit's handle slowly, carefully, as if the whole world depended upon the cooked meat. A line of stitches marched down the man's cheek, from the bottom of his left eye to the lower edge of his jaw. Even in the limited light of the camp fire, Gammin could see that the edges of the wound were puffy, red, still inflamed with the outrage done to them. Next to the fire, another man, this one no older than Gammin, was preparing another rabbit for the flames. He was stuffing it with leaves and what looked like rice or oats. That man's arm was in a sling. The knuckles of the hand holding the knife were crusted with thick scabs.

No one looked at the prince as he strode by. He was moving quickly and quietly, the tandem escort of guards his father had forced on him trailing discretely behind. As he moved on, Gammin heard a greeting in the Old Tongue. He caught the word *folan*—brother, countryman. Turning to acknowledge the greeting, Gammin saw that it had not been for him. One of his guards had paused long enough to slide a leather bag from his shoulder into the hands of one of the diners. Gammin noted it with pleasure. He stopped so the guards would have a little more time with the others.

Odd behavior for a prince? Yes, indeed. Branden, in the prime of his youth, had not displayed such compassion for his people.

It might have been Gammin's own command that had caused the generosity. He had been very clear on his expectations with the guards the king assigned to him. He informed them that he required only three things. First, they had to protect him; that was the king's command. Second, they must protect each other with as much devotion and commitment as they protected him. Gammin told them that he would give his life as readily for any of them. We are a unit, he had stressed. It is as simple as that. Finally, Gammin told them that, as a unit, it was their mission to spread help and compassion to everyone they met. It was the old way. Though he did not mention it to them, he had seen an example of such a society in River's Bend. As far as he was concerned, that was about as good as it gets.

Now, standing in the night, watching these simple acts of

sharing, Gammin was warmed against the chill. He watched as the diners passed the wine bag around their small circle. The last of them made as if to hand it back to the guard. The guard shook his head and held up a hand, refusing to take it.

The diner uttered thanks and handed the bag to a woman sitting on his left as a glob of rabbit fat dripped into the fire. A sudden flame licked upward. Gammin saw that a horse head had been tooled into the leather on one side. He knew that on the other was a rather abstract depiction of a horse and rider as seen galloping away from the rear. It was the same wine bag he gave the guards last night, the one he had received from Theros. Gammin wondered what the diners would think if they knew they were drinking the King of Arel's wine. He grinned and strode off into the twinight.

The grin did not last long. Sooner than he would have liked, Gammin left the smell of cooking rabbit behind. Now, he was smelling something that had obviously died but not been cooked. No, that was not right. The stench was warm and moldy, wholly offensive, but it was not the odor of something dead. It was the reek of death itself. It was a smell that did not belong here, even though there had been a festival of death in the area just lately.

The prince stopped abruptly, the tails of his cloak swirling around his legs. He turned and sniffed the air again, holding his nose up the way a dog will when it is testing the breeze. Try as he might, he could not catch the unearthly stink again. The smell of rabbit was behind him now. He could no longer smell it, which was in no way remarkable. But where was that smell of decay? There was no trace of the diseased stench that had caught his attention. He inhaled more deeply. No, it was gone. He smelled wood smoke mingled with the ever-present miasma of the army, but nothing worse than that, nothing unfamiliar or notable.

Gammin frowned. Without knowing it, he slid the edge of his cloak back from the pommel of his sword. His fingers brushed the hilt. His pace quickened.

The disquiet continued to grow with each step. Was he the

only one who could feel the impending calamity? Why wasn't the camp up in arms? Gammin was almost running by the time he came near the block that contained the king's tent. He burst into the open area of the compound, blinking against the sudden onslaught of torchlight, ready to pull his sword and join the fray.

There was nothing amiss. The tents and other structures were arranged in a square surrounding a central quadrangle. There were two sentries in front of the king's tent. Another pair of guards patrolled the area. Except for the snores and farts that rose like nocturnal roars, all was quiet.

As he entered the area, almost sliding on his heels to abate his progress, the sentries turned their heads toward him. He saw them recognize him. One bowed slightly. One raised his hand in greeting, only to snatch it back once he remembered who—or what, really—his old acquaintance had become. They had known each other in the Bend. For all the trappings of war, this scene was as peaceful as a night on the Bend.

Despite all these signs of safety, Gammin was propelled by a tide of anxiety. He experienced the feeling that someone was watching him. That was nothing special. As the king's new son, there were plenty of appraising gazes each and every day. But this was not like that. This feeling was tangible, visceral, hot with sweat and blood. It made the heart pound in his chest, sped his breathing.

Suddenly sure there was someone behind him, Gammin lurched forward and ducked. His right hand jumped to the sword as he turned. His left groped for the hand axe. But there was no one there. The lane was empty save for his two body guards. They were about twenty paces away. That was a little far, but Gammin had warned them about dogging his steps, at least when the king was not around. Even at twenty paces, they would have seen anyone, anything that menaced him.

After making a circuit of the area with his eyes, Gammin turned back to his original course. The king's sentries were watching him now, interested in his odd behavior for professional reasons. The young prince forced himself closer to them. His feet seemed heavy, as if a chain of uncertainty was tangled about them. There was nothing behind him. That was true enough. But there was something... somewhere. It was here. He just had to find it.

He had felt this same way before. When was that? His mind seemed muddled, cloudy. Why couldn't he remember? Then he did. Gammin's heart skipped a beat. He sucked a deep breath against his tongue. In great fear, he began to run. Frantic now, he bolted across the center of the quad, his cloak billowing behind him. He knew what he would find when he got to his father's tent. That knowledge made him cold with rage, hot with dread. Now, the only question was would he be in time or too late?

The sentries were showing concern. That was very reasonable of them under the circumstances. Gammin shouted at them. "Get away! Get away from the tent!" Just before he was upon them, he cried, "Send for Marin!"

Gammin heard two swords sing out of their scabbards as he blew like a searing wind into the tent. It was very dark, though not pitch black. Muted light from a strong moon fell like mist through ventilation panels in the tent's ceiling. Gammin knew where his father's pallet was even without that impossibly soft glow. Shouting, he moved that way, only to stumble immediately over a pile of furs. He collapsed, sending out a scurry of pillows. Clawing his way back to his feet, Gammin ripped his sword out of its scabbard and shouted again.

There was a muffled grunt that was choked off prematurely. Gammin could just make out a form crouching over the king's pallet. They were struggling against each other. Gammin could see the king holding off the knife in one of the assassin's hands while he clawed at his throat with the other hand. As the instants sped into eternity, Gammin heard his father gasping, choking. For all the young prince knew, it might already be too late.

Gammin tried to propel himself forward, but he could not. His arms and legs were mired in dread. An invisible wall loomed between him and the assassin. There was an almost overwhelming sense of loss, a cavern of darkness into which he would fall if he did not flee. The bitter taste of terror coated his tongue. He shuddered.

Almost screaming with rage, Gammin threw himself forward. The wall of fear did not disintegrate, but it did relent. It moved with him, enveloping him in a blanket of mental misery that clouded his heart, made it difficult to think straight. He was swimming through an ocean of horror.

The prince managed three steps. They brought him close enough. He would have liked to skewer the assassin with his sword, but he feared to harm his father. There was no way to tell where the assassin ended and where the king began. The prince clubbed the intruder on the head with the pommel of his sword, then grabbed him by the shoulders and hurled him to the side.

Gammin hit him hard enough to kill most men, but the assassin did not die. As Gammin pushed him away, the man twisted, spinning in a different direction than the one Gammin had intended. Much to his dismay, the prince found that his opponent was now behind him.

Gammin spun. His head turned first, and he saw the knife. Its blade was black as night. The prince's forearm stuck against the assassin's, turning it just enough so that the tip of the knife missed his chest by the breadth of an infant's fist. He slashed with his sword, cut nothing but air. The assassin had moved again.

Suddenly, the tent was filled with sound. Guards were screaming. Gammin recognized the voices. The tent flap opened violently. Light flared, making Gammin blink involuntarily. In that instant, the prince and the assassin each jumped back to avoid the other's strike. Then, their eyes met. Understanding flowed like water between them, and a certain grudging respect.

Gammin saw something else, something that tightened the growing net of fear constricting his heart. This assassin was an Old One. Even worse—by miles and miles—this murderer in the dark was one of the *Silanni*, the Silent Assassins of the Forest. The young price battered aside a rush of despair that threatened to engulf him.

Two guards loomed up behind the Silanni. Hadn't he, Gammin, warned them to stay away? No, those had been the king's sentries. These men were Gammin's guard.

As the prince's mind was trying to grasp what that might mean, the assassin attacked. Quick as a snake, the Old One spun on his heel and struck. The guard closest to him had no time to react. He recoiled, clutching his belly in the useless attempt to close the steaming fissure that had appeared there.

The Silanni struck at the second guard. That man had the benefit of the extra time it had taken to kill his squad mate. He stepped out of the way, putting himself between the intruder and Gammin. The knife missed him. He brought his sword up in guard.

The Silanni took no notice of the steel. He twisted, sank low under the defense, and struck. This time he did not withdraw the blade as quickly. He held on to the slumping guard, staring deeply into his eyes. As the dying man slid to the ground, his own weight caused the knife to cut deeper and farther into his abdomen and chest. Something that sounded like a mass of wet seaweed flowed down with him.

The Silanni laughed. It was a gay laugh, the excited appreciation of a young girl fawning over a kitten. He turned back to Gammin, who had not been paying attention to him. That is a very dangerous behavior when facing a Gryhm. For, that is what the Old One was now. The Silent Assassin was gone. The jubilant assassin had taken his place.

As soon as the Gryhm had turned on the guards, the prince bent to help his struggling father. The king's hands were clawing at a slender chord that was choking him. The urgency with which he was groping and the sounds he was making—or, trying to make—left no question as to what needed to be done or how quickly it had to be accomplished.

As the Silanni had driven his knife into the belly of the first guard, Gammin was trying to slide his fingers between the king's spasming throat and the garrote. It was much too tight to allow that easily. Pull as he might, the thing would not budge. In a last ditch effort, the prince jammed his fingers between the cord and the throat, yanked hard enough to bring the king's torso off the pallet with a lurch. It did no good.

While the Gryhm had turned on the second guard, Gammin reached for his hunting knife. He knotted the fingers of his other hand around the chord, pulled, and twisted. There was no slack to allow such a maneuver; something else had to give. The only other thing was the king's throat. Gammin's fingers pressed into the soft flesh, his fingernails raking out gashes that started to seep blood immediately.

Gammin set the edge of the knife against the garrote. It was a movement that deserved far more delicacy than could be given in that circumstance. The king's struggles were growing at once weaker and more frantic. Gammin moved the knife a fraction of a thought. The garrote parted with a jerk and left the king gasping for air.

That was all Gammin could do for his father. Now, he had to fight for his own life and the life of his men. He looked back over his shoulder in time to see the death of his second guard. The Gryhm was holding the man up, staring into his eyes with an almost loving gaze. It was obscene.

The Gryhm released the dead body and laughed. He turned back to Gammin and the king, a satisfied yet eager smirk on his face. The killing of those two guards had taken less than six breaths.

Gammin raised his sword, knowing there was only a single mistake between life and death for one of them. One could not hope to make any mistakes against a Silanni and live. Or, a Gryhm. Truth to tell, one could not hope to survive such an attack in any case. But hope was for later, like pain and regret. Now was for fighting.

Two bows sang. The assassin lurched forward as the arrows hit. Rage becoming action, the Gryhm whirled around. Ignoring the arrows protruding from his back, he stepped purposefully toward the men standing at the opening of the tent. There were three, two holding bows, one a torch.

One of the bowmen started to nock another arrow. His hands were shaking so badly that the familiar process was nearly impossible. As the Gryhm approached, the bowman gave up. He flung his bow toward the monster, then cowered back, raising his hands to cover his face. He was screaming inarticulately.

The other bowman retreated as fast as he could, dragging his partner. What had they seen, those two hardened warriors? Was it a ravenous wolf with glowering eyes? Was it a half-crazed fiend? Was it some combination of the two, half man, half wolf, a walking abomination bred by evil to serve evil?

The torch bearer did better than his fellows. He brandished the flame at the Gryhm, giving way only grudgingly as the fiend advanced on him. The fiery brand was in his left hand. He hid behind his right arm, which was raised to shelter his face from the Gryhm's gaze. It was like a scene from a horror story told to children while camping under a full moon in Magravina's Gamble. The story's unfortunate victim was holding off a monster with flame. Fire was good for that, so say the old wives. But how many old wives have faced a Gryhm?

Gammin saw only the last part of this. When the Gryhm turned back to the tent's opening, the prince knelt by his father's side. He searched for one of his father's hands with his own, running them over the king's torso. He found a hand, pressed the haft of his knife into it. Then, he stood and whirled back to face the action. Vaguely, his mind registered that his hands were wet with blood. Very wet. The king's night shirt was a sopping pool.

The Gryhm had chased all the guards away. Even the torch bearer had retreated. The creature was roaring in defiance, its arms held wide. He was standing in the opening of the tent, facing outward toward the last set of annoyances that had delayed him from doing his master's will. It was time to finish now. The fun was almost over. He would kill the kinglet and the young princeling, too—an impromptu bonus. Then, it would be time to move on again. The body of this accursed Old One had done the night's work well. He knew it would die very soon. That was part of the plan.

Gammin grabbed the hand axe from his waist and threw it at the Gryhm. The tip of the wooden handle struck the assassin in the back. That part was sharp too, for the Themera know that not every throw flies true. The point dug in before the circular action of its rotation carried the axe head forward into the space between the target's shoulder blades. It was not a bad throw, all considered. Gammin had not yet practiced much with that tool.

The Gryhm turned, enraged. He snarled at Gammin, spewing a spray of stinking spittle, and stepped toward him. Sword up, the prince went to meet him.

Another arrow slammed into the Gryhm, knocking him forward a step, sending him to his knees. He started to rise, struggled. A trickle of blood leaked from his mouth, depending like a red rope from between his lips. Roaring with frustration, he hurled his knife toward Gammin.

Gammin swung his sword with the same motion he used to hit walnuts with a willow branch. He missed the knife. It was dark. The knife was black. It flew past his upper arm, grazing a fold of his cloak, and fell to the ground somewhere behind. If Gammin's body had not been turned with the uncoiling of his swing, the assassin's stony blade would have struck him in the center of his chest.

Again, the Gryhm screamed. This time, a river of blood welled from his mouth. He turned cold eyes on Gammin, then on the king, who was struggling to rise. They were the eyes of a dead man. The voice, when he spoke into the sudden silence, was the voice of death.

"I will kill you yet, Branden, son of Brand. I will not stop there. I will have my revenge upon your seed long after you have ceased to be a memory. I will seek them out, one by one, family by family, until I wipe your line from the Crescent. It will be a lesson to all who defy my master. This I promise you, Branden the Upstart. This will I do. So says Rauchur. So says…"

The rest of the epitaph was lost. Gammin had had enough. Someone had told him that even the words of a Gryhm were poison. That was something he could well believe. Icy, seething malice coated every word, every syllable.

Gammin slid forward another pace and swung his sword. The body that had once been a Child of the Forest died. The foul thing that was Rauchur, the Gryhm, fled with a wail and a stirring of the wind.

10. OF GRYHM, MOTHERS, AND BODYGUARDS

I.

The young warrior prince gathered his breath. He focused on the lifeless body. He did not know where the Gryhm had gone, but he knew the fight with it was over for now. He also felt sure that someday he would meet that Gryhm again. He was correct about both.

Turning to help his father, Gammin said, "Are you all right?"

Branden struggled to rise without assistance. Finding he was unable to do so, he clutched at his son and pulled himself up using Gammin's arm as if it were the branch of a strong tree. As the king got to his feet, his knees buckled. He slumped down again all the way to his pallet. His right hand went to the pit above his left breast. Gammin knelt, pressed his own hand to the spot. It was warm and thick with blood.

Light burst in on the tent, a welcome explosion. Gammin's head turned toward it. The guard who had fought the Gryhm with a torch was there. The torch was in one hand. In the other was a bow. There was an arrow on the string. None of that caught the prince's eye. What he noted was the look on the man's face. It was unmitigated terror. But that was not the only thing written there. The fear-widened eyes also showed determination and resolution. Despite his fear, despite the certainty that doing so would mean his death or worse, the man had come back to do his duty. Gammin realized he was seeing bravery in motion.

Gammin recognized the face, though he could not place it. His mind searched for a name, did not find it. He was about to command the man to go for a healer, but he reconsidered. If the Gryhm had entered the torch bearer, it would be better to keep him close.

There was so much to do, so much to consider! And there was no time. The king was dying. The Gryhm might be even now taking over some other unfortunate victim. Gammin was paralyzed with indecision.

Then Marin was there. His face appeared in the opening like the dawning of a new sun after cold rain. For the first time since the horror had begun, Gammin allowed himself to relax.

At another time, Marin might have quipped with his friend, might have said something like, "Need a little help?" This occasion called for something else. Looking around the tent, Marin asked, "What do you need?"

"It was a Gryhm, Mar, a Gryhm in a Silanni." He was going to say more, but found that he was panting, almost gasping for breath.

Marin started to demand that such a thing could never be. The look on Gammin's face—not to mention the three dead bodies—was enough to quell the denial. He crossed to the decapitated body, turned it over with a careful foot. A look of pained disquiet clouded his face. That look grew to a storm when Marin examined the disembodied head.

"He is of family Meod," Marin said, holding up the head by its matted and bloody hair. "Maybe it was Druna. He is one whom I've never met. Or, he was before the Gryhm got him. The Meod are far from here, near the valley we call the Hidden

Vale. That place lies far to the east, where the Forest touches the root of the Great Mountains."

At that moment, the king's healer swept into the tent. She ignored the three other forms crumpled on the ground and crossed immediately to Branden.

"I am fine," said the king, his voice surprising both Gammin and Marin. "I am fine. Leave off, Elma!" The tone was less firm than the words, his voice thick, impeded. It had the quality of mud flowing over stones. He did not sound fine.

"You are not fine." Elma's hands probed. Her lips curled into a frown. "You are going to be dead if you don't settle down right now and let me do my job. By the Three, you are as bad a patient as Gilmarun. Now shut up and lie down."

The healer, whom he had first met in Daur en Lammoth months before, looked at Gammin. "Get his shirt off."

Gammin reached for his knife. It was not at his hip. He looked around. The man with the torch and bow was standing close. As the prince groped for his knife, the torch bearer dropped his bow and fished out his own knife. He handed it to the prince, who grunted thanks. With a wet slice and two saturated tugs, the rags of the king's nightshirt fell away.

Desperate to help more, Gammin ventured, "Do you need arrenil? We could find some."

Elma cut him off savagely. "Are you become a *nemen* since last we spoke, youngling? Have you served seven years as apprentice to a healer? Have you passed the Nine Tests? No? I thought not. Arrenil won't do the king any good. But this will."

Reaching into a satchel that hung from her shoulder, the healer pulled out a fist-sized lump that looked like a ball of yarn. With practiced fingers, she began to unroll the lump. It turned out to be something like a net woven from ridiculously thick spider's silk.

Cutting a hand-sized portion from the ball, she arranged the netting carefully, making sure the strands of webbing touched the bleeding flesh. The strands began to swell as soon as they made contact. She repeated the process twice more. When all the offended flesh was obscured by netting, she set a cloth over the wound and poured some kind of liquid over it, something with a sharp smell that was strong and reassuring. After surveying her work, she placed her hands against the bandage and pressed.

Gammin let out a dismayed sigh. Everyone knew that is what you did when someone was bleeding! You put pressure on the spot. Why hadn't he thought of that? An image of the healer holding her hands up to stop a waterfall presented itself to Gammin. He pushed it aside.

There was nothing more he could do. He offered, "It was a Gryhm, Elma. It used a garrote. I think it stabbed him, too, in the shoulder." He stopped talking when he realized he was babbling the obvious.

At his words, the healers eyes shifted from the shoulder to the king's throat. One of her hands touched the livid ring of blood and aggravated tissue. She put her ear close, listened, then set her face against the king's chest, ignoring the blood. Without comment, she returned her attention to the shoulder wound.

Gammin tried to wrench his own attention to where it might do more good. He looked around the tent, mentally cataloging the various activities. There were more guards now, more torches. A handful of warriors had taken positions in a protective ring around the king's pallet. A ring of warriors from the Fifth encircled those. The sounds outside the tent told the prince that the camp was astir. Try as he might, Gammin could not corral his thoughts. They stampeded back toward the man lying in front of him faster than he could rope them.

Fine then, he thought, frustrated with his own lack of self-control. Marin is here. He will take care of everything. He always does. Gammin gave himself over and watched the healer.

Elma was working incredibly slowly, or so it seemed to the prince. Gammin was wrong about that. She was working as fast as she dared and not a bit faster. She searched Branden's face, watched the rhythm in the hollow of his throat, felt at his wrist for the Three Pulses—shallow for the body, middle for the mind, deep for the spirit. She moved her hand to the center of his abdomen, just below his ribs. She closed her eyes and waited, becoming very still, imagining that her arm was the trunk of a tree, her fingers the roots. Her breathing began to coincide with Branden's. Soon, her breaths were as short and ragged as his. Gradually, both of them started to breath deeper, more slowly.

At last, when she had almost forgotten she was not a tree, Elma caught the Fourth Pulse, the Secret Pulse. She watched it flow, noting its color, its texture, its vibrancy—though none of these were accurate descriptions of what she was sensing. What she found set her mind at ease. There was no sign of the Gryhm. The king was merely human, as he had always been. Human, royal, and insufferable… almost.

With that concern dealt with, the king's nemen focused herself on the ailing body. She relaxed, let go, allowed Ea's healing grace to flow into Branden. She imagined, as she always did, a river of health flowing out of an infinite ocean and into her patient. If time passed, she did not mark it.

When she had done all she could, Elma opened her eyes, breaking contact with the shimmering vision in her mind. She poked here, prodded there, all the while asking the king questions in a voice that seemed disinterested. She reached out and touched the hollow of the king's right shoulder. The bleeding had abated significantly, but there was plenty of fresh blood. She held her fingers close to her face. She smelled them, rubbed them together as if testing the blood, smelled them again before bending closer to sniff the wound.

"There's no poison," she said almost casually. The statement might have been a checkmark on a mental list. "The Old Ones do not use poison, by and large. Gryhm do. It gives them some special kind of satisfaction, I think. Dirty buggers."

"Dirty buggers…" The king repeated her words. His eyes were closed, his tortured voice hazy.

Elma frowned. She reached once more into her satchel, which she had placed on a table next to the king's pallet.

Withdrawing a small vial, she broke the wax seal and popped the cork off with her thumb. Placing her arm behind the king's head, she lifted it slightly.

"Drink this."

The king's eyes eased open. "No… I…." His voice was weaker than it had been a moment before. The words struggled to make it past the damaged throat.

"Shut up. Drink!"

The king did, then settled back into quiet submission.

To Gammin, Elma said, "We've got to work fast. I can't risk any more of the sedative. It slows the breathing and might kill him in his current condition."

She removed the cloth bandage carefully, pausing to make sure the bleeding did not freshen. Most of the netting was gone. Gammin did not know if it had dissolved in the wound or been pulled away by the cloth.

He stared past the nemen, watching as she explored the king's wound. He saw her index and middle fingers slide into the bloody hole. Though she was probably probing quite gently, to Gammin it seemed like she was prospecting for trout with a sharp stick under a weedy riverbank.

After the assessment, she nodded and withdrew her hand. She wiped it on a piece of the nightshirt. Gammin did not have to ask if it was bad. The king's face and neck were as pale as old bones. A ribbon of violent red showed where the skin of his throat had been ripped open by the garrote. Gammin had seen enough men die from blood loss to know what was happening. But he had faith in this nemen. She had saved his life twice.

"Get him up on that table. I'll not be sitting on the ground when I am sewing him back together."

She looked up and around, as if expecting the others to do the lifting. While Gammin, who was closest, bent to the work, she replaced the cloth bandage over the wound. She began to apply pressure again, leaning into the effort to strengthen the effect.

Gammin started to call for help. Before he could, a hand

grasped the king's other shoulder. It was the torch bearer. The man was proving to be quite helpful. Gammin rued the fact that he could not remember his name or where they had met. Together, they lifted the bleeding king and laid him on the table.

Elma reached out and took one of Gammin's hands. She set it against the wound. While he applied pressure, she arranged several items on a clean cloth and selected a small bottle of greenish liquid. She peered into the king's face. He must have awakened during the short move. His eyes were open again.

"Stubborn, aren't you? There's no news there. Fine, if you want to be awake, be awake. Just be still! This is going to hurt."

Without waiting for an acknowledgement, she brushed Gammin's hands away, lifted the sodden bandage, and spread the green liquid over the shoulder wound. The king's body jerked.

Elma exhaled a scoff. "Not yet, you big baby. That was just a cleanser and something to make the bleeding abate."

She set the bottle down, picked up a needle. She threaded it with a strand of pale cat gut. At least, that is what Gammin thought it was; he was not really sure. Everyone knew that army doctors sewed armies back together with cat guts, right? Or, was it sheep's gut? Maybe that was it.

Wiping the needle and the gut with some of the liquid, Elma signaled for Gammin and the torch bearer to lay hands of the King of Ehrylan.

"Hold him down."

The torch bearer, who had already handed his torch to some other warrior, bent over the king. Gammin did the same.

As they started to comply, the nemen looked into the king's eyes with compassion and concern. Those two cousins vanished under the onslaught of a smile.

"The real fun starts now. Ready?

Without any further comment, Elma, the king's healer, bent to her work.

II.

"I'll have none of those heathen witch doctors in here!"

Elma, whose life was dedicated to healing, took two aggressive steps toward the cluster of Arelese. They were waiting for permission to enter the king's tent. She might have been an enraged butcher swinging a clever. The new-comers scattered like milkweed seeds driven by a sudden gale. Among them was Theros and his personal healer.

Elma surveyed the closed tent flap with surly satisfaction. She was shaking her head stiffly, but Marin thought he detected a smile hiding on her face.

"Bloody pagans," she said.

A moment later, the head and shoulders of King Theros insinuated themselves into the tent. The rest of him followed. Elma glanced at him, her lips already curling into a snarl. Her glare gave way when she saw who it was and that he was alone. She returned to tending King Branden's shoulder wound.

Theros looked down into his friend's sleeping face. Two days had passed. Branden looked much better.

"You are doing a fine job, Elma. He is almost well enough to ride." The twitch that rippled across Elma's face made him elaborate. "If he had to."

Elma ignored him. She extended a hand and laid hold of Branden's chin, thumb on one side, fingers against his other cheek. She moved his head marginally, peering at something no one else could see. Then she adjusted the bandage she had just reapplied after checking and cleansing the wound.

"That's true, King Theros. He could ride today if he had to, but that would be foolish. Even your barbarous dancers and hooters would see that."

Elma was again referring to the Arelese healers. As far as she was concerned, they relied entirely too much on the old song and dance. But she also knew, as did everyone else in the Crescent, that those dancers and hooters were skilled healers.

Taking a deep breath, the nemen patted Branden's cheek irreverently, then gave her full attention to Theros.

"I don't mean it, you know," Her voice was firm but placatory. "Your healers do fine, better than fine, in fact. They do well. But…"

Theros set a hand on her shoulder. "But a horse can mind only one rider at a time?"

"Something like that. The Ehrylain say too many cooks spoil the stew. Me, I say too many healers can kill even a healthy patient." She paused a moment, allowing the mood to turn. "That is why I didn't want them in here. I don't want to complicate the healing by mixing methods, not now that the king is on the mend. But they have been very helpful. I wanted you to know."

King Theros knew that already. After receiving word of what happened, he had set his army on full alert and come to the king's tent with a handful of healers, two priests, three wise men, and a contingent of fierce-looking warriors. They had arrived while Elma was working on Branden's shoulder. She would have used just about any trained help she could get at that moment and had allowed the king and one healer to enter the tent. Theros had watched as the two healers toiled over Branden that first morning. He had seen the mutual respect grow as they stitched together the offended muscle and skin.

That was then, and this was now. Elma had grown more intolerant as the king recovered. Why? Who knew? Who could safely ask? Elma controlled admittance to the king's unconscious presence with an iron hand. She did not answer stupid questions.

As if she were unable to focus only on talking, Elma began gathering her instruments, liniments, and bandages. Last of all, she lifted a small stone pot into her satchel. It was a supply of snake oil the Arelese healer had provided. She treated it with respect. Swayed by the Arelese healer's earnest demands, she had used it on the king, sparingly at first, more liberally when the results were beneficial. The effects were promising, so much so that she suspected there was more venom than oil in the salve. She was eager to study it, hopeful she would be able to add it to her formulary. She was always on the lookout for the healing graces Ea hid among his works.

As he watched her, Theros asked, "How long do you plan to keep him drugged?"

"No longer, I think. I've only kept him going this long to make him more accommodating. He's past the place where I need his cooperation now. It's high time he wakes up, though sad I am to say it. He always creates a mess wherever he goes."

Shaking her head wistfully and lifting her kit, she added almost to herself, "I am starting to think I should have just stayed at home in Stormhaven."

She nodded at the Arelese king and turned toward the tent opening.

"But no. I thought this was a chance to winter in the kind lands, where winter's gums have few teeth."

She talked herself out of the tent.

The king had been very close to death the first day. Though his condition steadily improved, the situation begged an interesting question. With King Branden wounded and unconscious, who was in control of the army? Annen and Gilmarun, Branden's two senior generals, were far away. That left the captains, the senior of which was Eamehr. He was also sedated under the Elma's care. The next in line could have assumed the baton, but there was a complication no one knew how to unravel.

The name I have not mentioned was the obvious choice. There was Gammin, the Prince of Ehrylan. Should he be in charge while the king was indisposed? And, what if the king died? That would make Gammin the King of Ehrylan!

That was a thought Gammin brooded over during the quiet watches of the night while his father snored on the nearby pallet. Gammin was not interested in being in charge of the army. He was less interested in being king.

If the young prince had grown up next to his father, and if that father had openly been reigning as the King of Ehrylan, there would have been little doubt what needed to happen.

Gammin had not yet reached his majority, it is true—that would happen in a few months if he was still alive—but there was ample precedent for his assumption of the responsibilities of king and the crown that went with them. There had been younger kings and older princes in Ehrylan's long history.

Gammin had not grown up in a king's court, under the watchful eyes of an adoring kingdom. There was only the king's word and the story of an admittedly curious Old One to substantiate his birth. Even more difficult, most of the Ehrylain had little or no proof that Branden was even the son of Brand. Only the man's charisma and the fortunate memories a few old coots—like Annen, for instance—gave any substance to that

The young, rapidly-aging prince was left to ponder the enormous burden of kingship. It seemed to loom catastrophically close as his father breathed in and out, hour after hour.

The others—the true friends of the ailing king—made the best of it. They visited when they could, though their efforts to knit together the threads of leadership left little time. Of them all, Theramina spent the most time with the ailing king. She watched the nights with Gammin, waiting and guarding. Some of the time, the cousins spoke with each other. More often, they sat quietly, one of them occasionally dozing while the other kept watch.

Branden awoke the afternoon after Elma had spoken with King Theros. The following day, he was well on his way to regaining his senses. At noon the day after, he held council. Elma insisted it was too soon. The king ignored her.

He chaired the small meeting from his pallet, which had been raised and made more comfortable since he had been injured. Theros, Theden, and Theramina attended. Gammin and Marin were there, too. At least one of the young men had been with the king since the attack. The reason was because they feared the Gryhm might attack again. They did not share this concern with the others.

So, the king lay in council. What he wanted to know most

was what had gone wrong. How had an assassin infiltrated so easily into the very center of their camp?

The answer to that question was easy. The assassin had been an Old One, likely a Silanni. One can more easily stop the wind from blowing or the rain from falling than deter a Silanni. The people with the king knew that. Accordingly, they wasted little time on placing blame or recriminations.

Hundreds had been questioned. No one knew the Old One. No one had seen him before. Where he had come from remained a mystery. There was no mystery as to how he had gotten into the camp or into the king's tent. A trail of bodies articulated that information quite clearly.

Marin had been the first to realize something was amiss that black morning. He had begun the day's activities upon arriving at the company's central command post, which was only a moment's walk from their tent. Almost as soon as he got there, a runner arrived from one of the perimeter guard posts. One of the roving patrols had failed to check in. The sentries at the post had followed procedures. Both members of the patrol had been found. They were dead, one with a cut throat, one with a stab wound at the base of his neck.

Marin sent word to alert the rest of the camp immediately. He sent a runner to notify Gammin and the king; that was the man who had tried to fight the Gryhm with his torch.

It was a long way from the perimeter, where the dead patrol was found, to the king's tent. Four more bodies were revealed the route; all of them were guards who had been on duty. Like the perimeter patrol, the second pair had been killed quickly and hidden under sparse cover. Another two bodies, these not hidden at all, were found just outside the rear of the king's tent. They had been assigned to walk circuits around that block.

It was still full dark when the searchers had found the bodies of the last two guards. They weren't even cold yet. Those same searchers found the man-sized slice in the side of the tent—from the outside in the dark. No one inside the tent noticed it with all the other excitement.

Those six deaths explained most of what needed to be

explained. No one thought earnestly to question whether the guards had been properly vigilant. It was, after all, a Silanni who had perpetrated the murders, though no one knew that for sure—except maybe Marin, and he was not telling. It had also been a Gryhm. No one who had seen it fighting with arrows protruding from its torso could doubt that.

Gryhm occupied much of the conversation that first meeting. As it continued, a blanket of anxieties wrapped Branden's mind. Old words, nightmare words often remembered and never enjoyed, rang out in his head.

There is a Gryhm among us!

What thought could be more chilling? He had heard those words in his own mental voice years ago, at a feast in King Theru's lodge. A decade later, he had said the same words to Eamehr, Gilmarun, and his other most-trusted captains and confidants. That had been in Stormhaven, when Therana was still with him. And now, sitting on a field of victory in northern Rath, the words had been spoken again.

There was—or had been—a Gryhm among them.

They were currently discussing whether or not it was the same Gryhm that Branden encountered in Arel. Of this, Branden was sure. The others, who, except for Theros, had not yet been born when Branden and Therana fought that battle, were not yet convinced.

"How could it be the same fiend, uncle?"

The words belonged to Theramina. She had been the picture of solicitude during the meeting, rising often to care for her pallet-ridden uncle, adjusting his pillows, massaging his neck and shoulders. If Elma had attempted the same tasks, she would have received the sharp edge of Branden's tongue. The young princess had tamed the lion.

"It was the same Gryhm," answered the king, his voice raw, broken like a rusty tree saw. "It was Rauchur. He told you his name."

"Gammin told me that Gryhm often lie for their own ends. Perhaps this one was lying?"

The king's eyes flitted to his son's face for an instant. How had this boy killed Rauchur? By all accounts, it was the third Gryhm he had faced, the second he had killed. How many had he, Branden, faced or killed? He knew the number. One never forgot an encounter with a Gryhm.

He said, "That is true enough, Theramina. They lie with every word. My father used to tell us that Gryhm deceive even when they tell the truth. But, I have no doubts; this was Rauchur. I could feel him when we were struggling. I could sense him."

"It is a dark cloud over the moon," said Marin, firmly. "It is the pelt of a wolf stinking with old rain and decay."

Branden eyed his seer. When no one spoke, he groped for his cup with an absent hand and took a tentative swallow. After another, he nodded.

"Yes, like that. You have fought Rauchur?"

"No, not him. Another. You know the tale, King Branden. Elma's magic potions have made you temporarily forget."

"I remember."

"I felt that, too," Gammin offered. "This time, I mean. At first, I thought it was a smell, but…" He had no need to elaborate, having previously related the events and feelings of that twinight morning to everyone in the tent.

The king cleared his throat in preparation to speak again. The effort sent a jolt of pain through his throat and chest, as if a giant hand had seized him and squeezed violently. Just as quickly, the pain was gone. Until next time.

"Sometimes the Gryhm and the Lessor Gryhm smell bad. Only the Arch Gryhm have a care for their victims, and that is not for their victim's sake. It might be because they plan to inhabit them longer. Or, it might be that they are smarter than the other Gryhm."

Gammin waited for Marin, knowing the woodcutter's son had something to offer on that account. But Marin was not talking. His eyes were looking at the space between his knees.

Gammin said, "Chilshan was an Arch Gryhm, or so I have been told. He was put together pretty well. I was not in very good shape when he interrogated me, but he seemed more like a prince than a monster. He was not at all like the first Gryhm we killed. What was his name, Marin?"

Marin looked up as if startled. His mind replayed what had been asked and retrieved the name easily. He knew Gammin remembered it.

"Grachul. The others called him Smiley. Llyren said Grachul was a Lesser Gryhm."

"I wish Llyren was here now," offered Gammin, running a hand through his hair. "He seemed to know a lot about Gryhm."

The moment passed without further comment. When no one else spoke, the king began again.

"Rauchur is a full Gryhm, not a Lessor Gryhm." He stretched the verb—is—reminding them that Gryhm, like all Everbourne, do not die. "He did not take care of the bodies he used when I met him before. What puzzles me is why this body should be different. You said there was no sign it had been neglected."

"Here's what I think," said Marin, interjecting with some force. He had realized that Gammin wanted him to participate more, so he was giving it a shot. He seldom volunteered words in the presence of King Branden. Accordingly, he had everyone's attention right away.

"The Gryhm was new to Druna. It must have taken him recently."

Gammin interrupted. "So recently that it had not yet had time to make poison."

Marin agreed. "That is consistent. Anyway, apart from the injuries inflicted on him here, Druna's body was in good shape. Most importantly, he was not yet forty. That is one of the reasons I think it was Druna." He saw by the looks in their eyes that none except Gammin knew why that information led him to that conclusion. He left them to guess if that is where their minds took them.

Again, Marin was interrupted, this time by Theros.

"How the fiend came to its last victory is less important than how it was brought to ruin. In its defeat, we have our victory. We must not forget that our victories are short, and their defeats easily mended."

"I agree," stated Branden, as if his words were an end to discussion. "Rauchur was still a young Gryhm, if that makes any sense. It hadn't had time to come into its full power in Druna. That is one reason he was so easily defeated."

Gammin, who, apart from his father, was the only one in the tent that had been present during the fight, had to restrain the almost irresistible urge to jerk. Easily defeated?

Branden's voice struggled on through a broken tunnel. "You are right, Theros. Victory over evil is always short-lived when that victory comes at the hands of men."

The king lapsed into a silence that was so long the others might have concluded he had fallen asleep. But they knew that was not true. His eyes were windows to emotions that floated there like lost minnows swimming among unshed tears.

When the silence became troublesome, Gammin said, "Sire?"

Turning to his son, Branden said, "We may have seen Rauchur's work before. There is much you don't know about your mother." The king stopped, shook his head. "That is foolish talk. You know almost nothing. What do you know of why your mother left Stormhaven?"

"I've heard only a little. They say that it is not talked about." He paused, then added, "That is what they say when they are not talking about it." He considered putting on his grin, decided against it.

The king watched him. He had heard about Gammin's sense of humor but had seldom seen it. The boy did not joke around him. That was just as well. The king did not know if he approved of senses of humor these days.

Seeing the serious aspect to his father's face, Gammin mentally sat up.

"They say there was a Gryhm involved and that she went away to keep the baby safe."

"The baby?" Branden's question had a jagged edge. But it was not hurtful. It spoke of sadness.

"Yes, sir," said Gammin. That part came out easily enough. The rest emerged in a gushing stammer. "The baby, your unborn son, sire."

"My unborn son?"

If Branden had not been allowed to see Gammin's humor much, he had plenty of experience with his son's flashing indignation. He was not surprised when Gammin's reply came in a stronger voice.

"Yes, sire, your unborn son. Am I saying that wrong? Missing something? What is it?"

The king shook his head. He sighed, massaged his face with the palms of both hands.

"That unborn child was you. You know that."

Gammin might have not heard his father's words for all the reaction he showed. He stared back into the king's eyes, undaunted, until the king spoke again.

"Have you never wondered why your father would send his wife and unborn son away from their home when she was so close to her time?"

"It has crossed my mind. To be honest, there has been a lot to occupy my thoughts these days. I knew you must have had a good reason."

The truth was that Gammin had avoided thinking about that situation as much as possible. As pleased as he was to have a father and to know who his mother had been, that knowledge had come with a heavy cost. It was a price he was not certain he was prepared to pay.

"I've wondered more at the thought of a Gryhin in Stormhaven than I have about why you sent your wife... us... away. As far as I am concerned, away from a Gryhin is a good place to be."

Gammin's face changed as if something new had occurred to him. "Marin and I talked about it. We thought maybe it was Charshan, since he was so close, there in Daur en Lammoth."

"Charshan came later," answered the king immediately, as if he was eager to leave behind the subject of Therana's departure. "He came when Dauroth decided to build a fortress in the Badlands."

The king's eyes blazed in sudden defiance. "It was our rage and toil that drove him to that." He raised a balled fist three hands high from the pallet and hastily set it at rest again. Pain chased him back into a more restful position.

"There had been several close calls in the castle, occurrences that threatened my wife but could not be explained—fires, falling stones and masonry, a stampede of horses. There were other attempts on her life, though we did not identify them as such. Not yet. It was Stryn who suggested a Gryhm might be involved."

Stryn was, and had been for as long as anyone could remember, the most famous faelyth in all the land. He was renowned for his wisdom and great age as much as his musical ability. He appeared here or there according to his whim, sometimes at a king or queen's court, sometimes at the hut of an itinerant shepherd. No king or queen in the Crescent would turn him away, save Dauroth only, and he was no real king.

"During those days, Stryn used to stop by Stormhaven from time to time. He said it was to give Therana another flute lesson, but he was keeping an eye on us. Those were early days. Dauroth's grip was strong and fresh. We were still fighting to establish a foot-hold. Stryn thought it might be a Gryhm that was troubling us, an assassin sent by Dauroth. I do not know how he knew that or even if he really knew it. But as soon as he said it, I began to understand.

"I do not know if it was the same Gryhm we killed in Arel. Whether it was Rauchur or not did not seem to matter at the time." He eyed his son. "It seems more important now."

Gammin spoke into the sudden quiet.

"Did the accidents stop, sire?" He held up a hand. "What I really want to know is if you caught the Gryhm." As he waited for an answer, it occurred to Gammin that he had learned to ask the wrong question from his old mentor.

"You sound certain that Stryn was right."

"You wouldn't have told us all this otherwise, sire."

"That is true enough. Perhaps I am wearier than I thought.

You may excuse my thick-headedness, if you please."

Gammin nodded. To Marin, the young prince looked decidedly regal in that moment, as if he, Gammin, were the aged king, his father the stripling. Marin had been watching and listening carefully, for he had begun to understand. Once again, the woodcutter's son was the first to see it.

His voice ringing louder than he had intended, Marin said, "How did you catch him?"

The king laughed and paid the price. His hand jerked before he could restrain it, though it did not make it all the way to his throat.

"Trust that you would know, Old One. It was the Children of the Forest who caught him, which seemed very ironic to me at the time. It was only a boy, a child Gryhm."

The unmistakable voice of Elma blew through the walls of the tent.

"He's doing what?" The question—more of a demand, really—was followed by a spate of curse words and phrases that would have delighted any collection of farmers, felons, and priests.

The king looked around the circle of his friends quickly. "My doom approaches. But it is not premature. I grow fatigued. I think I will rest now, willingly, and if my will prevails, without Elma's help." He coughed to clear his throat, winced with the pain of it. "On second thought, I might be able to wrestle some of the less loathsome stuff down."

The others got to their feet in poorly disguised haste. As Elma swept into the tent, the Arelese, followed by Marin, filed out with heads bent and eyes averted.

Only Gammin stayed.

III.

The next day the king met with all his captains. He laid the plans for departure. The fact that Elma did not resist much was a testament to the king's recovery, though he was still noticeably frail.

Theros and Theramina would be accompanying them to Arathai. Theden was staying behind to guard this part of the border. That's what the Arelese prince had been doing when all this began.

Marin did not share Gammin's delight when he heard the news. In the outer chambers of his heart, where darkness and light wait for admittance, Marin wished that Theramina was staying behind, not Theden. There was just something about her that he did not like. He could not quite pin it down. Perhaps it was the fact that he liked everything about her that disturbed him the most. But likes or dislikes did not matter. The seer had no vote.

There was something important—so said the king—that had to be accomplished before the march to the coast began. Gammin's bodyguard was now short two men. They had to be replaced immediately. The recent presence of a Gryhm among them was sufficient testament to that.

Gammin argued back that he was concerned for the safety of the men. The duty had already proved fatal. The king countered that it was the privilege of those men to die for their kingdom.

Gammin might have argued some other avenue, but he knew his father was right. Hoping to appease the king, he offered to let Marin pick two able warriors who might delight in such duty. The king agreed, with the stipulation that he have final approval.

That is where discussions broke down. Truth to tell, the process of discussion was the problem. Branden was frustrated that he had to argue for his will to be done; he was king. Gammin thought his father was intentionally being a turd in the kitchen. They were both right.

They were in the king's tent late in the afternoon. Marin was with them. In Gammin's mind, Marin was there to present the names of the new guards. The king intended that Marin was there to offer picks for approval, or more likely, rejection.

Branden, somewhat predictably, had not approved either

choice. That is when things came to a head.

King Branden knew he was becoming agitated. He could feel his pulse at the side of his throat, where the garrote had cut him worst, and in the hollow of his shoulder. The king did not want to become agitated, which was a little unusual for him. He enjoyed a bit of tension, usually. But right now, he was trying to be a good father—whatever that meant. In this case, it meant he was trying to forge a closer bond with the boy who was his son. It was proving more difficult than he had anticipated.

Gammin was currently responding to the king's rejection. "Yes, I do expect you to accept our decision. Marin doesn't need to justify his choices. I never doubt what he says. No one does."

"You trust him that much?"

Gammin tilted his head to one side and peered across the corner of his eye. The look was as good as a rebuke, though less aggressive.

King Branden barked a truncated grunt. "Not that way, boy. I know you trust him with your life. I trust him with that too, and mine, if you care to know. I mean can you trust that his advice is good without any evaluation of your own."

"Did you trust Annen's advice?"

The king answered at once. "Most of the time, I did. When I did not, I was usually wrong. But not always. What is your point? Calen—Annen—was a man by any measure. You and Marin are still young and making, not yet twenty summers old."

Branden held up a hand. He took a deep breath, pushed it out through a pleasant, if forced, smile. "Make no mistake. I do not say you are unskilled or inexperienced. You are one of my captains, the youngest, and of them, you have served in our army the least. That alone shows you have earned my respect."

Gammin produced a small bow. He recognized his father's genuine intention. Speaking more slowly than before, he said, "We are the same age you and Annen were."

The king considered. He knew he was beaten on that count.

A lessor man might have prevaricated. Branden just nodded slowly while he selected different ground.

"My son, we were brought up in the houses of kings, among men of battle and great experience, during a time of war. It was different."

"My father, it is the same."

Ea blessed their earnest hearts then, or there might have been trouble. Both were striving to find a peace amid tossing waves of emotion. Branden could have erupted there, or he might have just continued to build the wall, but he did not.

Speaking from his heart and without any rancor, Gammin's father said, "Tell me how it is the same. What king did you know? Where was his castle?"

"You were brought up a king's son, in a king's home, to be a king. I wasn't brought up in a castle or even a city. I didn't have a bed to sleep on most nights, not until I was older."

The king nodded to this apparent acquiescence. This was not his first confrontation of wits with his son. He knew there would be some unexpected twist, some sudden corner that changed the playing field. He was like Calen in that respect. And like Calen, he would eventually understand. He allowed Gammin to continue.

"Marin was not raised in a castle either, nor even a city. He was raised in the Forest by the Old Ones. He was raised by his own people, in his own land. As I was. As you were. We were not brought up in castles, but we were brought up among men and women of battle, men and women with great experience, in a time of war. That much is the same."

Gammin's arguments were inflaming his own emotions. They showed in his face as he continued to speak. "I will tell you a difference, though. You were young in the time of a king who loved you and cared for his people. We are young in a time when there is no king and where even the language you spoke as a child is outlawed. You tell me, father, that our upbringing might impose limits on our judgment. You are wrong. Our heritage is our strength. Certainly, that is true for Marin. Who better to read a man's heart by looking into his eyes than one of the Children of the Forest?"

Branden knew he could win this fight. He was certain he could impose his will on this young man, formidable though he was. The price would be high, much too high. He was at once disquieted and pleased by his son's firm stance. The boy stood his ground without becoming overly defensive. There was certainly hope for him, if he lived long enough to grow into it. Or, he corrected himself, if I live long enough to train him. Branden blinked away the thoughts of his own mortality, which were understandably more vivid lately.

He asked, "May I discuss it with Marin?"

"You are king."

Branden's growl started at once. The response was silenced when he saw the grin on Gammin's face. The king shrugged his shoulders and shook his grayish mane. At that moment, he looked more like a father than a king.

The frustrated king turned and stepped over to where Marin had been trying to seem transparent. He had heard every word, and the king knew it. It was no use trying to scamper like a lizard for some small crack in the floor. His only option was to bluff.

As the king approached, Marin stood up. He was on his feet when Branden said, "The prince is pleased to accept your recommendation. I am less so. One of your choices has had dubious reports about him. The other is no older than you two. Given the recent circumstances, I would like to know what, in particular, sets these men apart from the others."

Marin had been First Spear of Gammin's cohort among the Tallea, a rank that was roughly equivalent to a company's second in command in the armies of Ehrylan. He was used to making reports, even to kings—if the Elder of the Tallenlaust can be held to be a king.

"Dubious reports, King Branden? You are referring to Leanord?"

The king nodded once. The movement jumped across the space between them as a terse, impatient word.

"Leanord first came to my attention on the way to

Mendolas. He was part of the surprise attack. I watched him closely for a while, especially during the raid and the battle that came after. What I saw showed me that I was wasting my time. He was picked for the raid. He survived. Those are worth noting. It was no different in Elosai. He fought hard and with bravery." Marin broke with his self-imposed discipline and looked toward Gammin with a small chuckle. "It is true that his bravery outpaces his skill, but that will change."

The king did not speak.

"I came upon him when we went back to see if we could rescue Eamehr's men. Leanord and two of his squad mates had organized three units out of stragglers. They were fighting back toward where they thought you... where they thought the king would be. They were completely wrong, by the way. They were headed south, toward the enemy, but they were doing their best." As an afterthought, Marin added, "No matter which way they were going, they were killing the enemy."

The king nodded.

Marin continued, "He was with us when we came upon the King of Arel. Leonard went with me when I called for help against the soldiers Gammin told me to stop. The day you were attacked by the Gryhm, Leanord was at the command post waiting for his assignment when I got there. The report of the dead sentries came in. Leanord was there. I sent him as a runner to tell Gammin what had happened.

"King Branden, from what I have been told, Leanord was the only one who tried to face the Gryhm. When it drove him away, he came back again. He was smart enough to bring a distance weapon with him the second time."

The whole report sounded to Gammin like something his friend had already planned out. It had been delivered in the over-eager, yet still oddly matter-of-fact, cadence of a soldier. He kept his eyes solidly front for most of it. Both of those aspects changed when the woodcutter's son turned his head to look directly in Branden's eye.

"I chose Leanord for this post for one reason. He deserves it."

Gammin, and Marin too, had expected the king to bend under the weight of this report. The king did no such thing. Branden did not blink as he said, "He is one of the soldiers who came from Dauroth's army at Twofords. Can you trust him?"

"There is that. But there is also this. Seeing him rise to a place of trust gives hope to the others who share his recent past. But, more importantly, Leanord was in Dauroth's army; he has more experience around Gryhm than anyone here, except maybe you."

That argument penetrated Branden's guard. "You think that's why he was able to stand up to the Gryhm."

"I do."

The king apparently decided the subject of Leanord, though he did not share his decision. He shifted to the second recommendation.

"And the other, the young one?"

"Andryg."

"Yes."

Gammin said, "Annen mentioned him. You remember. He said some of your warriors were pretty young and pretty skilled."

The king said, "As I recall, Calen's words were 'some of the men are too young to be properly called men, though they have skill enough, and more than enough courage.' I remember the report. I do not remember the boy. He was with us at Stormhaven?"

"We were told he was, King Branden," answered Marin, intentionally forestalling Gammin's reply. He suspected the king knew all about Andryg already. "We did not arrive at Stormhaven until recently. He must have been there if he was in the riding—Annen's cavalry. That is heady company. They were the point of your spear."

The king's eye traced a line from Marin's face to Gammin's. "He fought at Twofords and at Mendolas? Here, too?"

Marin nodded, then seeing the king was not looking at him, added, "Yes, King Branden."

Beaten, the king shrugged. He looked back and forth between the two young men twice, unintentionally mimicking a large, stiff shaking of the head. "So be it, then. Let us hope past deeds are an accurate mirror."

That is how Leanord, who first came to attention as a rabble rouser, and Andryg, who was marginally too young to be considered a man, became members of Gammin's personal guard.

11. STRYN

I.

The kings fought three more engagements along the road to the Bay of Arai. They were only skirmishes, so said the older warriors. Certainly, they were much smaller than the Battle of Elosai.

The first occurred a day's march south of the valley along the River Road. A scouting party of Arelese riders came upon a few dozen soldiers who were holding a fortified camp. The Themera destroyed them. After searching the empty encampment, they rode back with what they thought was joyous news. Instead, they found that the kings were under attack.

Dauroth's forces hit Branden's column while the main army was negotiating a quagmire of three streams. It was a well-chosen spot for an ambush. They struck the column from the rear, after most of the army had passed through the marshy area. Gammin and the Fifth had been near enough to be among the first responders. The fighting was fierce as the Fifth struggled to deal with the foe until others could arrive to help.

The speed and mobility of the Themera, who encircled the attackers and rode them down, won the day.

The final skirmish happened two days later, when another group of soldiers assaulted the column. There was little planning or skill in that attack. It was more desperate than threatening, perhaps even a delaying tactic. The Fifth was on point that day, as it happened. They bore the brunt and turned the attack.

King Branden arrived at the gates of Arathai with more panoply than he had heretofore experienced. It might have been Brand—or even Andur—that King Kappelli was welcoming. The road, which runs in those parts near enough to the Silver River for travelers to see the water, was lined with cheering crowds. Banners and flags adorned the trees. Nearer the walls of the city, the Rathian City Guard were arrayed in ranks on either side of the gate, the sun glinting from their weapons and armor.

The peaceful arrival was possible only because Dauroth's forces had steadily—and literally—bled off during the last week. When Branden turned his horse's nose west toward the coast, the enemy troops had pulled up stakes entirely. It was not, however, a frantic retreat. The soldiers took the time to carry away their valuables. What they left behind was mostly useless, as were the scars their armies inflicted on the face of the land.

One likely reason for Dauroth's withdrawal from the immediate area was the size of the force Branden brought with him. With each victory, a tide of enemy soldiers and support personnel swelled his ranks. There was no problem trusting most of the previously conscripted, loyal Ehrylain. The joy on their faces and the spring in their step, even when encumbered by new weapons and gear, was testament to that.

With the addition of the Arelese cavalry, the rightful King of Ehrylan had, for the first time in this war, a respectably sized army. It was not yet as large as the armies of Brand, but it was growing almost daily. No one forgot that Brand, with his larger, more experienced armies, had been defeated by

BATTLE FOR THE SOUTHLAND

Dauroth.

King Theros rode west with Branden with only a token force, or so he put it. The escort was a thousand riders. That the King of Arel's personal escort was almost the size of Branden's entire army was not discussed where either king might hear.

Branden's army might had numbered more after the battle at Valley Elosai. He left many of the former enemies who wanted to rejoin their fellow Ehrylain. The new volunteers were recommended to the military leaders of Mendolas. The king did not leave unspoken his thoughts about how they were to be used. He also remembered the rest of his kingdom and sent many warriors to Twofords and to Gilmarun at Stormhaven.

As soon as they entered the gates of Castle Arathai, Gammin and Marin were whisked away to a suite of rooms that could have accommodated both of them, all six of Gammin's guards, and a litter of suckling pigs. Each young man might have had his own lavish suite, but King Branden had given up trying to separate his son from the woodcutter's some time ago.

Sleeping was what they most wanted after the long journey. Before that could happen, there was much to be done. It started with a long bath in a man-made pool of warm, flowing water that took up a whole room by itself. After that, they had been forced to dress in fresh, new, uncomfortable clothing. The clothing was necessary, it turned out, because they were paraded—literally—before King Kappelli. That had gone well, as far as such things go. Gammin did not talk much, which suited him fine.

Gammin was presented to and accepted by Kappelli, who was a bent old man with a close-cropped, white beard and a twinkling eye. The appearance of a previously unknown heir might have raised pointed questions. However, Gammin needed no proof that he was Branden's son. Branden's claim was enough to any who took Branden as king. Gammin made a different kind of claim to that unwanted honor. You had only to see him interact with people to want to be near him yourself. Once you spent time there, you were happy to know he was the heir to the kingdom. This was nothing new. The kinship that developed in Twofords between our family of misfits was knit together by Gammin as surely as pieces of a fine garment are joined by stitching. He made us one from many. We felt it when he was gone.

That first day had been arrivals, baths, meetings, and feasts. The feasts were not just for the stomach. There were banquets of smell, sound, and sight. Color was everywhere. It was captured and liberated in the architecture and the art.

Gammin and Marin had never seen so many paintings. They would like to have seen more but were too busy at other things. The fineness of finery was of no interest to them. They had no scale with which to judge it if it had been. They were taken by the brightness of the art, the colors, the sounds. It all seemed too untarnished to their stained eyes.

King Branden sat in the Castle Arathai's largest performance hall. A few days had passed since he arrived at the castle. He was enjoying the music. Having just left yet another improbably lavish feast, his stomach was full, his wine glass half-empty, and his desire to do much else absent. On King Branden's right was King Theros of Arel. On his left was King Kappelli of Rath, their host.

The performance had been superb so far. That was no surprise. Few kings in the history of the Crescent could have boasted of a more-celebrated stage. In addition to Nandea, who was performing at the moment, Stryn was in the hall. It was rumored he might perform tonight as well. That would be something to see. The two were the most-renowned faelyth of their generation. Of the two, Stryn was the superior. He had been the best faelyth in the Crescent for as long as anyone could remember.

At the moment, Nandea was the only performer on the raised platform at the center of the hall. She was playing her finalla and singing, or would resume doing so as soon as the applause lessened. As soon as she struck the first chord of her next song, King Branden knew she had embarked upon another retelling of the Battle of Elosai.

Having heard that tale a number of times already—he was not sure how many, though he knew the number could not be counted on a single hand unless he used knuckles instead of fingers—he was free to direct his attention elsewhere. His eyes automatically ticked off the faces of his senior commanders then turned to his son, who sat one row in front and just to the side of his position.

Gammin looked content. He was certainly entranced by the music. To either side, the young prince was bracketed by a princess. On his left was his cousin, Theramina. To his right sat Princess Karene of Rath, Kappelli's only child. She was a year or two younger than Gammin. When Kappelli finally died, she would be queen. The Rathians, like the Tallea of the Tallenlaust, care not whether a man or woman rule; their hope is in the beneficence of the ruler rather than the gender.

When Branden looked at Marin, what he saw took him by surprise. The young Old One's face resembled a quartermaster's face when she had been told there was a new platoon to be provisioned and billeted. The king, glad of the distraction, pondered. What would cause such a look? There could be no fault with the food or the entertainment. Perhaps the woodcutter's son had fallen for one of the princesses. They were both eligible, and why not? He was a seer, after all. Let him have one. There were two princesses and only one prince. If the four of them sorted it out among themselves, so much the better. That would solve a delicate conundrum King Branden had been considering lately. There was also a princess in Norlan. She was another interesting alternative. Gammin was assured of a good match.

That thought took Branden's mind on a pleasant journey during which he did not hear the rendition of his latest significant victory, which is a sad testament for poor Nandea. In the place where his mind went, there were legions of people from across all the Crescent. The air was a thunder of cheers as they celebrated the reunification of the kingdoms of the Crescent, united again for the first time in a thousand years. Above the cheers, and above the heads of the adoring subjects, lion banners danced and roared as the heir of Andur sat once again on the Throne and lifted the Scepter.

Would his son be ready when the time came, able when the need came, willing when the worst came? There was so much he needed to teach the boy and so little time.

Branden's grandiose ruminations were interrupted when Nandea, lifted up on a rousing dose of adulation, stood to take a bow. When the listeners stopped cheering, King Kappelli held up a hand.

"Honored guests, we have a special treat. As you have no doubt heard, Stryn entered the city yesterday. He has consented to play for us. Welcome him now."

The near-relative of the cheers Branden had just been imagining in his head erupted like a gushing waterfall. Nothing happened for a while. When the room had grown quiet again, a figure emerged from out of the shadows. He was dressed entirely in tight-fitting, comfortable-looking clothes of deepest black. His cloak was an ebony shadow, its edges trimmed in silver.

Stryn mounted the steps with quick dignity, too quickly for someone who was supposed to be the age of dirt. He kissed Nandea's cheek before turning to collect his finalla from its stand. Then he turned and captured the crowd with his smile.

His face was not the face of an old man.

II.

As the hall emptied, the four young companions found they had been forgotten by the three kings. That was fine with Gammin and Marin. They were tired of the endless meetings and audiences that seemed to delight their elders. What the two young men wanted most was to be left to their own devices so they could explore. They had never been any place that offered this castle's odd delights. Stormhaven did not even come close, though it was a better fortress.

So far, there had been less time for exploration than almost anything else. They had, as yet, seen only a small portion of the castle and its grounds. That was something Princess Karene was attempting to remedy.

None of the princesses, princes, or woodcutter's sons wanted to go to bed. Having sat for so long—first at the feast, then at the performance—they were tired of sitting. They wandered the inner castle, exploring enough so that even Marin and Gammin were temporarily satisfied.

Theramina was familiar with even this innermost part of the castle. The forced tolerance Gammin saw on her face reminded him of how he felt during the endless meetings. But even the hallways were impressive to Gammin, who was from a backcountry village that could have fit within the castle's curtain walls. He continued to be amazed the higher, deeper, or farther they traversed. Much of what he saw delighted him; some was more troubling, raising questions in his mind. Was this how King Brand had lived? Did Dauroth live this way in the castle, far to the north, in Kingsholm? Was this how he, Gammin, would be expected to live if he had to be king? That last thought persisted as they moved from one wonder to another, troubling him like the mental equivalent of a stuffed nose.

Princess Karene was an excellent hostess. She was a smallish person whose head came up almost to Gammin's shoulder. Unlike Theramina, Karene had no warrior in her. She was perky, though only in small doses that escaped the courtly aspect she adopted most of the time.

That courtly aspect might have slowed the process of working things out between the four of them. Apart from Theramina, who was nobody's idea of a storybook princess, neither boy had ever come anywhere near a princess before. Unlike Theramina, Karene was a princess to fit the stories. But they got on well enough once the two Southlanders saw the other side of her coin.

The weather being nippy, they stayed indoors. Eventually, they came upon a library. Marin thought it a cozy place and wanted to linger. A tapestry hung on one wall, a rug on the other. The tapestry depicted a trio of riders bearing down on the observer, their axes raised for throwing. The rug was the hide of some enormous animal Marin recognized only from his readings. He was wondering why anyone would hang a rug on the wall of a sumptuous castle when Gammin's voice pulled him out of his own thoughts.

"Is that Theros?" He was standing in front of the tapestry.

"Yes, it is," answered Karene. "He was young then, Prince Gammin."

"Who are the other two?"

Theramina answered, settling her hand around Gammin's upper arm. "You see Theru and his father, Thelas. Here are three generations of my family." She looked very proud. It made Gammin want to smile.

"I've heard a lot about Theru in the last few months," he said, "This must have been around the time King Branden...my father... was in Arel?"

Theramina bit her lip, considering. "The story I have heard is that this tapestry was commissioned by King Kappelli when Theru became king." The Princess of Arel looked at the Princess of Rath pointedly, as if Karene had told that story a few too many times.

Karene was oblivious to the look and to the implication. Focusing on Gammin, she nodded vigorously. "My father, who was also a very young man, had it made. He was new to the throne too, at that time. His mother, the queen, died during the wars." She took charge of Gammin's other arm. "There was much change in the Crescent back then."

"That is interesting," said Marin.

Gammin turned to him, breaking the subtle bonds the young ladies had placed on him. "Why didn't we think of that before?"

"Think of what?" asked Theramina.

Gammin said, "Dauroth was at war with Ehrylan. That's how we see it, anyway. He deposed King Brand; we all know that. But think about it. During the same period, Rath's queen also died, and Arel's king. Coincidence?"

Before the ladies could comment, Marin added, "I wonder if the King of Norlan was killed, too."

Gammin and Marin fell silent as they searched their memories. Though their education went beyond that of most persons of that day, what had happened a generation before in a kingdom far to the north was beyond them.

Karene knew. She had been forced to learn such facts. She could not tell you that a tree producing twenty apples a month for three months will give you sixty apples, but she did know how many bushels of grapes and casks of wine could come from each acre of land and which regions of her kingdom produced which product best. To each their own.

"I don't think so," she said. "Andheim was Scorl of the Norlaners before and after that war. They don't call their king a king, you know. He's a scorl, and he is never a she. Women are not allowed to rule in Norlan. It's insulting."

The young men nodded. They had known those facts in some far corner of their minds.

"Coincidence, maybe," said Gammin, returning the discussion to the subject of assassinations.

Marin finished the thought. "It's worth considering."

"Yes, quite!" Karene, agreed, though she did not understand the quick alteration in subject and mood. These two men were new to her, so grim and yet so courteous in their own rustic way. They seemed able to sit with silence in a way that the young men with whom she had contact could not.

As if he had not even heard her, Gammin mused, "In Ehrylan, we tend to think that we are the only ones affected by Dauroth. We don't remember often enough that other kingdoms were also affected. Who knows how much else happened, in places we've never even heard of?"

"You think that way because Dauroth won in Ehrylan," asserted Theramina. "History is rewritten by the victors. That is what Stryn says. That is why songs and tales are important."

No one made a sound for several heartbeats. Then, as the expectance swelled, Gammin said, "I never thought about that either."

Marin said, "We should come here more often."

A lively discussion of how the other kingdoms of the Crescent had fared during the last generation followed. There had been more conflict than either young warrior knew. Karene was pleased at the quick conversation. Assuring these guests had a pleasant experience was her primary concern. It was an added bonus that she was also having a fine time.

Eventually, their thoughts returned to the evening's performance and to Stryn. Theramina and Karene had met the man any number of times, knew him well. They were in no awe of him, save the reasonable respect that anyone feels for a skilled person. Gammin and Marin, on the other hand, had grown up with the legend of Stryn. They had never met him personally. They asked a stream of questions, listening happily as the two ladies regaled them with tales of the faelyth. This was a rare opportunity for the Southlanders, since these tales could—mostly—be believed. The ladies were describing events they had seen with their own eyes.

Marin took the opportunity to toss out the question in which he had the most interest.

"One thing I don't understand is the age thing. Stryn is an old man, right? Like your father, Princess Karene, if you will excuse the example."

Karene arched her eyebrows and lifted her chin. "I will excuse your temerity, Master Old One, only because to be called old by an Old One must somehow be a compliment. We shall construe it as such, at any rate."

"Good thing," said Gammin. He had already seen the young princess adopt her regal manner as a joke enough to know she was just having fun, or, as they say in the Tallenlaust, funning.

Theramina perked up. "Stryn's at least as old as my father. I remember him from when I was a child. He used to play tunes for me while I danced. Sometimes he would make up silly words to make us laugh."

"He did that here too!" Karene bounced in her seat. The mock aristocrat was gone.

The lighthearted moment developed a limp when the ladies asked how Stryn had interacted with Gammin at Stormhaven. Gammin had sensed it coming. He had devised an escape route by the time they realized their unintentional misstep.

He said, "Stryn has been around forever."

Marin agreed. "He always pops up in old stories. But, is it the same man, and is that the man we saw tonight, the one you knew as children?"

"Haven't you heard Andur's tales?" Theramina asked. "Stryn wrote them. He was there."

Gammin replied. "Yes, we've heard them. Marin could recite them for you word-for-word." A mischievous look overcame him. "He once told me that he wanted to write them out as a historical event, you know, do the research, all that." This was a false statement. Gammin had suggested it. He got the idea from Max, who had originally asked Marin to write skits for the group to act out.

Karene clapped her hands together.

"Where did you learn to write, Master Marin? I did not know the Children of the Forest could read and write."

Gammin did not let his friend answer. "That's a long story."

III.

Sometime later, the four were once again walking the wide hallways of Castle Arathai. It was twinight. They were winding their way back to a good night's sleep—or what was left of it. They had only just arrived at a corridor that seemed familiar to the two Southlanders when the sound of a finalla caught their ears.

Gammin stopped to listen. He recognized the melody

Nandea had used to accompany her Battle of Elosai story. He had heard it now so many times that he identified it in only a few notes. Nandea and Stryn had improvised a duet on the tune that very evening. This was the duet all over again, both parts being played with the gusto of a barn dance.

Marin and the two princesses clustered around Gammin.

When the piece ended, Gammin asked, "Whose room is this, Princess?"

"It is Master Stryn's room. He, like you, is an honored guest."

Karene fought the satisfaction from her face. An attentive host, she had noted the Southlanders' interest in the faelyth. She had taken this route past Stryn's apartment in the hope that they might meet him in the corridors. This would be even better!

"Who is in there with him?" Marin asked, then felt stupid as he saw the look that scurried across her face before she could contain it. It said as plainly as words, "I've been with you all night. How would I know that?"

To make amends, Marin did not wait for a reply. "Whoever those two are, they sure can play."

The Princess of Arel lit up like a well-trimmed lamp. All in a rush, she exclaimed, "Haaaa! One of them is Stryn. Can't you tell? No? The other, I am not sure."

Karene cried, "Let's go see!"

Before any of the other three could move a muscle, she turned, stepped up to the door, and knocked firmly. Gammin and Marin exchanged looks of dismay. They had not considered disturbing the occupants of the room, but that is not what had surprised them. It was the princess. Her spontaneity had a way of unsettling their balance.

A deep voice called from beyond the door. "By all means, enter, Rathia. Bring your friends, too. Why stand in the hallway when you can sit by the hearth?"

Looking self-conscious and delighted, Karene turned to her two new Southland friends, said, "He calls me Rathia. I always liked that."

Theramina, who had long-adored her own nick name, Arelia, said nothing. There was no time. Karene rushed into the room, pushing Gammin from behind as if they had been old friends.

There were two people in the room. Only one of them was holding a finalla. That person was Stryn. He was not particularly tall, certainly no taller than Marin. The hair was not white with age; it was a true silver. But even that was not right. His hair was not silver with age. Stryn did not look as old as legend made him. How old then? As old as King Branden? Yes. Was he as old as Kappelli? No way. Stryn's skin was tighter, smoother, less wrinkled. It was the color of river clay, darker than Theramina's. It was not the skin of an old man.

Stryn rose, setting his finalla on a stand. He gestured for them to sit. There was ample room on couches lining a sunken den. The young men were immediately reminded of Branden's hall in Stormhaven. They did not know that both chambers had been modeled after a hall in long-ago Tarabol, Andur's capital. Such a feature was almost a requirement for the accommodations of the land's most notable bard. These were the rooms Stryn always occupied when he came to the castle. They were his rooms.

"You are welcome, Rathia and Arelia. Welcome also are you, Prince Gammin. Last but not least, I welcome you, Marinsa, faenea of the Forest."

While Karene and Theramina took seats, Marin and Gammin stood next to each other, wondering how Stryn had known their identities. How he had known they were in the hallway? They were not allowed to ponder. The current continued to carry them along. They were corks caught in rushing water.

The allegedly old man said, "I present to you Caerlyn, an old acquaintance. Friend Caerlyn only just arrived. He tells me he has been on a long journey to far-off lands. He missed the feast, which is unfortunate for him, and the music, which is worse. I did not want him to starve amid the fertile fields of Castle Arathai."

A demolished chicken carcass and the remains of bread and cheese were evidence that Stryn was not speaking metaphorically.

Gammin stood and crossed the room. He bowed to Caerlyn, who was a lean man in a simple, travel-worn robe. He was about the same age as Stryn, which is to say, there was just no telling.

Caerlyn did not notice the courtesy. The Prince of Ehrylan waited patiently. What else could he do?

After a moment, Caerlyn said, "Good evening, young man."

"Sir," said Karene, with such perfect manner that her tutors would have been proud, "this is Gammin, son of Branden and Therana. He is Prince of Ehrylan." Karene had not been aware Stryn had a visitor. She made a mental note to chastise the head of her intelligence network.

Caerlyn's eyes flicked to Karene. They tarried a moment, then moved back to Gammin.

"There is a damn sight more to do before anyone can rightfully call themselves Prince of Ehrylan."

Karene, who might have been apoplectic otherwise, did not have time to react before Gammin said, "I could not agree more, sir. King Branden agrees with both of us. That is why he does not wear a crown."

"King? Riding out of a castle at the head of a few thousand soldiers does not make a man king."

"Ah, but it does in many lands, Caerlyn," laughed Stryn. He was unaffected by the social cataclysm yawning in front of Karene. "Well you know it."

Now Caerlyn moved. He stood up abruptly. To Marin, he looked like a resilient reed unbending after a strong wind. To Gammin, he resembled a mantis unfurling its long, hooked, appendages. When he was done unbending and unfurling, Caerlyn gazed down at the young prince. He was very tall.

"We are not talking about many lands. We are talking about Ehrylan. More importantly, we are talking about Dauroth, or whatever he calls himself these days. That one will not be defeated by a few thousands." He paused, his eyes shifting back and forth between Gammin and Marin. "Unless those thousands are as capable as these two might end up being if they live long enough."

Gammin, who had not known he appeared capable, offered, "Again, we agree. Surely you have heard of the king's victories at Twofords and Daur en Lammoth? Those were not the work of this army. The Tallea are not asleep in the Wood and Water. There is war there, too. You must have heard some word of these events."

Gammin was somewhat unnerved by Caerlyn's continuing pugilistic bent. He decided that the man's intention must be to put him off-balance. It was the only reason he could think of to explain the strange behavior. He resisted the urge to look at Karene, who sat trying not to wring her hands and wondering how she was going to remedy this situation.

"I have heard none of those things," retorted Caerlyn. "Weren't you listening? I only just arrived."

Weren't you listening? That was right up there with an outright declaration of intent to do battle, like proclaiming the name of your father in the face of the enemy. Now Gammin was sure the man was trying to provoke him. But what was to be gained? What was his motivation?

Gammin relaxed. All he had to do was wait.

Caerlyn pushed past Gammin with a swish of his robe. Stepping toward Marin, he paused to address the ladies.

"I bid you good morning, Princess Theramina, and you, Princess Karene. The fame of your beauties is too dim, and all that."

He turned on Marin.

"I am honored, Old One." Caerlyn inclined his head.

Marin had to reconstruct the greeting he had prepared as he saw the man coming toward him. What he had expected Caerlyn to say had nothing in common with what the man actually said. After a perceptible hesitation, Marin acquitted himself well. He was never the fastest on his verbal feet, but his words, when they came, were always worth listening to.

"The honor is mine, Caerlyn, though I don't know why yet."

He had no idea who this man was. The fact that he was here, in the innermost depths of Castle Arathai, gave Caerlyn a certain level of credibility. Stryn had called him friend. The Stryn of legend was Dauroth's bitter foe, unlikely to be in the company of one of Dauroth's allies—if the usurper had any. Beyond that, Marin was clueless. He had heard that name before; it rang the dim bell of a forgotten memory. Perhaps it was just a name in a rhyme his mother had told him as they played together in her garden or by the river or among the trees of his home.

Caerlyn looked him up and down. Then, abruptly, he went back to his seat, lowering himself onto it with all the grace of a white crane, somehow smooth and stiff at the same time. Ignoring Gammin, who still stood in the place he had taken in front of Caerlyn's seat, he peered across the sumptuous rug at Marin.

"Do you two know what you are getting into?"

Marin said, "Yes," while Gammin said, "No."

Caerlyn opened his mouth to say more. What he might have told the two young heroes remains a mystery because Karene had had all the rigorous language she could take. Almost desperately, the Princess of Rath blurted, "Master Stryn, where is Nandea?"

"Nandea? She is abed or perhaps roaming the castle, looking for a miracle cure for one of her imagined maladies. She thinks the healers do not take her seriously. I agree with her. And them. Last night, she wanted herbs, something to help her sleep."

"Is she ill?" It was unlikely something was amiss with the faelyth. Karene was asking more out of form than anything else, though she was interested to discover who had been playing the other finalla.

"Ill? Goodness, no. She is a right as clouds and honey. She thought the castle cold and feared to catch the Dribbles, so she said. She left wondering why the King of Rath does not heat his castle when there are guests."

"What did you tell her? It would be most unlike you to withhold the wisdom of the aged."

"I reminded her that there are always guests in Castle Arathai, most of whom do not expire prematurely from the Dribbles."

"Quite right," said the princess with a regal nod. "Now, dearest Stryn, please tell us who was playing the other finalla? Where is she?"

"Rathia, my dear, there is no one else here."

Caerlyn sighed. "Before you ask, princess, no, I was not playing the other part. I don't play the finalla or any instrument with animal bits for strings. There is only one finalla, as you can see. Stryn was playing both parts. He was showing off."

"Both? Never!" Theramina's face was sunny. "I don't believe it. He is much too feeble. Such an old man could never play both parts at the same time."

Stryn slapped his knee. "Ha! I do not know if you are being ironic or are just trying to goad me into playing for the sport of it. When you were younger, Arelia, I could tell. Not anymore. You have grown into a woman." He appraised her. "Either way, you win, as always. I shall demonstrate."

With a languid gesture, Stryn took up the finalla. He strummed a chord, adjusted the tuning. It was a familiar ritual.

"What musician could refuse such a *poldeferous* audience. I can think of no better way to end the day and to start a new one, both at the same time."

Theramina was not sure if he had just made up a word. She was unsure whether she had been lovingly slighted or not. Her only choice was to attack. "Go on, then."

Stryn did.

Gammin waited as the last note faded into a round of applause. If he neglected to show how amazed he was by the performance, it was because he had something else on his mind, something that had nothing to do with finallas, duets, or rude strangers. Knowing that he was cutting in on the faelyth's well-earned praise, Gammin finally allowed himself to ask the question that had been on his heart since the moment he had first seen Stryn in the performance hall.

"Master Stryn, is it true that you knew my mother?"

The faelyth took the sudden tangent in stride. He set the finalla back on the stand then leaned forward toward Gammin, placing his elbows on his knees.

"Yes, indeed. She was a fine young woman. There was more hope in the world when she was with us. I imagine you have questions."

"Only one. What was she like? The king told me you taught her how to play the Chinenyeh flute. I want to hear one. And, I want to know what songs she liked to play." To Marin, he said, "Merelina gave me the idea. She said one way to get to know someone is through the things they love. The…"

Caerlyn cut him off. "Merelina sounds like an uncommonly wise person. Maybe there is hope for you after all." He appeared to be talking mostly to himself.

Undaunted, Gammin pressed on.

"My problem, Master Stryn, is that I don't know what songs she liked. I guess mostly she must have liked Arelese tunes. I didn't know what those were like until recently." He nodded to Theramina, who nodded back.

"I think I can help you out with that, my lad," said Stryn. "First, allow me to clarify something. I did not teach Therana to play the flute. She learned from the Chinenyeh on her journey to Ehrylan. I taught her to play with more confidence. The Laughing People gave her a flute at their parting, a very great honor even for a Princess of Arel, though she did not know it. She was newly wed, freshly set out on her life's true adventure. It was her wedding journey. She was leaving her land, her people, her life. The Chinenyeh do not allow such significant events to go unadorned.

"Can you imagine that?" Karene mused. "Going to a new land where you did not know anyone?"

Theramina finished the thought, "My aunt left everything

behind to go with a strange man to a land where they would be homeless and outcast."

"She must have loved him a lot," crooned Karene happily. She was relieved, thinking they had turned the corner from tense to relaxed. She was wrong.

"He must have hated her."

Caerlyn's comment fell like a sheet of ice over recently stirred embers. It destroyed the mood, which had been threatening to become romantic. This time, Stryn could not allow the affront to go unnoted.

"Caerlyn, must you be so grumpy? These young people have done nothing wrong. They did not summon you or bring you here. You came of your own will, to do what you know needs to be done."

Caerlyn considered, his fingers pushing at his beard, which was the color of dirty snow.

"I suppose you are right, though it does seem malicious to take a maiden princess from the lodge of her father to the subjugated remains of your war-shattered kingdom."

Theramina laughed. "You see it as malicious, sir. I see it as brave. Brave love, maybe."

"I think it is romantic," added Karene.

She was trying—yet again—to get the tone of the gathering back on track. The stranger was no help in that regard, though he certainly was interesting. She knew the name Caerlyn; it was part of a certain important list. What she did not know was whether this Caerlyn was the one on the list. If he was, his behavior made more sense.

"Romantic?" Caerlyn gaped at Stryn. "The kingdoms of Rath and Eluylan are at war with a demon king, and all these pretty ladies can talk about is romance. I hope these boys understand better what they are part of."

Gammin's mind flitted back to Daur en Lammoth. Something Elma had told him there returned to him. She had said it was not good policy to slight warriors who have just come from battle. He thought he understood what she meant.

He stood up, turned on the rude stranger, and said, "You

don't understand. Marin and I are not just part of this war with Dauroth. We started it."

Caerlyn waved him off with the back of a hand. "Oh, calm down, puppy. No one doubts you or what you have accomplished, though that is certainly a bold claim. I said before that you were able enough." He shook his head, looked at Stryn again. "Why do we always have to repeat things with the young?"

Stryn held up a finger—an artist's version of visual intimidation—to forestall further interruption. "The topic, before you murdered it, friend Caerlyn, was flutes. I don't seem to have a flute in my pocket, but there just might be one in my bags. While I am gone, Rathia, you can entertain your guests by asking Master Caerlyn where he studied charm and if it took him very long to become so pervasively agreeable. He used to be really disagreeable, I assure you."

Stryn returned before anyone opened their mouth. Reverently, though with no ceremony, the silvered man held out a wooden tube. It was a flute such as those used by the Chinenyeh, a nomadic people who traversed Rath and northern Arel according to season and to their whim. What feature made it different from other flutes was still a mystery to Gammin. It was almost as long as his outstretched arm, simply crafted from what at first appeared to be a single piece of wood. A rich, polished grain flowed over its length like a natural carving. Gammin was mesmerized for a moment. He sat staring.

"Take it!" Caerlyn admonished. "It's not going to bite you. It's just a piece of wood."

Gammin reached out, said, "I was thinking it might be fragile, like a puppy or a chick."

"It is not an animal; it is a piece of wood with some holes in it."

"Caerlyn," announced Stryn, "if you can't be more pleasant, please pretend to be someone else for a moment." The look he threw across the room shut the irascible stranger up tight. The faelyth turned back to Gammin.

"You are absolutely right, Prince Gammin. All musical instruments should be treated as if they were priceless, no matter how fine or plain they might be. This is one of the plainer, though I love it. It plays nicely."

He placed it into Gammin's hands. The prince saw that he had been correct to be gentle. It was more complex than it looked at first sight. He held it across his outstretched hands, gazing at it quizzically.

Stryn plucked it out of Gammin's grasp, turned it so that it was pointing side-to-side rather than up and down, then handed it back. "Like this. Cover the holes with your fingers, seven of them. One is for the thumb, you see? What makes a Chincnyeh flute different from others is these little levers, here and here. You can think of them as longer fingers that cover far off holes. And, one other thing. You don't blow straight into it, not the way you see in Ehrylan. You blow across the mouthpiece." He pointed with articulate fingers to each item as he named it. "Like this."

As if he was unwilling to let Gammin actually hold the thing, Stryn snatched the flute. He set it to his lips, holding it so that it extended to the side instead of down along his chest, and played a series of notes. Gammin watched the faelyth's fingers exactly as he had watched the soldiers' feet when he was very young. He watched with the same happy, contented gleam in his eyes that had been there when Breanna taught us Corn Gathering Dance.

IV.

A week or two later, Gammin could play Farmer's Husband, the most simple of the tunes his mother had liked. To be sure, he was no prodigy. He would never be Stryn's star pupil. But he did learn to play—poorly, at first, at first being a very long time. He might have become a better player if they had stayed longer in Rath. But, now, after decades of excruciating delay, the wheels of war were turning fast.

Branden was chaffing to pick up his sword again, and Gammin had plenty of other duties to attend.

Chief among these other duties seemed to be meetings. There were meetings about what to do in Rath, meetings about what to do about the Southland, meetings about Dauroth. The situation moved from annoying to disturbing when one of Kappelli's advisors suggested a meeting to discuss meeting attendance. But they weren't all bad. Gammin looked forward to discussing the campaign in the Westland.

Most mornings started with King Branden, who made a habit of breaking his fast in the company of his confidants. Usually, Marin attended, as did Eamehr and a few other long-time friends. Other times, it was just Gammin and his father. Those were less enjoyable.

The morning after Stryn gave Gammin his first flute lesson, the bleary-eyed prince was sitting at Branden's table next to Marin. There were no others present, which was a good thing. Gammin had not slept at all. He spent the time between when he left Stryn's quarters and when he appeared at the king's table practicing the flute. Marin hadn't slept either, also because Gammin was practicing the flute. He had not even tried. With Gammin torturing a cat with a hot poker in the next room, what was the point?

Today was starting off with a whimper instead of a laugh. Not that there was likely to be much laughter around King Branden's table. The king had little use for laughter. Silence was the rule rather than chit chat when serious matters weren't being discussed. Thanks be to Ea, that made the breakfast part of the meeting shorter.

Gammin, having waited until his father was finished detailing the day's events, said, "We met Stryn last night." The faelyth was not what he wanted to talk about, but it was a good place to start.

"So I heard."

Gammin, wondering when his father might have had time to hear such a thing, continued. "There was another man there, someone I never met before."

"You have never met almost everyone, so that is hardly an uncommon honor." Because there was no harm in the boy knowing that he, Branden, had eyes everywhere, even in Castle Arathai, the king said, "You are talking about Caerlyn."

"Yes, sir. I was wondering if you knew him."

"I do not. Kappelli mentioned him. He came for Stryn, or so he said. What about him?"

"I don't understand him. He doesn't seem to be from around these parts, but he talks like he has been fighting Dauroth all his life."

"I have not spoken to him. My understanding is that he arrived during the performance last night. Kappelli posted an honor guard for him while the bard was away in case he needed anything. I posted cautionary guards, in case he wanted anything else. You may have noticed them."

Gammin had noticed the extra guards—smiling men sauntering idly in pairs, not saying or doing anything in particular as they passed by. Why hadn't he considered what he noticed? Chastising himself, Gammin committed to working harder at being more observant.

The reason for the extra care was evident. One could not say that Stryn's friendship with Caerlyn put the man in unquestionable territory. Stryn did not owe his allegiance to Ehrylan or to Brand's heir. Stryn was not Branden's subject, or Kappelli's, or Theros'. He was a faelyth of the Crescent. One thing was sure, however. Stryn would not align himself with someone supporting Dauroth.

If giving a stranger access to the most-tender parts of the castle pleased Kappelli, so be it. It was his castle, after all, and his tender parts. Branden knew how to defend his own.

"Anything else?"

"Yes, sir. One thing. We have not gone to Ehrynai yet."

The king wiped his lips with a cloth. He picked a bit of egg shell from beneath his finger nail. "No, we have not. Is that your one thing?"

"No, sir. I just don't understand. Those are our countrymen, yet we stay here in Rath."

"I am glad you noticed." Branden lifted his mug. The juice in it was tepid orange juice. One thing nice about living in the Great Mountains was that there was always ice to be had. Branden liked his juice cold and his kef hot.

"Did you notice also that there's no war in Ehrynai right now?"

"Yes, sir."

The enemy had withdrawn completely from the area. Ehrynai was free for the first time in a generation. It was a huge victory for the loyalists, but there was still a mountain of war to climb.

"It's a tricky business, reclaiming a kingdom. You saw some of it in Twofords, more in Mendolas. This part is the hard part."

"Hard? This part?"

Gammin's incredulous look made Branden smile in spite of himself, spoiling his feigned glower.

"Waiting is the hard part. I will fight to the end, but don't ask me to sit around and wait for it."

The startlingly human admission made Gammin laugh. He wished that he had more opportunity to see the man behind the king. Often, Gammin was not sure there was one. At those times, he thought Branden was all king.

There had been plenty of waiting recently. Messengers had been sent and received from the leaders of Ehrynai. The military was in charge there, led by someone named Fothyr. The messengers had been followed by envoys and all their annoying trappings.

In the normal course of events, Fothyr should have come, but he refused invitations, offering instead to meet when the king came to Ehrynai. Such a refusal might have been construed as belligerence, even out-right defiance, but Branden was not concerned. Calen had told him about the Resistance. Fothyr seemed to be the main instigator of that, perhaps where it all started. If Calen trusted the man, he could be trusted.

The king grunted, shifted in his chair to ease his shoulder, burped into a loose fist. "The waiting is almost done. The army is rebuilding; winter is passing. But, never fear, my son, we will not wait here in comfort while our people are in chains. One week, maybe two, and we will be off to Neath."

The city of Neath was the army's next goal. Dauroth's forces had taken a stand there, it being their nearest fortified asset, a few day's ride up the Coast Road. After reclaiming Neath, Branden would either continue north to Kingsholm or east through Norgap and down toward Twofords. But no matter what, the king and his army would stop at Ehrynai first and do there what needed to be done.

In the meantime, they were left to enjoy a small window of peace in lives that had been full of war. Castle Arathai could be very tranquil, sitting as it did like a jewel on the rim of the ocean. Because the two navies had gone north, Kappelli's chasing Dauroth's, the Bay of Arai was blessedly clear of the trappings of war. It was a welcome change. But as seemed to be most-often the case, peace in one place meant conflict in another. While Branden and his army recovered in Rath, the good people of Ehrylan languished under Dauroth's grinding heel. Back home things were growing more difficult by the day.

Branden cleared his throat. It was a harsh sound, one they had all become accustomed to since his injury. A new thought jumped to the front of Gammin's mind.

"How is your shoulder?"

The king had cast off the sling a few days ago. He was, for good or ill, treating the wound as if it had healed completely, which it had not. Nemen Elma had refused to speak with him since. If Branden had known that's what would have happened, he would have lost the sling much earlier.

"It's nothing."

"It's not nothing, father. I was there. I held my hand against it. I watched them sew it back together."

The king watched his son, letting the silence close in. His eyes shifting to Marin, then back, he said, "It's my throat that bothers me."

That was nothing new for Gammin or anyone who had spoken at length with the king since he narrowly avoided death by the Gryhm's garrote. His voice had remained rough though the flesh of his throat was healing. No nemen ever cured that condition. He asked many, and they tried their best, but he spoke as if through a slow river of rocks and sand for the rest of his life.

V.

The rest of that day was filled with work. So was the next and others after that. The nights were full of work too, though of a different sort. The Rathians make great efforts to pursue leisure. Evening commenced with supper and an appearance by one or both faelyth. After that, the kings usually wandered off to do whatever old kings do when they are together. It had come as a relief to the older men when they saw that the younger set did not need babysitting. Therefore, Karene and her charges were free to please themselves so long as they did not cause a commotion.

Some nights, to the delight of Gammin and the chagrin of the young ladies, Stryn invited his new pupil to drop in for a lesson. After the second lesson, Marin excused himself from further participation on those nights. He spent the time with the men and women of the Fifth. The ladies lasted through the fourth lesson. After that, when Gammin reported for music, his friends scattered in different directions.

Another week passed. In Rath, winter deepened to a moist chill. The same was true in much of Westland, where snow is uncommon except on the Western Mountains. Still, they waited. The army drilled, built, and mended.

Gammin was up and on the way to his father's apartments. Unless Gammin was mistaken, the messenger for whom the king had been waiting had arrived during the night. If it wasn't that, it was something else big, judging by the summons he had received before dawn. Report to the king's chambers. Come alone.

When Gammin arrived, he saw that the other captains

weren't present. The table was not set for a meal. There was bread, honey, and butter, but no plates.

"Sit," commanded the king.

Gammin seldom received a more civil greeting from his father, even when the king was in a good mood. As he obeyed, Gammin watched his father, unsure what this was all about.

Branden took a hunk of toasted bread from the basket. He pushed the basket toward his son and dipped his portion in the honey pot after smearing it with butter.

"You should eat more. You are too thin."

"Yes, sir," replied Gammin, who was not too thin and who ate plenty. He had discovered that his father did not like it when you failed to make a reply.

The king drained his mug of kef. He glanced around the room. His eyes found the vertical slit that was the only window. They lingered there, the eyes of a hawk hunting.

"We leave in three days."

Gammin nodded. "Marin and I have been expecting that, the other captains, too." He searched his father's face. "It is nice enough here, but we've got a job to do. The men are ready."

The king did not reply. He kept his gaze on the window.

After waiting as long as he dared, Gammin said, "There is a lot to do between now and then. I'll get to it."

The king's reply stopped Gammin from rising. "Less than you think, Gammin, and more."

"You sound like Annen." Gammin's spirits had been lifted by the news of departure, his tongue made careless.

Branden let the comment pass unrebutted. He turned his eyes from the window, focused them on Gammin's. His gaze might have been the honed edge of a killing blade.

"I am giving command of the Fifth to Eamehr."

That was King Branden to the core. Go right for the heart. "What?"

"You heard me. As of now, Eamehr commands the Fifth."

Branden observed his son, eager to see how Gammin would react. The king knew he had struck deeply and without warning. Would his son understand the lesson? It was a lesson he needed to learn.

Gammin took the news as a blow he had failed to redirect. It struck him squarely. He was staggered, but he did not falter. He kept his mouth shut and waited for the riot of thoughts and emotions to abate.

When his son did not respond, Branden was pleased. The boy had learned self-control, at least.

Branden said, "We are reapportioning the Fifth to bring it back to where it needs to be. You lost quite a few at Elosai and after."

Gammin could make no argument with that. He had lost a larger portion of his company than most of the other captains, with the notable exception of Eamehr. The king had failed to mention that the Fifth had performed miracles as it was used to plug whatever hole developed, sent wherever the need was greatest. They had been shot across the battlefield like arrows from a quiver, the same arrow—picked up and dusted off—for each shot. One of those little miracles had been rescuing Eamehr.

"Most of the additions will be new recruits from Elosai," continued the king. "Those men need to be trained correctly. Eamehr is the man to do it, now that he has recovered."

Recovered? Eamehr had been injured worse than the king. True, he was up and about, but the man had some mending to do before he could be rightly called recovered. Gammin stared at his father, his eyes growing harder with each passing breath.

Because he was expecting to be defied, Branden mistook the silence for defiance. Without those preconceptions, he might have seen that his son was genuinely aggrieved at the news and at the way it had been delivered.

King Branden was not accustomed to explaining himself. He had been born a prince, was a prince all his youth. He had ruled his roost as the Defier for most of his adult life. Branden's father had not made a habit of explaining his decisions, either. In Brand's case, this was because he had such perspicacity that his decisions were mostly self-explanatory.

Yet Branden was father as well as king. He was as new at one as he was the other. Truth to tell, if there is truth about such things, he was better at the fathering than he gave himself credit for and less kingly than he hoped. That is why he failed miserably when he tried to explain himself to his son.

"It is very important to train new recruits properly. You run your company as if it's a Tallean border patrol. This is not the Tallenlaust. We are not the Tallea."

Gammin found his center. He took a mental stance, started to speak. Branden held up a hand.

"I do not need to be reminded of your many successes. That is not the point. I want you with me. That is a proper place for a prince."

When it was safe to speak, Gammin said, "Is the Fifth so different? I have only been captain a few weeks. We haven't changed anything important."

"No? There was an extra man at the guard post. He took the message to the watch commander. You remember?"

"You are talking about the night Rauchur came? Yes, I remember the reports."

"Who ordered an extra sentry at the post that night?"

"You're angry because we posted too many guards? The night you were almost killed?"

"Answer the question."

Finding that his hands had balled into fists, Gammin relaxed them. He picked up something from a table to occupy them, set it down again immediately.

"One extra guard makes sense. One night in five, each warrior takes a turn sleeping at a post. That way, there is someone to run messages." He knew that he should stop there, but he didn't. "It worked pretty well."

Gammin lapsed into silence under the weight of his own words. It worked well? A Gryhm had stabbed the king in the chest while choking him. That was not a good measure of success.

Branden slammed his fist against the table. "Answer the question, captain."

There was only one correct answer, but it did not matter to Branden. This was just a pretext. Gammin would recognize that—his father saw at least that far into his son's character—but it did not matter.

"I don't even remember what the question is!" Gammin's voice was a hammer. He stood up, looked from his father to the door. In a calmer voice, he added, "If I understand correctly, I am no longer a captain."

Branden, son of Brand, was neither a young man nor a new leader of men. This was not his first battle. As soon as he heard the bitterness in his son's voice—he had been trying to draw it out the way a healer draws puss from a wound—he knew he had won. It was only a matter of time now. The king had already prepared his final stroke. If he waited for the right moment—there was one in every conflict—and delivered it just right, the boy would be set back on his heels enough to be pliable, at least for a while. Then he might actually learn something instead of thinking he already knew everything.

"You are still a member of this army. Or have you decided to go home now that you can't play with my toys the way you like?"

Gammin became angry. A shower of heat washed over his head and filled his body. His voice lost its edge. The tension in his body bled away. He took two slow steps toward his father. When he spoke, his words were very quiet.

"Go home? Run away? Is that what you think of me? You are mistaken. When have you seen my back?"

He was referring to the Sulanese, far to the south, who were known for turning and running in the face of force. They had a habit of showing their backs to enemies and allies alike. There was a saying in those days, "The enemy of my enemy is my ally, except for the Sulanese. They can't be trusted in either army."

"You refuse to answer my question?"

Calmly, without a hint of sarcasm, Gammin repeated the words. "I don't remember what the question is."

"Who gave the order to post an extra guard, a sleeping

guard?"

"You are wasting time. Why? You know very well that I command the Fifth. Who gives the orders is not important. I have the command... had the command. The decision was mine."

Gammin hadn't made a conscious decision to post extra sentries. It was something the Tallea did, one extra guard at each post, sleeping, to be used in emergency as a fighter or a runner. It made good sense as far as he could see. He could not understand why his father would object.

The truth of it was that Marin had implemented the procedure as a matter of course. Gammin had noted it without comment and approved wholeheartedly. He wondered what the king would do if he knew that little tidbit.

"The decision was yours? You decided to start changing the armies of Ehrylan into the brigades of the Tallenlaust?"

"That was not my intention, as you know." Gammin suddenly realized that he was done with this man. "Why are you wasting time? What do you want from me?"

The king had to stop and think. His son, who was taking this remarkably well, had not yet become indignant. That is what Branden wanted. He needed Gammin to be self-righteous, thinking only of himself, when he made his final assault. The king knew such emotions were not typical of his son. He would have to press hard to break this young colt. Any regret he felt about that was tinted with more than a little satisfaction.

"What was your intention, Gammin?"

"To do the best we could. To do better than we should have been able to do with what we had."

The response tarried as Branden, who had not expected that kind of answer, found his tongue.

"A captain of the Ehrylain is telling me that the ways of the Tallea are better than the ways of his fathers."

"That is not what I said. Why are you being so dense?"

Inwardly, Branden smiled. He brandished the steel in his eyes and said, "I am not the one who is being dense, Gammin.

You are. An extra sentry at each post on the line means you have at least four warriors who are not sleeping well each night. That is four of a hundred, four percent. But there are four watches. That means sixteen percent of your company is guaranteed a poor night's rest every night. Or, did you change that, too? Maybe you have an extra watch each day as well?"

"I did not change that. We still have four watches." Gammin could see that his father was toying with him. He did not understand why, but two could play as easily as one. "It is worth thinking about. Why should there be only four watches?"

"Why not two hundred in a company, or six, or eight? Gammin, there are reasons we do things the way we do. They have stood the test of time."

"Maybe."

Gammin's terse reply fell like quiet thunder. King Branden got to his feet. It was the first time Branden had seen the man in his son on equal terms. The king was pleased and more than a little disquieted. Mentally, he squared his shoulders and bent his knees.

"You mean the results would have been different if we had changed things, broken a few rules?"

Gammin was tired of dealing with this strange king. If times had been different, he would have departed long since. But times were not different. His wagon had become hitched to Branden, and there was nothing he could do about it. Not yet.

Had he meant to imply that events would have unfolded differently if King Brand had taken different actions? No, not at all. That was an obvious irrelevance. What had he meant? And, more importantly, what did his father want? Not one part of him believed this was about the extra sentry.

Gammin formed a reply in his mind, tested it, changed two words.

"Sire, that is not what I was thinking. It is true, though, now that you mention it."

"Of course, it's true. Don't be an idiot. Now, what were you thinking?"

In that moment, the king sounded so like Caerlyn that Gammin did a double-take. He was relieved to see that it was indeed his father. Then he laughed at himself for that.

"The traditions didn't stand the test of time. If they had, you'd be sitting on a comfortable throne in a city I have never seen, and I... would not have been born."

In his mind, Gammin saw the fireball explode between Branden's ears. But the king did not move, except one tiny twitch under his left eye.

There was a very long silence.

When the king spoke, his voice was controlled, unnaturally calm, a frozen waterfall.

"Sit down."

Branden watched his son obey, thinking that this was better than he could have hoped. Gammin had forgotten that his command was taken away. Time to remind him.

"You point out the obvious. I had a teacher in Kingsholm who said that habit was both useful and harmful, so it must be used sparingly. I think we can spare some more. Tell me something else obvious. What harm is there if the Prince of Ehrylan runs his company differently than all the other companies?"

The king waited until Gammin tried to respond, then held up his hand again. He did not want anyone else's answers to the questions, particularly right now. The trap had been laid, the quarry enticed. It was time.

"Gammin, when will you stop thinking only of yourself?"

Branden knew his son was not selfish. He was generous to a fault. That was the key, the soft spot. Having delivered the stiletto to the target perfectly, the king sat back and watched. He did not have long to wait, and again, when Gammin started to speak, Branden forestalled him.

"You are prince of Ehrylan. You will be king someday. You cannot afford the appearance of favoritism. Do you understand why that is important?"

Gammin's heart was beating very fast. He did not speak.

The king said, "Overt or unjustified favoritism destroys

morale, especially when the leader is young and new. You are prince. You must move among all the companies, not one only. And I want you by me."

The thoughts Branden left unspoken were more important. They were the real reason for all of this. He wanted Gammin close, where he could keep an eye on him, where he could show him what it is to be king. No matter how sturdy a warrior the boy might be, there was only so much he could have learned in Twofords. He had never really been out of the Southland. The rest of the Ehrylan was foreign to him, the rest of the Crescent just the rumor of a wild place. As Branden had discovered for himself, the world was impossibly large. There was just so little time.

"Do you understand, Gammin? You cannot act or believe just as you like anymore. You act and believe for a whole people, even when they cannot see you. Do you understand?"

Gammin nodded. His eyes were as blank as a slate rubbed clean.

"I understand, sire. There will be details I need to give to Eamehr personally. You will let me tell the company myself?"

The king smiled a painted smile. "Of course. That is usually best. Certainly, there's no harm in it, in this case."

He lifted a hand off the table just high enough to gesture toward the door.

The motion caught Gammin's attention. The image of Charshan sitting on a throne flitted across his mind. A shudder sprang from the center of his chest to his toes. He shook his head to clear it, knowing the king would see. Fine. Let the king think it was some kind of response to the reassignment. It didn't matter.

One thing was sure. Breakfast was over.

12. THE WELLING

I.

Gammin was furious at the man who was his father. It wasn't because the king had failed to offer a nice breakfast. Gammin knew there was sense in what Branden said. That only made things worse. What he needed to do was get to Eamehr, Marin, and then the men and women of the Fifth. What he wanted to do was think.

Gammin knew that the company would be no worse off than they had been with him as captain. Probably, they would be better off. Eamehr was a true survivor. If the man was confident in his own abilities, he had earned that right.

With that decided, Gammin was free to direct his thoughts toward a more interesting question. Why had the king delivered such delicate news in such a brutal manner? Gammin felt like he had just been through a major battle.

He was no closer to understanding by the time his feet delivered him to his own door. Nodding to the guard, he pushed the door open and went in.

Marin was still there. That was good. Maybe together, they

could run off and go… where? It was a good question.

Gammin grunted a greeting. As he collapsed on to his bed and began to tug at his boots, he realized the answer to that question. If he could, he would go home, back to Merelina, back to Dara and Marn, back to Simon, Max, Temay, and little Bre, who wasn't quite so little anymore. Arica would be there, too. And… he knew that was all a fantasy. He wasn't going anywhere near home for a good, long while.

Marin, who had been putting his boots on, said, "Trouble at the mill?"

"You won't believe me when I tell you. I am glad you are here. We need to go see Eamehr, then the Fifth."

Gammin stopped. He had been thinking only of himself. The realization rocked him. Marin might not, probably would not, be Eamehr's choice for First Officer.

"You are going to tell me," said Marin, tugging at the top of his boot, "that Eamehr's captain now. I will tell you, no, I will not be First Officer. That's Tallep. He was Eamehr's First, has been forever, or so they say. He's a good man. He was with King Branden on the immortal voyage, which, as we know, was the definitive test of a sojourner's mettle."

Gammin, who was well aware of who Tallep was and where he had been, shrugged. He breathed deeply and began to relax.

"I don't know which to be more astounded by, that you knew about Eamehr or that you know about Tallep."

"Don't' be foolish." Marin used Branden's voice and tone. He regretted it as soon as he saw Gammin's head jerk around. The woodcutter's son did not need to see the motion to know his friend was wounded. He looked for an apple. Those always seemed to take Gammin's mind away from hard tidings.

"I'm a First Officer. Tallep's a First Officer. We First Officers, we stick together like arrows in a quiver, if you get my point." It was an old soldier's saying, uttered most often by soldiers who had never been a First Officer.

Marin knew his friend understood what he meant. All leaders have spies and other ways of generating intelligence, even squad leaders, platoon leaders, First Officers, and bullies.

"Eamehr mentioned it to Tallep," continued Marin, "the what, not the why, which I still don't know. That's the way it is supposed to work, right?"

Gammin peered out through the web of fingers he had laced across his face.

"Yeah, Mar, it is. Will you be able to keep your sources? I don't want to lose touch with what is going on. That is what is important."

"Time will tell. Your guess is as good as mine."

Marin waited for more, knowing it would not come, not just yet. He pulled off the boots he had just put on and kicked himself into his bed. He hunkered his back up against the wall.

"You alright?"

"Me? I'm fine," said Gammin. "It's the Fifth we need to think about. They need to be told as soon as possible."

"Yes, they do. We will get to them. How can you be fine?"

Now there was a really long silence. Marin watched it, waiting like a child of the forest.

Gammin kicked off the rest of his boot. He lay back, as Marin had done before he answered.

"How can I be fine when I am no longer captain of the king's Fifth Company? That's easy. Before I met Annen, it was a big deal just to make sure I had food or, sometimes, a place to sleep."

Marin started to protest. Gammin waved him into continued silence.

"I stayed with you lots of times, and I was never going to starve. That is true. It is also true that there were times I had nothing to eat, and it wasn't possible to get to you. During storms and such."

Marin looked at him dubiously. Gammin flashed him his mother's grin. Talking to Marin always made him feel better.

"Anyway, that's not the point I was making. Stop interrupting. Do you want to hear this or not?"

"Yes, please continue."

"My point is that, with or without the Fifth, my life has been changing for the better at a pretty good rate."

"You mean becoming a prince?" The question was genuine.

Gammin shook his head only slightly. "Not at all. You are thinking way too big. That is the way a king would think, or someone who wanted to be king. I am talking about something more important, more basic." He closed his eyes, took a very deep breath, then another.

"I eat every day now, even when we are on the march, most days twice. As much as we complain about camp food, it's not bad at all. That's just when we are campaigning, which seems to be most of the time, now that I think of it. When we are in a city, I eat like… well… like a king."

Marin said, "Yes we do, though I have never heard you complain about camp food. Or much else, really. Complaining's not your way, is it?"

Gammin shrugged. "We lost the Fifth. There is a war on. We are getting farther from the ones we love every day. All those are true. In spite of all that, things are still going pretty well for me. If King Branden gets so mad that he kicks me out, so be it. I know where I will go, what I will do. On the other hand, if the worst happens and I end up on a throne somewhere, we'll make the best of that, too."

Thinking back to his recent conversation with the king, Gammin asked, "Does that answer your question about how I can be fine? We are fine. Yes, there is a war on, but, right now, at this minute, we are fine."

Marin did not answer. He let the silence speak. It was something his father had tried to teach him, a tool he was only beginning to understand. Not realizing what he was doing, Marin thought, in the distant corners of his mind, "So much change, so fast. How can we keep up with your wave?"

Gammin and Marin were on their way to see Eamehr when they happened upon Karene. Normally, Gammin would have been pleased to see her. She was an excellent companion. He enjoyed being with her. However, he was on the way to relinquish his command responsibilities and not in the mood for enjoyment.

They paused to greet each other in the hallway. Karene, a promising diplomat, saw that Gammin was in a hurry. She must also have seen that he was greatly troubled. She reached out and took his hand.

"Theramina and I are going to see the Orb tonight after supper. Come with us!"

Gammin stopped to sip from a moment he had intended to bypass. Andur's Orb? He had forgotten about that. It would be the thing to see, now that time was short. It had been a gift to Andur, so the legends told.

Gammin was forming an answer when Marin said, "We would like to see that! Yes, we would. That is something we would like to see."

Gammin looked sideways at his friend. "I thank you, Temay."

The words did not match Gammin's somber face. The moment almost found awkward as a playmate while Karene was at a loss what to say. Marin was many things, enticingly odd among them, but he did not often act like a simpleton. A smile spread over her face as she realized why Marin had been playing the fool. He was a true friend. Gammin was fortunate.

"Good, then," she said, retracting her hand. "See you at supper!"

Princess Karene hurried off. As she had not been in a hurry when they had first seen her, Gammin suspected she was hurrying away for their benefit, which was remarkably considerate. He stared after her, momentarily distracted by the thought of seeing the Orb. It was something from legend, something Andur had touched, had put there.

Like every young person in Ehrylan, Gammin had been born into a society where such topics were not openly discussed. But he had heard the legends. The loyal were careful to pass those along, knowing that was how truth was preserved.

What little Gammin knew of the true history came from his studies. The Orb was reputed to be a very large piece of

Dragon's Eye that had been worked into a rough sphere. How Andur had come to select a cavern in northwest Rath as the Orb's final resting place was still a mystery. Both Southlanders would have been thrilled at the prospect of a visit to the artifact—chaffing at the bit, really—if their moods had not been so murky. Hard news has a way of darkening the road.

The meeting with Eamehr went well. Marin's reminder of Temay—of home—and the possibility of seeing the Orb turned his mind from his frustrations and helped Gammin focus. The older man understood more than he let on. He was gracious. The two of them knew each other and had quickly come to agreement on the important particulars.

Then it was off to meet with the Fifth. That is where things got difficult. The new recruits had not yet started to arrive. The sixty or so survivors were all blooded veterans now, at least compared to what they had been a few months ago.

Gammin made the best of it, and Marin, too. Most of all, they tried to encourage. Eamehr was a senior commander, one of the king's closest friends and confidants; it would bring them great honor to serve under such a seasoned veteran. They would learn much, do much.

When they had done all they could think of to do, Gammin and Marin took their leave of their companions from the Fifth Company. They made the longish walk back to the castle-proper with what felt like rain clouds moving overhead. It was, however, as fine morning as anyone could have wished up, cold, windless, and clear. There was not a cloud in sight west of the mountains across the river, which marched northward, a parade of jagged peaks swathed in white.

Gammin led the way to their quarters without speaking. They did not meet anyone with whom they had to stop and chat. Gammin has relieved by that. He did not want idle chatter or even purposeful discussion. What he wanted most was to dive into a clear mountain lake, perhaps from the bough of a shoreline tree. Since he could not have that, his next preference was to get something to eat, and then a while to think. After the thinking, if there was time before they had to meet Karene and Theramina, he might be able to make some plans. The plans were the most important. He was free now. Free.

He pushed open the door to their apartments with the same preoccupied distraction that had possessed him earlier. Then, he had been rushed by the need to transfer the command. At that point, there had been warriors and support crew that depended on him. Now, when less than a handful of people had a tentative commitment to meet later, he felt that same lack of time.

He hung his sword on its peg. Casting himself on the bed, he thought, "Why is time so short? How can I find more?"

Then, because worry did not stick to him, he called to his dearest friend, who had just closed the door.

"Do you have any apples?"

II.

By the time Gammin arrived in the Chamber of the Orb— or whatever the place was called—he was glad they had found the time. None of it was what he anticipated. He had expected guards, locks, and rigorous controls, but the whole affair seemed uncommonly casual.

The oddities started the moment the four young people stepped out of the castle. Gammin and Marin had assumed the Orb was enshrined in the main keep. That would have made sense; the keep was the most-fortified and defended part of the castle environs. But the Orb was not in the keep. It was not even in the inner ward, an open area that contained most of the castle's living areas, the great hall, and the wells. Andur's Orb rested in the outer ward, which was separated from the rest of Arathai only by the moat and the ring wall.

Karene led them through the stables, granaries, and workshops to a mound near the north wall. Coming nearer, they saw that the mound was little more than a rough face of rock about the size of a wagon. It was surrounded by a cape of grass. The hillock stood at the center of a park or, as it is called in Rath, a garden, though nothing to consume was intentionally grown there. There was a low tower to one side of the rock. A stream sang merrily between them. It seemed an ideal place to throw off the disappointments and frustrations of the day.

An assortment of people were already doing just that. Some looked affluent, others not. A few were seated on benches or under trees near the stream. Others wandered through the park and in or out of the tower. There was no loud talking. Now and again, the voice of a person or an instrument lifted in song above the tumbling cadence of the stream.

Karene greeted each person they encountered with genuine affection. The people nodded or bowed, depending on some etiquette Marin did not know. They did not shy away from their princess or her guards, who followed discretely. She was often among her people, and, here, near this tower, there was no need to be afraid.

Marin entered the tower not knowing what to expect. The structure was not large enough to be where the Orb was kept. The only thing he saw in the tower, apart from torches, was a stairway leading under the mound. There were no guards.

"Why would you build a stone tower over a stairway and then leave it unguarded? There must be a good reason." Marin spoke into the empty stairwell. He felt the weight of the close walls as he began to follow Karene down the dry, well-lit stairs.

"It might be a bad reason," said Gammin, who was feeling better. Just being out like this at night was enticing. And, they were going underground! The only thing that could have made it better was a full moon. Or if Arica were here with him.

Karene pretended to think. "I am not sure if it is a good reason or a bad one."

The Princess of Arel arched her eyebrow. "It is a simple reason. That is why they do not see it."

Neither young man could tell if she was feigning the knowledge or not.

Marin asked, "Why, then?"

"Why, to keep the rain off, of course," said Karene. "Stairs are slippery when wet."

She shook her head at the simpletons, winked at Theramina, and led them down. It was a long way down.

As they came to the foot of the stair, Marin expected some sort of opulent throne room with a giant ball taking up the place of honor. Maybe the Orb would be hanging in a harness or supported on a giant plinth. It might even be hovering in the air without any support. You never knew what you were going to get with Dragon's Eye, and this was supposed to be the biggest hunk anywhere.

What the woodcutter's son saw was nothing of the sort. The rough stone walls and floor of an antechamber still separated them from whatever was beyond. Out of habit, Marin glanced at Gammin. He saw that his friend was as excited as he was and looking much better.

Gammin was certainly feeling better than he had. The Orb was very near. They would get to it soon enough. Why rush it? The antechamber had obviously been made centuries before. It was very interesting and had a nice feel to it. To start with, there was an open doorway. It was truly an open doorway; there was no door, just a rough, arched opening. That was as far in his inspection of the antechamber as Gammin got. Without thinking, he stepped toward the archway. The others moved with him, an expectant cluster, boys in front.

The air was delicious. Gammin stopped to experience it, Marin next to him. They breathed. It felt very fine just to stand in front of that opening. Two breaths stretched to six, six to ten.

Karene emitted something too dignified to be called a giggle, though that is what it was. She said, "It disorienting the first time."

"It is disorienting every time, but in a good way," said Theramina. "You will see." She pushed Gammin between the shoulder blades. "Go on."

Gammin was not concerned about how disoriented he might be. He wasn't concerned about anything. He stumbled a bit as he was propelled through the doorway. The minor clumsiness made him grin.

Andur's Orb was not enshrined in a throne room—or any kind of room in the true sense. The space was a cavern, and it made no apologies for it. This part of the cavern, which was thirty or forty steps across, appeared to be natural. It was mostly uncut and completely unadorned. There were no paintings, no carpets, no cabinets, and no guards. There were no benches or chairs. It was just an underground cavern that felt as fresh as a mountaintop. Gammin thought the air was pregnant with the promise of rain, wind, and sunlight all at the same time and all in perfect, pleasurable measure.

A few people sat on outcroppings of stone that had been worn to excellent seats over the centuries. A man, woman, and their two children—farmers, Gammin somehow knew—were standing in front of an angular boulder at the center of the cavern. The boulder was white, maybe quartz or granite. The surface was uncut and unpolished except on top where it had been sheared off to a sparkling sheen.

Once again, and for the second time that day, Gammin had a brief vision of his troubled past. He saw a jagged black table surrounded by dragons of stone with gemmed eyes. In a flash of insight, he understood that the black table was an obscene perversion of this white boulder.

No such vision could stand up against the presence of Andur's Orb, which sat on top of the boulder. It was big enough that Gammin thought he could only just put his arms all the way around it if the need struck him. Based on how he felt, it just might. The Orb was not white or clear as he had expected, which was silly of him since he had seen more Dragon's Eye than most people. At the moment, it seemed to be several colors at once, its various facets glimmering like rainbows through fog.

Gammin watched Andur's Orb while they waited. Really, they were not waiting at all. They had already arrived.

When it was their turn, Karene took them forward. As he got closer, Gammin saw that the Orb was not really a sphere.

It wasn't even close. Much of its surface was unworked. Some of it was faceted. The rest was dressed in curves and angles that pleased the eye.

"Go on," repeated Theramina.

Gammin shook his head. "You first." He knew that, at another time or in a different place—which was the more accurate of the two—Theramina would have argued that point just for the sport of it. He also knew she would not do so this time, in this place.

He waited for Theramina and then Marin.

When it was his turn, Gammin approached the Orb with an open mind and what should have been a quailing heart. He knew what even a small piece of Dragon's Eye could do to him. He should have been uneasy at being this close to so much of the stuff. Truth to tell, Gammin was not feeling uneasy. He did not feel anything, but in a good way, a quiet way, a still way.

The Orb was already gray by the time he stood before it. That was one thing he had expected. It was the color he engendered from Dragon's Eye.

What he had not expected was the water. He had not noticed it before stepping close to the Orb. A pool lay close around the base of the boulder. Gammin could not see how the liquid was contained or how it was brought up to flow back down over the Orb and its table, which were really nothing more than two wet stones. The upper-most surface of the Orb was just below the level of Gammin's eyes. He gazed at it, trying to see where the water came from. But it was difficult. Soon, he lost interest in that question entirely. What was important was the Orb and the way the sculptured Dragon's Eye... felt.

As he gazed down on Andur's Orb, the Prince of Ehrylan felt very young and also very old. Deep inside, beneath the layers of muscle that knit him together, he felt a click, as if one part of him had suddenly shifted, allowing a door to close. Or was it opening? Was that music he heard? A finalla? Voices? Singing?

Gammin stared at the Orb, watching the water wash over it, hearing its song. After a moment, he perceived that the flowing water was the source of the freshness in the cave. That made sense. It was nice, very nice.

In a moment, he would have to leave this place—the real place—and go back to the dream, where wars raged and winter winds blew. He had purpose there and things to do, many things. He knew he needed to get to them. But there was no need to hurry, not yet. That would come later. For now, he just wanted to listen to the water and the song of the stones. Perhaps they were one and the same.

As he extended his hand to touch Andur's Orb, Gammin thought, "We have time to worry, even when there is no time to wait."

III.

"They should make treaties in there," said Gammin.

"I think that was the point," replied Theramina.

The four friends were sitting in a parlor within Karene's quarters. Actually, they were in the garden that grew within the parlor. A garden seemed very fitting for how they felt. They had not spoken much after leaving the cavern. Now that they were seated and back in familiar territory, things were loosening up.

Gammin, who was in no mood for a contest, started again. "It reminds me of the spring in Bendwood, only hundred times more, or a thousand."

"I see what you mean," replied Marin. To him, it had felt like the deep heart of the forest. "Now that you mention it, water sounds perfect." He turned the Karene. "I guess you can't just create a spring in there, but you might make a pool."

Gammin said, "I thought the water was already perfect. I can't stop thinking about it. Karene, do you know how they made the fountain work?"

As he finished speaking, Gammin realized what he thought

must have been the truth. "Oh, I see. There's a natural spring there? Andur just put the Orb on top of it. That was clever."

"What are you talking about?" The question came from Marin. There was a hint of disquiet in his voice.

"The water flowing from the Orb pooled around the base of the boulder. There wasn't much, but you couldn't have missed it." No one spoke. Gammin reconsidered, imagining what he had seen. "Now that I think about it, there was lots of water."

Marin saw where this was going. "There is no water."

"You didn't see it?" Gammin turned to Karene, intending to ask her about the water. The look on her face stopped him cold.

"What is it, Princess? Are you unwell?"

Karene's eyes were as big as Rathian silver crescents, which are a good-sized coin. She managed to say, "You saw the Welling?" Her voice was small as a whisper.

"I saw the water. What is going on?"

Karene's hand crept toward the base of her throat slowly, as if it were frightened of what it might find there.

"There is no water in the cavern, not around the Orb."

"Then what is the Welling?"

Karene's eyes shifted from face to face and landed on floor in front of her. "There is an old rhyme. It is mostly nonsense, I think. I don't remember it exactly."

She closed her eyes, appeared to concentrate. That was a sham. She was trying to determine a way out of the trap into which she had stumbled. She had, to some extent, created it herself, albeit unintentionally. Who wouldn't have stumbled? It was not every day someone saw the Welling, or even every lifetime. Not by a long shot.

Deciding that honesty was the best policy, she said, "I couldn't tell you anyway, even if I did." She bent low, held a finger to her lips. "Shhshhh! It's a family secret."

The distraction worked. She was able to continue before being questioned further. Now, unless she was careful, she would have to say things that were less truthful and therefore more risky. She didn't like that. These people were friends now, maybe more than that. Still, each of them had their secrets. They would understand.

"Somewhere in the rhyme, it talks about the water from the Orb. It's called the Welling. That is all I can say. Gammin has seen the Welling. He is not the first."

Princess Karene remembered more than she was saying. She remembered everything. The rhyme was mostly a list of the names of the individuals who, over the centuries, had reported seeing the water. The kings and queens of Rath had been keeping that list since Andur's time. According to the lore she had been forced to learn and promised to keep secret, they had been commanded by Andur himself to keep the list. That is, if the tales were true. And, if the tales were true, then…

Karene was excited and frightened at the same time. Much to her chagrin, she was sure these emotions showed on her face. Which they did.

"Oh, vulture turds," muttered Gammin, drowning his face in his arms. "Does this mean I am destined to mount Andur's throne and lead the reunification of the kingdoms of the Crescent?" He looked up from his nest of forearms and biceps. "I just want to go home."

The poor boy looked so genuinely aggrieved that Karene wanted to laugh, especially since he'd got it all wrong. With a quick smile and a hand on his arm, she told the Prince of Ehrylan the truth.

"Not that, I assure you. There is no mention of Andur or his throne." She thought for an moment, then, when she was sure there was no harm in the admission, she added, "No thrones at all are mentioned, for that matter."

The list had nothing to do with rulers and kingdoms. As far as she knew, none of the names on the list belonged to people who had been kings or queens. Or princes.

The ramifications of her new-found knowledge left her a little giddy. The news was not bad. She would be the one who got to add the new couplet to the rhyme. That opportunity did not come around often. It was a very great honor, even for a princess. Only her direct descendants, the rulers of Rath, would read the words.

Karene decided to put an end to the evening's festivities. That would not be such an odd thing. People typically wanted to be alone after viewing the Orb. This news was in no way urgent, but she wanted to tell her father as soon as possible.

"If the rhyme does not foretell the reuniting of the Crescent, then what does it say?" Theramina's demand jarred Karene out of her ruminations.

Karene was not moved. She had to suppress a smile. If they knew the truth, the questions would stop right away. "Gammin has seen the Welling. Since there is no water there, it must be some kind of vision, right? There have been others over the years. It's nothing to worry about. And, it's nothing to trouble us tonight!" She concluded by straightening her already straight back, placing her hands in her lap, and smiling brilliantly. Then, she let the smile fade as her hand rose to the middle of her chest. "I seem to be uncommonly tired. Prince Gammin, how do you feel?"

The response was immediate. There was no attempt to disguise the relief it contained at the hint. "Honestly, Princess, it has been a long day. I've got a lot to think about. I think I'll go back to the room if you can't remember any more about that rhyme."

She shook her head. "Sorry."

"No worries," he said. "I thank you for taking us to see the Orb, water or no water."

Gammin wished Theramina a good night. He rose and bowed low to the two ladies.

Just before Gammin turned away, Karene said, "There is one thing I know, Gammin."

He stopped. "What do you know, Karene?"

"I know your color. Gray. I saw it in the Orb. It is the same gray that is in your eyes."

IV.

The four were together only once more. That happened the night before Branden's army departed. All of them—even the two young ladies—had become friends. The parting was tearful.

When the streams of their conversation had run dry, Karene sighed. No one had spoken during the time she had drunk her last goblet of wine. It was time for the moment each of them had quietly grown to dread as the days passed and the bonds of love grew between them.

"I think it is time. You will be taking an early start, no doubt."

"No doubt," repeated Marin, rising. He straightened his tunic, which was richer and stiffer than he preferred.

Karene took his hands in hers. She raised them to her face, placing them against her cheek. Gazing into Marin's eyes, she released his hands and placed hers on either side of his face, cradling it with her fingers. Without the least hesitation, she leaned in, kissed him on the lips, and set him free.

"The wine of my life, Marinsa, is richer because of you."

Marin replied, "I will see you again when the paths cross."

"Is that a foretelling?"

Marin did not answer the question. The subject of his appointment as Ea's primary herald wasn't one they had discussed much—on purpose. He did not intend to start now. Instead, he said, "May your children sit at the feet of Ea and play there together with mine."

Karene reached out a last time, touched his cheek with the end of her fingers. It was a timid caress, given that she had just put one right on his kisser with some authority. To Gammin, who stood waiting, the gesture resembled something from a dream, as if she were reaching out to see if the Marin was real or imaginary.

Then, in her capricious way, Karene turned and held out her hands to Theramina. By-passing the extended hands, Theramina embraced her. It was not an embrace that grew from courtesy only, but also from the friendship that had grown between them, replacing what had before been merely familiar acquaintance. It was as if Gammin and Marin had been the mortar that solidified the relationship between the two princesses. This was not a true farewell between them, not yet. Theramina would be back, if only for a short time.

The Princess of Rath turned at last to the Prince of Ehrylan. He opened his arms to her. After a long hug, she pushed herself back. Her left hand stole up and cupped Gammin's cheek. After a pause, she said the words she had prepared some days before.

"In Rath, farmers say that the best fruit comes from bitter soil. I've always thought that meant good things come from bad. Now, I see there is more. If I were less sad at this parting, it would only mean that I loved you less." She dropped her hand, looked at Theramina and Marin. "All of you."

Setting her hands on Gammin's shoulders, standing on the very tips of her toes, Karene kissed his cheek.

Branden, his son, the seer, and the army left at dawn the next day. There was no need for an early start, but the breaking of light upon the day seemed to be the preferred commencement time for marches and battles. Gammin wondered why. Perhaps it was just another tradition.

13. THE CONQUEST OF EHRYNAI

I.

It was a wet, gray afternoon when King Branden and his army arrived at Ehrynai. With Fothyr behaving so strangely, no one knew what to expect of the negotiations. Ehrynai was one of the largest cities in the kingdom. There would be many loose ends to unite before they could move on to the real objective, which was to drive the enemy out of the Westland. The delay, though necessary, chafed Branden. With three quarters of a kingdom still to reclaim, he had little interest in cities that had already been won.

The king arrayed his forces beyond the north and eastern walls of the city. The other sides were bounded mostly by water. With Neath—only a few days ride north—firmly in enemy hands, vigilance could not be relaxed. Dauroth's commanders might even now be embarking on some kind of counter strike.

Taking with him his son, a few of his captains, and a hundred or so of their closest and most well-armed friends,

King Branden made his way to the prearranged meeting spot, Ehrynai's Council Hall. Theros, Theramina, and Marin stayed behind, holding themselves in readiness for good or for ill.

The king encountered none of the ceremony or panoply that had accompanied him on his three previous victorious entries. He had not fought a battle in front of the gates to drive off besieging enemies. His string of victories elsewhere had done that. Gammin wondered if that simple fact accounted for the difference.

That is not to say the townspeople failed to notice them. Even in that time of constant warfare, the passage of so many able-bodied warriors turned heads. Many townsfolk assembled at street corners and along the wider streets. Some tried to approach. They were turned away by City Guards who, though they were unobtrusive, seemed to come out of nowhere at the least suggestion of need. Apart from the effective security system, there was no official response.

The way from the city gates to the hall was long. As has been noted, the city was large, both in size and in populace. Their hall was at the top of a hill, which is where such meeting places seem to crop up most often. Taking only their two personal guards, the king and his son entered the imposing structure. Their booted footsteps echoed as they were ushered to the place in which they were left to wait.

It was not a waiting room or any kind of antechamber. The room resembled a large, comfortable office. It was the kind of place in which a town's senior clerk or treasurer might process rivers of paperwork. The king eyed the plush, leather-covered couches lining the walls. In what appeared to be an intentional contradiction, a pair of uncomfortable chairs cowered in front of an enormous desk.

The king sat on one of the couches, his truculence thinly-veiled. He had been aware of Fothyr's strange ways, but this treatment was unnerving. The longer they sat, the more the corner of Branden's mouth twitched.

Gammin used the time to ponder why Fothyr would act

this way. Fothyr had picked Annen to be in the Resistance. That was the story. Gammin knew that Annen had been in touch with Fothyr recently. So what was the issue?

As he tried to puzzle this mystery out, Gammin's mind stole into a very dark hole. The progress down was slow, each step more furtive than the last. Perhaps Fothyr was not loyal to Brand, the old king. Maybe he had intended all along to grab the throne himself, once Dauroth was killed—or whatever one did to an Everbourne to be rid of it. What if Fothyr was playing both sides? He might be luring King Branden into a trap with intentions of delivering him to Dauroth trussed up like a Snow Moon turkey ready for the fire. Or worse, what if Fothyr had been taken over by a Gryhm? How would they know? How could they trust him?

The prince caught himself. What was he thinking? Such ideas were so alien to Gammin that they felt wrong despite their validity. Where had such thoughts come from? That was the question he was pondering when the inner door to the chamber opened and Fothyr stepped in.

Fothyr was exactly what Gammin expected. He was tall, thin, and rugged—an ancient pine tree that had withstood many harsh winters and stood fair to outlive several more. Shutting the thick, heavy door behind himself with a satisfying thud, the old man held his arms wide.

"Welcome to your city, Prince Branden. I'll call you that only once. It is how I knew you when you were but an insolent little peep, always getting underfoot, chirping to be at the front of the action. Henceforth, I will call you king, as will every loyal citizen of this, your city. Welcome home, my king."

Branden stood. He crossed the room with sure steps. Planting himself in front of Fothyr, he raised both hands to his hips, striking a pose.

"Insolent peep?"

"Insolent little peep, sire. My apologies. I wanted your attention. It seems I have it. What I said is true, however. You were much smaller back when the war started. And, you did always want a place on the front line, even when a more able warrior—you were only a lad, then—was the better choice. Not that King Brand gave in to you all that often, even when you pitched a fit."

"Pitched a fit?"

"Sire, we are not going to get anywhere if you just continue to repeat what I have already said."

Branden's hands abandoned their perch on his hips to make tight fists. When he realized it, he opened his hands again and flexed the fingers, wishing he could curl them around the pommel of his sword and poke this old fool with it a few times. However, he suspected such an overt act of intolerance might be construed in a bad light. He passed over the desire in favor of a less violent course of action.

"You know me?"

"Yes, sire. I know you very well. I saw you often back when times were just starting to turn sour."

"Stop talking in riddles!"

"I am not talking in riddles, King Branden. I am just not moving as fast as you are. Slow down for me, please. And, do you mind if we sit? I am not as young as I used to be. It's been a long war."

The king stepped back. As if intentionally throwing fuel onto a bonfire named Impatience, the old man refused to sit until after Branden did. As frustrated as he might be, the king could hardly argue against proper protocol. Furthermore, the old man was not resisting at all. The situation was so absurd that the brewing mash of frustration and impatience bubbled out in a single, irresolute laugh. Then, he recovered himself.

"Now, who are you, and how is it that you had such access to the castle in Kingsholm?"

Fothyr shook his head. "Nay, not yet, sire."

The king's silence spoke eloquently. Fothyr was forced to continue.

"It's a story that involves your father, sire. I was thinking you might care to hear it in a less public setting."

Branden considered the words, signaled the guards to leave. For one terrified instant, Gammin was sure Andryg, who had the duty today, would look to him for approval. But Andryg was young, not stupid. He had lived in Stormhaven all his life and was familiar with Branden's ways from the many stories that had circulated about the Defier. He followed Branden's guard looking very proper.

Gammin let out the breath that had caught in his throat. These rituals of respect were insane. They were courtesy and honor taken to absurd levels. When he had read of such things in the history books and scrolls, they hadn't bothered him. Now that they were slapping him in the face, it was another matter entirely.

Once they were alone, Fothyr said, "Forgive me, majesty, for the lack of courtesy. There is a reason. I believe you will agree with it once it is known to you."

"Proceed," replied the king. "I am less interested in slighted courtesy than in learning how you knew me. I wish to know how you created an organization that is, in my estimation, wholly successful. My own intelligence people could determine little about the Resistance, other than that there were pockets in isolated areas. We thought them disjointed and un-unified, when we thought of them at all."

"Exactly!" The old man slapped his thigh. "That is how we had to appear. If Dauroth had known we were organized and moving forward, operations would have been even more difficult than they already were. Your man, Annen, by the way. He didn't think we were moving fast enough."

The old man was going to add more. Branden cut him off. "We are not Dauroth."

"The student cannot exceed the master when they are both playing the same game. You see, King Branden... No, how could you? I'll start again. I must ask you to forgive an old man, sire, one whose family has been in your service for generations. It is just such a pleasure to see the results of our expertise!"

Fothyr rubbed his hands together happily. "I am not referring to this present occasion only. I refer mostly to the past."

The king waited. His hand tightened on the couch's arm. His fingers dug in.

Fothyr nodded and blinked slowly. "I see your impatience. Do not worry, sire. I will reveal all. The fact that you do not know me means I was good at what I did. That is satisfying, even in the face of this cursed war, maybe because of it. You must allow me to tarry in the rosy light of my own success."

"You see my impatience. You knew me when I was younger. You must know I have little tolerance for wasted time. Baste in the fatty drippings of your success all you like, but do it later. Answer my questions now."

Fothyr sat up in his chair. He looked the king in the eye without either defiance or entreaty. He said, "I was the head of your father's secret service. I don't think you even knew he had one."

Branden did not miss a beat. He said, "I knew, but only because any ruler must have such organizations." He might have said more, but the flow of words was caught in his damaged throat. He swallowed hard, looked for a cup, frowned when he did not find one. "I have always thought secret organizations turn out for the worst. Perhaps I was wrong. I have been wrong before."

"King Branden, you asked how I created a successful organization. Perhaps this will answer your question more fully. Consider. Where did your senior security people—the ones who put together your intelligence network—come from?"

Branden took the time to consider. After he decided there was no harm in it, he said, "One of the men who came back with me from the western seas had been in my father's secret service. His assignment was to watch over me. He was just one of the warriors as far as the rest of us knew. After we lost Calen and the ship, he revealed himself to me. There weren't many of us left by then. He is the one who suggested Stormhaven. He is with me still, though he has given over his responsibilities to someone else, someone younger, his daughter, in fact."

The king stopped abruptly, realizing he was saying too much. It didn't matter, or such a thing wouldn't have happened. He trusted this man, and he trusted in his own judgment. What Fothyr said next secured that trust further.

"That would be Rylf?"

The king did not answer.

"I picked Rylf for that mission, sire, with a little help from your father and Calen's."

Off-balanced by the turn this conversation had taken, Branden murmured, "I always thought Calen's father was head of the secret service." To cover his lack of composure, Branden shook his head vigorously and said, "You expect me to believe this?"

"That is not my problem, sire. I am your man. I have told you truth. I will answer your questions. Here is Ehrynai, your city. Command me or kill me, do what you will."

"Tell me more. How could you be the head of such an important organization without me knowing you? Or Calen. He would have remembered you, surely, when you met him after he returned. You saw him often enough."

"Sire, there is a reason I remember who we sent on the ship with you. It was a big moment in my life. Rylf was taking over an assignment that I held when you were a baby and again later. You could not have known me. You must have been almost twenty when I became head of the service. After that, I did not appear in the castle often." The old man chuckled, looked at Gammin. "I did haunt it, though."

For a time, Fothyr drifted on his memories. Now that he had the answer to his question, Branden was able to wait more patiently.

"I was with you long before that. I stood over your crib when you were a baby. That was before the war. Times were peaceful. Life was good. I was just a guard then. It was a family honor. I did that for about three years. Then I was invited to join the service. Later, when you were grown, I was picked as your personal attachment. The king knew me. I had held you for him while he attended your bottom on more than one occasion. The honor was presented as a promotion for meritorious service; it meant I had to follow you to all the different battles you tried to win single-handedly. I had to do it without you—or anyone else—knowing about it."

"That isn't possible. I would recognize you if you'd been so often near me. I am good with faces." The king studied the older man. "I will say that you have a familiar look. That can be because you are from Ehrylain stock."

"Do you remember every water boy who carried water—or, was supposed to—to the warriors in battle? Do you remember all the men who chopped the firewood, built the camps, and buried the dead? I did each of those things and more in your service. Maybe it was in your father's service, or even Ehrylan's. It did not matter back then. It does not matter now."

"Why didn't you send word to me at Stormhaven as soon as you knew?"

"I did not know you until recently. You were just the Defier until, what, Harvest Moon? That was only two or three months ago. It wasn't until Annen's messages got through that I found out the truth. By the way, he's a good boy, that Annen. I don't think we'd be here today without him. I remember when he dragged himself in, all leg-broke and half-dead. We weren't sure which would live longer, him or the old, ragged horse he rode in on. He was all sword wounds and broken bones, but his eyes were full of that crazy purpose, like he was hearing a song no one else could hear. It drove him wild and made him focus all at the same time. He used to frighten me. Anyway, Annen's the one that got the Resistance started in Mendolas and Twofords. That was after he was with me for a year or two, if I recall."

"Even you call him Annen? No, I see. That would be right. You have been calling him that a long time."

"Yes, sire. That is how I have known him for years, though we each had many names in the Resistance. Does it aggrieve you?"

"No. It confuses me. Why didn't you reveal yourself to him?"

"To Annen? There was no need. What would it have helped? The less he knew of me, the better for me. The same was also true for him. The less I knew of him the better—if I were caught. You understand."

King Branden allowed that he did. His tiny nod, despite its diminutive size, was a giant victory in the battle for patience.

"Even if I had known the true king was in Stormhaven, I would not have revealed my identity to Annen. I would have sent word to you. I would have told you of Annen."

"That is logical, Fothyr."

"Yes, sire."

There was a long silence. Branden was thinking, plotting. Finally, he said, "I believe your story, Fothyr."

"I thank you, King Branden."

"No, sir. It is I who thank you. It has been a long war. I am glad to find a friend unlooked-for at this end of it. I do not have enough of my kingdom to reward you as well as you should be rewarded." The king put a flash of hard steel in his eyes. "Don't bother claiming you cannot accept or do not deserve. I will not tolerate such talk. Here is talk that matters. I name you Fothyr, Lord of the Westland."

Branden made the proclamation with such nonchalance that Gammin, who was busy thinking about something else, almost missed it.

"Meredan, sire," said Fothyr, interrupting.

"What?"

"The name my mother gave me was Meredan. I would like to start using it again. Meredan was what King Brand called me. It would be ample reward just to hear it from your lips, your majesty."

Now—finally—Branden was moved. He had not intended to make a show of this, not right now. There was time for that later. Now he thought better of it. The old man, who had spent his whole life in Ehrylan's service, deserved better, just for himself.

"Arise," he said, motioning regally with his arm.

They all got to their feet.

"Who was your father?"

"Owen, sire, son of Sten."

"Meredan, son of Owen whose father was Sten, you have been of great service to this kingdom and to the House of Brand. You are Meredan, Lord of the Westland, whose heirs will continue to serve the House of Brand. Your heirs are granted right of immediate audience with the king in addition to their roles as nursemaids to our babes and as silent servants of the service."

Branden, pleased with himself, reached for his sword. It was back in camp. He felt suddenly vulnerable. He had left it behind on purpose. A king with no sword appears stronger than a king with a sword. That was the principle. In practice, this king felt naked.

"Sire." Gammin moved his left hand down to his left hip and pushed back the edge of his cloak. It was red velvet or some such material. It wasn't the war cloak he favored. Another mandate. The heavy, embroidered edge of the cloak danced back revealing first the pommel and then the scabbard of his sword.

Branden nodded.

The blade came free, a whisper singing. The carpets and hangings prevented what might have been a nice echo, but there was a swift arch of light. A sudden stillness sprang into the already quiet office.

The prince held out his sword. It had been made just up river and not so long ago, as swords go. The king took it the only way a hardened veteran could take such a plain and true weapon. His grim countenance melted under the heat of a fierce smile. He gazed at the unadorned steel with such ferocity that poor Meredan had to stave off the urge to scramble for one or two swords of his own.

Quick and unexpected as an accident, King Branden thwacked Meredan on the upper arm with the flat of the blade. The blow would have broken the walls of a thick, clay pot. It might have cut cloth if the edge were set.

"Lord Meredan."

"Sire," replied Lord Meredan.

Branden said, "You have been instrumental in the victories we have won so far. You will be a big part of the victories to come."

"My days of being a big part of anything are passed, King Branden. Notwithstanding that, I will do my best. How shall we start?"

Meredan, for all his protestations of being half way in the grave, did not look ready to die.

II.

In Ehrynai, the local head of the Resistance was also the head of a purely titular town council. The will of Fothyr had little opposition and a weighty vote. Now, Fothyr was Lord Meredan. He held the king's mandate. As importantly, he controlled an extensive security apparatus and Ehrynai's army, which was significantly larger than the one Branden brought to the Westland.

There were feasts, banquets, dances, and doings of all kinds. Marin, Theros, and Theramina arrived before any of those began, having been notified of the developments as soon as that first meeting ended. The festivities went on for days.

At one feast, the two Southlanders had a nice surprise. They had lost track of what this meal was for—and where, exactly, they were—when they noticed a stout, leathery-looking man. He could be mistaken for nothing but a life-long sailor. They hurried over, abandoning whichever important personage they were seated next to without caring for their discourtesy.

"Captain Norbet!"

Captain Norbet looked up from his plate. He focused on the two strapping young men across the table from him, recognizing them the instant his vision penetrated the fog of ale that clouded it. He knew he had seen them before, but not who they were. Maybe they had been involved in important business. That was like-enough true.

He stood up abruptly, his lap spewing bits of half-chewed food. He gaped the way the besotted do, as if he was trying to remember what he was trying to remember. The food he had been eating—the leg of some bird in one hand, a long knife skewering a roasted potato in the other—was forgotten. Then he found what he was looking for.

"Why, ho there. You be those two young knights from the Destra!"

Gammin laughed aloud. He extended his arms.

Norbet looked back and forth from Marin to Gammin. He tossed his feast back onto the table, careless of where it fell. The leg managed to overturn two containers of ale, something no one noticed in all the excitement. But it got worse. Or better.

"Didn't I say you'd be lookin' a'ter yourselves just fine? What are you, generals now?"

Norbet thought he was giving the two a compliment. The only better thing he could have called them was Admiral as far as he was concerned. He had no idea that he had shot low. The two Southlanders did not even notice.

Norbet started to reach out for Gammin. At the last moment, he remembered his hands. He retracted them, stared at them for an instant, then wiped them on a generous cloth draped across his jacket. That was the last impediment to disaster.

With hands that were only a little less greasy than before he wiped them, the elegantly scruffy sea captain seized Gammin. Captain Norbet, who had worked hard on ships and in dockyards literally all his life, pulled the Prince of Ehrylan over and across the top of the table as if he were a fifty-weight sack of grain. Revelers and food scattered everywhere. Laughter was plentiful. No one minded. It was a great day where all were satisfied, and on, and on.

Gammin and Marin saw the captain and a dozen other old acquaintances. Some they remembered, others not. The ones they recognized mostly came from the inns, taverns, and merchants they had been to with Annen, and sometimes with Merelina. Gammin came to understand that Annen's choices in mercantile and exchange had been part of the web he and Meredan wove. Gammin might have seen it sooner, but he, Marin, and Arica had left Twofords early on.

Gammin and Marin were exhausted by the time they were allowed to go in search of sleep. Fortunately, there was no return journey to the camp. Rooms, compete with their own gear, had appeared for them as if by magic. They laid their heads down in comfort that night.

Gammin lasted longer than Marin. He drifted off eventually, listening to the snores, knowing there were not many comfortable nights left in the immediate future.

III.

Captain Norbet managed to survive his public display of exuberance. As it turned out, he had been part of Meredan's web, which was not all that unexpected. Meredan had performed his first truly official function as Lord of the Westland by appointing Norbet to be the First Admiral of Ehrynai's navy. The sturdy seaman had been doing that job already without the title. The appointment had the effect of making him First Admiral of the King's navy as well, since Ehrynai's navy was the only one in the kingdom at present.

BATTLE FOR THE SOUTHLAND

Two days before the army of the king departed its last safe haven that side of the mountains, Theramina took her leave. She was headed back home, where, said Theros, her people needed her. She sailed away rather than rode, which was not something Gammin or Marin anticipated. Old King Kappelli came in his flagship to collect her and to meet Meredan. With him came an escort of military frigates. Rath did not have a big army. They had the best navy.

Theramina, her horse, and a suitable escort of Themera took ship with the old king the same day Branden marched. From there, she was headed back to Rath, but only to change ships and join with a different armada. That one would take her quickly and comfortably home with as much safety as winter seas allowed. There, with the help of the elders and chieftains, she would rule until her father returned. Theros did not expect any trouble. Arel was well defended.

Six Rathian war frigates stayed in Ehrynai after King Kappelli sailed away with Theramina. Those ships would escort Ehrylain troop ships containing warriors from Ehrynai's army as Brand marched toward Neath.

Stryn rode with Branden, claiming there was no better place for a faelyth than at the king's side, particularly when that king was fighting for truth and justice. It was a reasonable offering if a bit flowery. What else could you expect? Caerlyn came as well, his horse draped under blankets to protect its thin, southern blood. He did not state his reasons for coming. Gammin did not ask. The king seemed to trust the man, so Gammin put his doubts on hold.

Gammin rode in the vanguard with his father. Now that he no longer had a company to occupy him, his full attention could be on the king. Theros, King of Arel, rode with them. At least five thousand fought under the King's lion pennants now. They were a proper army with a navy to supply them and a cavalry to be their eyes.

14. THE ROAD TO NEATH

I.

Winter can be a raging beast in much of Ehrylan, but it is only an inconvenience on the ocean side of the Western Mountains. Not that it mattered. King Branden did not heed weather, inconvenient or not. He set out for Neath on a morning when there seemed to be more water in the air than in the sea. That surprised no one. Dense, moist air is well-known in those parts. It is only marginally less uncomfortable than the driving, coastal rains that come later.

What had taken King Brand's messengers less than three days to ride took his son's army more than twenty days. Mostly, the slow progress was not the result of the weather. Branden had to fight his way to the walls of Neath.

The first battle happened where the Coast Road turns truly north for the first time. They were only a day or so from Ehrynai. The king's army, rested and spoiling for a fight, battled through a force of similar size as their own, tested but not bested. To some, it was just like many another battle. To others, it was a first taste of victory in their fight for freedom.

The Coast Road stays between the coastal bluffs and the valleys to the east, which climb steadily toward the mountains. The valleys yawned above the army as it marched. The folk of that beautiful country had long ago settled in the mouths of those valleys. There, close to the sea but set back from high bluffs, ridges sheltered them from the cruel winter winds.

As the army moved northward, it encountered many farmsteads. At some of these, the farmers and their families came forward eager to celebrate the prince—now a king—who had returned to them. At others, the farmers were resistant, even belligerent. These held no allegiance to the old order. In most cases, they were Outlanders who had arrived with Dauroth or their now-grown offspring.

It was the same with the settlements. Some were loyal to Branden. Others were willing to fight against him. In either case, there was little the settlements could do to aid or deter the king's progress. Only a few were large enough to be thought of as proper villages.

For the most part, the settlements loyal to the king were well-known to him. He had been to many of them in his youth. They had been there for centuries upon centuries. They were on old maps.

The new Outlandish settlements were places where Dauroth's victorious soldiers had planted themselves after their conquest a generation ago. The younger people of those settlements had been born in Westland villages that did not exist when Branden sailed away. Other settlers had arrived since, using sea roads to come to this fertile land. They had found it free for the taking. In those settlements, few, if any, were loyal to the king's banner.

Those people—soldiers who had settled here after the war, children and adults born to parents newly arrived in this place, criminals or wanderers who had fled their own lands to make new starts—were fighting for their homes. And, they were fighting fiercely. Branden's intelligence gatherers had not missed this development, they underestimated it. The farther north the king went, the worse it got.

The second of the Westland's major battles happened where the Coast Road touches the harbor that is sometimes called Fana Haven by the locals. That is only a day's ride from Neath—if, that is, the day does not include thousands of opposing swords. That battle was not like the first. Branden's forces smote a superbly organized enemy who outnumbered them substantially. It stopped the king's advance. His army had to entrench.

That is where the weather, inconvenient or not, asserted itself. Torrents of rain were cast from a sky tortured by wind and lightning. Whole days passed without a single sword thrust, except those aimed at reluctant embers or soaked wood. Nights were spent huddled in dripping tents, trying to stay dry. Neither slumber nor vigilance was to be had in great quantities on either side of that storm.

When they were able, the king's forces made war on the Outlanders and Westlanders who opposed them. Maybe the weather helped limit casualties; maybe it increased them. Either way, the dead and wounded multiplied while the armies and cavalries dwindled. The kings gradually pushed Dauroth's forces all the way back to the Westvale River, which flows eagerly all the way from the mountains to the sea.

There, on the south bank of that wide river, Dauroth's commander made a stand. The location had been prepared. It was waiting to accommodate the retreating soldiers. The Ehrylain and the Arelese were forced to dig in as best they could south of there.

The fighting continued sporadically. When the weather permitted, one side would make an assault. The other would respond. The fighting would rage back and forth for an hour, or a morning, or a whole day. Men and women, horses and dogs died. Blood flowed from the dead and wounded, mixing with the sandy mud to make a viscous, roan mess that was almost clay-like. The thick goo made identifying survivors difficult and complicated retrieval efforts. Then the skies would open and wash the whole mess with a fresh deluge. It was awful.

Branden had yet to ride amid battle since he was wounded by the Gryhm. There is no telling what motivated him to take to his horse again. Maybe Branden had swallowed his limit of giving in to Nemen Elma, or maybe he just felt better. Whatever the reason, ignoring the counsel of his captains and his healer, on a morning with nothing to differentiate it from the ones that had come before, the king rode out with his warriors.

Branden took a place at the rear of the action. Even this small concession required the concerted urging of those who knew the king well enough to risk an argument. Before the sun broke through the clearing clouds, he was moving forward into the battle.

One thing led to another. Soon, Branden was in the thick of it. Shortly thereafter, he realized how right his captains had been. He could keep his seat well enough, but there were issues with his sword arm. The wound in his shoulder was nowhere near completely healed, though it had been well on its way at the start of that day. He switched the sword to his other hand, not stopping to consider.

The arrow slammed into him high up on his left arm. As the sudden shock punched through him, Branden's fingers, at once nerveless and screaming with pain, lost purchase on the sword. It fell from his grasp. He had nothing to block the battle axe he had been fending off.

The king wrenched himself to one side. The only part of the blade that hit him was the lower corner. It bit into the flesh of his side just before the haft slammed into his abdomen, knocking him from his horse.

Gammin was there when the king went down. He was off his horse in an instant to stand over his father's body. Marin took a place next to the prince as soon as he finished gutting the soldier who had knocked the king from his saddle. With help, they fended off the other enemies until the king's inert body had been removed.

The prince had only the briefest moment to wonder why the king was unconscious. Gammin had heard a series of profane and unambiguous expletives that suggested his father had not died from the fall. Maybe he had bled into unconsciousness. There was no time to investigate, not even if such an investigation would save the king's life. Gammin had to fight for that in other ways.

Though it cost him personally, Branden's thrust forward stopped the enemy's assault. By the time the battlefield healers were ready to carry him away, the Ehrylain had control of that part of the muddy, bloody battlefield. The fighting raged for days to come, but the enemy did not again push so close to Branden's encampment on the south side of the river.

Gammin stayed with his father until the orderlies carried him away. He took the opportunity to talk with the healer who seemed to be in charge. He got a nice surprise, considering the circumstances.

"Peryn, son of… Lor."

"Lorn, your highness. It is good to see you!"

Gammin had met Peryn, who was a year or two younger, in Daur en Lammoth. The had come to know each other better in Stormhaven, even becoming friends. But this was no time for a reunion.

Peryn said, "Is it just the side, apart from the arm and the head?"

"I don't know about any of it. I saw him get knocked off his horse. He was conscious for a while, I think."

"It looks like a horse kicked him in the head. I don't know how bad it is. His breathing is strong, and his heart is beating well. We stopped the bleeding in his side and arm. I need to get him back to Elma. I'll be back for the others."

Guilt pulled Gammin's head around. He searched for his warriors, the men and women of the Fifth. Then he remembered that he had no official place in this battle. The Fifth was elsewhere, marching under Eamehr.

The prince of Ehrylan spared one more look at the healer. "Find me later, when there is time after the battle. I'd like to…" Gammin could not finish. He didn't know what he would like from Peryn.

"I understand, Gammin. I will. Ea be with you."

Peryn, an apprenticed healer but not yet a full nemen, returned his attention to Ehrylan's king. Someone found the king's sword and placed it on the stretcher with him. Peryn frowned, then shrugged. Kings need swords. Healers need bandages.

II.

When Gammin and Marin returned to camp, they went immediately to see the king. Elma's rebuke was cut short when she saw who had entered the tent. She had learned they could be trusted, even useful. They didn't ask questions when the work was at hand. She gifted them with a curt nod, which was about as close as Elma came to civility. Peryn was there. He was stirring a small, bubbling pot that hung over a hinged contraption containing coals. His eyes did not move from the work as the Southlanders entered.

When she was done with all that needed to be done, Elma placed herself in front of Gammin and Marin. Her eyes were red and strained. Her face was damp with sweat, though it was cold outside.

"He'll be alright, I think. He'll do as well as any fool who disregards his nemen's advice."

"Don't call me a fool." There was no power behind the king's words. He was almost too weak to push them through the torture of his throat. They emerged in a growling whisper.

Elma replied, "You shut it. Sleep is what you need, Branden, not talk. Don't make me dose you." She said that without looking down at the king.

To Gammin, she said, "By the looks of things, we need our king up and aware as soon as may be. I think we can get him there, but not if he doesn't cooperate. Are you getting this, Branden?"

The king did not reply. His breathing had become deep and regular. He was obviously asleep.

"You already dosed him," admired Marin.

Elma nodded. "Clever, aren't you, Old One?" Her gaze shifted to Peryn. "If that mongrel got the proportions right, he'll sleep through until morning, then be his troublesome self again, or near enough. He'll not be riding into anymore battles for a while, not if he wants to stay this side of what comes after."

Elma's practiced eye saw that Gammin was mildly alarmed by what he heard. She had tended him twice before and knew his heart. He was a good boy. She took pity on him, mostly because he did not ask.

"Don't worry, Prince Gammin. Peryn got it perfect. He usually does. Why else would I let him near the king?"

Gammin laughed, said, "Elma, when it comes to you, I've learned not to worry."

"Fine, then. You'll not worry when I tell you that I am leaving Peryn to tend the king. There are hundreds wounded worse than he is, maybe thousands."

"No," said Marin, "not thousands, not today. It was too muddy for anything that big. King Branden rode right in to the middle of the worst of it."

"That's nothing new. Anyway, my apprentice will stay with the king. I am needed elsewhere."

Elma remained where she was until Gammin said, "Nemen Elma, did I forget something?"

"You forgot you are in charge. There are injured Ehrylain waiting. I can help them, or I can do whatever you wish. What is your command, highness?"

There was an assault at dawn the next morning. It came with sudden ferocity, as if the commander of Neath was trying to take advantage of the king's indisposition. The captains of Ehrylan were prepared. They beat back the attack with the help of the Themera.

There was even a little advanced notice from Lord Meredan's folk inside Neath. The network of spies and informants Lord Meredan had created extended into the captive city and even into a few Outlandish settlements. His informants had reported changes within the power structure of Dauroth's army, changes in Neath, as well.

The new ruler of Neath was a woman who had been in Dauroth's service for a very long time. Her name was Vila. She deposed the previous governor—who had shown no disloyalty to Dauroth—with a gesture. Literally. He died on the spot, first screaming as if in agony, then withering like a dried-up vine. Vila imposed strict marshal law, rounding up those who were suspected of being Branden's sympathizers and isolating them in parts of the city where they were easily monitored and controlled.

Meredan's spies did not know this activity—and the brutality that followed—was nothing new for Vila. She had been with her master when he defeated Ehrylan the last time. She led the roundup of the multitude of loyalists in those early days. They had been mostly women and children, the widows and orphans of those who had fallen in their struggle against Dauroth. It was no different this time, other than that she was on the cozier side of the city walls and sleeping in a bed. The current crop of hostages was also predominately women and children. She did not care. Vila cared about defending this city, defeating Branden's army, and getting things back the way they were supposed to be.

Vila knew Ehrylan's king was injured. His troops would be in disarray. If she attacked now, she could put this matter to rest before the so-called king's army crossed the river. But that did not really matter. Help was on the way by land and by sea. All Vila had to do was hold the city until it arrived. The lives it would cost did not matter to her. Ruining lives was her business, now and forever.

She ordered the forces arrayed outside her stronghold to strike with everything they had. It was still dark and drippy when the first wave of soldiers came squishing out of the north. There was no hope of surprise. To Branden's sentries, it sounded like no one really tried.

Eamehr commanded Ehrylan's army for two full days and nights. The weather cleared to cold, blue skies, as if to encourage the carnage. The days were filled with strike and counter strike, the nights with raids and scouting missions that taxed both armies.

The next day, the skies opened again. This time it stormed for a full week, reducing the fight to forays rather than full-on battles. During that time, Gammin had a chance to catch up with himself. He was feeling poorly. He needed to take stock.

Gammin had killed many people since leaving Twofords. He did not like the taste of it. Dealing death was a bad business, even when killing enemies. Here, in the Westland, it was worse, much worse.

In the Southland, Dauroth's soldiers had been mostly mercenaries or conscripts. The soldiers in the Westland weren't like that. Most of them had been born in the Westland, lived here all their lives. Such people did not necessarily look upon Dauroth as a rightful or just king; he was simply the king that had to be bowed to at the moment. The people Gammin was killing were fighting for what was now their homeland. It was the same motivation that drove Branden and all who followed him.

Gammin's trouble was not with the trained soldiers. They knew how to defend themselves. It was the others who were hard to take, the farmer, the villager, the child. They were untrained, had lived hard lives, and died easily. This was the first time Gammin had fought against untrained, willing combatants. Both parts of that mattered. The untrained swineherds were as willing to die for their homes as he was willing to die for the Bend.

That difference affected the fighting, too. In the Southland, there had been a moment in every battle when the enemy soldiers realized that, if they just stopped fighting, they would be out of Dauroth's control and back with their countrymen. Gammin had come to rely on that moment, to anticipate it and use it to his advantage. That moment had not come during the battles here in the Westland.

III.

Gammin was brooding, but he did not let his rising gloom rule. To combat it, he decided a visit to Peryn was in order. The prince and the seer sought out their sometime companion when he was not on duty tending the king. The Southlanders had managed to reacquaint themselves with Peryn before the king reasserted himself. But, until now, there hadn't been time, and they were more than ready to speak with Peryn about his journey from Stormhaven and the doings in the rest of the kingdom.

What the young healer told them was not encouraging. Branden and his army in the Westland seemed to be the point of the spear. There was little change elsewhere. Stormhaven was, as yet, free of conflict. Twofords and Daur en Lammoth were holding the line. There was conflict at both and all through the lands between them. South of that line, there was a wartime peace all the way to Rath. As far as Peryn knew, everything north of Magravina's Gamble was still firmly in Dauroth's hands. That included Kingsholm, Norgap, and Erowain—the other large cities of Ehrylan. Of Darkhold, far north in the eastern corner of the kingdom at the foot of the Great Mountains, there was still no reliable word.

Peryn was unable to answer any of the Southlanders' many questions about Twofords or its people. He hadn't accompanied Elma when she left Stormhaven with Branden and his army. Nemen Elma, for reasons she did not disclose to the apprentice, left him to winter in the castle. Under the oversight of a senior nemen, he was to assist the healers who remained behind. At this stage in his training, such a thing was not out of place. The message summoning him to Elma's side had told him to make all speed. The commander of the troop sent to escort him took that as a command. They hadn't stopped in Twofords, even to switch horses or re-provision. They had been in a hurry to catch a ship in Mendolas.

"I arrived," he said, "when the king's army lay at Arathai. It was the first time I ever stepped on foreign soil. I had never been west of the Rift before that."

Having concluded a lengthy account of why he was unable to answer questions about Twofords, Peryn added, "Those Rathians know how to do it, don't they?"

The young healer sniffed the pot he was tending. He peered into it more closely, then stirred it with a long-handled wooden spoon.

He, Gammin, and Marin were in his tent. Andryg was there, too, though as the bodyguard, he was standing rather than relaxing. Gammin had picked him for this particular duty because Andryg and Peryn were friends.

Gammin got up from the camp chair into which he had settled some time ago. He looked into the small pot, which was swinging on its handle above the mobile heat. He grimaced, turned his gaze back to Peryn.

"The Rathians are nothing to the Arelese."

Peryn grinned. "For fighting and riding, maybe even singing and storytelling, I'd agree. But if you want a good party, go to a Rathian merchant's home."

"Have you ever been to an Arelese party, Nemen Peryn?" The question came from Marin, who had been through as much Rathian and Arelese revelry as he could take.

"Please don't call me that, Marin. I am not a nemen. Call me healer if you want; I can take that, and Elma won't remove one of my ears if she hears you saying it." The young man looked so aggrieved, almost alarmed, that his listeners considered the possibility he was not exaggerating.

All nemen are healers, but few healers are true nemen. Those who settle for the title healer usually have some amount of healing grace augmented by knowledge learned from their grandmother or someone else. To be a nemen, one had to undergo rigorous learning and years of service.

Gammin said, "He did not mean it, Peryn, not that way. Besides, you are a nemen to us. Healing flows through you either way, right? What is in a name?"

Gammin was thinking of the Water and the Stone. That is

how he thought of the Orb now—the Water and the Stone. He was also thinking of fruit and soil, and of life and death. Watching Peryn stir his creation, he realized they were all the same.

Marin said, "I agree. What do you think, Andryg? Do you agree that Peryn is a healer?"

Andryg, who was standing near the tent flap, said, "Begging your pardon, sir, it's not my opinion that counts. It's the king's. Or maybe Elma's."

There was a trio of nods. Marin chuckled.

Peryn grunted. "As I was saying!"

The apprentice nemen with the sunny disposition glared at Marin, then at Andryg. He brushed aside the Prince of Ehrylan so he could more thoroughly sniff and stir the pot. Gammin and Marin had pestered him for his story almost from the moment they had come to his tent. They just wouldn't let him tell it. He was, however, almost done. And, he was not displeased. The constant interruptions made it easier for him to prolong the uneventful story until his concoction was ready.

"I came to the army at Arathai. I am guessing you were too busy with other things to notice. I saw you a few times; I was with Elma, and you were with the other things. Both of them, each prettier than the other. Unlike you two, I didn't have a room in the castle."

Peryn stopped what he was doing and focused on Gammin.

"Do you think there is any chance I'm a prince, too? Maybe we're brothers separated at birth? Not that I am complaining. I've got this whole tent to myself. Being Elma's apprentice buys me that much."

The apprentice tasted his concoction by timidly touching the tip of his tongue to the end of the spoon. After a moment staring into empty space, he drizzled something thick and golden into the mixture, stirred it, then swung the pot away from the fire.

"Seriously, though. I don't deserve that title."

"Not yet, but you will."

Peryn laughed. "We are taught not to say yet. There's a

reason, but let's not get into it. Yet."

It was a very good reason. That was something he studied a lot with Elma—reasons as opposed to causes. He had not appreciated the difference before he began his studies, and he knew from experience that such subjects were of great interest to these two adventurers. If he opened that door, there would be no turning back.

"Anyway, I thank you for your faith in my abilities to release the king from his discomfort. Give me a moment. I have to time this right."

"How do you know when the time is right?"

"Believe it or not, by the size of the bubbles, but that is not until after you smell the butter blossoming. This is one of Elma's own recipes, not something the apprentices of other healers get to know. It takes a sure hand and brave heart."

He held out his right hand, fingers splayed in pantomime, and peered at it. He turned it over so he could see both sides, pretending to make certain it held no trembles.

"Now, hush."

Gammin turned, said, "What is Elma's thing, Andryg? Why does she get away with so much? I'd ask Peryn, but he is too busy."

Marin asked, "Was Nemen Elma part of King Branden's adventures in the Sundered Seas?"

"There were no women but the Arelese when they came to Arathai."

"How do you know?" Marin asked with a frown that was really just a smile on end. "You weren't even born then." It was not a serious question. Peryn had a way of relaxing him.

"There is a painting in Stormhaven. It shows everyone who arrived at Arel. Twelve of them? Or, was it twenty? I can't remember the story. What I do remember is that there are wrecked boats in the background and Arelese warriors on horses. It's kind of vague, the way Arelese art seems to be, but there aren't any women in it."

Wishing he had paid more attention back then, Gammin said, "You were saying, Andryg, about Nemen Elma?"

"I wasn't saying anything about Elma, your Highness."

"Well, whatever you weren't saying, say it now, if you please!"

"I really don't know anything, and I don't please. It's just the common talk."

Marin said, "Let's have that, then. That's what we're after."

Andryg truly didn't know much more than he was saying. He did know that gossip was always fun, seldom helpful. A hand full of gossip was an empty hand.

"Nemen Elma is famous, as you know," he began, an unguarded smile breaking across his face, "is a little older than the Defier... ooops, sorry.... I mean the king." He cast an anxious glance at Gammin, who cared not at all. "He was always just the Defier to us. We didn't know he was king until... well, until you came back with the people from Twofords, Prince Gammin. There was a joke in the castle when we found out he was a king and you were a prince. No one was sure whether the Defier being the king made you a prince or whether you being the prince made him the king."

Andryg's tongue stumbled to a halt. He was wondering if he had gone too far. He saw that Gammin had not noticed. That made him feel better. He hurried on, glad now to talk about Elma rather than the king. With an apprehensive look at Peryn, who did not appear to be listening, he said, "Most people think Elma is older than King Branden, but not me. I think she just didn't weather as well as he did. Anyway, the connection is not with the king, not directly. It's Gilmarun. Nemen Elma is supposed to be involved with him somehow. You can imagine all the speculation. She is his wife or his lover, something like that. Nobody really knows. One of my friends back in Stormhaven thinks Elma and Gilmarun are really the same person. Think about it. Have you ever seen them together?"

Gammin, who had eaten with both at the same time more than once, cocked his head and tried to look as if he were considering the possibility.

"I have heard she's his sister," said Peryn dryly. His voice, long absent from this conversation, sliced through the moment with a calm resolve. He didn't take his eyes off the pot into which he was crumbling a pinch of dark-tinted crystals. "I have also heard that she's his mother. Many tales involve illegitimate children, if your highness will excuse my bringing up a delicate subject."

Peryn instilled the flavor of secret knowledge in his words. He was Elma's apprentice. It was a special bond. If anyone knew the truth, surely he did.

"Oh, shut up. You're just an over-stuffed bag of pig dung."

Andryg, body guard to the Prince of Ehrylan, glared at the apprentice healer. His words chased the mock-solemnity from the tent. Peryn, who had been accused of being worse things than digested food by Andryg, did not look up as he replied. He was counting.

"I'll have you know, sir, that I am not over-stuffed." He waited a single, expectant breath, then said, "You take that back."

Andryg and Peryn had known each other since they were babies. They were both born in Stormhaven and had been around warriors their entire lives. In those years, there few paths open to the young, the chief among them being the waging of war and the defense; the promulgation of knowledge or healing; and the production of food and shelter. Andryg had loved horses, steel, and the fine edge of a new cut. The army had been his path to this chamber. Peryn would rather heal a horse than ride or feed it; he had undertaken to become a nemen.

Andryg took back his words. Marin smiled. Peryn grinned, breathing deeply as if of a cool breeze. Then he lifted the pot and poured its fragrant contents into three waiting mugs.

"As I said, I thank you for your faith in my abilities to release the king from his discomfort. Perhaps this will release us from ours, if only for a time."

Gammin held his mug up, looked at Andryg. "Sorry." Guards were not allowed to eat and drink on duty, even in Gammin's circle.

Andryg said, "I thank you, your Majesty. Peryn's canella is better than good. I know that from experience."

Soon, Gammin and Marin knew that from experience, too.

15. SEEING

I.

As it so often does in those parts, the weather shifted with the wind. The clouds were pushed aside, and the sun peered out. If it wasn't warm, the weather was unseasonably fine. It was especially fine for killing, except the mud.

Branden's troops had not been disarrayed by his injuries. The core of Ehrylan's western army was well-trained, and, by now, quite experienced. They were tried and true. The leaders and senior warriors were capable men and women. The lesser-experienced looked to the more-experienced for guidance and took strength and courage from them.

King Branden was back in the saddle the day Eamehr and Theros broke the enemy's army and pushed it back across the river. The king's saddle was on a horse that stood apart from the fighting. That was just as well. The horse had been selected for its calm temperament, not its battle training.

Now, after days of fighting and storm, King Branden held the south shore of the Westvale River uncontested. They could recover. There would be another battle, that one for control of the north shore. Then, there would be a siege of some sort, which was exactly what Branden could not afford.

He would worry about that later. Now was the time for resting, the time for celebration, if only for show. There was little real call for celebration. The success of opening up this walled city, when it came, was only one piece of the victory pie. But warriors need revelry to balance out the horror of their lives.

Gammin and Marin accompanied Branden to Theros' camp. It was east, farther up the valley where the grass was more suitable for horses. They went straight to the large pavilion. Stryn was there already, and Caerlyn. Eamehr and others from Branden's close circle arrived after the king and took places near him.

The floor of the pavilion was already festooned with nests of Arelese warriors, all of them men. Ehrylain warriors, male and female, began to filter in once the King of Ehrylan seated himself. In almost no time, the trickle of Ehrylain became a flood. Veterans know better than to show up late to a feast. Soon, the pavilion was full.

It was not a small gathering, though it was intimate and informal. The meal was plentiful. Rivers of wine were poured into cups that seemed to have no bottoms. Despite this and in spite of Stryn's best efforts, the revelry remained more subdued than was usual. The boasts were fewer, less grand. Many and many in the gathering bore wounds, some much worse than others.

The mood weighed down proud words, making them too heavy. Theros recognized what was happening. It was his party and his responsibility. These warriors were sitting on a field of victory, small though it was. They should be laughing at the wounds they had inflicted on their vanquished foe, not licking each other's wounds like timid dogs. These men and women would be better served by light thoughts. He cast his eyes around the circle. They lit upon Gammin, who was staring at his full cup of wine as if it were a mirror or a window. Theros, seeing his opportunity, swallowed some wine of his own, then spoke above the cloud of ambiguous voices.

"You are quiet these days, nephew. Do you tire so easily of victory?"

Some of the men laughed outright; other's waited to see how the Prince of Ehrylan would reply. Would he choose to play? The prince had been uncommonly reserved of late.

When the chuckling abated, Gammin said, "I tire of battle very easily, uncle."

There was an almost audible lament as listeners who had been hoping for entertainment swallowed their disappointment. Theros noted it. This was not the place and time for disappointment. He was about to say something when Caerlyn spoke.

"I would say the poor boy has been smitten. Now he is bereaved."

There was a mixed medley of cheers and jeers. Several of the older warriors froze, only their eyes moving as they watched to see how King Branden would respond to such audacity. Those were the people who had known him as the Defier and, in a few cases, even before that.

King Branden was not put out in the least. He understood Caerlyn now. While he was convalescing—again—the king had talked to Stryn. The faelyth confirmed what Branden already suspected. That understanding bought the irascible stranger named Caerlyn a lot of lee-way. It wasn't just a matter of tolerance. For the first time in a long time, Branden was in the presence of someone to whom his tolerance was irrelevant. He found it enticing.

Branden waved his hand dismissively. He was relieved at the opportunity to liven things up. They had a long way to climb before the celebratory energy could begin to replenish the depleted stores of the captains of his battered army. This was a good place to start.

He said, "Smitten and bereaved, is it? By whom and by what?"

"The princesses, of course," responded Caerlyn.

Branden noted the volume and character of Caerlyn's voice.

He could tell that the man, like Theros, was trying to liven things up. That bought him more credibility with the king.

Theros did not allow anyone else to speak. The King of Arel moved his hand in a way that no one could misinterpret for anything other than, "Keep it shut. I am about to speak."

The hush was so quiet that the crackle of the struggling fire could be heard. That was perfect as far as Theros was concerned. He wanted to make the first response to Caerlyn. To do otherwise would be risky. One never knew what that man was going to come out with. Theros thanked the stars. This time, Caerlyn had thrown a perfect axe. The warriors gathered here were the leaders of their armies. Theros needed them energized, not contemplative or grave.

Theros put a skepticism in his voice that he did not feel. His words issued a challenge.

"Which princess?"

"Theramina, Princess of Arel," exclaimed an excited Arelese voice.

"Princess Karene," offered another.

A third voice spoke. "You are wrong."

Marin's words were loud, clear. They captured the moment the way ice does, freezing it in place until the thaw. He had not intended to speak. He had been thinking—with an air of internal humor—that Gammin's new love was the flute, not a woman, princess or otherwise. That flute had been returned to its owner, Stryn, when they left Castle Arathai. The words had come out all by themselves, with an attitude that was misleading at best.

An expectant silence hung in the air. Marin decided that his best bet was to finish the thought honestly.

"It's the flute he's pining for. He likes it better than food these days." After allowing the jeers to settle, he added, "But not his sword. He likes that best of all."

Cheers and laughter delivered Marin to a safe haven. The word he used for flute was common slang for a certain part of a man's body. He had chosen it intentionally as a pun. It fit the situation.

Someone asserted that, if the Prince of Ehrylan was going to pine for someone, the Princess of Rath was worth a pine or two. She would be a good match, a good queen for Ehrylan.

A voice from the back of the pavilion rang out above the general agreement. The words were painted with a rolling accent. "Why not Theramina?"

Support and contempt for that suggestion mixed in an unlikely chorus. As the level of sound and conversation swelled, Theros allowed himself an internal pat on the thigh. Now they were headed back in the right direction. Things were heating up.

To fuel the fire, he turned to Branden and said, "Theramina is the daughter of a mighty warrior, a noble chief of his people, with many lands and many horses." It was another challenge.

Now the raucous could not be outspoken. Branden's father had taught him that few successful kings wasted words in such situations. He knew they would grow quiet again, their attentiveness and expectation multiplied all the more.

When the din had settled, Theros said, "You disapprove of Arelese women, brother?"

Obviously, King Branden approved of Arelese women just fine. Truth to tell, he had thought about that particular match a lot lately. Such a union would be a huge step in the reunification of the Crescent. But marrying cousins was one thing; bandying it about in public like it was a joke—or a prize—was another.

With a wave of his hand, Branden said, "Not that, Theros. I was just thinking that our customs in Ehrylan do not allow us to marry closer than the second cousin."

An outrage of cat calls and rudeness blotted anything else he might have added. They included things like, "Oh yeah?" and "You need to get out more!" The general consensus seemed to be that marrying cousins were a bit more common than the king suggested, especially here in the Westland.

Theros was quite happy to add his own voice when the volume made it less futile to speak.

"The doings of your family, way up here in the far north,

are not unknown to us, Branden, my brother. If I remember the tale of your fathers half as well as I think I do, there is precedent. Such unions are at the foundations of both our kingdoms."

Branden laughed only little more loudly than was necessary. He was relieved that the mood had brightened. And, though Rath or Norlan might have been his first choice, he was warming to the idea of joining with the House of Arel.

"I know the escapades of my ancestors, Arel. You have the right of it, of course."

There followed a lively discussion of the customs of queens, kings, and their offspring. The dialogue took place mainly between the kings for the pleasure of their commanders and friends. The lively part came from the commanders and friends, who took it as their natural right to keep things stirred up to a celebratory level.

Sometime later, well after the banter had turned to a different subject, Gammin got up. He wandered away from the revelry on a path that many had used already and more would use as the night went on. If anyone noticed, they were sure to think he was on his way to relieve personal necessity. Marin, who had been watching his friend carefully, suspected Gammin wasn't going just so he could relieve himself.

Marin observed the revelry the way a hidden scout watches an enemy patrol cross a river. The further along they went, the safer he became. When they had gone far enough across the river of their own mirth, he would steal away, leaving none the wiser.

Marin waited for the right time. Eventually, someone across the pavilion made a witty remark that brought a storm of laughter and caused every eye to turn toward the clever wit who had spoken. Marin stood up and melted into the darkness like so much smoke from the fire—which had been restocked a few moments before. After a short search, he found his friend.

Gammin was sitting by a stream, his back resting against a boulder. Above and below, the icy water tumbled down an incline of white rock in a joyful cascade on its way to the Westvale River.

There were several guard posts in sight on either bank of the river, which was a bow shot away. Marin picked them out by their small fires. There were others, he knew; those would be fireless, cold, well-hidden.

He sat down, his back against the same boulder Gammin was using. Several moments passed. Marin listened to the river, trying to decipher its message. Finally, he had waited long enough.

"What are we doing?"

"Thinking."

"Of what?"

"Life," said Gammin with finality. "My life, specifically. I don't seem to have much say in it anymore."

"I don't need to remind you that, only a few days ago, you told me your life was going pretty well."

"Then why did you remind me?"

Marin thought about that. "Sometimes, even someone as sensible as you needs reminding."

Gammin tossed a stone at a nearby puddle. The ripples were sluggish against a thin crust of ice. That is how the Prince of Ehrylan felt. He was cold and sluggish, not physically—he had on his battle cloak—but emotionally.

He said, "When did I lose the right to choose my own wife?"

"Do peasants have rights?" Marin spoke with a Rathian accent. It was a fair approximation of Karene. He expected Gammin to laugh, but he didn't.

Gammin said, "One of the advantages of being a peasant is that you get to run your own life."

"Is that what you think?"

"No, but that doesn't make it any easier. Those people are talking about me like I am a piece of meat or a sack of grain."

"You are, aren't you? You are their sack of grain, their seed. You've given them new hope."

"We have done that," said Gammin.

The young prince thought about the farmers and dairymen he had killed recently, imagining the faces of their wives, daughters, and sons. Exhaling softly, he said, "Hope is expensive."

Marin nodded. He listened to trees chat with the night winds. There was a nice-sized stone by his hand. It had been half-buried in the loam before his fingers dug it out unconsciously. He brushed away wet dirt, hefted it, handed it to his friend.

Somewhere near, a she-fox ventured from her den. Marin felt her as she tasted the air. She was wary. She was confused. There were many good smells, but there were many men and many dogs. It was tantalizing, yet frightening. Marin felt her decide. She had eaten well of late. Her kits could have whatever small thing she could hunt up here, near the stream, where it was safer.

Gammin did not know about the fox and her feasts. Presently, he said, "Did you know that Arica loves waterfalls?"

"I think so."

"I wonder if Micah knew that."

The admission startled Marin. It was not often they truly surprised one another. Where had that come from?

Gamin tossed the stone Marin had given him into the water. There was a distinct clatter. Farther down the slope, he glimpsed a blur of fur as some animal that had been hunting by the stream scurried through the bushes, leaving behind only the rustle of its passing.

"Do you ever think of Melani?"

"All the time. Sometimes more. I think of her when I see Annen thinking about Merelina. I think of her at times like this, when I see that the Prince of Ehrylan is missing a woodcutter's daughter."

Gammin looked up. "It is uncomfortable, isn't it?"

"What? Love? You bet."

"You've been waiting for a while. Does it get more comfortable?"

Marin shook his head. "It gets harder, but you get better at dealing with it. My mother taught me that. She was talking about life at the time, but it's the same."

"So, there's good news and bad news, huh?"

"You bet. There is always good news and bad. In fact, I am starting to think that everything is like that. Life's just a crooked path through gardens and thistles."

Then, unaccountably, Marin laughed as if he found his own words delightful.

"What's so funny, Old One?"

"It just occurred to me that gardens and the thistles are the same. It's only time that's different. The gardener digs out thistles and plants joy in his garden. In time, he eats the fruit of his labor, and life is good. Eventually, the fruit trees die, or the floods come and wash everything away. After the good stuff is gone, the thistles grow again. You could make the case that we are the weeds in Ea's thistle garden."

Gammin made no reply. Marin waited. After a long time, he said, "Best get back to the gathering. You will have been missed by now. There will be rumors that I spirited you away somewhere".

Gammin started to get up. He stopped, said, "I am sorry for the way he treats you. You don't deserve it." Gammin was referring to his father, King Branden. Marin knew it.

"No worries. It is no different than how he treats you or any number of the people he loves. He's got his job; I have mine. It's best just to focus on that."

"So his job is making you and me uncomfortable? What's yours?"

"Me? I have to keep you straight."

Gammin did not return a jibe or a quip. His mind had turned. He was considering how dispassionately he thought about his father. Gammin had never had a father or mother to love. He did not know how that kind of love should feel. He was pretty sure it was different from how he felt about the king. Maybe that was to be expected. They had not known each other long.

Gammin and his friend, the woodcutter's son, made their

way back to what was now a roaring bonfire. Branden saw them as they approached. He eyed his son. Marin, who was watching the king to see how he reacted, saw the appraisal. It was cold, the assessment of a sculptor inspecting the rock from which he intended to chisel his masterpiece.

The woodcutter's son was staring directly at Branden when the king turned on him. Their eyes locked.

II.

The battle for the south shore of the river had taken everything Theros and Branden had. Even if the horrors that followed had started a few days earlier, there was nothing they could have done about it. Their armies were too depleted. They needed rest and good weather.

Only one of those two was a possibility. The weather turned wet again, though less cold. Warriors settled in, grimly preparing for a siege, hoping that either the wet or the cold would stay away while they tarried. One of those they could deal with. Both together meant danger.

They weren't yet into the siege-proper. That would not happen until they held the north side of the river and had access to the city walls. Even then, there was not much hope of starving the city dwellers this close to the ocean. The freshwater springs of Neath were well-known. The whole region was dotted with them. Food and water were not difficult to come by in the Westland, even in the worst of times.

Branden's plan had not included a long siege. He was chaffing at the delay. If Vila had not acted so grievously, he might have left the siege and proceeded on his planned course. The Rathian navy was battling off the coast somewhere. They must have taken shelter from the storms in one of the small bays and inlets along the Westland coast, else they'd have been blown to flotsam. They would defeat the enemy's ships and join the battle for Neath as planned. Meredan's transport ships would land the hundreds of Ehrylain who were now probably quite sea sick and eager to be on land, no matter how wet it was.

All that changed the night Vila hung ten men from the towers of the city. There was no demand, no announcement. The bodies were tied and suspended by wrists, or in some cases, feet. Some of them held their silence. Most pleaded for mercy or for help. When the moon was at its height, they were set afire. The oil that had been soaked into their clothes made them into hideous, screaming torches, even those who had before been silent.

The next night, it was ten women. All the next day, as the kings tried to put together a battle plan, the warriors wondered. Would it be men again tonight or children. It was children.

That night, Marin dreamed. He realized he had been dreaming as soon as he opened his eyes. He was thankful at the realization and terrified.

Gammin was sitting cross-legged on his cot, staring at him intently. A knife, unsheathed and polished, rested across his thigh.

Marin said, "I had another dream."

"No kidding."

"Was I talking in my sleep?"

"A bit. You and I are going somewhere. I am not sure where. There was something about Arica. That's the bit that concerns me. Is she alright?"

Marin sat up abruptly. "I've got to tell the King of Ehrylan to abandon the hostages, and you want to hear about Arica?"

Gammin held up both hands. "I did not get that part. You'd better tell me the rest. Do you feel up to it?" He could see the water bag hanging on the end of Marin's cot, so he did not offer any of his own.

"To tell you the truth, I feel fine. I expect this is as good as I am going to feel for a long time. It's not going to get better. That's for sure."

Gammin remained silent.

"It was a dark," began the Seer of Ehrylan, then faltered.

Gammin said, in his most helpful voice, "There's no stretch

there. I can believe that."

"The rest is harder. I could see campfires, thousands of them, or maybe just hundreds, I don't know. It was a lot. I knew it was an army, bigger than ours, for sure. I was high up on a ridge in the Western Mountains. An army had marched right out of Kingsholm. They were coming to free Neath."

After waiting for more, Gammin said, "What else? There's nothing unexpected there. We don't have any scouting reports of an army up there yet, but you'd know better. You always seem to know that stuff before me."

"That is the easy part, I am afraid."

Gammin could see his friend really was afraid. That was not uncommon as these things tended to go. Gammin had been with Marin when he had each of the seeings. He was used to the odd behavior; in his quiet heart, he felt Marin's fear did not come from the dreams. The last dream had sent them from Twofords and everyone they knew and loved.

Marin continued, "The king is supposed to abandon the hostages and leave Neath. He needs to head north, toward that army."

"Wait." It was a needless request. Marin had already stopped speaking and did not look like he ever wanted to open his mouth again. "Did the dream command him to abandon the hostages?"

"It comes to the same thing."

"No, it doesn't."

There was a long pause as Marin considered. Then, he said, "You're right. I'm getting ahead of myself."

"What was it Merclina likes to say? When you get ahead of yourself, you're likely to trip."

A little smile drifted across Marin's lips. "Yeah, that was it."

"What else?"

"The what else is the worst part. We are going to Twofords."

"What's bad about that? We can ride north with the king and head through Norgap alone if he decides to go anywhere else." The possibility of getting away from Branden and back to his home seemed anything but ominous, especially if it came at Ea's mandate.

"Not that way. You and I have to take the Narrow Road."

"The Narrows? The Narrows?"

That was all Gammin could say. He was dumbfounded. The Narrow Road led through the mountains to the Narrows, a lonely gorge that opened on to central Ehrylan on the east side. The road was not named for the gorge, though it could have been. The Narrow Road stretched like a sunning serpent between steep-sided cliffs, at times lacing up and down one of the faces in precarious switchbacks. It was no place for an army, as Dauroth had found a lifetime ago. Nor was it a place for anyone in winter, even two experienced travelers.

Neither of them saw that part of the dream as the biggest difficulty. Heading east was heading home, though the route they were to take was the coldest possible way to get there. Both were relieved at being free of the king. The need to convince Branden to break the siege was the hard part. It should not have been, given how Branden was chaffing at the delay, but….

Marin said, "The army needs to take the low road north. If the king doesn't head north, something bad will happen, not necessarily to the army or to your father, but to Ehrylan. I am sure of it."

"I believe you. I think you have done your part. What else can you do? The king will make his own decision. We make ours."

Marin's face showed the appreciation that welled within him. Then it sagged again against the pull of his anxiety. "If the king turns the army, and if we make it safely through the Narrows…" His words dribbled to a stop. He sat worrying his hands together, staring at the floor.

"I know," said Gammin. He waited a few breaths, added, "Say it, Mar."

Marin looked up without moving his head. Only his eyes moved, and his hands. They writhed against each other like the emotions he was feeling. "I don't want to. It's too much."

"I know," Gammin said again, "But you need to say it."

Marin did not respond immediately. Then, with a heavy sigh, he sat up straight. Wiping the sweat from his brow, he said, "If we make it safe through the Narrows, and if the king taking his army north turns out to be the right thing to do, it means Ea has made me a seer."

"Yes." Gammin smiled at his agonizing friend. "And no. Ea made you his seer long ago. This is just the first real test."

"The first?" Marin's voice was louder and higher-pitched than he'd intended. "Have you forgotten we left Twofords on the strength of one of my dreams?" He shrugged, shook his head. "I know you haven't forgotten. Sorry.

"What is wrong with Marn's son that he should not be Ea's seer?"

"Marn is a woodcutter, and I am a woodcutter's son."

"What is wrong with that?"

"For starters, it's nothing so grand as being a king or a Farseer, or even a lowly prince. All the seers of legend were important people."

"So what? Did they become legends because they were important, or did they become important people because they did incredible things?" Gammin was thinking about what Peryn had said the night they shared canella.

Marin did not answer. Gammin picked at the scab covering a sword cut on his forearm. It wasn't deep, but it itched something fierce. For some reason, scabs were fun to molest once they were dry and crusty. Wondering if it was true that scabs you worried at turned into worse scars, Gammin muttered, "What do the legends say of Teryn before he became a seer?"

Marin frowned as he gave the question a cursory examination. He looked at Gammin sidelong and dug deeper into his store of legends and history, which was larger than most.

I don't know," he admitted.

"Neither do I. Maybe Teryn was a shepherd or a fisherman. Or, maybe he was a baker or a sailor. Who knows? The point is that it doesn't matter."

Marin said, "There are no stories about Teryn, Andur, or anybody from those times being uncertain, not like I am about being... called."

"The legends don't record that part. Two men sitting in a tent on a wet night talking about self-doubt is hardly the stuff of legend."

Gammin fiddled with the knife he was holding for a while, then said, "Maybe this is where we find out what legends are really made from. They are just normal people trying to do what has to be done. Maybe the people named Andur or Teryn—or even Annen—had the same doubts as you do." Gammin was thinking of his own doubts as he spoke. Knowing that Marin was well aware of them already, he did not voice them.

Marin blew through pursed lips. "If Ea was going to send a dream, why didn't he send it straight to the king? For that matter, why not solve the problem directly? Why mess around with us at all?"

Gammin shook his head slowly. He was thinking deeply. "Why does he insist on working through us? I think that's the right question. I don't know the answer."

Marin looked disconsolate. He might have been a sad-eyed puppy.

Gammin started a new thought. "Do you have any real doubts that this dream was like the others."

"No."

"Is it ambiguous? Are you unsure what we're supposed to do?"

"No."

"What choice is there, then?"

"You make it sound very simple. I am glad you will be there to look after my bleached bones when they are done drying."

"That's my job. Someone's got to take care of the king's seer. It might as well be me. I've got nothing better to do."

II.

Branden was as furious as they expected him to be.

"You have to do what?"

The king's outburst was very similar to the one he had voiced when Marin told him Ea wanted the Army of the Westland to move north immediately. They had already argued about that.

The king glared at Marin, then at Gammin. "The Narrows would be insane this time of year. It's probably not even passable."

"That's true," replied Marin before Gammin could say anything. "I am going, nevertheless. My only other choice is to argue with the Infinite, and that seems pointless. It is what I must do. You have your own tasks."

"My own tasks? Who do…"

The king broke off. It was too late to stop himself from getting angry, really angry, but he could keep from acting like it. Unfortunately, it was also too late to stop the argument that followed.

Branden had not become angry for being awakened in the twinight. He had listened to the dream willingly enough, at first. The response from Kingsholm was expected. The trouble came when Marin mentioned the requirement to move Branden's army northward. When Marin mentioned he and Gammin were supposed to head east immediately, the inevitable storm had been unleashed. It reached its peak just after Gammin mentioned that heading north had been Branden's intention all along, so it should not be difficult to swallow.

After that, no one was in the mood to listen to anything reasonable. There came a time when each of them had fallen silent. The sudden lack of contention smote them almost like a blow.

After a long moment that dripped with all manner of charged emotions, King Branden looked at Marin. He raised a hand and pointed. "Get out. I will talk to my son alone." The torchlight glittered off the ruby eyes of the horses on a ring he was wearing.

"No," said Gammin flatly. "He stays."

Branden's eyes flared. Fists balled and jaws clenched, he squared on his son. Once again, the lion saw that, though it was still a young one, he faced a dragon.

"That is not the tone of my son or my subject. What are you?"

"I am not here as your son or your subject, sire. I am here as someone who wants to do the right thing."

Branden turned amidst a swirl of the cloak he had thrown over his shoulders. He stepped away from Gammin and relaxed his hands. After a moment, he spoke.

"What would you have me do? Shall I leave the good people of this city? You want me to abandon them at Marin's whim?"

"I want you to head north because it is Ea's will."

"Ea's will out of Marin's mouth. You lay upon me a big decision."

"I think it is the same decision Andur had to make when Teryn said he needed to take an army through the Narrows and down into the Old Forest. Maybe that is why we remember him the way we do. He made the right decisions."

"Good kings," said Branden, "are heroes for their good decisions, villains for the bad."

"Sire, why don't you trust Marin? Why don't you trust me? The Elder of the Tallenlaust trusted us enough to make me a captain even though I was still young. We have been fighting for Ehrylan since before we knew you were alive. How have we failed you?"

The father and son stared at each other in a blaze of silence. Marin could feel the heat of their glares. He was trying—and failing—to recall a time when he had ever had such a confrontation with his own father when the king spoke.

"Your eyes accuse me."

"What do they say?"

"They say that Calen would heed Marin's words. They say Calen would turn the army and leave the innocents to die."

"That is what you see in my face, sire?"

"That is what I see."

Gammin thought for a moment, then said, "Your eyes are telling you Annen's council, not mine."

The king's face spasmed. He took three swift breaths, then three more, which were measured.

When he had put away his quick anger, King Branden said, "What you ask of me is difficult. The plans are made and the way is open. I can feel the road to Kingsholm and to victory; it lies along the northward road. All those things are true. But I cannot leave these people to die undefended."

"Undefended, sire? Are you the only weapon in Ea's quiver?"

Branden's gaze held steady as fury coursed through his veins. Gammin did not shy from the brutal stare as many an older campaigner had done. Branden lowered his eyes first.

The king sighed. "The road to the Narrows is treacherous. There are innumerable places for ambushes. Where it leads is only death. I have been there; you have not."

Gammin took a deep breath, considered how far he could safely go. Firmly, he said, "Who's death? Is it the battle you fought there in your youth that you dread or the battle you fear we may have to fight there if we take that road?"

Branden's shoulders slumped. He brought a hand up and pushed it across his face, over his eyes. He shook his head.

"You think I don't see that?"

The king seemed to be melting, his anger giving way to internal torment. It was evident he felt like one of the unfortunate loyalists who were being burned alive. Finally, looking at each of them in the eye, Marin longest of all, he said, "Leave me now. I must think on this."

III.

Marin and Gammin talked it over time and time again. Each iteration ended in the same conclusion. They could not wait for the king to make up his mind. They had to go now, as soon as possible. So, without consulting the king, they began preparing for their journey. Why not? By the king's own command, they had no official duties to perform.

The two young Southlanders were not used to kings and their ways. How could they be? To them, a king was some far-off demon who inhabited the throne in Kingsholm. They were not used to living at the whim of other people, as strange as it sounds. If any of the oldsters had known how the young men continually questioned the king's judgement, those oldsters would have taken them in hand and taught them the way of it.

Having told their closest confidants of their plans, the day before they departed was spent more on partings than on provisioning. First to come was Stryn, who arrived in their tent before the evening meal.

When they were all seated as comfortably as possible in the tent, Stryn looked around with a beaming face. His words, when they came, seemed to be a song without music. "Isn't this just the thing? Here we are, sitting on the banks of the River Edgling—that's what it was called when I was younger—besieging the castle just like Andur did. It's a city in your case, not a castle; Neath came later. But it's the same. Exciting, isn't it?"

Exciting was not one of the many words Marin might use to describe this experience. Nevertheless, he nodded. It was difficult to disagree with Stryn. The faelyth went on to describe the events of Andur's day. At the time, it did not occur to the young men to ask how he might know such details. Their thoughts were hiding in different rooms.

Stryn saw his companions' distraction. He understood what was happening more than they did by a long way. Rathia had told him that Gammin saw the Welling. Stryn knew what that meant. The knowledge thrilled him and made him simultaneously pity and envy these boys. They were in for a hard road, but it would not want for excitement.

"So you are leaving us."

Gammin nodded. He did not want to be rude, but he didn't

have any words to offer. Stryn saw. He exhaled a soft chuckle and leaned forward to touch Gammin's knee.

"Don't worry, Gammin of River's Bend. All will be well, and all will be well. Trust the road upon which the Almighty has set your feet. I suspect your father will remember that sooner rather than later. Ea has other ways of moving people than seers and dreams. What do the Stonethanes say? The Maker has many hammers."

Gammin did not respond, so Marin did. "Don't worry, is it? Fear not?" He was thinking of his first seeing, the one where Andur had told him not to fear. They had been standing at the top of Tarabol's walls, which were about to be breached by uncounted hoards. It was well known that Tarabol had fallen.

"Yes, fear not. Two easy words, one impossible demand."

Gammin pulled himself from within and said, "How do we do that, Stryn? How do you win the battle against the fear that you are not doing the right thing?"

"You don't. You never defeat fear's army. But you can win a victory every day just by trying. That is all it takes." The faelyth displayed his most disarming smile, which vanished abruptly as he thought of what Gammin had said.

"Is that what you are afraid of, my boy? Afraid of doing the wrong thing?"

"No, not exactly."

Marin laughed. It was real. The sound fell over them like a summer shower, sweet and cool. "You don't know him well enough, Stryn. Gammin isn't worried he'll do the wrong thing. He's worried he might not do the right thing. There is a difference, you know?"

Stryn looked surprised. Then, his head giving a little cock to one side as his eyes widened, he said, "I suppose there is. I have never considered that before. Never had to, I guess. That is one benefit of spending time with young people. It keeps one growing."

Stryn looked at them, saw he was not managing to lift their spirits. He thought he'd give it one more go before he did what he had come to do.

"Listen!" Despite his command, Stryn said nothing more. When he was sure they would not interrupt, he continued.

"Funny I should start that way, isn't it? Have you ever noticed that faelyth usually start their stories with that admonition? Listen! Attend! I am talking now!"

The boys were listening, but they were not buying what he was trying to gift them.

"Attend me, Gammin of River's Bend, Prince of Ehrylan, son of my friend, Therana, who I called Arelia before she came here with Branden. I can't help you with your self-doubt. You come by that naturally, I am sure. What child with no mother to care for him could have confidence in the god who made him? Not me."

"What is your point, Stryn?" Gammin regretted the words as soon as he spoke them. He was not sure if Stryn's barb was a hit or a miss.

Stryn relented. He could see real pain in Gammin's face. What was the harm in making it simple, just this once?

"Gammin, stop worrying about your worries. Go do what needs to be done. The truth of it is that you know what you are supposed to do. It's just uncomfortable. Sometimes I wonder if the wheels of Ea's wagon are named Discomfort; other times I am sure."

That got the smile Stryn wanted. It was not Therana's grin—which he had seen on Gammin more than once—but it was close enough. He inhaled deeply through his nose and bent to pick up a bag he had brought. He extracted a bundle and extended it to Gammin. Both Southlanders knew what was hidden within the wrappings.

"Why don't you take that with you? It is yours, and you are most welcome."

"Sir, I could not take this from you."

"I have another, as you know."

"Yes, but..."

"Yes, but nothing. How can I persuade you? I would not have all my hard work go to waste. Nor yours. Making music is like boiling water. It requires tending."

"I thank you, sir, but I can't. I appreciate the honor you do me."

"Is there nothing I can do to convince you?"

"Nothing, Stryn, but I thank you again."

Stryn took back the bundle. He unwrapped it and lifted out the flute. The dark-hued wood was lustrous.

Holding the flute at arm's length, he admired it. "I always liked this one. Your mother played it. To tell you a truth, she made it."

The faelyth held it out to Gammin. The reluctant prince took it at once. He looked at the instrument as if he had never before seen it, as if he had not played it a dozen times and more.

"Therana gave it to me the day she celebrated my birthday. It took her two years to make, as I recall. That wasn't so very long before she was killed." Stryn did not look away or apologize for touching a tender subject.

Gammin appreciated that. He said, "You drive a hard bargain, faelyth. You've been planning this all along? Is that why you didn't tell me earlier?"

"I knew you would take convincing. Remember, I knew both your parents when they were not much older than you. They had stubborn streaks, too."

"You held the information in reserve so you could exchange it later," said Gammin. Respect danced with surprise in his voice. Knowledge as a hostage was something to ponder!

"That would be one way to say it, I suppose. You are still thinking like a warrior. When you make music, you will be thinking like the wind."

Gammin did not notice the artistic language. Marin did. He wrote it down in his journal. He always did that with phrases he liked. He was a good boy.

Gammin was inspecting the flute, a collection of love and wood his mother had put together in the years just before he was born. "This is your practice flute?" He asked without taking his eyes from the instrument.

"Practice? I don't practice, young man. I just play. And, no, that is not my practice flute. That is the flute I play when I am on the road and encamped by myself. It has a pleasing sound. I like the memories it brings. The other flute is for kings and audiences who would feel slighted if I showed up with a trinket like that. Listen, it's yours now, Gammin. Take it, and who better to have it? Perhaps it only came through me so that it could get into your hands. Yes, let's look at it that way. It is poetic, no?"

"My mother made a flute this fine?"

"You have me there. She made the flute. I made it fine. It was playable when she gave it to me. Now it is a pleasure to play and to hear. Or, it will be when you have practiced, Master Prince, half as many hours as you have practiced skewering soldiers on your pointed objects."

Stryn brought the negotiations to a halt. After rewrapping the flute, he re-handed it back to Gammin. He was pleased that his ploy had worked. Gammin accepted the gift with both hands. Not knowing he did so, he cradled it against his chest. The bundle might have been a newborn puppy. Or, a chick.

IV.

It was the dark before dawn. A mist hung in the air. Marin felt a shift. He turned in time to see the King of Arel appear out of the moist darkness. Theros looked at Marin, jerked his head to one side. The woodcutter's son understood. He patted his horse on its flank and moved off to give his friends space.

Gammin had already made a long parting with the King of Arel. Theros knew about the dream and of the dilemma it caused both king and prince. Though he was not surprised to see his uncle again, he was touched. He started to speak. Theros didn't let him.

"This is a good horse." He ran his hands over the beast lovingly.

"The last one I had died beneath me at Elosai." Gammin's words were heavy, betraying how he felt.

"So, he died well. Good for him. And, nephew, good for you. It gladdens my heart to see you set out on this journey."

"Uncle, why is it good for me? It feels like I am running away. I am displeasing the king. I'm letting down the men and women who…" He stopped. He had been going to say he was failing the men and women who depended on him, but he realized there weren't any, not any more. Instead, he asked again, "Why is it good for me?"

Theros did amazing things. First, he grinned. The grin turned into a smile that soon spilled out as good-natured laughter.

"Nephew, I am very glad that I am no longer young. Of all things, youth is the hardest." He held up his hand to forestall reply in the familiar gesture. "I have come to tell you two things. First, it took real courage to stand up to your father. It takes real courage to do what you think is right when others are telling you it's wrong."

"I thank you, sir. I don't feel courageous. To tell you the truth, I thought you would agree with him, with King Branden."

"I do agree with him. Your absence will be felt in our armies. But, you cannot be in two places at once."

"You believe Ea sent the dream?"

"That is the other thing I came to tell you. Ea is not my god, but I know he is strong. What is the word? Oh, yes. Mighty. I saw what he did in Arel, back when your father and I were just babes like you are now, maybe even a bit older. Back then, an old man claimed Ea had sent him a vision in the fire. What he foretold came true, just as it always had. One way or another, this mighty god of yours seems to have his fingers on the pulse of the future. I think you do well not to anger him by disobeying."

They talked a while longer. The sound of damp footsteps reached through the mist. King Branden followed.

Theros had been expecting the king. It had taken all his wits to get Branden to commit to bidding his son farewell. Theros set his hands on Gammin's shoulders.

"Your father is a hard man, a stern king. He is what the Ehrylain need to free themselves of Dauroth. Eventually, they will need a different kind of king. If they are lucky, that will be you. I think your father will see you for what you are before the end. You do not have to wait so long. Try to see him for what he is now." The King of Arel held his nephew's eyes for a moment longer. "I will try to sway your father after you are well away. We can hope to see the ships now that the storm is resting. If they come, perhaps the warriors they carry can free the city while we ride north."

It looked to Gammin like Theros wanted to say more, but Branden was hard upon them.

Theros dropped his hands and said, "I go now. I hope to see you again, nephew. Fare you well."

Theros headed off to take his parting of Marin, giving Gammin's horse a final caress in passing.

As Branden approached, Gammin said, "I did not expect to see you. I thank you for coming."

The king stood without speaking for a time, then began, "You are leaving." It was obvious he had more to say and was struggling for the words.

Gammin said, "Now, who's stating the obvious?"

Quite unaccountably, the king laughed. It was almost a relieved exhalation. "You see? You demonstrate what I came to say, and I have not yet said it."

Thinking the King of Ehrylan was going to make a prolonged statement, Gammin finished what he was doing before giving Branden his full attention. He was adjusting the length of his stirrup. He and Marin would be riding in a different kind of terrain almost as soon as they turned east, up the Narrow Road. This small change should make a big difference by the end of the day.

As Gammin worked, the king said, "I have been struggling with how I am going to raise a son. Now, I realize I do not have to. You have done well on your own. I don't like what you are doing, but it took a man, a strong man, to make the decision you made. I hope it works out for you and for the kingdom."

Caught off-guard, Gammin dropped the stirrup and focused on King Branden. He thought for a moment, then said, "I'm just not ready to be a prince."

"But you are able. You will never be ready, I think. I am learning not to hold that against you. A man could have worse failings." The king shuffled his feet. "I regret the loss of your sword more, at the moment."

"Yes, I know. This is hard for me, as well. I think you know how it feels. It seems like I am running away. But that's not the way of it, at least, I hope not."

"I do not doubt your courage."

The prince started to say it was Marin that Branden doubted, or maybe Ea, but he thought better of it. "I thank you," was what he said.

They talked a while longer. It was a short while. Both son and father were trying to do what was right. It was very hard. It felt like an invisible force was urging them to conflict, eager for dissension. When the well of their good intentions ran dry, they stood silent, neither of them wanting to prolong this agony. Then Branden shrugged.

"I do not enjoy partings. I charge you with this only. Remember, whether you like it or not, you are the Prince of Ehrylan. Remember your people. They will be watching you. I wish you well, Gammin of River's Bend."

Turning amidst the swell of his cloak, Branden stalked into the darkness. Theros jogged to catch up.

ABOUT THE AUTHOR

John Douglas Day lives and writes in northern California's San Joaquin river delta. Before retiring to write full time, he spent decades working in the Tech industry. He enjoys music, martial arts, animals, and language. He relishes the outdoors and spending time with his incredible Labrador Retriever.

More information is available on the author's web site:

jdouglasday.com

BY JOHN DOUGLAS DAY

<u>Annals of the Everbourne</u>

Book I-   *A Justice of Ehrylan*
Book II- *Warriors of Ehrylan*
Book III- *Battle for the Southland*
Book IV- (forthcoming)

Made in the USA
Coppell, TX
08 September 2021